NOSTALGIA

NOSTALGIA

Hope Jennings

GRAND RAPIDS, MICHIGAN

www.RawDogScreaming.com

Cover Image "The Flapper" © 1922 by F. X. Leyendecker

Interior Layout by D. Harlan Wilson
www.DHarlanWilson.com

Anti-Oedipus Press
Grand Rapids, MI

www.Anti-OedipusPress.com

TABLE OF CONTENTS

"... such as mouse-traps, and the moon, and memory, and muchness—you know you say things are 'much of a muchness'—and did you ever see such a thing as a drawing of a muchness!"

—Lewis Carroll

An old man sits in his garden surrounded by his sons; he is not sure why they are there. Perhaps they are only luminous mirages, demonic imagoes of the prodigal boys who ran away from home; yet here they are, all of them for the first time since their sprightly childhoods collected and pinned in the same frame of time and space. The old man shifts his weight and ignores the creaking of his lawn chair, all the sagging folds of flesh he refuses to accept as his own. He is distracted by the bruised-blue-and-black and yellow-limned wings of a *Nymphalis antiopa* fluttering past his peripheral vision; her appendages should have faded by now into a desiccated white, and so she can only be a figment of his imagination. He returns his attention to the men sitting in their own lawn chairs, each of them shifting uncomfortably in each of their own small ways, and the old man decides that this, surely, must be the last time they will be forced to meet. Meanwhile, he is reduced to silently simmering in the September haze, envying his sons their slim, supple youth.

The eldest, however, has sloppily attempted to disguise his middle-aged paunch with an oversized cambric polo shirt. Even now, after everything the boy has suffered, the old man feels insulted by the existence of his eldest child, as if he is a blotch in his dazzling vision he would like to erase. He glances over at the youngest, who offers one of his conspiratorial, feral grins, and the old man is struck by a familiar pang in his chest because this is the child of his heart. So he regards the middle child, stiffly slouched, fastidiously sipping his chilled tea, and also studying his father with detached interest. They both hastily, haughtily turn their eyes away, and the afternoon passes slowly, insufferably, if only because of the boredom that usually accompanies such family reunions, at which no one had expected or desired to be present. None of them, in fact, know why they are there. Each of the boys calculates in his head the timetable for the next departing train that will transport him into his inevitably unforeseen future. As for their father, he buries himself further in his chair. He smiles slowly, reticently, recalling a preciously hoarded secret, the smile concluding in a catlike curve until it vanishes with the unwilling knowledge that the woman he'd loved and lost years ago may never be recovered.

The woman standing at her kitchen window observes her husband and sons. She remains inside where she does not have to listen to their silence. In a rare twinge of maternal sentiment, she longs to gather to her breast this assemblage of a family she is quite certain never existed. Then, one of her sons (it couldn't possibly matter which one) detects the gleaming pinpoints of his mother's eyes and returns her gaze, his lips twitching into the ghost of a precocious smile. Suddenly she desires their departure, and turns away from the window, her slim unforgiving spine receding into the shadows of the house. Her foolish son continues staring at the empty space beyond the kitchen window, which now contains only the blurred reflected features of his own befuddled, fading grin.

"Part of the problem with the neutral observer, who is in fact romantically involved with his subject, is that some time must always elapse between the experiment and the record of the experiment. Infinitely tiny, perhaps, but even without a lover's gaze, how many fantasies can force themselves into an infinitesimal space?"

—Jeanette Winterson, *Art & Lies*

CHAPTER ONE
A Prodigal Daughter

Mina's sixty-eighth year began and ended the night she slipped out into a winter storm, and I can only imagine why she felt compelled to go wandering in the middle of the night in the middle of a snowfall. Perhaps she'd been awakened from a dream, in which she roamed, forever ageless, through a grove of blossoming tulip poplars. A man she'd once loved and lost led her by the hand, black pearls dripping from the ocean of his eyes. Butterflies chased stars through her hair and a small beloved child ran laughing before them in a field of crimson poppies, tainted only by the slanting shadows of a sun setting on a horizon that could never be reached.

The dream disintegrated in the emptiness of Mina's bedroom when a phone rang and forced her out of sleep. She sat up, groping for the receiver, only to be confronted with one brief familiar husky hello and then silence. She breathed into the crackling static of collapsed time, waiting to continue a conversation that had been severed too soon, too long ago. When the mechanical, automated voice broke in, advising her to try that number again, she set the receiver down on the bedside table, abandoning it off the hook. Disorientated, Mina stumbled barefoot down the moonlit corridor of her hall, intending to calm her nerves with a late night snack or a cup of the bitter, black coffee she loved. Instead, she discovered an unexpected visitor sitting at her kitchen table, the unruly ghost of a man smiling recklessly, challenging her with a sly tilt of his dark head to follow him outside into the wintry unexpected landscape of his return.

Determined not to lose sight of him this time, Mina vacated her premises, leaving the front door ajar and a small drift of snow to sweep across its threshold. Once Mina caught up to him, where he stood beneath the looming skeleton of a tulip poplar that no longer existed except in her memory, she allowed him to take her hand and twirl her through the silent swirling snow descending from the bright star-strewn sky. Revolving in each other's arms to the swooping dives and swelling, anguished notes of *O mio babbino caro*, Mina was transported to a late summer evening when she'd waltzed barefoot along the sloping lawn of a Tuscan villa, impossibly happy despite the knowledge that she would vanish, abandoning him in the morning. Forgiven now, after so many years (for why else had he come back to her?), she smiled up into the vast infinity of stars and falling snow, as she spun further into the past, sinking finally to the ground where she lay trapped in the blinding glare of the headlamps of a passing vehicle as it cautiously made its way down the winding mountain road adjacent to Mina's property.

The driver was fortunately a level-headed local; he wrapped her in a spare blanket stored away in the trunk of his car, brought her to the hospital, and supplied the overnight nurse with a name, which helped her track down the number to call in the event of emergency. That number went unanswered and Mina was filed away under the general category of elderly woman whose sanity had cracked and split open from the burden of a life outlived. Nevertheless, the nurse dutifully paused on her rounds to check her patient's fading vital signs and was later able to report, mildly perplexed, that in Mina's last moments she had mumbled repeatedly, feverishly, that she knew where she was going, she knew how to find her way, and at last, slipping into sleep, murmuring, it's through the looking glass . . .

On the other side of that glass, Mina returns to the memory of her childhood. Exiled to the sprawling overgrown garden pocketed behind the Devonshire cottage in which she was born, she lies down on her back, sinking into the springy bed of unmown lawn, eyes closed, and summoning sufficient courage to gaze unflinchingly into the sun. Her mother has informed her, most likely during one of their abbreviated bedtime stories, that if she looks directly into that scorching ball of flame, her vision will become terribly damaged; she may even suffer incurable blindness. When

Mina musters the courage to open her eyes, there is no flash of lightning, no bolt of retribution, only a murky overcast haze. She longs for the day when she might run away to a warmer, sunnier place where it never rains, and resentfully studies the clouds, fashioning grotesque shapes out of their pliable, evaporating bodies. She thinks she is dreaming, or that she has, in fact, been blessed by a message from some inarticulate god, when a small tear in the oppressive blanket of cumuli frays into a transparent, ragged hole. A gigantic eye opens onto the world below, and streaming from its blue pupil, the sun tumbles down through the sky as evidence of its existence, as blazing tribute to her presence. She wants to cry, but decides otherwise, rising from the crumpled lawn and disdainfully brushing aside the crushed blades of grass clinging to her behind.

Tiptoeing into the empty kitchen, she is aware of having been transformed into a new creature, which she must keep secret from the arrogant disregard of her father and the eccentric inscrutability of her mother. If she told them, they would translate her vision into something they could possess for themselves. She slowly chews a slice of toasted pumpernickel smeared with marmalade, and listens to the impersonal clacking of her father's typewriter in the study down the hall. From above, she detects the whirling leaps and thumping descents of her mother rehearsing a bizarre contorted dance no one will ever have the privilege of seeing. She does not try to decipher the meaning of her vision, but is certain she has been singled out for some life-long sacred mission. She considers briefly Jeanne d'Arc, and though she accepts that she too may be sentenced to a tediously misunderstood and ostracized fate, she will refuse anyone the opportunity of burning her at the stake. She will grow up to be quite unlike any woman who has ever lived before; for now, though, she softly hums along to the internal rhyme and rhythm of the continuously stitching fabric of her flesh and rapidly evolving marrow of her bones.

The following Sunday in church she sits beside her mother in the front pew, listening listlessly to the droning of her father's sermon, which is a flawlessly structured homily on the possibilities and limitations of man's transcendence. He should have remained a tutor in philosophy at Cambridge, since he obviously begrudges his economically imposed decision to tend this bleating flock of irreligious country folk, before whom he squanders his gleaming pearls of wisdom. They'd much rather receive booming tirades and terrifying bombardments, the spectacle of eternal hell, fire and brimstone wreaked upon the exiled and wicked children of this earth, who have been cast out of paradise by a merciless and vengeful god who is our father who may or may not be in heaven. Turning to his wife as their example, they belligerently yawn, glance impatiently at their fellow congregants, skim distractedly through the hymnal, and are equally resentful towards the social obligation of attending Sunday service.

Not one of them appreciates the reverend's measured, atonal voice reasoning quite uselessly on the benefits of considering their metaphysical aspirations. They are confused by that word, *metaphysical*, leading each and every one of them to the conclusion that he is mocking their ignorance, which, admittedly, he is. She, however, adores her father, and decides her metaphysical aspiration might someday be to exceed his pure embodiment of pure intellect. Such a lofty goal has the discouraging effect of making her feel a very lowly earth-bound creature; the usual Sunday ennui tempts her into disregarding, along with everyone else, her father's vain exhortations to strive beyond all physical desires.

Averting her gaze, she locates the image of the stained glass window just directly above and to the left of her father's receding hairline. The virgin mother sits where she always sits, holding the wizened infant in her lap, the same two self-satisfied incipient smiles glazed onto their stiff lips. The archangel Gabriel hovers over them, observing mother and child with an equally smug rather too-human grin. They all look so happy with themselves, this ludicrous trinity. Happiness like that simply cannot exist, she muses, even if you are a winged messenger of God or God's singular child or that child's sanctified mother. Perhaps this is a delusion of happiness that can only be gained through spiritual aspirations, or perhaps this is the aspiration we must transcend. Mina would have continued ruminating on these conundrums, but the sun crashes into the stained glass, splintering the image into a thousand prisms of colored light. Kaleidoscopic shards scatter across her pale upturned face, and the carefully constructed mosaic of cut glass, illuminated by the sun, miraculously shifts so that the dumb lifeless smiles of mother, child, and angel are transformed, distorted but now beautiful, believable, promising the infinite possibilities of art and nature in perfect union with each other.

In that moment of comprehension, the beatific smile Mina offers her father causes him to lose his place, allowing for a distracted pause that prompts the congregation to break out into a lusty rendition of the closing hymn. Her mother also observes her daughter's beamish grin and generously mirrors the smile. Together, they leap at the opportunity to raise their voices in song, blessedly bringing to an end her father's tortuous speech. After the final resonating amen, Lauren stoops to whisper into her child's ear: "Mina, my love, you must never forget." It is never explained, however, exactly what she should remember; and Mina never once thought to ask.

Shortly after Mina's death I discovered a box of several unfinished manuscripts that she had left for me, none of them dated as to when they'd been written, but once carefully sorted they provide a rough chronology of Mina's life. The first of these manuscripts, *Laman Duare* (the eponymous title of the text's heroine and clearly an anagram of Mina's parent's first names), presents a fragmented narrative that nevertheless allows for an overall impression of her childhood. Mina's representation of this, however, was perhaps as distorted as that stained-glass window, a scene borrowed from Laman Duare's recollections and inserted above with some of my own revisions to indicate that this episode more accurately belongs to Mina's own life.

Although this might seem a dishonest move on my part or even a clumsy attempt to turn fiction into fact, if one did not know anything about Mina, then the literate reader of *Laman Duare*, upon opening its first pages (if it ever gets published), would immediately suspect its narrator's memories to be thinly plagiarized from another novel (and admittedly a more masterfully written novel). The reader could hardly be at fault for this hasty assumption, since we are told right away that just when Laman, a bohemian artist living in Paris, is feeling securely free from all ties to the past, she is forced to attend some insipid soirée hosted by one of her fellow expatriates where she is offered a cup of unsweetened Earl Grey, and with one sip of its milky bitterness, she is transported to the claustrophobic landscape of her English childhood. There she revisits the uneventful experience of growing up in a home where all dreams and desires have been stifled, yet where love is the ghost haunting that home's inhabitants; and here is where the narrative diverges from familiar terrain, at least for our assumed reader.

For those of us who are familiar with Mina's biography (which admittedly is an obscure text since it has yet to be written, though I am obviously at this very moment in the process of writing it), we might be justified in substituting Laman's depiction of her childhood for Mina's formative years while also saving Mina from the accusation of shamelessly stealing from another author's memories. As such, the impossibly messy manuscript of *Laman Duare* might be salvaged and rewritten here as the first chapter of Mina's biography (though admittedly I must steal from Mina's memories in order to write anything that unearths her earliest years, including her origins, of which she never spoke, as far as I know).

As revealed, then, in the manuscript of *Laman Duare*, Mina's father, the Rev. Adam Byrne, was of grubby Anglo-Irish stock; against all economic disadvantages, he had succeeded in winning a place at Cambridge where after three years of endearing himself to the more eminent dons of his college, he was assured of a small but coveted parish within St. Albans. He then made the ill-considered choice of marrying the daughter of a Hungarian-Jewish investment banker, whose father had been an importer of exotic fabrics, and his father before that a successful draper. Lauren Lowell had enjoyed all the advantages of a pampered childhood. For the past three generations since immigrating to the beating heart of Empire, the Lowells had accumulated enough wealth to have become one of the more affluent and respected Jewish households that had managed to escape their grubby East End origins. The Cambridge dons and Lowell patriarchs, however, were in harmonious agreement that there could be no earthly advantage to such an interracial, never mind interfaith, alliance. It was the popular belief of their time that the miscegenation of Gentile and Hebrew would only lead to a mongrelized nation of children poorly-suited to recognizing their proper place within the British scheme of things.

Forced to take a living beneath his ambitions, and disowned by her family, Mina's parents found themselves exiled to the intellectual and social backwater of rural Devon. Lauren made an initial good-faith gesture of converting to the Anglican Church, then promptly disengaged from all communal activities of charity, tea-hosting, and hypocrisy expected of a vicar's wife. The insulated, sophisticated world of Lauren's London upbringing had not prepared her for the ignorance of the ruddy-faced, coarse wives of the local farmers, whose grumbling whispers conjecturing over the mystery of her exotic dark looks and stilted mannerisms were maliciously intended to be overheard. By the time Mina was born, within the first year of her parent's marriage, Lauren had stopped leaving the house altogether. Her only concession was to attend the required weekly appearance at her husband's Sunday sermon where she would give such a studied performance of disinterested resentment that her presence did not in any way inspire further affection towards her from either the vicar or his parishioners. By the time Mina began toddling about on her own, no longer requiring the sustained attentions of her mother, Lauren and Adam Byrne no longer shared a bed, or even the same existence.

In all the years of her unconventional upbringing, throughout which the members of the Byrne household held no sustained contact with each other, or any society outside the vicarage's inner walls and unspoken rules, Mina took for granted her family's peculiarly estranged cohabitation. She thought this was how all families endured each other's enforced presence. There was, after all, no visible proof that her parents had once been passionately in love before they had wildly, unadvisedly married against all better judgments, and then discovered love was not enough to sustain them in the face of overwhelming social and familial disapproval.

Mina was left to spend her days wandering in and out of the cramped rooms of the vicarage, seeking in each of them proof of her parent's presence, only to discover they were always located in some other part of the house, behind closed doors and in chambers Mina was never allowed to enter. She sniffed out the fading perfume or whiff of pipe smoke her parents left as traces of themselves; she listened to footsteps pacing along hallways, a typewriter tapping away in communication with itself, a gramophone repeatedly scratching over the same grooves of a finished record no one bothered to lift and turn over. Often, the sound of her mother singing an old Hungarian lullaby drifted down the long passageway separating Mina's bedroom from Lauren's locked room; or, the dry, emotionless voice of her father offering unwanted advice to one of his begrudging flock could be overheard when Mina pressed her ear to the door of his study. Whenever she did come into contact with her parents, it was always on opposite ends of the day and never with both of them together.

Her father, who had taken Mina's education upon himself, set aside several hours of every morning to meet with his daughter. The first lessons began when she was three, and as soon as the rudiments of reading were accomplished Mina was expected to master a more demanding set of ABCs. After proving a diligent student of Aeschylus, Boethius, and Cicero, she was rewarded with Augustine's *Confessions*, or the *Letters of Abelard and Héloise*. Although Adam expurgated the racier bits, for the most part he was not very attentive, so Mina also became acquainted with the tales of Scheherazade and Shakespeare, the metaphysical wit of Donne and the rambunctious digressions of Sterne. If these liberal borrowings from her father's library were discovered, then as long as she could demonstrate an intellectual response to her illicit choice of reading, Adam decided he had no reasonable justification for further censoring his daughter's education.

As for Mina's minimal contact with her mother, this usually took place on those evenings when Lauren remembered to visit her daughter's bedside. She would do so with the intention of bestowing upon Mina a bedtime story, something Lauren vaguely felt was a maternal obligation, yet discovered herself incapable of providing without some kind of preparation or assistance. Mina was thus left to spend her unsupervised afternoons daydreaming in the privacy of the neglected garden while Lauren sat at her desk in her bedroom trying to think up some fabulous story that she might write down and then read aloud to her daughter at the close of yet another dull, empty day. When her imagination failed her, she attempted to compile into a journal various nuggets of wisdom that she believed, or rather guessed, every mother should pass down to her daughter. In the end, the most Lauren ever managed was a distracted kiss on the brow and sometimes, in her husky voice, a few inaudible phrases concerning the weather or the roses or the nesting sparrows or any other mundane, momentary thought that flitted through her head.

Eventually she gave up trying to speak to Mina. Some maternal mechanism had miserably malfunctioned, though Lauren persisted in her need to communicate the profound love she felt for her child yet was incapable of articulating. She began perusing lists of books from a mail-order catalogue, carefully dissecting their titles and abstracts to discern which ones might allow for a more meaningful dialogue with her daughter. She knew the girl was mad about books. Whenever Lauren accidentally entered a room where she did not expect to discover Mina, her daughter was usually sprawled out on the floor with several books keeping her company; thus Lauren had decided books were the way forward. It took several months to make her tortured selection, and when she finally gave Mina the seven-part set of *A Child's Progress, or, the Trials, Tribulations, and Triumphs of Bertram Benson*, a popular series of children's stories by the esteemed Mrs.

Fiona Beresford, Mina accepted the gift with feigned gratitude, disdainfully frowning down at the gold-embossed title of the first volume, *Bertram and the Goblet of Temptation*. Lauren was devastated, and swore never to make a similar effort again.

Lauren, however, had not read the *Bertram* saga, and because she had no idea that its aim was to indoctrinate every good little boy and girl into becoming upstanding, moral Christians, advising them in patronizing tones how to tell the difference between right and wrong, how to honor their mothers and fathers, and always obediently, meekly turn the other cheek, she had no idea how offensive these books might be to her daughter, who'd already learned such lessons from reading *The Oresteia*. Lauren also never knew that, as soon as she left the room, Mina did not cast the books aside but gulped down the entire *Goblet of Temptation* in a single night, drunkenly thrilled by the epic adventures of that sniveling Bertram Benson. It was the first time Mina had been allowed to participate in a character's adventures for the purely vicarious pleasure of sharing in his perils and downfalls, his battles and victories, and without the portending doom of failing her father's examination of her intellectual growth.

Of course, Mina could not help inwardly cringing at Mrs. Beresford's stilted prose, or heartlessly critiquing the convoluted plot. Bertram's advancement into adolescence and its accompanying picaresque sequence of ludicrous traps and snares was inanely improbable, and little Bertie was a silly, dim-sighted, and annoyingly priggish public school-boy who inspired very little sympathy in the reader (likely an unintended flaw on the part of Mrs. Beresford since each book's dedication identified the author's son, Billy Beresford, as her inspiration). Mina had no other childhood friends, and so she was inevitably as fascinated by Bertram as she was repulsed, and compulsively reread the Bertie books countless times over the course of countless nights in the privacy of her bedroom after her mother had kissed her goodnight.

She became Bertie's greatest antagonist, playing out the many nefarious roles of villains who stood in the way of his moral progress: the Witch of Wolves; the Mage of Maleficent Mire; the Horrible Harpy, responsible for most of the hapless boy's trials and tribulations; the slithering Melusine, who shape-shifted from an emerald-scaled sea-serpent into a green-eyed temptress (though Bertie inadvertently managed to triumph over her when he barged in on one of her clandestine baths, a dirty trick if there ever was one); and lastly, the most wicked of them all, the monstrous Lilith, who gave birth to demons and dragons, and haunted Bertie's nightmares until he took some sleeping potion that made him nearly comatose. Mina began to think she existed in this fantastical world more fully than Bertie himself, and to the point where she stopped reading the books entirely. Instead, the lights remained turned down, and with the room descended into a blank darkness, Mina projected into its void an epic adventure of her own making. Bertie was quickly written out of the story, as he so rightly deserved. Mina now became the heroine, who thanks to her wits and beauty, her bravery and wisdom, rarely suffered a tribulation and always, in the end, triumphed.

Around the time of Mina's tenth birthday, though, a series of events as fantastical as those found in the Bertie books threatened to defeat her. Adam received an unexpected inheritance, declared himself an atheist, gave up his income (yet managed to purchase the house that had come with his parish), began writing his philosophical treatise (which would remain unfinished at the time of his death twenty-one years later), and enrolled Mina in a pretentiously overpriced conservatory, which specialized in finishing off London's hothouse blooms, or so Mina once quipped. Lauren had been given the thankless task of informing her daughter one evening that Mina's father would be taking her on the train to London, where she would be expected to receive a real education, and then she promptly kissed her child goodnight for the last time.

Lauren did not want Mina to see her tears since those tears were not for Mina but her own miserable existence. She deeply resented Adam's new-found atheism, and having thrown away a richly secular life for his insubstantial faith, the least he could have done to repay her sacrifice was to relocate somewhere, anywhere, out of this godforsaken hell called Devon. Sending Mina away to London, which Lauren had regretted leaving every day of their marriage, was exceptionally cruel, and he had not even allowed her a say in Mina's future, believing his wife could not be bothered with such trivial matters, an assumption for which, Lauren knew, she had only herself to blame. Mina certainly blamed her, and would never forgive her mother's lack of sympathy, her cold, disengaged heart, her self-centered absorption, and this, by the way, is where *Laman Duare*'s narrative ends, since Mina seems to have abandoned the manuscript as soon as her simmering fury towards her mother became mired in inarticulate rage.

NOSTALGIA

Mina's next attempt at fictionalizing her life can be found in another unfinished manuscript of a novel that deals with her student days in London. Much of the text lapses into feminist polemic, which never makes for compelling fiction, but it usefully describes the six awkward, lonely years she spent at the Regnauld Conservatoire. Here Mina was forced into a sphere of social activities for which her own isolated childhood had not sufficiently trained her; deposited among a gaggle of girls incapable of measuring up to Mina's level of intellect, she was nevertheless made to feel in every respect their inferior. She did not know how to pour tea or properly set a table, or how to embroider, or even darn a sock; she was completely inept when it came to selecting the most flattering ensembles of clothes, accessories, and style of hair; she could not flirt or dance or flutter her eyelashes; she did not understand the etiquette of saying the very farthest thing from the truth, but blurted out exactly what she thought when someone else behaved stupidly; and she was a failure when it came to sharing secrets about herself, which is an art every girl masters if she wants to make friends of other girls. Mina did not think she had any secrets, and if she did then she would have kept them to herself, or else what would be the point?

Mina did learn she had one secret she should never disclose. As soon as the headmistress discovered the Byrne girl's maternal connections to the Lowell tribe, which explained why she received such low marks for her slovenly comportment and dirty fingernails, Mina was called up to Mrs. Cole's office and accused of being Jewish. Mina coolly replied that as far as she knew she'd been baptized and thus came from a Christian family, at least until her father's recent conversion to atheism; yet it was carefully explicated, for Mina's benefit, that the Jews pass down their blood from mother to daughter, ad infinitum, and so this was a taint from which Mina would never be free, no matter how much she insisted on playing the Judas, Barabbas, or Queen Esther. Although slightly confused by this mixing of biblical allusions, as well as the woman's primly self-righteous tone, Mina comprehended that the real point of this lesson was to impress upon her the necessity of denying she was her mother's daughter.

There seems to have been a photograph taken of Mina at this unhappy time in her life, captured during her only visit home after being sent away. She had looked forward to this visit, if only in anticipation of going down

21

on her knees and begging her father to let her indefinitely return home. When Mina arrived, though, she was unsettled by her discovery that they had a house guest, and she could not determine whether this guest was herself or the colleague her father had invited to stay with them over the summer. Mina's mother made her feelings known concerning this unidentified invasive presence by refusing to come out of her room, and would only emerge at night when everyone was safely abed. Mina could hear her tiptoeing down the stairs, like a thief in her own house, to make herself some tea and a plate of scraps left over from the evening's supper. Mina assumed Lauren spent the rest of her days asleep. Regardless of what she did, she made no effort to see her daughter.

Mina also never had the chance to speak alone with her father. He was either locked away in his study or attending to his old Cambridge chum, an esteemed logician and amateur photographer whose predilection for photographing pre-pubescent girls inspired him to extend an invitation to Mina to sit as one of his models. Her father thought it an excellent opportunity to preserve an image of her as a child before she outgrew that role, and gave his permission for the photograph to be taken. She was instructed to wear one of her old white, linen shifts, and assemble herself in an alluring yet innocent pose out in the garden among the honeysuckle vines. Mina did as she was told, and upon viewing the developed negative, both Mina's father and her father's friend exclaimed it was the most charming likeness. I've been unable to locate the image in any known archive, but I assume Mina's expression was not a happy one.

The night before she was sent back to London, her mother finally knocked on her door. Lauren did not receive permission to enter, and so left a parcel for her daughter to discover in the morning. While on the train, Mina unwrapped the brown paper clumsily tied with a piece of twine, and though she could not understand why her mother would give her a book written by her father's friend, as soon as Mina began reading, she forgave this unfortunate choice of author, for it was not the book's fault. She eagerly tumbled down its rabbit hole of disorientated wonder, slipping through its looking glass of a world where contradictions were permitted to make perfect sense, because this, really, presented the most accurate reflection of a world so violently antithetical to a little girl's desire to feel at home in the universe: when what she was told who she was did not mirror who she knew she was.

Mina decided never to return home again until she'd learned what was needed to survive in a world that expected nothing more of her than to grow up and become a respectable woman with a respectable husband and respectable children. By learning how to achieve these things she would know how to avoid them in the future. Mina conformed very nicely to the standards and prejudices of her classmates, gained the sour approval of Mrs. Cole, and flourished under the tutelage of Maître Regnauld, who seemed determined to transform Mina into his most accomplished artist, though Mina had no idea why or how she'd inspired such ambition in the man. She'd never demonstrated any talent or desire for becoming a painter, but decided she may as well do her best to become one, since this was what Maître Regnauld wanted.

Five years later, during the annual exhibition of graduating students, Mina's submission was unveiled to an audible uproar of outraged gasps. At first glance, at least to the discerning eye, there was nothing disturbing about her painting, a very tame watercolor demonstrating a delicacy and precision of hand and line rather than any scandalous originality. It was not even a full nude, though this might have granted it some respectability, since nudes have been the standard representation of the female body since time immemorial. What so many found offensive was the seated woman's vulgar state of half-clothed coquetry, her breasts spilling out of her tightly cinched waist, not to mention the subject's coy tilt of the head, her neck and head stretched at a grotesque angle, and her smile offering a lewd hint of sexual rapacity. The title of the portrait, *Consider My Mother's Corsets*, clearly announced Mina's intentions: portraying her mother in the reckless dishabille of a prostitute, she had not only debased the sanctity of motherhood but also exposed the bare bones of the feminine education she'd been expected to absorb.

For hadn't she, like the rest of her classmates, and like her mother before her and her mother before that, ad infinitum, been expertly trussed and lavishly dressed for display at the marriage market, where their delectable and preferably virginal cunts were the only currency they had to exchange, their flesh no more than fresh meat auctioned off to the highest bidder? Mina did not think there was anything very ground-breaking in her statement; she was only pointing out the obvious, observing her world with an unflinching gaze, just as Maître Regnauld had taught her. She was promptly sent home with her offending portrait, and without a graduating certificate of completion or commendation for effort.

When she showed her father the evidence that had led to her expulsion, he studied it calmly before asking his daughter to explain why she'd felt the need to produce such an oddly disproportionate and repulsive figure. He had never before questioned her without demanding an answer to something he already knew, and so Mina replied, with enough sincerity to be convincing, "Because I want to be a great artist, papa, and great artists must not be afraid to show the ugliness in this world." Adam shook his head, sighed, and apologized, because this was not something he could teach her, but he would look into finding someone who could.

In return for the books Lauren had bestowed upon Mina, books without which her imagination might never have flourished, she decided to give her mother the painting. Lauren studied the portrait for no more than a few seconds, visibly shuddered, and then consigned it to the closet. Mina assumed her mother had misunderstood, and Lauren as usual made no effort to explain that she was not at all insulted by the portrait; rather, she was worried by what it foretold of Mina's future. When it appeared Mina would be allowed to go to Paris to continue her artistic studies, Lauren knew her daughter would end up just as she feared.

The night before Mina left home, Lauren tiptoed into her room and perched on the corner of Mina's bed. Moonlight made her mother's features seem ghoulish, a presentiment of the tumor already eating away at her thorny breast. Mina shut her eyes, wishing she could also shut out Lauren's languid, husky voice, offering her the last obscure words she would ever communicate to her daughter: *Darling, don't fall in love with the first man who chases after you. In fact, don't fall in love at all, if you can help it.* Convinced the woman had been half-mad for years, Mina disregarded her mother's unprompted advice; besides, what did this emotionally withdrawn and stunted woman know of love?

Three months later, Mina discarded her virginity in the locked bathroom of a Parisian duplex. A few obligatory tears squeezed themselves out of her dry, disappointed eyes while her mother's throaty laughter mocked her for those profligate tears, because Lauren had of course known the idiotic girl would persist in discarding her heart until it was inevitably, irretrievably lost. That, I suspect, is how my mother's childhood came to an end, with the ghost of her own mother's voice haunting her for years to come.

CHAPTER TWO
Une grande démence

Mina once told me, when I was far too young to understand, that her life began the moment she met Jerôme de Voile, which occurred the very instant she left her father stranded on the station platform watching his daughter depart without even offering him a wave goodbye. Although this seems an exaggerated coincidence, by Mina's own admission, she insisted that she did indeed meet Jerôme de Voile on the 10:37 morning train from Calais to Paris, and that the train's departure time was hardly a super-fluous detail since she'd missed the 9:17 due to her father's misreading of the timetable. Thus, as Mina concluded without ever telling me the full story, the precise train is crucial in getting the facts right, or else the rest of her life might have unfolded quite differently, and with excruciatingly unimaginable consequences, since I might not have been born, but that comes much, much later . . .

In an effort to understand why she insisted Jerôme de Voile was the true origin point of her life, and since she never thought to explain it to me, I imagine Mina that morning sitting in a first-class compartment, depos-ited there by her father because he believes first-class is synonymous with safety. Regardless if he resents the exorbitant fare, he feels the price was worth it. He wants to see his daughter transported away in the illu-sion of chugging off into a first-class world of genteel propriety, where young women traveling without supervision might remain unmolested.

Mina appears oblivious to her father's anxiety; she is gazing at her face reflected back at her by the window, envisioning the new face that is already emerging to meet her in an unknown future that belongs to no one but herself now that she's escaped the dull, loveless confines of her childhood. For a brief moment, though, Mina, unmoored, is overcome by fear. She steals one last glance back at her father, but the pained look in his eyes is unbearable; his own disconsolate wave of farewell slips into the past, unseen and unacknowledged.

Mina turns from the window and meets the gaze of the man who has sat down in the seat across from her. His eyes are black, contemptuous, and thinly veiled with predatory desire for this lovely, young girl who boldly returns his stare instead of coyly looking away, as any other lovely, young girl would be expected to do. Mina is thrilled by the man's wolfish appraisal, and in her naiveté, is determined to proceed fearlessly. Love will not consume her. She will consume love. I wonder what might have happened if she'd acted on such a courageous impulse, and picture her, briefly, rising, locking the door to the compartment, lifting her dress, and consuming the man she has chosen to be her first lover. Such a scene might have saved her the embarrassment of the one in Jerôme de Voile's bathroom three months later, but a woman enters and sits beside the man across from Mina, immediately attempting to steal the spotlight.

Let us resist the assumption that this woman is the typical matron, stale with musky perfume, jangling with ostentatious jewelry, heftily waggling her hips as she settles into her seat, sniffling disapprovingly as she eyes the unchaperoned Mina, and taking it upon herself to protect the poor girl from that ravenous wolf. Rather, she is a different stock character: slim, elegant, and wilting with worldly ennui. After flirtatiously crossing her legs to reveal an elegant ankle encased in sheer stocking, she attempts to engage the man in conversation, but soon enough, their words come to a halt, and the journey continues in silence. The woman whips out a ladies' fashion journal in a performance of disinterest, refusing to admit her insignificance.

Meanwhile, Mina becomes increasingly immersed in the complicated game now playing out between her and the Frenchman. Caught up in the newly discovered rules of look, look, look at me, you cannot touch, but only look at me, she is enraptured with herself as the object of his lust, seduced by his eyes that are telling her soon, soon, very soon, he shall touch her in all the undiscovered places existing on the map of her body. One glance is enough to achieve this intimacy. His hands are in his eyes, and though Mina has never fallen for that bit of nonsense, claiming the eyes are the windows to one's soul, she thinks perhaps they are the windows reflecting one's desire, which she neglects to admit may more or less amount to the same thing. She muses dreamily upon a small poem set to the rhythmic metronome of the train's churning gears: my desire is my soul, my soul is my desire, my desire, my soul, you, only you, *mon semblable, mon frère, mon cher, mon plaisir* . . .

"*Mon plaisir, mademoiselle,*" he smoothly assures her when the train's jarring halt nearly throws Mina across the aisle into his lap, her face blushing rosily as he steadies her and releases her hand while pressing his business card into it, all achieved in one fluid motion of practiced seduction, which of course Mina is too young to recognize. Then he vanishes and time is returned to its past tense, the immediacy of their mutual passion lost and impossible to recover.

"I'd watch out for that type," Mina was admonished by the older, more sophisticated woman, who was perhaps no more than the ghost of Mina's future self. "He's the sort who'll take everything and leave you with nothing."

Mina, confused, ignored this advice in favor of staring down at the small cream card in her hand. She traced its bold black embossed lettering with her fingertips, *Jerôme de Voile*, and then slipped the card into one of the blank pages of the diary her mother had given her as a going away present, indicating that Mina must now write her own story, which Mina had thought at the time an exceedingly trite gesture. She now relished the thought of concealing Jerôme de Voile's name between the diary's virginal lined leaves that would someday be filled with the story of their torrid affair, an equally clichéd fantasy that Mina was not permitted to pursue further, as she stepped off the train and into the cloying embrace of her Tante Rosalie.

Seven years ago when Lauren had informed her that it was not Adam who was responsible for sending Mina off to London but rather a Mme. Louvel who wished to sponsor Mina's education, Mina had merely supposed this Mme. Louvel an imaginary godmother. This was precisely the sort of thing her own batty mother would concoct rather than acknowledge her father's existence. Then, after Mina had been expelled, the letter from Tante Rosalie had arrived, apologizing for ever having sent her great-niece off to the Regnauld Conservatoire, which in her day had been a very fine place to learn French literature and art but had clearly lapsed in standards if they could not recognize her niece for the great artist she would someday become, and so Mina must without delay come to Paris where she might further her art studies, all expenses paid. Though reluctant to see his daughter travel so far abroad, Adam was not one to stifle another's higher aspirations. He thought Mina should take this opportunity to transcend her provincial childhood, and whether or not she turned out to be a great artist, she surely was intended to achieve greatness at something or other.

Lauren, however, had reacted to the news with unexpected passion. She tore up Rosalie's letter before burning it in the fire, a futile gesture of censorship since it had already been read, then proceeded to scream, babble, and weep that it would be over her dead body before she let her daughter go. When these melodramatics proved unsuccessful, she went on hunger strikes and silent protests, but all to no avail, as this was not so different from her usual routine. Lauren's unspoken fears were based on her certain knowledge that she'd never see her daughter again. As a child, she'd grown up with the threatening stories of Aunt Rosaleen as an example of what happened to wayward girls who followed their wicked desires, and as a woman, Lauren had learned the inconvenience of choosing the life of an outcast, the romance soon disintegrating into regret. Yes, Lauren knew all too well that her only child would never return home, just as she and Aunt Rosaleen had never been allowed to return, but what Lauren did not know was that her waywardly wicked *mume* had never wished to return.

When she was barely seventeen, and on the eve of her marriage to a diligent dull boy from one of the more respectable Jewish families in London, Rosaleen Blessing Lowell had absconded to Paris with her lover, Marcel Gabriel Arnaud, the black sheep of a degenerating aristo-cratic line. Marcel would eventually make his fortune in collecting and selling art, but before that profitable venture rescued him from a sea of debts, he'd been forced to cross the Channel and pass himself off as a tutor to young bourgeoisie girls whose parents believed their daugh-ters could do with a bit of cultural improvement before passing them off to men who, not unlike Marcel, found themselves floundering in dire financial straits. When Marcel first saw pretty, petite, raven-haired

Rosaleen, of the chocolate brown eyes, impish smile, and lilting laugh, he knew that if he were to find success in his foul, tarnished life, then the girl would have to be his first glittering acquisition.

Rosaleen, the only daughter of a successful importer of exotic fabrics, was fluent in five languages, played an entrancing tune on the harp, and proved an avid reader of Marcel's native literature, her favorites ranging from Voltaire, Dumas, Mme. de La Fayette, Diderot, and Flaubert. She had a judicious eye for art mixed with a passionate love of color, light and form, and she could charm even the stingiest of old codgers. After espying the dashing Frenchman who'd been hired as Susan Jacobson's tutor, she'd convinced her father to procure M. Arnaud for herself, even though Mr. Lowell suspected his daughter knew more about art than some scoundrel down on his luck. Rosaleen also knew far more of seduction than poor M. Arnaud or her father might have guessed, and Mr. Lowell would blame the influence of Mme. de La Fayette and all those other French courtesans who'd written cheap romances in order to lure good English-Jewish girls into a life of hedonistic sin.

During one rainy afternoon of reading Rimbaud rather than taking their usual perambulation of the National Gallery, Rosaleen collapsed sobbing in Marcel's arms begging him to rescue her from a dreaded forced marriage. Rosaleen exaggerated the forced marriage bit, but it *was* dreaded, a long life unfolding before her with a man whose ears belonged on an elephant and who still trembled at the mere sound of his mousy mother's voice. Marcel was not at all shocked by the looming marriage; rather, he had not expected to win her over so easily, but here she was, eagerly possessing him with her lips. Two weeks later, they were living in a corner garret at 13 place Emile-Goudeau and enjoying all the pleasures of sin the flesh had to offer.

When they finally got around to setting up business, Rosaleen took on the responsibility of luring prospective clients and painters, all the while perfecting her skills of seduction. Her indiscriminate tastes led to the detection of genius before anyone else looked twice and amassed for them a small fortune that made possible their relocation to a more spacious *appartement* in the environs of Saint-Germain-des-Prés. Although Marcel did not live past the age of forty, succumbing to cirrhosis of the liver, Rosaleen kept up the enterprise on her own, which was not so different from how things had always operated. Marcel's death, however, allowed her a rebirth: she changed her name to Rosalie Louvel, opened a gallery in Montparnasse, presided over a literary salon, introduced numerous writers and artists to each other over late dinners at les Deux Magots, and generally enjoyed herself with all the men and women who passed in and out of her bed. The freedoms of her so-called middle age suited her very well indeed.

By the time she reached her sixty-ninth year, she'd decided it was time to find someone suitable enough to carry on her legacy. Most of her relations, with whom she'd had no direct contact during the past five decades, had predictably gone the way of all flesh. She knew this because for some bizarre reason Nathaniel Jacobsen had sent her the obituary clippings for every successive death in the Lowell family since her scandalous departure from England. She'd always assumed Nathaniel had done this due to some morbid desire for revenge against the woman who'd left him at the altar clinging to his venerable mummy's apron strings. However, one day she received Nathaniel's own obituary along with the postal address for a Rev. Adam Byrne, as well as a lovely handwritten note from a Mr. Jonathon Redpath, who had been honored to spend the last thirty years living in his own particular sin as the companion of the dearly departed Mr. Jacobsen. It seemed Nathaniel had done the service of keeping the exiled Rosalie informed of her family out of sheer gratitude for releasing him from an unnatural union that had been dreaded by both unwilling participants. Mr. Redpath went on to write that shortly before his death, and knowing his time was upon him, Mr. Jacobsen had gone to great lengths to track down Mme. Louvel's last remaining relative, since all of her brothers but one had failed to leave behind any progeny, which explained the name and address of the Rev. Byrne.

But, no, that did not explain nearly enough! Mr. Redpath had neglected to inform her why this unlikely nephew went by a name and religious denomination entirely unconnected to that of his forefathers. Intrigued, Rosalie immediately responded to Mr. Redpath's letter, and after offering her condolences and thanking him for such a thoughtful missive, inquired as to whether he might make a further study into the matter of this mysterious nephew. From there, Mr. Redpath and Mme. Louvel began a warm and extended correspondence, upon which their friendship was formed, providing a comfort to both parties during the last years of their lives. We shall shortly be meeting Jonathon Redpath in person, and so the more pressing matter of Rosalie's nephew demands our attention.

Although it took several months of discreet detective work before Mr. Redpath reached any solid conclusions (an investigation that might have been foreshortened if he'd been less circumspect), he discovered the Rev. Adam Byrne was not in fact Rosalie's nephew, but merely an in-law, whose surname had concealed the identity of her biological relation (a paternalistic convention Rosalie despised for both its inconvenience to the female sex and deplorable associations with the slave-trade), which now brings us back to Mina disembarking from the train and into Rosalie's ecstatic arms, as if Mina were the long-lost daughter she had never had.

"Oh, *ma fille*, you are the precise image of your mother!" Rosalie proclaimed idiotically, because if she had ever in fact seen Mina's mother, then she would never make such an absurd comparison. "Jonathon, love, doesn't she have the very look of her mother?"

Mina smiled politely, extricating herself from Rosalie's grasp, smoothing down her skirts and tucking a stray curl behind her ear while surreptitiously observing her aunt's companion. He was tall, thin, rakish, and despite his sixty-two years, still boasting a thick head of peppery black hair, a smoldering glint in his dark eyes, and a cynical smile perpetually turning up the corners of his mouth. He looked not at all unlike an older version of Jerôme de Voile, and Mina forever fell in love with him when he lifted a silver-rimmed monocle to his left eye, gave Mina a thorough once-over, and then slyly threw the girl a wink before turning to Rosalie and drawling lazily, "Not a bit like the woman. Perhaps you'd like to borrow my spectacles, you old bat, because our Mina looks like no one but herself."

"You watch yourself, Mr. Redpath," the old bat squeaked. "Our Mina is too clever a girl to fall for such shameless sycophancy."

Our Mina was thrilled to have that pronoun attached to her by two strangers who laid claim to her purely in the recognition of their sharing kindred spirits rather than any biological ties. Mina did not consider Tante Rosalie to be her real aunt. She had lived for so long in the claustrophobic trinity of father-mother-daughter that she could not quite believe in the existence of any other familial relations.

"Come along, my dear girl, we haven't a moment to waste," Rosalie tittered cryptically, taking Mina by the arm and leading her out of the station in the general direction of the *appartement* on rue des Saint-Pères, where the old woman had now resided for the past fifty years, refusing to die until she found a suitable student whom she might remodel into the image of her own youthful decadence.

"Shouldn't we wait for Mr. Redpath?" Mina glanced back anxiously at where they'd left Jonathon arranging the delivery of her luggage, though she could also have been hoping for one last glimpse of Jerôme de Voile, as if he might be lingering somewhere in that midday crowd jamming every platform in the Gare du Nord.

"We shouldn't have to do any such thing!" Rosalie cackled. "The first lesson, *ma cherie*, is never wait on any man, no matter how deplorably charming he might be."

And that is how the miseducation of Mina Byrne began. She hardly imagined the invitation to Paris was all part of Tante Rosalie's plan to pry the poor girl free from her supposedly repressed English childhood. Thus, Mina slyly performed the role of innocent ingénue: she dutifully visited all the recommended museums and Parisian landmarks, attended countless tedious soirées, dressed in prudish ensembles, and made herself as unremarkable as possible, thoroughly disappointing her aunt's high expectations of her. Whenever Rosalie invited for tea the most outrageous and interesting people she could find, her niece would indiscreetly yawn, excuse herself with a limpid smile, and disappear to spend a solitary afternoon in the Jardin des Plantes, always coming home with the same studied sketch of an ape sorrowfully staring back at her through the bars of his cage. Rosalie would have forgiven the uninspired sketches, the dull clothes, the utter lack of character, if she'd known they were only a charade. In fact, she would have been very pleased indeed had the girl thought to confide in her, but an affair with a married man twice one's age wouldn't inspire the same illicit thrill if condoned or encouraged by one's seventy-six year-old aunt.

Only two days after her arrival in Paris, and misinterpreting Rosalie's first piece of advice, Mina called upon Jerôme de Voile at his place of business listed on his card, bluntly informing him in her stilted schoolgirl French that she'd like to continue the acquaintance initiated on their shared journey from Calais. Monsieur de Voile, not even remotely the kind of man to turn down such a brazen, unanticipated offer, whisked her off to a sordid, dimly lighted café where he began his drawn-out seduction. This was hardly necessary since Mina was more than willing to fall in love with the first man to go chasing after her.

Let us fast forward through the details of Jerôme de Voile's carefully calculated onslaught of Mina's virginal barricades. If the reader is interested in such things, then refer to the novel by Choderlos de Laclos, which, upon his first perusal of it as a boy of twelve and plotting out the seduction of his mother's chambermaid, had served as Jerôme's textbook manual for all subsequent affairs. Having now matured into a seasoned lover, he believed he'd perfected the Vicomte de Valmont's tactics of conquer and destroy, since unlike Valmont, he never fell in love with his prey. Mina, unaware that she was any man's prey, enthusiastically engaged herself in the twilight strolls, the whispered endearments, the yearning gazes, the protestations of devotion, the feverish stolen kisses, and was ripe for the picking when at long last Jerôme proffered the invitation to his duplex on rue Racine. This is where he resided when he wanted to forget he had a wife, and where Mina anticipated they would consummate their mutual lust, which for her had been elevated into *une grande passion*. (More like *une grande démence*, Tante Rosalie might have quipped if she'd been asked.)

The moment she arrived, Mina knew that it was all a horrible mistake, and that she'd entered a foreign world where nothing made sense. Another woman answered the door. Mina had not suspected Jerôme's invitation might include anyone else, and although she had taken great care to wear what she'd assumed to be the height of sartorial splendor, she was immediately diminished by the other woman's glance of scathing pity. This sentiment was further reinforced by all the other party guests laughing away in the rooms beyond the foyer, not exactly laughing at Mina, but making her feel absurdly small. They seemed to her a blur of exotic glossy animals bedecked in a mélange of slinky gowns and crisply tailored dinner jackets, and having arrived in what she now realized was only a childishly prim and pleated frock, Mina was suddenly no longer herself but Alice unwittingly crashing a party where she was neither expected nor wanted. Jerôme also appeared surprised to see Mina standing before him; he too was laughing over some inane joke with some doe-eyed minx who now quickly wandered off to a herd of other gazelle-like creatures after excusing herself from the lumbering silence Mina had brought with her.

"Well, little girl, what do you want of me?" Jerôme asked, one brow arched in a manner she'd thought so attractive only two days ago.

"To be loved," Mina blurted out, because she did not understand this game.

"*Alors*, that perverse old man may have been on to something," he sighed affectedly for an imagined audience who might appreciate his pretentious wit. "It is a misfortune, yes, but a woman's desire is always narcissistic."

Mina, who'd always tuned out during her aunt's endless teas, and had therefore missed the ludicrous debate that took place one day between two surrealists engaged in the endless war of the ego and the id, was now at a complete loss for a response.

"I suppose you want to be the only woman loved by me?" he prompted.

"Yes, of course," she replied, because she had not thought there was anything inherently pathological about her desire and thus there was no point in concealing what seemed to her a very simple, uncomplicated truth.

"Ah, but little girl, there is something I must love in everyone!" he burst out laughing, appearing very pleased with his absurd declaration.

Mina dumbly stared back at him, suddenly bewildered as to how or why she'd fallen for the crass charms of such a transparent man. This egalitarian desire of his was supremely selfish and illogical, because to love everyone must surely render each of his lovers into no one. Mina shut her eyes, painfully, and when she opened them Jerôme had been magically, fatefully replaced by a complete stranger who for some reason knew her name.

"Miss Mina, you are not to be ill," the man pronounced with misplaced inflection.

In a sudden flash of inspiration, she decided to settle upon the most repugnant person immediately available as an antidote to Jerôme de Voile, and disregarding how this apish fool knew her name (he'd attended one of Rosalie's teas where he'd been introduced to a somnambulant Mina), she affected a wavering, winsome smile, and replied, please, if you could assist me in finding *la toilet*, thankyoueversomuch, and the man was ever so quick to oblige. With her back pressed against the locked door, Mina listened to the garbled voices of party guests on its other side; she refused to cry when he clumsily shoved his prick into her, biting her tongue and stubbornly keeping her eyes open throughout the entire ordeal, which only lasted a matter of seconds before he expelled one final grunt and disengaged from Mina to observe the unexpected and unwanted proof of her proverbial maidenhood streaking his hirsute thighs. He begrudgingly offered her a beige monogrammed hand towel before attending to his own excretions. After swabbing away all traces of blood, Mina studied the stained towel, realizing this may not have been the wisest response to Jerôme's humiliating rejection.

"You will forgive us," the swarthy man demanded. "I did not know of stealing your . . . um . . . well . . . your purity."

"Don't be ridiculous," Mina retorted. "You haven't stolen anything."

"I insist to differ," he grumbled, obdurately seating himself on the commode. "A man never must steal . . . um . . . ah . . . well . . . unless intended for wife . . . or unless paying . . ."

"*Nothing's* been stolen," Mina insisted. "It's just a silly bit of blood, quite natural for any woman during her . . . well . . . um . . . you know . . ."

"Ah . . . yes . . . ah . . . harrumph," the man inarticulately reached the conclusion to which Mina had vaguely misled him, his face slowly contorting with disgust. "Then *you* must be forgiven . . . to tempt me to . . . um . . . yes, to lie with you . . . *unclean* . . ."

"Oh, please, you're talking utter rubbish," Mina angrily, irritably waved the bloodied towel in his direction. "And if you must know, I'm clean as a baby's bottom!"

He stared at her blankly, something clearly lost in translation, as if he were envisioning a baby's diapered bottom sitting in its own shit. Then, realizing where his own posterior was perched, he leapt to his feet, and in a vain struggle to recover his dignity, slipped one of his broad, meaty hands into the inner breast pocket of his now badly rumpled, sweat-stained jacket and retrieved a calling card with gold embossed lettering, which he forced upon her. Mina glared down at the spidery script informing her that he possessed the improbably alliterative name of Besim Berisha and that he lived on some shady street off Place Blanche, where syphilitic whores, con artists, pornographers and the dregs of bohemia freely roamed. So much for Besim Berisha's obsession with purity, Mina wryly observed, bursting into a fit of giggles.

"The day will be you must desire some need for me, Miss Mina," he stiffly informed her, confused and embarrassed by the girl's hysterical laughter. "Mayhap you are feeling shame at present but with my insurance, I will oblige to you an honest woman's making."

"You will make an honest woman of me?' Mina was so astonished by the preposterously clichéd sentiment rather than his strangled syntax that her laughter had now turned to tears.

"Ah, yes, such is the phrase, ahem," he cleared his throat yet again and muttered one last invitation before blessedly leaving her alone. "And you may oblige to me for making photograph. You have face of avenging angel, yes, ahem, much to be obliged, thank you."

Mina locked the door upon Besim Berisha's hasty, fumbling exit, and then, with towel in one hand, and calling card in other, she dried her eyes and deliberated over what she should do next. Placing the card aside, she picked at the embroidered lettering of the monogrammed towel displaying an ornately stitched ~ J de V ~ until the thread began to unravel. Once the initials were completely mangled, she refolded the cloth so her virginal blood was conspicuously revealed in a rust red smear, replaced it in the linen cabinet, and then deposited the calling card in her tiny tasseled handbag. Mina, however, doubted Besim Berisha would ever hold enough magnetic attraction for her to be lured north into the dubious eighteenth arrondissement.

Somewhat dismayed, Mina realized that despite the manner in which she'd made free use of her body, she had not yet cut loose from her childish faith in romance, that true-love-at-first-sight-butterflies-in-stomach sort of romance, which she'd read many times in many books was the natural condition accompanying all consummations of desire. Choosing, for the moment, to forgive her shortcomings, Mina briskly splashed her tear-streaked face with a handful of icy water from the chrome faucet and patted her cheeks dry with a freshly laundered towel boasting the same regrettable initials. She discarded the cloth in a corner and walked out of that bathroom forever, though this too, like her mother's knowing laughter, would haunt her for years to come. When one is seventeen, freshly deflowered, and eager to bloom in such luxurious newfound freedom, the smallest detail hardly matters, such as a faux Albanian émigré comfortably cloaked in one's handbag, just waiting to be retrieved, recalled and redeemed as one's ticket out from all romantic obligations.

Emerging from the bathroom, Mina glanced at a wall-clock vaguely resembling a rooster, and noted the hour. Less than twenty minutes had elapsed since she'd last spoken with Jerôme de Voile. She found him whispering into yet another woman's ear, a seductive smile on his lips as he elicited from her a low, provocative laugh, his hand resting possessively on the low dip of her spine, the bare flesh exposed by a backless emerald silk dress. While Mina stood there, unnoticed, observing Jerôme de Voile and one of his many mistresses dripping from his arm, she promptly decided there was nothing to envy in this other woman because she, Mina, could not possibly be in love with a man who monogrammed his hand towels and insisted he indiscriminately loved something in everyone.

"Thank you for inviting me to such a lovely party, Monsieur de Voile," Mina murmured in her most proper English, rudely interrupting the lusty tableau. "I've had a most memorable evening, for which I am not in the least grateful or obliged to you."

"You are not departing already?" he blandly smiled, not entirely following Mina's words or why she was in such a rush to leave. "Would you not like a glass of wine, *ma petite fille*?"

"No, thank you, I believe I've had enough." Mina offered a prim, trium-phant smile and then vanished into the summer night, leaving Jerôme de Voile in some confusion; he could not recall what he'd said to upset her silly sensibilities, but there were always other little girls to seduce, and so he swiftly forgot all about her.

Mina, on the other hand, would always recall his name thanks to a bloodstained towel embroidered with his abbreviated identity; his face would not fare so well, eventually becoming a blur of features, and even now, the insult of J de V's cruelly dismissive smile was already consigned to a dim corner of her memory. She was more concerned with the aching throb between her legs and the sticky discomfort of blood still trickling down her thighs as she walked up Saint-Germain before turning right onto rue des Saint-Pères. Out of everything from that night, she would remember most clearly the walk home and the sensation of simultane-ously inhabiting and having been evicted from her body.

As soon as Mina walked into the room where Tante Rosalie and Mr. Redpath had sat sipping crème de menthe while waiting for her return, she collapsed in a chair and wept for the loss of her dignity rather than her virginity. Rosalie directed Mr. Redpath to pour out another round of crème de menthe, and after Mina slurped down the treacly liqueur as if she'd been forced to take a teaspoon of medicine, she spilled out all the lurid, humiliating details of her activities over the past three months. Neither of her elders betrayed the slightest whiff of disapproval. They were more than happy to relive their youths through the girl's first flawed romance, and knowing it would not be her last, thank goodness, liberally offered their advice as to how she should proceed. Tante Rosalie proclaimed Mina must now fearlessly throw herself into the business of living life to the fullest of her imaginative capacities. Mr. Redpath suggested the only way to follow through on such high ideals was to embrace all that was most repugnant to her, because that, ducky, is the only means of achieving absolute courage, with which Mina complaisantly agreed before trundling off to bed.

When she woke the following morning, Mina borrowed one of Rosalie's old gypsy skirts and peasant blouses, which seemed the most suitable ensemble for the task at hand, left her hair unbraided beneath a broad-brimmed floppy straw hat, crossed the Seine and walked up into the seething, seedy, southern fringes of Montmartre, unchaperoned and determined never to look back. With the help of some very good-natured and garishly painted women idling about on a corner that had been left unlisted in her out of date, borrowed Baedeker, Mina found the address she was looking for, climbed three flights of a steeply spiraling staircase, knocked upon the intended door, and when it opened, refused to flinch. Besim Berisha glared down at her as if he'd been expecting someone, anyone, other than Mina, who merely placed into his hand the calling card he'd forced upon her the evening before in his bungled attempt at social decorum, and then stepped silently, purposefully, across the threshold of the door.

Mina discovered herself stranded in the squalid privacy of this stranger's too cramped, too cluttered, too fetid abode, as well as the suffocating, sordid intimacy that had already been established between them. She came to a halt in the middle of the room, and refusing to take in the details of the studio's chaotic disorder, or its malodorous musty maleness, she turned and faced her astonished host, who was far more embarrassed by her presence than either could have anticipated. Just as Mina had walked away from Jerôme de Voile utterly disillusioned with regard to her romantic fantasies, so too had Besim innocently arrived at the de Voile soiree without the slightest preconception that he'd be dragged up into that bathroom and tricked into relieving the girl of her virginity only to be mocked and discarded immediately after she'd made use of him. Indeed, Besim had spent a sleepless night mulling over the collapse of all his carefully constructed illusions concerning appropriate relations between the sexes.

By the time he'd met Mina, he had cultivated a healthy degree of machismo, and having invested a great deal of faith in the magnetic compulsion he seemed to hold for the opposite sex, Besim had long since accepted that the female body existed for no other purpose than the satisfaction of his invariable and somewhat tamely bourgeois desires, and that as soon as he'd finished with one woman he would inevitably move on to the next. Thus, Besim did not know how to react to this presumptuous twit who'd taken the initiative to continue what could only become a messily obsessive and ill-defined affair. Besim in fact failed to respond to the body she seemed to be offering him the moment he shut the door and turned to discover her disrobing. In almost any other circumstance, he would have gratefully accepted her offer, but his spine stiffened with rejection and he was at a loss to explain why she left him so unnerved, unmanned, so unlike his usual blustering braggadocio self.

"You have come for photographing," he grumbled, desperately hoping this was the only reason for her unprompted display.

Mina stared at him blankly, though not because she misunderstood, clearly recalling his invitation to take her photograph; rather, his manner of speech now seemed a clumsily transparent charade. Several years later Mina would have confirmed for her this initial suspicion that Besim's odd accenting of syllables and supposed Eastern European pedigree were no more authentic than his name. In that moment, however, she realized her body had taken Mr. Redpath's advice rather too literally, but instead of embracing what was most repugnant to her, a retching turmoil began to rise from her belly and into her throat.

"I'm afraid I'm going to be ill," she whispered hoarsely.

Besim took her by the arm and directed her to the basin, into which Mina lowered her head and emptied the contents of her stomach. Afterwards, in a repeat of the previous night's encounter, Besim handed her a towel, which did not boast a single stitch of monogrammed initials. It even smelled freshly laundered, without the slightest trace of its owner's scent, for which Mina also was grateful, or she might have continued being shamefully sick. While she pressed the towel to her face, dabbing the corners of her mouth and the perspiration gathered at her brow, Besim placed his paisley silk dressing gown over her shivering shoulders, sparing them the continued discomfort of her nudity. Mina did not shrug off this kindness, and decided to accept from him a glass of chocolaty claret, although the sun had yet to reach its meridian.

The rest of the morning slid into an afternoon lazily unfolding to the accompaniment of three bottles of wine and their voices circling around various topics that avoided the more substantial subjects of themselves. A phonograph recording of *Eroica* repeatedly turned itself over, and Mina tried to ignore the absence of the missing consonant in the symphony's title, which in her mind threatened to turn it into the erotica surely unintended by Beethoven or the man sitting beside her. Several poems were read aloud, but when Besim began to suspect his familiarity with the literary past severely lacking in comparison to a girl who could recite by heart entire passages from Virgil, Dante, and Shakespeare, he whipped out a tarot pack, which he claimed to have inherited from a gypsy woman, and proceeded to invent Mina's future. The Hanged Man made an ominous appearance beside the Page of Cups, and Besim warned her to fear death by water, to which she lamely quipped, if one were fated to drown then at least one might escape death by fire. A game of chess was played, which Mina allowed Besim to win, and in the violet light of dusk she disrobed once more. They had nothing more to disclose, nothing more they wished to know about the other, and although the only discernible objects in the room were the shadowy contours of the furniture Besim had accumulated from rummaging in the junk shops of Montmartre, he'd taken out his camera and begun photographing her.

When Mina asked why he was taking pictures of her in the dark, he explained: "I am learning the better how to see you."

"But there's nothing to see," she replied, her tongue thick and furry from the wine.

"Quite," Besim confirmed. He sounded distinctly more British than Albanian.

But Mina was too drunk to bother challenging this clipped shift in accent, and was hardly disturbed by his curt summation of her existence; she merely assumed they would become lovers, and that through repeated physical contact with a man from whom she felt entirely dissociated, the sexual act would become reduced to two bodies sparking a feeble light off of each other. Unfortunately, and despite Mina's many embarrassingly lazy efforts at seduction, Besim perversely withheld from entering into any relationship more physically intimate than photographing her in the nude. Although she pursued other romantic entanglements, engaging in unmentionable sex that left her partners reeling with adoration, Mina would always return to the Montmartre studio and Besim would always allow her to return, as if they both held some privileged claim over the other, a claim that neither in fact desired or admitted (even years later after they'd been married).

NOSTALGIA

One day, Mina found herself sitting in the Jardin des Plantes making innumerable sketches of an ape staring back at her through the bars of its cage. The drawings were as uninspired as the ones she'd made when she first came to Paris, and on closer inspection, she reached the conclusion that this was the same ape she'd been drawing two years ago. When she received the telegram informing her that Lauren Lowell had died from an undetected tumor in her left breast, instead of returning home to attend the funeral, Mina boarded a ship optimistically headed for the new world. Tante Rosalie provided her with tearful blessings, generous financial assistance, and the Madison Avenue address of an old friend who used to do the high-kick at the Moulin Rouge in her more gamine days.

Mina arrived in New York in the sweltering, eternal haze of August. She aimlessly wandered the noisy, invasive, filthy streets, until one afternoon she stumbled into some squalid pub where she was accosted by a distraught, drunken man who offered her a poem and the promise of that impossible true-love-at-first-sight-butterflies-in-stomach sort of romance. As she looked into Andrew Brennan's hazel eyes, she realized, awkwardly, that up until this point in time she had barely skimmed the surface of madness into which it is said fools plunge and drown when they have helplessly, hopelessly fallen in love.

CHAPTER THREE
Of Marriage and Muses

The very day Mina stepped off the ferry from Ellis Island, Andrew Brennan decided to marry a woman who was not at all an appropriate choice. Before sending the telegram informing his father of this fateful decision, he stood at the Western Union counter deliberating over all the excuses he might use in his defense. It would eventually have to be *some* woman, and so it may as well be *this* one. She wasn't all that bad, though he wasn't certain what qualities a woman should possesses in order to inspire a man to claim her as his wife. All Andrew knew was that his choice, by virtue of infinitely infuriating his father, would excuse Andrew from the occasional obligatory holiday visit home. Nevertheless, he continued studying the telegram, which he could not yet bring himself to push through the slot and sign over to the clerk, who in a series of exasperated sighs was audibly expressing his eagerness to get on to the next customer.

"*Proposed stop Accepted stop Small Ceremony stop RSVP full stop.*"

Andrew did not like all those stops; they hinted of defeat, and as soon as the clerk snatched away the slip and receipted his payment, Andrew realized that he had not written the telegram as it should have been written. He'd omitted the name of the woman who had accepted his proposal, defeating the whole point of the telegram, which was to inflict upon his father (with the specific name of a very specific woman) the realization of all his worst fears. That his eldest son indeed had no sense, good taste, or judgment, and that a child of his should turn out so disappointingly was painfully unimaginable to the great Vasili Vasilievich Novikov. And so Andrew stood paralyzed, trying to decide if it was worth writing a new telegram or if he were better off forgetting the whole matrimonial farce; he continued staring blankly for some time at the clerk's jaundiced complexion mapped by a volcanic landscape of erupting pores. In return, the clerk eyed Andrew suspiciously, unable to comprehend why this person refused to behave like all his other customers and amenably step aside. Finally, Andrew's gaze focused on the white crease of the clerk's scalp, revealed by the black pomaded slick of his parted hair.

"I'm sorry," he mumbled. "I gave you the wrong message. I need to correct it."

"But it has been sent," the clerk blandly informed Andrew from behind the barricade of iron bars on his stall. "There is nothing to correct."

"But I just gave it to you!" Andrew blurted. "In fact it's there, right there, on the counter, to your right, top of the pile. You haven't sent a goddamned thing!"

"Sir, it is sent if I have said it is sent," the clerk smirked before venomously narrowing his eyes. "Are you, sir, questioning my tenacity, or even my veracity, in successfully carrying out the functions of my occupation?"

"What the fuck are you talking about?!" Andrew exploded, inspiring a wave of startled gasps in the line of customers waiting behind him.

"Sir, if you feel the need to make an amendment to a previously transmitted telegram, you may step to the back of the line and when it is again your turn, you may submit a revised message," the clerk droned before pursing his lips, staring Andrew into seething silence.

Andrew's clenched fists were about to grasp and force the bars apart into two inverse arcs so that he might smash to a pulp the clerk's smarmy face. He was quickly forced into relinquishing this fantasy upon reevaluating the material reality of those bars and his own estimable strength in altering their vertical attachment to the clerk's stall. They were there, after all, for this very reason. So he walked away, ignoring the bewildered expressions of the other customers studying him as he departed; each and every one of them relieved to have him vanish, as he'd certainly disrupted the routine of things.

Andrew sidled down the next few blocks, hugging the walls, avoiding the cast of his shadow, and stepped into the first bar he found. By the time he'd finished his third bourbon, he couldn't recall why he'd felt the need to improve the silly telegram. His parents would know implicitly the identity of the woman in question; there had never been any need to name her. By the bottom of his fifth bourbon, and as he was ordering the sixth, he discovered his double reflected back at him in the mirror across the bar offering an inanely smug grin. By not naming her, Andrew had accomplished a very neat trick. His evasive allusion to a small ceremony that did not precisely name a second participant was in the nature of many of his father's own well-crafted narrative loopholes. Yes, just as the great magician of fictions, Vasili Novikov, always gave himself enough room to pull out of his hat all sorts of unexpected tricks, Andrew had perfected the art of leaving open an escape route from reality. His telegram now appeared a clever contrivance allowing him to produce just about any woman as his wife. His father would show up expecting a certain future daughter-in-law, only to be met by a complete stranger, and he would have no choice but to applaud his son's ingenious talent for surprise.

The following morning, when Andrew woke with a hammer pounding nails into his skull, he decided that if he had a choice between this reality and the one found at the bottom of a bottle of bourbon, he would choose the liquid mirage. To make matters worse, the buzzer persisted in ringing until someone agreed to answer. The woman beside him moaned into his armpit, assured that he would be the one to silence the buzzer. It was the Western Union boy, wearing a goofy, optimistic grin, as if it were inconceivable that he should ever be the bearer of grief, tragedy, and doom. Andrew blearily signed the slip, and slammed the door with an insensitive thud. He sat down on a ratty armchair, and proceeded to read the over-hasty reply.

"*How lovely stop We shall do our best to attend full stop.*"

Andrew winced. His mother's perfunctory response was as insincere as could be expected and was intended, if anything, as a prescient balm for her son's blistered pride, which was about to be scorched by one of his father's cruelly dismissive rebuttals to whatever drivel his son had proposed. This time, Andrew was prepared; he noted the time, closed his eyes, and wagered Vasili's telegram would arrive in approximately twenty-eight minutes; seven minutes later than expected, the same Western Union lad yet again received the door slammed in his face as quickly as it had been flung open. The woman in Andrew's bed groaned irritably, rising groggily to confront him in all her naked abundance of bosom and torso, the sheets inconsequentially having slid down to her broad hips. Sara, to whom this bed and this apartment belonged, confronted her fiancé with a bleary eye.

"Andrew, my dear, *must* you go banging about so goddamned early in the morning," she muttered in the general direction of the clock. He ignored her complaint, flopping back onto the bed with the unopened telegram held against his brow as a semaphore of despair. Sara snatched it, read it and then flung it onto Andrew's chest, laughing crudely, remarking carelessly, as she ambled off into the bathroom, "Well, darling, what else did you expect?"

Andrew listened to her running the taps for her bath and then the trickle of water as she used the toilet, having, as usual, disregarded his need for privacy. He brought the telegram up to the level of his eyes, and read, relying on anything that might now serve as a distraction from living with a woman who never felt the urge to close the bathroom door.

"*Fool stop No Marriage stop Are you mad question mark exclamation full stop.*"

The roar of the flushing toilet gurgled into the room and then the rippling splash of Sara's flesh sinking into her steaming bathwater. As she released intermittent gasps and coos over the hot pleasure in which she now found herself immersed, Andrew nearly concurred with that full stop; yet he knew there was only one role expected of him. Vasili's supreme enjoyment in this life was violently scrimmaging against his sons, and Andrew's filial duty was to participate in these occasional conflicts until either his father won or lost all interest in the game.

Later that afternoon Andrew stood once more before the same odious clerk, slipping him a crudely phrased reply intended to provoke his father even further, perhaps to the point of apoplexy, and then Andrew could marry whomever he damn well pleased without the hassle of Vasili butting in with his officious opinions. The battle had now begun in earnest. Over the proceeding weeks, Andrew spent entire afternoons shuffling back and forth between the Western Union and the *The Triple N*, a shadowy dive he'd discovered on West 54th Street. He would sit in what soon became his regular booth and scribble away in a notebook that held nothing more than doodles and overheard scraps of inebriated dialogue shared between the other customers at the bar. Andrew claimed if anyone asked (though no one did), that he was collecting raw material for his first play. After consuming a series of iced bourbons, he would then tramp down the three blocks to receive his father's latest challenge, also becoming quite a regular with Alan the clerk, who shrewdly refrained from commenting on the absurdity of the convoluted slurs and slanders passed back and forth between father and son. Alan's silence was purchased with an extra fiver Andrew slipped over to him at the end of each day before making his way home, careful never to return until Sara was sure to have stepped out for the evening. Luckily she was playing in some obscure more-than-off-Broadway production, so she barely noticed his absence from her life. They simply shared a bed.

As expected, Vasili eventually lost interest, or Deirdre had prevailed upon him to get back to work on his latest novel. When the terms of his truce arrived, it was such a momentous occasion that Alan had the document run over by the delivery boy to Andrew's booth. Andrew read the message, expelled a heavy sigh, then generously tipped the boy, who snatched the dollar out of Andrew's hand and bought a swift shot of whiskey before skipping off to deliver more tidings of either bliss or woe, for it was all the same to him. Andrew meticulously went over again each word, each gloriously irrelevant and perfectly placed stop.

"*I relent stop only if postponed stop one year full stop.*"

A year, a year, everything could happen in a year. Only a year ago he'd sat at a table in a tavern much like this one, though slightly more upscale, surrounded by his brothers, his mother, and his father. All of them had been uncomfortably restrained, unable to resist snatching appalled glances at the woman Andrew had decided to bring along to this farewell dinner in honor of his brother, Jamie. His family, of course, had assumed the familiar faux pas had been motivated by Andrew's infernal desire to upstage his younger brothers, still resentful that they'd ever been born, though this was not his reasoning on this particular occasion.

He had brought Sara because, in the brief blush of their affair, Andrew was enraptured, head over heels, gob smacked, and refused to imagine anyone else incapable of comprehending those feelings or accepting the woman responsible for inspiring them. Andrew should have known better, and realized too late that if he ever fell in love again, he must conceal all evidence of that woman's existence; that she should remain at all costs a buried treasure undetected by his family, especially his parents. Because as soon as Vasili and Deirdre, in unison, studied Sara with their narrowed eyes, Andrew's own vision became tainted. Clearly she would never belong within the enclosure of their inner, exclusive circle. Sara, however, was unaware of the fatal blows working against her, for which Andrew was also to blame, as he'd done nothing to prepare her for that deliberate unified gaze, which mercilessly skewered anyone who did not meet Novikovian standards of intellectual sophistication.

Large boned, amply bosomed, broad faced, lusty, blunt, braying, simple, oh, so simple, she appeared blithely monstrous, a genial ogress battering her vulgar presence against a refined, steel-tempered wall of disapproving silence. She clucked and gushed in a show of maternal fondness over Andrew's adolescent brother, Colin, flirtatiously teasing out of him a sweetly mortified grin. She interrogated Jamie, departing for his studies in philosophy at the Sorbonne, as to whether he'd devised an adequate response to Hamlet's rhetorical quandary, *être ou n'est pas être*? She professed a passionate interest in reading his father's new book, the one he was still in the throes of composing, and then confessed her personal library primarily consisted of historical romances. Thus, she didn't know if she'd be able to endure his *playful style of dense erudition*, reciting an absurd phrase from a recent review in *The New Yorker*, and mistakenly believing that by demonstrating she'd done her research she coyly flattered Andrew's father, who scorned any and all criticism of his work as mere piles of piffle. Finally, she committed the worst blunder imaginable, and complimented his mother on the three fine boys she had produced, as if the two women shared some common ground in the trifling fact that they both owned ovaries.

His mother's thin, contained, patrician face gleamed with condescension, as she accepted perfunctorily, politely, the crude compliment, because that is how Deirdre Novikov managed to float above the muck and mire of philistines such as Sara Sorrell. Jamie's pale, grim expression exhibited one of detached interest, as if Sara were an unclassified bug that had been placed before him. Colin was simply determined to devour everything on his plate and then move on to the untouched food on everyone else's plate, blissfully ignorant of the rising tension around the table. Andrew seethed with envy, for who was this bumbling, rambunctious boy? He could not possibly belong to this family, and yet, their mother never once reprimanded his barbaric table manners, and their father visibly adored him.

Vasili, at that moment, was sharing in Colin's gusto for the food. His eyes gleamed with adulation for his youngest son, and whenever he thought to address Jamie, his voice surged with an underlying tone of pride and respect. For Andrew, he had only vitriol and venom. He ignored the outlandish woman's incessant, mindless chattering by concentrating his seething wrath onto his eldest son, who had dared presume any interloper would have been welcome. Andrew wanted to protect poor, common Sara from this hostile group of snobs, while simultaneously suppressing the urge to disown her on the spot, kick her under the table, and brush off the crumbs of her presence with a sharp flick of his napkin. Instead, he slouched lower in his chair, twisting the table linen violently in his hands, his face drained, colorless, because he was furious, helpless, and terribly ashamed: all the emotions his father usually provoked in him, no matter what he did, no matter how he behaved. He was convinced he could not be his father's son.

"I am relinquishing your name," Andrew finally exploded.

Sara's nervous titter threatened to turn into an astonished bray, but he was gripping her hand under the table, pinching her into silence. Colin looked up from his plate in awe and wonder, admiring the drama his older brother always seemed capable of spontaneously creating. Jamie displayed the glimmer of an envious smile. His mother sighed impatiently, though she had the grace and good manners never to roll her eyes in exasperation over her son's sporadic tantrums. His father was the only one who thought to laugh.

"What on earth . . . are you . . . going on about?" Vasili dismissively waved his fork in the air, still in the process of finishing a mouthful of food.

"I've decided to take mama's name," Andrew persevered. "Yes, I'm changing my name from Novikov to Brennan," and then tacked on insensibly, "I think this shall be best for all."

"Andrej," his father chuckled, folding his napkin neatly down beside his now empty plate. "You are free to call yourself whatever you like, but it still does not change you are my son. Now, while your mother, your brothers, and your *guest*, order some dessert, we shall enjoy a cordial at the bar, and a cigarette, yes?"

Andrew's mother glanced disapprovingly at his father; she'd recently demanded he give up his three-pack-a-day-habit, but knowing a greater battle needed, for the moment, to be waged, she promptly brought over the waiter who had their plates cleared and desserts served. Andrew and Vasili stood at the bar, sipping a smoky cognac each, inhaling their cigarettes, and performing as if they were the two closest comrades in the world.

"She's a deplorable actress, and a married woman, no less," his father remarked.

"She is being divorced," Andrew proffered.

"Being?" his father huffed intolerantly at Andrew's choice of verb tense and the ambiguous position in which it placed Sara. "Is this something she has decided to pursue or is it *being* inflicted upon her against her will?"

"How could it possibly matter?" Andrew inexpertly exhaled a cloud of smoke into his father's blandly arrogant face. "She getting a divorce and I love her, and I may even marry her, eventually. And she is a damn talented actress!"

"She is older than you," his father reprimanded.

"You are younger than mama," Andrew riposted.

"Your mother is a different breed altogether," his father pronounced. "Look, Andrej, this woman, she is not worth our time quibbling. I do not begrudge your youthful and indiscriminate tastes. Yes, experience as many women as possible from as many varietals to be found in this life. Just do not, and I repeat, do not ever bring one of them to my dinner table again."

"So you aren't offended if I change my name?" Andrew clutched onto this small act of revolt, even if his father reduced it to an empty gesture.

"You can change your name to Oblomov, for all I care," Vasili impatiently flicked his hand, parting the sea of smoke between them. "All I ask, if you take your mother's name, is that you do not shame her with your habitual laziness and squandering of talents! In fact, I demand you produce within the next two years a substantial piece of work. I do not send money every few months with the benevolent wishes for you to spend it all on booze and your latest showgirl folly! Now, let us rejoin your mother, and congratulate Jamie; he's your brother and leaves for Paris in the morning. We should all be proud of his accomplishments!"

Andrew bit his tongue, he bit his lip, he would have bit down on his knuckles, but the usual performance of infuriated anguish was unnecessary. He knew when to concede to his father's greater will and when to challenge it. Andrew also knew he should be grateful for any truce Vasili might offer him; nevertheless, a year later, he buried his head in his hands, staring bleakly at the telegram, clutching at his hair as if he might tear it out of his scalp. Could he, should he, cower humbly before his father yet again, abase himself at the altar of Vasili's smugly superior intellect and wisdom? Andrew drained his bourbon and sketchily gestured to the bartender for another. His eyes glazed over while he considered Sara, deliberating over all the excuses he might offer her, weighing all the pros and cons of proceeding with the engagement, untangling the reasons why he'd proposed in the first place, and failing to notice the glare of the sun briefly invading the dank interior of the bar as its front door opened and closed, which might have saved him (and us) the trouble of the following two paragraphs.

One year. Postponed. Sara would be annoyed, suspicious. After achieving the glamorous status of *divorcée*, and quickly bored by any charade that had indeed been forced upon her, she once again wanted to experience the joys of wedded bliss. She'd taken Andrew under her wing when he'd been struggling to survive on his father's stingy allowance (thus Vasili had no one to blame but himself for Sara swooping in to protect his poor son). She'd offered the cohabitation of her loft, which Andrew often suspected (now and much, much later), was the only reason he remained with her, for where else would he live? Presumably, Sara expected in return a proposal and the patter of tiny feet soon to follow. Dangerously nearing the age that would exclude her from all chances of genuine motherhood, she felt personally threatened by a diminishing range of roles in which she was required to play a woman on the verge of barrenhood. She wanted to exult in postpartum depression, not postmenopausal caricatures.

Andrew had finally caved after an exceptionally vigorous session of sex, followed by a rare spurt of creative inspiration, during which he'd begun writing, as demanded by his father, something of substance, which had been enough to tempt Andrew with the small hope that Sara might actually be his muse. Now, he was not so sure. Andrew had always accepted the premise that a muse must remain an object of sublime detachment, impossible possession, and divine silence. Sara was too real, too knowable, and too damn noisy. Regardless, he attempted to negotiate how he might keep Sara as his wife and discover his muse elsewhere, which was, he realized, though ignoring that the logic behind such a conclusion was tenuous at best, perhaps the source of his father's violent opposition to the idea of Andrew marrying Sara. Hadn't Vasili claimed his own wife as muse; had he not dedicated every book *To Deirdre*; had Deirdre not fulfilled the obligations of her role, remaining detached from every one of Vasili's public and private squabbles, always appearing the elusive element within every family mystery? How could Sara Sorrell, with her bawdy guffaw, gushing sentiments, and voluptuous appetites, ever embody any museline or melusine attributes?

Andrew raised his head, and blindly swept his gaze about the room, knowing he must send his father a reply before Alan barred him from his counter. Then the answer to his dilemma miraculously materialized before his eyes, as they finally focused on the far corner of the bar. His Muse, his Melusine, had slipped in unseen, and to his astonishment, even from across the hazy distance separating them, he could perceive that she was the embodiment of all his desires. He was in love. At first sight. He rose from his booth, abandoning it as a sailor might jump ship, crumpling his father's telegram in his slippery, perspiring fist. He waded through the room as if in slow motion, entering a realm of mystical underwater translucency, a shimmering of aquatic desire, helplessly drawn to the siren shored on the edge of the bar where she languished, solitary, her long legs gracefully twined around the stem of her stool, her dark head bent over a book, her mind entrapped by its enchantment while she delicately, inter-mittently, sipped from a chilled martini with olives to be gnawed on after she had greedily drained its briny, oceanic liquor.

Andrew stood at the other end of the bar, dithering, willing her to meet his gaze. He needed to see her face, even if he knew this would be the face that launched more than a thousand words. Impulsively, he grabbed a bar napkin, scrambled for a pen, and scribbled the first subaqueous syllables that filled his head:

An angel has fallen from the sky
She is the sky and I am the bird
Fallen from its home
The earth has been wrenched
Impossibly above my head
Now I am drowning in reversals
Shattered, enflamed, and incomplete

Upon completion, he told Phil the barman to pass the elegiac napkin to its source of inspiration. She stared down at it, confused and slightly embarrassed, and then raised her head, her eyes anchoring on the only man who could have dared grasp for her attention, since he was, fortunately, the only other man at the bar. One did not include Phil as a contender for the girl's affections, as he appeared beyond any possibly concupiscent age, and furthermore, he did not reveal the slightest flickering of poetic inclination. However, because Phil had seen many a strange and unexpected love story in his time, which was simply an occupational hazard, he grunted decisively in Andrew's direction to avoid any confusion between the three of them. The room rippled with her shy smile. She was beautiful beyond words and Andrew was mortified by the ones he'd given her. As much as Andrew tried, he could not describe her; and the phrases he began formulating around her ineffable, exceptional beauty became bogged down in piles of purple prose belonging in one of Sara's cheap, paperback bodice-rippers.

Sara. He'd forgotten. The charming smile he'd intended to offer his newly discovered beloved involuntarily transformed into a grotesque grimace of pain. He glanced at his watch. It was nearly five. Andrew rushed over to the girl and grabbed her hands, disregarding the alarmed saucers of her eyes.

"There's something I must do, urgently," he informed her. "I'll be right back, swear, less than ten minutes!"

He pivoted out of *The Triple N*, composing the message effortlessly in his head, stumbled up to Alan's window, and wrote down the words sloppily, but legibly enough. He attempted to shake the clerk's hand through the bars of his window, announced breathlessly that it would be some time before they saw each other again, if at all, and then spun on his heels, racing headlong and blindly into his future. Alan stared at the words Andrew had left behind.

"*Fine stop Postponed stop For now full stop.*"

Alan was sick at heart of all these stops, and questioned for the first time their necessity when it seemed just as easy to delete them altogether. A week later he resigned from his desk at the Western Union after obtaining a position in the customs department at the seaport, where he took great pleasure in emphatically, silently stamping the passports of the huddled, wretched, homeless, teeming and tempest-tossed masses arriving on the squalid promised shores of New York. Never again did he need to concern himself with the inevitable disappointment of endings but only the infinite hope contained within beginnings.

CHAPTER FOUR
Claudia's Revenge

I do not know why Mina so recklessly fell in love with Andrew Brennan. Why indeed do any of us choose, in the inexorable pursuit of love, the one other person in this world who is incapable of ensuring our lasting happiness? The long, drawn-out, miserable affair between Mina and Andrew begs the question; though I have asked it, I am not about to presume to have come up with a reasonable reply. Far more gifted poets, playwrights, and philosophers have failed to comprehend the various vagaries and barbed insults of love, though this did not stop Andrew from declaring he'd solved the mystery of why Mina chose to wait for him in *The Triple N* and follow him home that very same night.

Fortunately, his fiancée was on a three-month tour of *Medea*, but not Euripides' masterpiece. Sara point blank refused to play in a tragedy. This was a modern vaudeville revision, replete with dancing, singing and a happier, harmless resolution, everything that was antithetical to Andrew's vision of his and Mina's future.

"You were born for me, you are my other half," he whispered feverishly in her ear as they lay naked on the floor, reassembling the other's face in the shadows of the room. "It terrifies me, because I already see how this will end. You will destroy me."

"Andrew, we've only just begun, and besides, I wouldn't even know how to hurt you."

"You will," he promised. "Someday you will leave me."

"But I'm here now. I'm not going anywhere."

"Let's run away together," he pleaded. "Let's go where no one else knows us."

"And where would that be?"

"A place that doesn't exist, where no one can ever come between us and where you are exactly the woman I dream you to be."

"Does this magical impossible place have a name?" she teased, trying not to laugh.

"Antiopa," he smiled mischievously, because he knew Mina knew her Shakespeare. "Where there is nothing either good or bad, but thinking makes it so."

"Well, my sweet prince," she sighed. "I'm thinking that I am perfectly happy here, with you, and have no desire to be anywhere else."

"You'll be the end of me," Andrew murmured into the dark river of her hair. "You will drink the life from my veins, and I will remain eternally a husk of my former self."

"So now I am to be your vampire?" Mina finally laughed. "Or is it a succubus?"

"You are my muse, my masterpiece, my melusine," Andrew rhapsodized, yawning repeatedly with each possessive endearment.

Mina wanted to poke her finger into his mouth, only to see what might happen when he clamped down on it, if he even would. She'd often dared herself to do this with her cat when she was a child, but had always been afraid. Cats never did what you expected of them. Once, when she was older and braver, she attempted to jab her finger into the gaping yawn of the cat's wide, bored mouth. He had not bitten off Mina's finger, but was deeply offended by her silly experiment, snatching his mouth away and scuttling off under the relative safety and privacy of the sofa. Mina thought Andrew might do the same.

"I am only myself," she insisted, but Andrew continued to propose otherwise.

"You are my fate, Mina, but sadly we were born under the influence of crossed stars."

"And when you die, sadly, I shall cut you up into little stars, and then all the world will be in love with me," Mina purposefully, playfully misquoted.

"And they will pay no worship to the monstrous sun," Andrew also misquoted, accidentally, as he was probably thinking of how, with Mina as his inspiration, he would write something so brilliant that it would outshine anything his father had ever written.

"Seriously, though, Andrew, this metaphor of crossed stars is ridiculous," Mina lectured, since she had little patience for some bedtime fairy tale stolen from one of Shakespeare's more dissatisfying romantic tragedies. "There are billions of stars and they do not intersect. They simply descend, they fall, or they hang on to their tiny notch in the firmament and slowly burn out. Besides, most of the stars we're capable of seeing have already died millions of years ago. They are only illusions from the past clinging to our present, and they will continue to remain visible illusions long after *we* are dead."

To this, Andrew had no response. He preferred the clichéd romantic tragedy and did not want to acknowledge that Mina had just unintentionally created a much more perfect analogy for their affair. He felt threatened by her cool, dissecting, glittering intellect and her ability to interpret and construct the world with meanings independent of his meanings. As long as he refused to believe in this other version of Mina, or that she might have an existence divorced from the one he'd created for her, as if she'd arrived tabula rasa from some other world, then he could keep her safely contained in the umbrageous corners of his imagination. Mina played along with Andrew's fantasies only to the extent that she believed he was the great love of her life, and that eventually Andrew would recognize, cherish, and love her for who she truly was, and not merely his other half reflecting back to him all his desires and fears.

It was nearly a year into their affair when Mina began to realize that, for Andrew, the differences between truth and fantasy were impossible to reconcile. The first glimmering of this insight into what would eventually become the terrible, frightening reality of Andrew's madness occurred to her on the night she attended the opening of his first play, *Dusk*, which turned out a tremendous success, although Mina could never understand why. She sat in a darkened theater witnessing Andrew's transformation of the private intimacy of their romance into a monstrous spectacle, in which his distorted view of Mina was put up on display, whored out by her lover for an evening's brief and cheap entertainment. Although she was capable of rationally recognizing that Andrew's dialogue had been written in code with invisible ink that only she knew how to decipher, all the while Mina could barely suppress the urge to scream at the credulous audience that none of this was real or true or even close to an accurate version of her.

Nevertheless, the play received several laudatory reviews: a rough gem promising a brilliant future for its young author; a slice of theater that unflinchingly exposes the terror yet irresistible compulsion of forbidden love with an ironic, shiver-inducing twist at the end; a mordant revelation of the heart's dissipative, if not sadistic, desires, while also hinting at the possibility of redemption for the lover's sins. The plot is broken down as such:

A man, who happens to be a famous writer, is kidnapped, held hostage and beaten by a woman who has obsessively read all of his novels, deeply admiring his genius yet enraged by his profanely brutal portrayal of the female sex. His conflict is one of desire and derision for this avenging angel whilst his sole motivation is to survive his present ordeal without ending up dead by dawn. For the entirety of the play, the man sits bound in a chair as the woman prowls around the stage, gloating in her power, circling ever closer to her victim, seductively torturing him with the reenactment of all the strip-tease fantasies found in his books. Her resistance to his own circular, seductive debate arguing for the freedoms of the imagination over respect for the truth eventually breaks down until the action is resolved with the man slipping loose from the straitjacket in which she has imprisoned him, and then strangling her in a death grip that may also be perceived as a perversely tender embrace of love.

It is a harrowing play, for it aged Mina by several years in a single hour, and by the drop of the curtain and before the lights rose, she'd swiftly slipped out of the theater, a phantom dissolving into the fading mauve of dusk. It was just as well that she left before congratulating the playwright, since his fiancée and his parents were in attendance, praising his success, and so Andrew would have been too distracted, and deliberately neglectful, to think of acknowledging his muse. After all, muses are by their nature required to remain in the shadows, and this particular muse should be forgiven for fulfilling the stereotype, since when confronted by an ugly truth it was Mina's first impulse to run and hide. So upon returning home, she locked herself in her room (which she rented from an elderly, eccentric deaf lady who danced every night to music she could no longer hear and with a lover she had never known), and spent the rest of the evening bawling into her pillow, considerately, irrelevantly, muting her sobs.

Andrew did not see Mina again for several months, and never realized that she would have (probably) refused to see him if he'd attempted to resume the affair. This is not to say his passion for Mina had diminished; he fervently loved her even more now that he'd transcribed her existence onto the page, but fate had intervened and was conspiring against him. Apparently, he'd written a substantial piece of work, and recalling Vasili's absurd terms (which Andrew had insisted upon fulfilling before following through on his proposal), Sara demanded their marriage immediately take place. She'd already wasted a tedious year patiently listening to Andrew weave and unweave a million improbable excuses (though we'll never understand why a sensible woman such as Sara so stubbornly remained with Andrew). The simple truth of the matter is that Andrew felt confessing the truth would end up causing him more trouble than it was worth, and Sara couldn't give two hoots for the truth as long as she got what she'd been promised (even if it was something she no longer wanted).

So on the morning following his glittering debut, Andrew stood in City Hall signing his name to a piece of paper he had no business signing, yet taking a perverse pleasure in watching his father, who'd been maneuvered into acting as legal witness, also sign his name to the documented travesty. As for Sara, she cheerfully ignored Vasili's sullen disapproval, and her spirits were not in the least dampened by Mr. and Mrs. Novikov's hasty departure on the 11:39 morning train back upstate. Mrs. Novikov limply shook her daughter-in-law's hand and declined to embrace her son, all the while clutching onto her husband's arm as he muttered beneath his breath that it was all quite impossible. How could they expect him to stomach a celebratory luncheon after his son had achieved so much and so little within the mere span of twenty-four hours? Andrew, as usual, wanted to vanish, or weep, because now he was sure he'd never see Mina again, and it was not until Sara traipsed off into another musical touring the broad North American continent that he summoned the courage to go looking for his long lost missing half.

He found her in the squalorous shadows of their usual booth at *The Triple N*, scribbling away in a notebook, refusing to lift her eyes until he took her right hand so that her arm stretched across the surface of the table, the extended limb appearing as if it were a lifeline unwillingly flung out to a drowning man.

"Mina," he rashly, emptily proposed. "Let's elope."

"You're already married," she observed, indicating the ring on his finger with an arched brow. "Besides, why would I ever want to be married? Especially seeing what it's done to you."

"What are you talking about?" Andrew blustered.

"You've clearly lost all sense of yourself," she pronounced.

"So help me find it again," he pleaded, missing, as always, the double entendre.

"No," she sighed. "But I'll help you find me."

"Have I lost you?" he asked, anxiously.

"There was nothing to lose," which to Mina seemed a cryptic enough answer leaving her adequate room both to forgive and condemn his betrayal.

Believing she'd bestowed upon him the necessary forgiveness, Andrew grinned, and then asked, "What are you writing?"

"For the moment, nothing, and none of your business," and for the moment Andrew felt sufficiently reassured.

That night, he woke shivering on the thin, worn rug in Sara's loft, reaching for the space where Mina should have been, but was not. He heard the faucet running from the kitchen tap, and when he found her naked, gleaming in the moonlight, gulping down a glass of water, she lowered the glass and stared emptily into Andrew's face. They studied each other as if neither knew where they were or how they'd arrived, bumbling about in a house in which they did not belong. This can't possibly continue, she murmured, lifting the glass to her lips, draining its contents, and then refilling it once more. Andrew returned to their makeshift bed and fell into an uneasy asleep. When he woke the following morning with Mina curled perfectly, peacefully, into the curve of his shoulder, her arm flung across his chest, her left knee pinning down his legs, and only the slightest trace of tension at the corners of her mouth (but Mina always slept with a kind of concentrated intensity), Andrew lulled himself into believing nothing had changed.

Two months later, after a flurry of adulterous afternoons drunkenly debating with Mina the language, lunacy, and lust she inspired in him, Andrew presented as proof of his devotion his second play, *The Harker Affair*. It was, as its title suggests, and its five acts confirm, nothing more than a rehashing of the Dracula story, which Andrew Brennan was incapable of leaving alone in nearly all of his plays. In this version, Nosferatu is convinced Mina Murray is the resurrected ghost of a woman he once loved and lost, her angelic soul now adorned with limbs of flesh. As for Mina Murray, although she coolly resists his powers of seduction, she is determined to save the old devil from his eternal damnation and allows him to swoop her off to his castle in Transylvania where he forces her into playing some kind of erotic game of wit and words, and this is where the sense of the play begins to unravel. The two go on for quite a stretch philosophically disputing something or other having to do with Plato's cave; the gist of it is a bit garbled, but somehow works to the effect of Mina tricking her adversary into running like a bereaved madman out into the unforgiving glare of the sun. After leading him to his suicidal demise, the perfidious ingénue places a lingering, triumphant kiss on the lips of the grizzled vampire; yet Andrew refuses his heroine a happy ending. She rises from the corpse of the forgiven undead, confident she may now move on into the bright horizon of her future, only to discover that her fiancé, Jonathon Harker, who has come chasing after her, turns out to have been the wily bloodsucker's last victim; he is, in fact, his vampiric heir. The distraught Mina must choose between destroying the man she loves, and from whom she had so optimistically expected the promise of mortal bliss, or pragmatically baring her neck to him so he might drag her into his immortal darkness. Mina, in the end, chooses the darkness.

This time the real Mina had wisely read the play before its production, and refused to grace any of its performances with her presence. Again, she prolonged her inevitable acquaintance with the *real* Nosferatu, who'd learned the trick of walking about undetected in broad daylight, always casting his oppressive shadow. Vasili could not resist draining the flush of accomplishment from his son when he remarked that the boy's latest endeavor was of course very clever, but must he always be so morose? Was it necessary to persist in displaying such cruelty towards his characters; did he not think compassion, even for fictional people, even for *repugnant* fictional people, the range of an artist's true genius? Mina, if she'd witnessed such a scene, might have been torn between empathizing with her lover (destroyed by his father's slightest critique), and vehemently agreeing with Vasili (since she was the repugnantly clichéd character upon whom the author had refused to bestow any compassion or authenticity).

After reading the script, Mina decided that in the interests of self-preservation she needed to disentangle herself from the entire affair. Besides, she'd lost patience with playing in what she'd once thought was a romance but had now become a farce. None of the parts made any sense and not all of the actors were aware of performing on stage with each other.

"I refuse to be the other woman," she informs Andrew after arranging a final meeting at *The Triple N*, admirably resolved to walk away, but hoping he might actually become some other, braver, saner man.

"It's impossible, all of it is impossible," he exclaims, not really sure what Mina is asking of him, clutching onto his empty glass of bourbon sweating out its final ice cubes.

When the silence stretches out unbearably, Andrew lifts his head to observe Mina on her side of the booth, observing him with a blank stare. She brushes aside a loose curl, and in the same graceful, unconscious movement of her hand, averts her gaze to study the lurid, color-tinted photographs hanging above the bar as if she'd never noticed them before.

"I will not become *that* woman," she murmurs.

"What the hell are you talking about?" Andrew grumbles, since the woman looks nothing like Mina, but she only offers him a ghostly smile, sliding out of the booth, fleeing from the cavernous depths of the bar without a single glance backwards. Eurydice freeing herself.

Andrew did not attempt to chase after her, but sat sucking on an ice cube, bleakly staring up at the photographs. For the record, he did attempt a serious contemplation of these images. They were coy, teasing film stills of some buxom blonde who'd once been a famous sex symbol. She smiled directly, guilelessly into the camera, as if she were a child and had nothing to conceal. The more intently Andrew stared at that smile the more it disturbed him, its inviting innocence trans-forming into the smug contempt of a leer; in spite of the surface impres-sion of a woman so overwhelmingly evocative of lush femininity that she achieved a transcendence of her gender, the depth image of these photographs presented an abject, soiled, degraded piece of flesh selling itself on the market for a few tarnished coins. Andrew realized he could no longer distinguish the visual representation of *this* woman from the images he'd seen elsewhere, those obtrusive photographs documenting her death. She'd been discovered alone in a Hollywood bungalow, the phone left mysteriously abandoned off the hook beside the bed where she lay sprawled, bloated, overweight, stuffed with pills and vodka, scantily clad in a nicotine-stained, tatty silk robe, her brown roots eating up the peroxide glory of her hair; then that same body covered by a coroner's sheet as she was wheeled off to the morgue; the only sign of her previous existence a pale arm, indiscriminately left unconcealed, hanging limply, lifelessly over the stretcher.

Andrew shuddered. Was Mina contemplating suicide? If so, would he be to blame? As much as he wanted one, Andrew could not tolerate another drink. He leapt out of his seat, also fleeing *The Triple N* without looking back. For nearly a year Andrew played the role of faithful husband, and although Sara wasn't quite sure why he suddenly seemed so attentive to her needs, she initially welcomed the change. When it became clear Andrew was no longer writing but spent all of his time moping about the loft, depending on her as his only form of amusement, Sara no longer found his sobriety very charming.

One late August afternoon, after Sara suggested, inconsequentially, or so it appeared at the time, that perhaps he might write a play for her, Andrew scrambled out of bed, hastily threw on some clothes, and raced out the door. Sara simply sighed, refusing as usual to question her husband's bizarre leaps and bounds out of inertia. Sooner or later he would descend to some level of normalcy, and if this latest exhibition of tormented genius resulted in a new play in which she might star, then all the better. She welcomed the evening's solitude, slipping into one of her long, steaming baths, and gurgled down a glass of pink fizzy champagne.

Sure enough, he returned the following morning, bleary-eyed, stinking of bourbon, and with a handful of notes for his next script, and all thanks to Sara's encouragement, which had indeed inspired him to track down his long-lost muse, though finding her had turned out to be much more difficult than expected. After eliciting the necessary information from a blind, deaf loon of a hag who'd once been Mina's landlady, Andrew trekked all the way down from the Upper to Lower Eastside, and then circled several blocks before locating the studio Mina now rented. He was about to knock on the door when it was flung open by an unexpected stranger, who thrust the door ajar, shouldered Andrew aside, and shambled off into the penumbral recesses of the stairwell. Andrew failed to ask about the man's identity, because as soon as he stepped into the studio, there was only Mina, her dark hair veiling her pale, beloved face.

Without wasting words or time, they did what any estranged lovers would do when reconciling after a year's absence from one another.

Afterwards, when they lay naked on the floor, listening to a sudden thunderstorm pelting a tattoo of rain against the windows, Andrew admitted he could no longer imagine a life without her, and that he wanted her and only her, whoever that might be. As usual, Mina did not respond to this romantic declaration as Andrew had thought, or at least hoped, she might. She merely extricated herself from his embrace, rose from the floor, and put on a frayed silk robe, its paisley print mottled by stray flecks and streaks of random paint. After seating herself on an overturned crate, she lit a cigarette and proceeded to inhale and exhale clouds of smoke as she stared down at the ashes dropping one by one to the floor. Uncomfortable in his nakedness and her silence, Andrew began clumsily dressing himself.

"It's too late," she finally replied.

"What's too late?" he demanded, baffled, tying double knots into the laces of his shoes, prepared to flee the moment he could no longer bear listening to her voice.

"For any of this, well, for you, for me, oh really, Andrew, for you to show up here making ridiculous declarations of love," she explained clumsily, tritely, as if she were a woman who could only exist in a badly written book. She struck another match to yet another cigarette before the first one had been extinguished. Andrew scowled. She hadn't taken up the habit of smoking before, and it certainly didn't suit his image of her.

"What the fuck are you going on about?" he asked irritably, standing above her.

"It's just, oh, it's just too late," she sighed, exasperated, before more bluntly informing him, "Besides, I've agreed to be married, the day after tomorrow."

"Married?! How could you . . . how could you, Mina, after everything . . ."

"You married Sara."

"I knew Sara before I met you."

"Precisely."

Her infuriatingly dry retort left Andrew no other choice than to make a silent, speechless study of the large canvas propped against the far wall, the sheer size of it overwhelming an entire corner of the room, attracting yet repelling his interest so that he nearly forgot Mina's presence. The painting appeared to be a rendition of Eden, the central background space containing a massive tree inhabited by fanciful birds and butterflies, and blotted with bright red globular fruit. At the base of the tree stood an emaciated, raven-haired woman, starved to a sagging sack of flesh and bones, her gaze ravenously focused on Eve, a voluptuous nude, blonde, with hooded eyes and plump greedy lips, seeming both earthy and ethereal, a pre-Raphaelite figure wearing the expression of a woman lost in a trance of either religious or sexual ecstasy.

Twined about her broad hips and rounded belly, and resting its narrow head against her pendulous breasts, the serpent lapped with its forked tongue at the fat rosy aureoles of her swollen nipples, its tail provocatively inserted into the wilderness of her pubic hair. Eve openly offered temptation to the smudged, unfinished contours of a male figure standing in the foreground, a visible dribbling of juice from the freshly bitten fruit trickling from her outrageous, orgiastic grin. Andrew nearly gagged, overcome by the violent urge to turn away.

Mina stood beside him, her eyes shifting uncertainly between the canvas and Andrew, and Andrew was about to ask Mina who, or what, had inspired her to paint something so offensive, but the door to the studio abruptly opened. The same disgruntled, churlish figure who'd accosted Andrew had returned, scowling his way across the room, hair now dripping wet and plastered across his blunt brow. He peeled off his soaked shirt, leaving his coarse, hairy chest startling bare, and discarded the sopping garment into the embrace of a tattered Victorian armchair copiously spilling out its stuffing. The man then poured out a glass of Chianti from a faux *taverna* decanter into a chipped glass, muttering in displeasure, "Mina, old girl, I am soaked, downright miserable, and in no form to entertain, as you can plainly see."

The man's deep-barreled, orotund, perfectly clipped English accent did not at all match his slovenly appearance, and Mina did not bother replying, but faced Andrew, her mouth ominously stretched in a thin travesty of a smile. "Andrew, this is my fiancé, Lord Beresford, or Besim, whichever you prefer to call him, although I prefer Besim, since that's how I've always known him, and long before I ever met you."

Andrew's stomach suddenly turned, as if he'd been caught doing something horribly wrong. His eyes searched the room, looking for an escape route, his coat, something to put on with which to conceal his embarrassment, though of course he had not brought a coat. It was

August. Their entire affair, in all its arrivals, ruptures, and departures, was trapped in some eternally hellishly hot season, endlessly repeating until they finally got it right or gave up. He wanted to clasp Mina's body against his own, some gesture to claim some part of her as irrevocably belonging to him. She could not possibly marry this ogre, who now sat slurping his wine and perusing a book, as if Andrew and Mina were no longer in the room, having dismissed them from his lordly concern. Andrew observed the man's broad, filthy hands, as he raised the book and wetted one of his fingertips to turn over the next page, and when Andrew saw the title of the book, the name of its author, something in his mind splintered and cracked.

"*How did you get your hands on that book?!*" he barked inanely, and in reply, Besim glanced up at Mina, raising one dismissive brow in Andrew's direction, indicating that he expected her to respond, and then returned to reading his book.

"Besim brought it over from Paris," Mina murmured distractedly, silently strategizing how she might avoid later having to explain Andrew to Besim, who would want to know, for his own amusement, why Mina chose to consort with such ridiculous characters. "It was a gift from my aunt. She thought I might enjoy it, or learn some kind of valuable lesson."

"And did you?" Andrew laughed in a kind of strangled apoplectic gurgle.

"Enjoy it? I can't decide, though I should probably read it again, since the narrator is obviously untrustworthy," Mina explained nervously, concerned with the increasingly pallid tint spreading across Andrew's face, and so she continued babbling on about the silly book. "As for any valuable lesson, I haven't the slightest idea what that might be. Tante Rosalie abhors all forms of didactic art, a term she claims is oxymoronic in any case, and so would not recommend any novel in the hopes of reforming me. Rather, knowing Rosalie, she probably thought I would find its erotic content inspiring, on a purely aesthetic level of course, but I didn't think it was very romantic or erotic, really, and I don't see why they've censored it over here with such puritanical sniffling. In fact, I thought the whole thing rather sad, that impossible little girl . . ."

"Why impossible?" Andrew pounced. "Why is she *impossible*?!"

"Because she's not a real person," Mina ignored a dismissive grunt from the Besim beast, and raised her voice slightly, as if she were defending an old argument between them. "We only see her through the distorted viewpoint of the narrator, who ends up being a raving lunatic, and so the impression he gives us has nothing to do with her as an actual, feeling person."

"But she *is* only a fiction," Andrew exhorted, and their silent audience grunted once more, now in approval. "There is no *real* person to know."

"Well, then, I'm sure that's why it's so unsettling," Mina muttered, reaching for another cigarette, exhaustion overcoming her; she did not want to continue this conversation any further, yet she persisted in continuing. "Honestly, Andrew, there's nothing offensive about any of it, so I don't see why you're so upset. Even the vague descriptions of the sex scenes are hardly titillating but more or less the same dull stuff you might find in the Marquis de Sade, especially the incest and sexual bondage, or perhaps the author is playing a joke on the whole driveling genre of romance novels and those who enjoy reading them."

"Perhaps you should ask the great Novikov himself," Andrew lamely spat out, incapable of ordering the confused jumble of his thoughts or finding the perfect words that might condemn Mina to a long miserable life without him. "He might even consider you his ideal reader, which he's never admitted actually exists!"

"Oh?" Mina exhaled a waft of smoke. "Have you read him?"

"That would hardly signify!" Andrew released an absurd yap of a laugh and then scampered clumsily out of the studio without explanation, apologies, or farewell.

He assumed Mina would simply continue to sit there, smoking her cigarettes, smugly certain he would show up again when he could no longer bear to live without her. He could never have imagined, while racing towards the nearest bar, his mind fragmenting painfully in his despair, his dejection, and his inspiration for a new play, that Mina, now miserably regretting ever letting Andrew through the door, would fling herself across the room to a corner opposite the man heartlessly reading in the shadows, burrow herself in the unmade bed, and weep out yet again what she believed to be the shattered remnants of her love for him, which is exactly, actually, what she proceeded to do.

Three months later, Mina received an invitation printed on a postcard announcing the opening of a new play, *Claudia's Revenge*, by Andrew Brennan. For some perverse reason, Mina felt obliged to attend, and as expected, she received very little pleasure from watching the tortuous plot unfold. The eponymous heroine was supposedly an old woman trapped inside the body of a seven-year-old child due to a curse placed upon her by a vampiric pedophile, who had imprisoned his child-lover in a perpetually pre-pubescent body. The dénouement was achieved by the nymph/hag thrusting a dagger into her own breast, her suicide evidently the intended revenge. Never mind the play was a disastrous pile of drivel (and no more than the author's laughably derivative comment on the great Novikov's latest novel); the more visible insult was the actress cast in the role of Claudia, who turned out to be Andrew's bawdy, broad-hipped, ambling, drawling and unintentionally droll wife. Never mind that such an inconceivable character might only believably be represented by a dwarf, or, a precociously talented little girl; that Andrew had finally conflated Mina and Sara into the same monstrous role was more than Mina could willingly, silently withstand.

As soon as the curtain closed, the audience made a hasty retreat either to the lobby bar or the nearest exit. Mina refused to feel embarrassed for Andrew's sake. She stood patiently in a dim corner of the bar, waiting for Andrew to appear, and when he did, looking pale and alarmed, already aware the play would never receive another performance, and helplessly immobilized by the transparently false enthusiasm of those who had been brave enough to remain, Mina began moving towards him. He saw her weaving through the feeble crowd, his eyes desperately locked onto hers, because only she could save him with just a few small words of praise. Realizing this, Mina could have been kind, and she would always regret that she had not chosen kindness.

She was about to offer him such generosity, and as she stood in front of him, her mouth opened, and she was about to tell him . . . what? What would she have told him? It couldn't possibly matter, because Sara had materialized beside him, and Mina was reminded of the insult Andrew had inflicted upon her and the wound she wanted to inflict in return.

"Hello," Mina extended her hand to Sara. "I apologize for not being able to congratulate you on your performance, though it's no fault of your own, since your character was so badly written. Andrew never could get me right. By the way, I'm Mina."

Sara accepted the proffered limb, giving it a firm squeeze while narrowing her eyes onto her husband, whose gaze was glued to Mina in a look of abject horror, which was more than enough to confirm Sara's suspicions; she decided to display a deliberately breezy smile. "Well, my girl, I can't say I'm very pleased to meet you, and as for Claudia, you're more than welcome to her."

"I've already been playing her long enough," Mina dumbly smiled, and though no one else standing there watching this exchange understood what she'd meant by this, Sara was sharp enough to catch on.

"And good riddance to the whole goddamned mess," she burst out in one of her hearty guffaws, and then sauntered offstage, still chuckling to herself, striding confidently towards home and a hot soothing bath, and with every inch of her dignity intact.

The same could not be said of her husband. Andrew continued standing there, mortified, mouth gaping open and then closing like a floundering, suffocating fish. Mina however was no longer looking at him, but at someone hovering over his shoulder. Andrew did not need to acknowledge who this person might be. He was always intervening, poisoning everything with his critical glare. Stupidly, Andrew shuffled aside and so was forced to observe the old man studying Mina with insatiable curiosity, and, unbearably, a small flickering . . . of desire . . . for Mina, corrupting her forever with this one small glance.

Mina met the old man's gaze, suspecting this could only be Andrew's father but never imagining he was also the great Novikov himself, since Andrew had only spoken of his parents once, describing "Papa" with childish confusion and wounded affection, as someone who was quick to find fault no matter how hard Andrew tried to please him, and of course "Mama" always sided with "Papa," both of them expecting the worst from their son. Mina glanced at the mother, clutching onto her husband's arm, and briefly back at the father, and then lowered her eyes in shame. She'd just hurt Andrew in the cruelest and most vengeful manner she could have devised: announcing her existence, enacting the role of the woman scorned, a scene full of clichés, and one that was all the worse for Andrew's parents having been present to witness it since she had exposed his secrets to the two people who would be the most unforgiving of them.

"I'm so sorry," she mumbled, ignoring Andrew's parents, their eyes boring into her; she looked up at Andrew who was now glaring at Mina with revulsion and fear, an utter lack of recognition. "Andrew . . . oh . . . I didn't mean . . . I don't know what I was . . ."

"Is everything all right here?" his father interjected in a befuddled effort to ease the obvious tension between his son and this unknown, lovely, wretched girl.

"For the last time, stay away!" Andrew blurted. "Don't ever come near me again!"

He vanished from the bar in a crazed sprint, leaving those who'd witnessed his departure with the impression that his words had been directed towards Mina, as if she were some obsessive mistress stalking him to the point of madness. She glanced once more at Andrew's father, who offered her a lame smile of commiseration, and then at his mother, her face drained of all color, staring at the empty space where her son had been standing. Mina could not tolerate their injured expressions, and so she also fled, also aware that everyone would assume she was chasing after Andrew, extending the distraught scene to its conventional, histrionic end.

When she returned home, Mina was relieved to find Besim absent, and hoped he would never reappear. She raided the cupboard beneath the sink and proceeded to consume the motley supply of vodka, gin, whiskey, and rum, whatever it took to put her into a comatose sleep, but sleep would not come. Instead, she was confronted by the offensive images of her paintings, all depicting morbid distortions of famously fictional women: a withered Sybil, her desiccated flesh crawling with white maggots emerging from raw suppurating sores; a black and blue Ophelia floating naked, monstrously bloated; a nude and flayed Magdalene, scrubbing with her shorn hair the feet of her redeemer; the emaciated Lilith and voluptuously omnivorous Eve. Mina wanted to forget she'd ever created these images, forgetting what statement she'd intended to make other than some empty critique of the cruelty men inflicted upon women.

Naturally, her response was to find the largest kitchen knife and begin attacking the women as if it were a fight to the death. She ripped into Eve's engorged breasts; disemboweled Ophelia's distended belly; severed Mary Magdalene's meekly lowered head; chopped and quartered the Sybil's decaying limbs, and slit open Lilith's scrawny throat. The knife had a will of its own, yet the only blood it drew belonged to Mina, who was wounded while slashing paradise into slivers of paint encrusted canvas. In one swift swipe, which had been intended for the figure of an absurdly affronted Adam, the blade opened a deep gash across the inner flesh of Mina's forearm. Swearing loudly, she dropped the knife on the floor, which in its descent nicked her thigh and barely missed severing her big toe. Mina might have then come to her senses, but when she lifted her eyes, Adam remained unscathed, staring back at her, displeased and defiant, mocking the apocalypse she'd brought down upon his representative world, of which he was determined to stand as the lone survivor. Mina shrieked a curdling banshee scream, took the canvas in her hands, raised it above her head, and brought it crashing down many more times than necessary, until every bit of it was shredded beyond recognition.

She then whirled through the room, flinging frames and lacerated paintings into walls, furniture, corners, until every single one of them was obliterated. She never heard the couple below furiously pounding on their ceiling with a broom handle, or the reclusive transvestite from across the hall threatening to call the cops, which was an empty threat in any case. Eventually, she collapsed on the floor, sobbing noisily, gulping for air, hoping to lose all consciousness, forgetting to bandage her wounds, and ignoring the abrasion on her cheek and the slivers of wood embedded in her palms; because she would not ever be able to erase from her memory the grotesque parody Andrew had made of her throughout their affair, and her disgust for willingly playing the part he'd expected of her.

When Besim finally appeared some time past midnight, he discovered Mina passed out among the debris of their wrecked home. Though she was spattered in blood, Besim failed to discover any significant injury, and was thus relieved from having to blame himself for his wife's anguished suicide, never realizing that if this had been Mina's intention, he would hardly have been the one to inspire it. Mina, if she'd been conscious, would have been shocked by the fretful tenderness Besim lavished on her. He neatly bandaged her arm, extracted every sliver of wood from her hands, treated her scrapes with antiseptic, bathed her, put her to bed, and all the while hushing and cooing her in muted admonitions and affectionate nonsense words. The following day Mina slept while Besim restored the studio to a habitable space, and that evening, as he held her in his arms, spooning her beef broth, she gazed up at him drowsily, wondering painfully, *who is this man?*

CHAPTER FIVE
Besim Berisha

As it turned out, he was the son of the famous children's author, Fiona Beresford, and upon discovering a first-edition of *Bertram and the Hall of Mirrors* tucked away on a bookshelf in Besim's Paris studio, where she'd shown up one day demanding to be photographed, Mina had recovered the memory of reading the Bertram books when she was a child, and thus decided Besim must be a necessary numeral in the equation leading up to the sum of her existence. Or rather, this is the slightly disingenuous anecdote Besim presented to anyone who asked how he met his wife, which most people found charming in its superficial but satisfactorily simplistic logic. No one bothered confirming the truth of Besim's story with Mina, who merely offered her cool, circumspect smile and abruptly changed the subject at hand.

For Mina, those coincidental accidents random pairs of lovers contrived in order to explain all the fateful paths leading them into each other's lives were exasperatingly insulting, especially after the debacle of Andrew Brennan. That she would end up marrying the man whose mother was responsible for writing the very same books Mina's own mother had bestowed upon her daughter was neither here nor there; in fact, Besim Berisha was not even his real name. At least it was not the name Fiona Beresford had used when dedicating each of the Bertie books to her son. Thus, Mina never would have imagined any connection between Bertram Benson and her husband without him having confessed to her two weeks before their marriage the reasons why he thought Mina should become his wife, which necessarily entailed revealing to her the abbreviated narrative of his banal childhood. This was in some respects not so different from Mina's childhood, since Besim also was the product of a briefly passionate then subsequently loveless marriage.

His father, Charlie, hailed from one of the more prominent Anglo-Irish families in Belfast, and had been in the robust flush of his youth: a charismatic playboy, celebrated wit, and competent spin bowler. His mother, Fiona McGarrity, the only child of an ex-convict who'd struck it rich in the Australian gold rush, had been appointed as the singular object of Charlie's desires after the entirety of the Beresford ancestral estates and incomes were lost due to the current Lord Beresford's predilection for making reckless bets at the tracks. Fiona, impatient to be rid of her father's tainted name and scramble rapidly up the social ladder, ardently encouraged the lustful attentions of the future Lord Beresford, who was only too eager to be rid of his father's debts. When they returned from their three-week honeymoon on the continent, Fiona was assuredly pregnant; seven months later a lustily squalling, healthy, nine-pound, full-term Beresford heir was produced, and that was the end of the Charlie-Fiona romance, since both had obtained what they wanted.

Soon enough Charlie tired of his wife's middle-class aspirations, which she betrayed the moment she confessed the vulgar desire to write novels, and Besim's father replaced Besim's mother with a much younger woman of even more disreputable origins. This bubble-brained showgirl would later become Lady Beresford after Charlie's own father finally expired. Naturally, the first Mrs. Beresford, outraged by the theft of the hereditary title, and discovering Charlie had spent the three years of their marriage depleting her inheritance on whiskey and whores, took the drunkard for all he was worth, which amounted to nothing more than the Belfast townhouse. Unfortunately, Fiona was forced to give up her high artistic ambitions and make a living off writing a popular series of children's stories tracking the trials and tribulations of a bespectacled, priggish schoolboy who with his magic wand banished evil from the world, all of which carried a pungent whiff of plagiaristic desperation.

And what of the real little boy one day destined to become the last of the Lords Beresfords? Considering the state of the Beresford patrimony, neither parent expended much energy in haggling over the future of their son, and Charlie was only too eager to escape the greedy, scheming clutches of his first wife. He managed to achieve through his second wife, the Lady Bess, his only ambition, which was to spend the rest of his sorry existence safely sloshed and in the company of a woman who desired nothing more than an easy laugh, some cheap sentiments, and the luxury of sleeping in a feather bed with the same man rather than a different one every night. As long as he knew where his next drink and his next fuck were coming from, Lord Beresford believed himself blessed with all the necessary provisions life could offer a man. He swiftly forgot the first Mrs. Beresford or that there was a boy they'd magically conceived during their honeymoon, and other than the annual birthday pub lunch, Besim forgot he had a father.

As for his mother, Fiona Beresford was consumed by sustaining the life of her adored Bertie Benson, and so Besim was more often than not left to his own devices, which is indeed a dangerous indulgence for any snot-nosed, intellectually lethargic, chubby child who is without friends or adults investing something of their limited concerns in his education and moral growth. When not shuffled off to St. Dymphna's, where he exhibited no substantial evidence of academic, athletic or social agility, the scope of his recreational activities were restricted to half-heartedly yanking the limbs off daddy-long-legs, stuffing his face with sweets, stealing sips from his mother's laudanum, and groping the pert-breasted housemaid before wanking off while she watched in scornful amusement.

The worst part of Besim's unhappy, uneventful childhood was that he could not escape the sniping, ever-present reminder that his existence wholly depended upon his mother's imagination. Fiona could not comprehend why her son failed to establish his reality as precisely the same as the one she'd so painstakingly reconstructed for him in the persona of Bertram Benson. The slovenly and seemingly retarded child, who occasionally made an obtrusive appearance at her breakfast table during his school holidays, had no likeness to the hero of her children's books. Bertram did not gobble his food like a greedy peasant. Bertram wore perfectly pressed shirts and creased trousers, and never forgot to tie his tie or to comb his hair. Bertram did not grunt monosyllabic answers to questions asked of him by his elders. He had friends to play with. He was athletic and liked the outdoors. He did not mope about all day trailing after his mother who had deadlines to meet and needed to finish writing the next chapter in which he vanquishes the Horrible Harpy.

The only remarkable event of Besim's childhood was the morning of his sixteenth birthday when he absconded from Belfast, leaving a note informing Fiona that he had finally run away in search of all those adventures she'd been harping on him to pursue. Keeping in mind, however, the promised inheritance from the Bertie books, which his mother had always informed him he did not deserve, he swore to return by his twenty-first birthday. Throughout the following fourteen years, Besim fondly addressed Mrs. Beresford as Dearest Mother in every one of his letters mendaciously describing how he got on in the world, and in spite of her repeated requests that he return home so she might forgive her prodigal son, Besim never saw her again.

Although I know little to nothing about those adventurous, itinerant years of his youth before he stumbled into Mina's life, the one thing of which I have no doubt (because he once told me as much) is that Besim learned this was a world where, in his own words, "the fraudulent fantasist, the fanatically megalomaniac, and the manipulative misanthropist were best equipped to survive." So he discarded the name his mother had given him (William, or Billy, as the dedication in each of the Bertram books diminutively refers to the author's only beloved son), adopted a number of aliases, learned the tricks of the long con, and dabbled in the illusory pleasures of photography. Supposedly he learned the techniques of this burgeoning art form during his stay in Berlin. There he was briefly apprenticed to a filmmaker of avant-garde pretensions whose surrealist adaptation of *Alice's Adventures under Ground* had been silently funded by Rosalie Louvel. Besim had been given her address when he decided to move on to Paris. The very day of his arrival, he showed up unannounced at one of Rosalie's overcrowded soirées, blending in easily enough amongst the motley bohemian vagabonds whilst also standing out in his fabricated role of the exiled Albanian aristocrat, Besim Berisha.

If anyone made inquiries into the origins of his makeshift English, Besim would shudder, lean in with a sorrowful sigh, and admit the recent loss of his beloved motherland to a maniacal band of Fascist communist bourgeoisie was too terrible a burden of memory to recount for the gossipy pleasure of those who had no direct experience of such historical tragedy. His interlocutor would lean back with the requisite gasps of pity one usually offered in response to the plight of the émigré, as so many were marauding the Parisian boulevards, cafés, and salons in those days, and Besim's bumbling explanations were accepted as proof that he was yet another outcast from one of those politically troubled and confused lands that lay veiled in mist across the Ural Range; never mind Albania was situated southwest of this geographical demarcation, no one actually wanted to know the history of such people. In this way Besim enjoyed the delicious freedom of remaining unknown and unfettered, and relished his absolute control over an identity he knew was not real but became so in the disinterested eyes of others.

Until Mina Byrne stole from him with her cold, black eyes any pleasure he took in the charade. The first time he met her at the *appartement* on rue des Saint-Pères, Mina had stared straight through him as if he were an object that she was required to maneuver around in order to proceed with the more relevant tasks of her day. It viscerally reminded him of the same look he'd grown up facing every morning when forced to attend his mother's breakfast table. Then, the first time Mina met Besim in the marbled claustrophobia of Jerôme de Voile's bathroom, she'd burst into laughter, immediately recognizing him for a fraud. This seemed to explain, at least for Besim, why he allowed Mina to return repeatedly to his Montmartre studio, determined to convince her of the authenticity of his disguise. When Mina abruptly abandoned her obsession with Besim to discover another one in New York, he was relieved to see her go, since keeping up the act had become thoroughly exhausting, and soon he happily forgot Mina.

Then he received a letter informing him of his mother's death. From this letter, Besim learned that in Fiona's final years she had become a mad Havisham, shutting herself in the house with only a mottled jack terrier to which she bemoaned all her failures—her books out of print, no fans or fame to speak of, no son to look after her in her dotage. The only one to make an occasional house call was Lady Bess, who did not come to gloat over Fiona's downfall but to mollify her own grief, as old Charlie had finally drunk himself to death, leaving his second wife as penniless as the first. So it seemed only natural, at least to Bess, that the two women should belatedly discover commiseration in each other's company. The first Mrs. Beresford of course refused to acknowledge the second, at least until it appeared Bess had all but moved in. She then directed all communication between them to the jack terrier, its peevish whimpers, half-hearted growls, and insistent yaps translated by the good-natured Bess as an indication of Fiona's reluctant gratitude for the other woman's companionship. Bess cheerfully played along, pursuing endless conversations with the runty lapdog, and when he died not long after his mistress collapsed of heart failure, Bess mourned him equally if not more than she did Fiona, believing she might have inherited the dog just as she'd inherited the husband.

The only thing bestowed upon Lady Bess was the daunting mission of finding the new Lord Beresford so his mother's sizeable monetary estate, earned from royalties on the Bertie books when they were still wildly popular, might be disposed of as she'd intended. The task proved simple enough as soon as Bess rummaged through Fiona's desk and found a collection of letters addressed to Dearest Mother. After copying out the Parisian return address provided on the most recently dated letter, Bess could not help skimming over its confession of the author's prolonged despair of ever discovering a woman worthy enough to become his wife, at least one who might meet his mother's approval; thus he'd consigned himself to the lonely life of a bachelor.

"Oh, what a pickle you've gotten yourself into you naughty boy," Bess chuckled, knowing the terms of Fiona's will, of which Besim clearly had no inkling. She sat down to write her lugubrious letter detailing the circumstances of Fiona's sudden death, as well as the drawn-out dejection of her final years (which Bess had done her best to mitigate through her constant though unappreciated attentions), and then the more significant information concerning the provisions Fiona had made for her son. By the time he got to the point of this letter, Besim was soon absolved of any half-hearted twinge of pity he might have felt for Fiona the moment he comprehended the sheer absurdity and downright pettiness of the stipulations in her will.

Realizing the action now required of him, and believing he had only one available pawn that might allow him to checkmate, at long last, his mother, who even from the grave seemed determined to control his fate, Besim immediately tramped off to the *appartement* on rue des Saint-Pères in order to beg from its cohabitants Mina's address in New York. Rosalie and Redpath had also recently received a letter, in which Mina had described her intermittent affair with one Andrew Brennan, an alcoholic playwright ensnared in a marriage to a vulgar vaudeville actress. Rosalie insisted Mina would soon come to her senses, and that sending Besim as an intervention seemed an unnecessary measure, especially since she'd recently cut Mina's allowance in the hopes that this would force her to return to Paris. Redpath argued, however, that Besim's abrupt arrival on

Mina's doorstep would act as a palpable *aide memoire*, prompting her to recall her past failures in judgment when it came to choosing such deplorable lovers. Rosalie chose to ignore the misplaced logic of this cockamamie strategy; nevertheless, Besim sailed off to New York with a gift for her niece, accompanied by strict instructions from Rosalie that Mina devour it immediately upon receipt.

The fateful gift was of course *Dolores*, recently published by Ophélie Press, an imprint catering to softly pornographic proclivities, thus guaranteeing the novel's author an uproar of popular and critical acclaim, and not only in Paris but also back in the country where the work had been censured. The novel's nebulous heroine, who eventually triumphs over the solipsistic monster keeping her prisoner in his perverted palace of lust, was intended by Rosalie as a literary example to which her niece might aspire. If we follow Rosalie's rationale to its equally illogical end, it seems she believed that, if one read the novel as a cautionary tale, then Mina would be reminded of the glorious heights of her own romantic destiny, which was far above anything the beastly Besim or that asinine Andrew might have to offer.

Queasily cloistered in his cabin during the heaving trans-Atlantic journey, Besim's boredom and prurient tastes inspired him to read the book, which ended up a disappointment. Since he was hardly the literary aesthete, Besim was incapable of appreciating the novel's linguistic virtuosity, nor could he have guessed that its erotic content, as Mina later deduced, was only a transparent parody of *Eugénie de Franval*. He was thus reduced to transposing Mina's face onto its heroine's as he relentlessly engaged in an onanistic diversion timed to the cresting and descending rhythm of the ship's tumultuous passage over the ocean separating him from his object of desire. As soon as he arrived in New York, with nothing but the clothes on his back (having sold most of his possessions in order to pay for his passage), a single remaining camera (but no film) wrapped in his old paisley silk robe, and a copy of his mother's will slipped between the dog-eared pages of a slightly battered novel, he directed a taxi to 359 East 11th Street, where he intended to claim the woman he now believed would be the answer to his financial quandary.

He thought it a propitious sign when he discovered the door to her apartment unlocked. Besim blithely hallooed and let himself in, assuming Mina had stepped out for eggs or milk. By that evening, he began to worry, not so much over whether she would show up but if he'd be allowed to remain as a co-occupant of the studio for what would surely be an unspecified length of time. The only way to relieve his discomfort, then, was to make her home his home; besides, it was early August, the heat insufferable, and the studio lacking proper ventilation. Besim stripped off all his clothes, put on the paisley robe, drank several bottles of sour red wine he'd found stashed in the back of a cupboard, and began taking photos of the space so irritatingly devoid of Mina's presence, disregarding that his lack of film would fail to document her absence. When he glanced up from his empty camera to discover Mina silently, blankly appraising him, for the first time in Besim's amatory life, his stomach lurched and his heart beat erratically at the sight of a woman whose desirability might place her beyond his grasp, and so he greeted her as if the distance of two years and so much more could not possibly ever stand between them.

"Hello, old girl! I thought it jolly well time I made an honest woman of you, what?"

Mina was not shocked by this plummy, demotic, public-schoolboy, Wodehousian inflection—of course, she'd always known that the mangled Eastern European accent was a clumsy ruse. Rather, she was transfixed by the sight of Besim suddenly present in more flesh than she'd ever hoped or truly wished the opportunity of glimpsing. In his mindless romping about her studio, the sash of his robe had come undone and he seemed unaware or unfazed by the full frontal view he offered Mina. She continued standing in the open doorway, through which she might have fled and never returned; instead, she shut the door behind her, collapsed on the floor, and began retching in more or less a precise reenactment of the first time she'd barged in on Besim, who also duplicated his original role perfectly, bringing her a basin and a clean towel before wrapping his robe around her shivering shoulders (further disregarding that this now left him entirely naked). Mina, however, was grateful for Besim's small kindnesses, his reassuring familiarity as he blusteringly explained his mother's ludicrous will, as well as the fact that he never thought to ask Mina for an explanation of where she'd been the entire day (wandering Lower Manhattan looking for work but ending up drinking in a Bowery dive), and as soon as they'd polished off the last remaining bottle of wine, she impetuously accepted his proposal.

Two weeks later, as Mina was not one to break a promise (and was obviously in need of funds), and Besim never doubted the practicality of his scheme (with only the slight disruption of what everyone incorrectly assumed to be Andrew Brennan's final appearance in Mina's life), they were married at City Hall. Promptly thereafter, once all the required documentation had been submitted to the executor of his mother's will, which demanded Besim marry respectably and resume the title of Lord Beresford before receiving a single penny, and after the right to retire to the Belfast townhouse had been legally conferred upon the Dowager Lady Bess as reward for services rendered, the funds of Besim's inheritance were transferred over to him in their entirety. These were of sufficient means to permit the Beresford-Berishas to live comfortably, at least financially, throughout the ensuing eleven years, although they remained married for some considerable time longer than either ever expected.

CHAPTER SIX
Antiopa

I once asked Besim Berisha to sum up his marriage to Mina Byrne in five words. Counting the words on each finger of one hand while vocalizing aloud, he replied: "A series of unexplained absences." He had never nurtured the delusion that they might one day fall in love, but their agreement had been founded on the assumption that they were capable of living together for at least the sake of financial convenience. Consequently, neither Besim nor Mina invested one iota of his or her identity in the question of whom he or she chose to fuck outside of their own tepid sexual relations. Besim, however, relied on Mina as an audience for those self-affirming performances only a spouse could appreciate, yet she refused all pretense of listening to the various quiddities that inspirited his daily existence.

Whenever he arrived home to complain about the poor quality of cigarettes in America, or recount the event of unexpectedly running into so-and-so while out buying the dailies, or how a street sweeper on his lunch break had rudely cut him off in the queue waiting to make use of the public toilet, Besim was forced into the posture and tone of delivering a dully inconsequential soliloquy. In a desperate attempt to produce some kind of response, he would tack on various interrogatives, such as: hadn't she ever noticed that Virginian tobacco smelled like manure, or that so-and-so wore the expression of a constipated parrot, or that the lower classes always seemed to be in such a rush to take a shit? Besim believed he was offering Mina amusing anecdotes artfully embellished by his own quirky sense of humor, but the ever-so-slightly-perceptible clenching of Mina's jaw as he delivered one of his scatological punch lines clearly indicated her seething desire for him to vanish and never reappear.

So Mina shut herself up in the studio producing ever more disturbingly macabre images of women from myth and literature, sublimating her murderous impulses into a frenzy of creative activity. Meanwhile, Besim obliviously traipsed in and out, bringing wine and food, futilely attempting to solicit Mina's attention, before falling into bed and snoring loudly enough to disrupt her concentrated solitude. She had no choice but to lie down beside him, taking infuriated pleasure in pinching his nose or jabbing his ribs while he comatosely, vociferously slept. Mina would violently toss and turn until the sheets became tangled and Besim shifted onto his side and scooped her up into his arms, since he'd come to learn this was the only way of ensuring they both received a decent night's rest.

This state of affairs continued for three months until the night of *Claudia's Revenge*, or rather the following evening when Mina woke in Besim's arms after Andrew's disastrous play had driven her to destroy all of her paintings (for which Besim was silently grateful). Gazing up into his eyes as he fed her beef broth, confused as to why he offered such kindness when she didn't deserve it, Mina buried her head in the crook of his shoulder and confessed all the garbled shameful details of the previous evening, clutching onto Besim until she incoherently broke down into repeated, wrenching sobs.

"I don't know . . . I don't know what I'm supposed to do . . . I don't know anymore . . . I don't know how . . . I don't know . . ."

"Mina, old girl, you really can't go on like this," Besim gruffly, awkwardly assured her.

"But I won't ever love anyone as much as I've loved him," she wailed childishly.

"Yes, quite right, so you may as well learn how to love him less," he grumbled.

Mina's tears dissolved; she hiccoughed, raised her head and stared at Besim as if he'd expressed something both incomprehensible yet intellectually intriguing.

"How can you possibly quantify such a thing?"

"You could learn to love yourself more."

Mina thought this was a particularly trite answer, but did not have the energy to argue a more complex point of view; she didn't think there was one immediately at hand, and so she dryly remarked, "Well, I will at least have to learn how to do something other than paint."

After she'd curled up in a ball with her back turned to him, Besim slid further down in the bed, stretched out on his side facing the curve of her spine, and watched the rise and fall of her breath until he believed she was sleeping, until he might safely close his eyes without having to decide what he should do with his hands. Eventually Mina lifted her own hand and found Besim's hand, pulling him closer so that his body rested snugly against hers, his mouth snoring softly into the nape of her neck. From that point on, for as long as they were married, both comfortably conceded to the other's presence, and even occasionally, on those rare nights they shared a bed, enjoying an intimacy most couples take for granted.

This is not to say Mina magically, effortlessly discovered what she should do in place of painting or loving Andrew, and Besim hadn't the faintest idea what she did with her afternoons while he was out photographing the freakish denizens of Lower Manhattan or meeting moneyed married women at the St. Moritz. These were the sort of affairs that made no demands of his evenings, which he never spent apart from Mina since that night he'd returned home to discover her bleeding from self-inflicted wounds. Mina, however, seemed safe from any further suicidal or hysterical impulses, her activities now reduced to sleeping, reading, or sitting on the ledge of the windowsill absently staring down the airshaft, a journal in her lap, yet no pen in sight.

Once when Besim found her in this pose he asked if she'd decided to take up writing. Without removing her eyes from the nonexistent view, she handed him the empty journal, in which he discovered a small rectangular calling card slipped into a crease separating two of its blank leaves. Besim studied the black embossed lettering of a name—*Jerôme de Voile*—and then dimly recalled meeting a Parisian banker whose family owned a vineyard in Bordeaux. After buying seven cases of the de Voile Cabernet, Besim had been invited to one of the man's soirées. This must have been around the same time Besim and Mina first met, for he clearly remembered drinking two bottles of the supremely quaffable stuff that afternoon she'd shown up uninvited at his studio in Montmartre. He had no idea how Mina might have known Jerôme de Voile or in what capacity or why she would still have in her possession his antiquated calling card. He could have asked her, and Mina would have reminded him that it was in this man's house, or to be precise, his bathroom, where Besim first had the pleasure of fucking his wife. Besim simply chalked it up to the fact that he and Mina inevitably shared several acquaintances from their Parisian days, and forgot Jerôme de Voile as easily as he'd been recalled.

No wonder Besim misplaced from time to time the whereabouts of his wife. Several weeks after *Claudia's Revenge*, he came home to the mild shock of discovering Mina was gone, but she appeared less than an hour later, and after this initial reentry into the outside world, she continued her afternoon forays. Although she never ventured further than the seven blocks south of East 11th Street, where she sat in a quiet pub tentatively scribbling in her journal, or conversing with a much older man who bought her glasses of wine, Mina went out of her way to avoid piquing Besim's curiosity. At first she always arrived home not long after him, then she gradually began stumbling in later and later by weekly half-hour increments until it was often past midnight and either Besim had already fallen asleep or had failed to show up and would most likely not do so until the following morning or afternoon, by which time Mina would already be out again for the rest of the day.

In this manner Mina eased Besim into a routine that allowed them rarely to cross paths, which lasted a little over a year until without warning Mina changed the rules. Besim found her one evening seated at the kitchen table, her head bent low, fingers ink-stained and blotched while tearing across a sheet of paper in brutal jagged spurts of messily scrawled script. He sat down across from her, and was slightly disturbed when her face suddenly lifted and pinned him with her black eyes that nevertheless failed to focus properly upon the man before her. She dropped the pen, shoved the pages towards him, rose from the table, and collapsed into the bed, leaving Besim to confront on his own (and with comprehensible confusion) the following poem:

Beyond Berating

belladonna's bosom booms berserk
barrenly bantering in beastly brevity
baiting a booming barbarous baboon

shamelessly seducing his sanity
sauntering her simmering sordid sex
seedily sipping his sedentary stream

arranging attenuated answers
assigning asinine allegations
ambitiously adulterating our ardor

between both bumbling buffoons
baring a bruised and battered butterfly
bound to the blowsy bourbon of my breast

harlequin harlots harbinger hopeful halos
hanging on the hinge of hemispheres
hermeneutic happiness happens hermetically

After reading through this alliterative nonsense several times, Besim realized he could not interpret a single word of it, but recoiled from questioning Mina further when the next morning she refused to get out of bed. He did not want to suffer through yet another suffocating period in which she sank into a stubbornly silent depression, and so refused to acknowledge there was anything wrong. Later that afternoon, Mina was still in bed, gazing dully up at the watermarks in the cracked and stained ceiling. Besim would have gladly left her alone, but he had nowhere to go; it had rained all day and was threatening to do so again.

Because he was the sort of generally affable bloke who turned into an obnoxiously irritable grump when denied any and all sources of amusement, Besim began loudly banging about the studio in a pretense of tidying up, hoping this might at the very least rouse Mina into screaming at him to give it a rest. When that didn't succeed, he pulled down a copy of *Hamlet* (Mina's favorite out of all of the tragedies because it was not at all a tragedy, she claimed, but a very witty collection of memorable quotations), and proceeded to read aloud all the best lines in various comic voices, but Mina only sighed and turned her face to the wall. Finally, after he'd resorted to fiddling with one of his cameras, loudly cursing the lack of sufficient lighting not only in the studio but all of smog-infested New York, Mina sat up, her eyes glittering feverishly. She called across the room to Besim to deliver a carefully calculated question, one she'd been waiting all day for the opportunity to ask.

"What do you think of California?" she asked.

Besim had never thought of California, but as soon as Mina introduced the name of this unimaginable place, he took up her suggestion as if it were a magical key opening onto some enchanted kingdom that had always been awaiting their discovery. "All right, old girl, California it is! The sun will do you some good."

"Yes," Mina smiled tremulously. "And no doubt, Besim, if we try our luck in Hollywood there must be some film set or other where you might find a bit of camera work."

"No bother trying, eh, old thing?" he cheerfully agreed.

"Quite," she primly demurred, beginning at once to pack their luggage for what she'd already planned to be no more than a three-month sojourn out west. This, or so she'd been told, was roughly the length of time most films expended in making themselves, and as Besim discovered upon their arrival, there was indeed employment waiting for him, which Mina had also orchestrated so that it all seemed entirely coincidental.

While browsing the latest copy of *Variety* during the long train journey, Mina had spotted a blurb announcing the imminent production dates of *Dolores*, and after exclaiming how wonderful it was that her favorite book was being filmed, she persuaded Besim to make an appearance at the studio's production lot as soon as they arrived so that he might inquire about getting hired as an assistant cinematographer. Surely whoever was in charge of making such decisions would be more than happy to take him on, considering he'd already read the novel and once assisted that famous film director from Berlin, what's-his-name. Besim agreed, taking the rare opportunity to be responsible for Mina's happiness, and was pleasantly surprised to discover how simple this turned out to be. After five minutes on the set the job was offered to him, and Besim never doubted the relative ease with which he and Mina settled into a new routine, which was not much different from the one they'd established in New York. His only regret was that Mina refused to allow them to remain settled, and that he had somehow been maneuvered into arranging his life so that it followed whatever direction her capricious moods might take them.

As soon as the last reel of film had been shot, Mina, who had not once visited the set, suddenly stood before him and announced she'd had enough of the artificial California sun and wanted to return immediately to New York. She'd already purchased two train tickets that afternoon. Instead of accompanying Besim to the wrap party, she would be spending the evening packing their belongings for an unreasonably early departure the following morning, scheduled for 7:52. Besim had no urgent desire to resume their lives in New York, but agreed in the interests of avoiding an argument; he just needed an hour or so to say his goodbyes and then he'd be right along to help her pack.

The next morning he staggered blearily back to their bungalow at 9:27 and discovered Mina had left without him. His train ticket waited for him atop his packed trunk, as well as a note informing him that he'd be able to exchange the now defunct ticket for a new one, as long as the request was made within the first twenty-four hours of the missed departure. Besim sat on the edge of the bed, staring at the ticket in his hand, and questioned whether Mina actually intended for him to come chasing after her, or if this was her way of leaving him a way out, not of their marriage but the pretense of living together in the same relative field of time and space.

He considered staying in California, but then regrettably recalled how he'd broken things off with the snub-nosed starlet who'd played the role of Dolores, saying something or other about how she may as well shove off since there wasn't much more between them than a few fumbling fucks. After receiving the standard slap across the cheek, he'd been accosted by an officious old toad who snappishly reprimanded Besim for the lack of pity he'd shown "his poor little girl," and then expounded in the dry tones of a professor condescending to impart his wisdom to a hopelessly dense student: "It is inevitable that our sexual affairs should heap indecency upon indecency, something I find too tedious for words, but since we have only words to play with, then we must learn to master our playthings, a skill, my dear man, you apparently have little likelihood of achieving."

Besim was about to defend himself, struggling through the perplexed haze of far too much wine for a few choice words that might repudiate the man's infuriatingly obscure accusation, but a severe, silver-haired, spectacled woman appeared at the old codger's side, taking him by the elbow and dragging him away with stentorian disapproval; whether this was directed towards her husband's outburst or Besim's supposed provocation, Besim had no way of knowing. Likewise, he had no idea that this belligerent interloper into his private affairs was none other than the author of *Dolores*, since Vasili

Novikov had not once graced the set with his presence, despite the fact that he'd agreed to serve in an advisory role and had been generously compensated for this. Besim assumed the old man was the father of the scorned starlet, and that his verbal attack, delivered in the burred accents of a Russian émigré, had been provoked by the misplaced desire to defend his daughter's honor according to some old world code of pedantic paternalism. To be fair, the girl had been the one to seduce Besim, who rarely found anything attractive in the puerile charms of adolescent twits. Already missing Mina, but since he'd had no real desire to assist in packing their belongings, Besim left the party drunkenly lugged along by the more mature and amply proportioned actress who'd played the role of Dolores' nagging mother.

To discover the following morning that Mina had refused to wait for him soured his entire view of California; it had now become the gloomiest spot on earth. Without further delay, he took himself to the station, exchanged his ticket for another heading out East, and arrived in New York only twenty-seven hours after Mina's scheduled return. When he unlocked the door to their studio, boisterously calling out Mina's name, he was disappointed, but hardly worried, when she didn't reply. After lighting the lamps, and while waiting for the rattling pipes to hiss out some warmth into the November damp, he observed yet another note left for him on the dust encrusted table, and after reading, Besim's heart palpitated briefly with the devastation of undeniable loss.

I don't know when or if I'll be back. I don't expect you to wait or understand. I've only just realized that we, or at least I, cannot go on like this.

No salutation, no signature, no indication of where she might be. Besim did not attempt to go looking for her, to hire a detective, file divorce papers, or wallow in grief. He resumed their usual habits, as if Mina had not left such a ludicrous letter, as if she still resided in the studio and they simply kept different hours, their comings and goings failing to overlap in a relay race of absence and presence. In this way, Besim had resolved to wait for her, and it did not at all seem a foolish endeavor, or even an act of blind faith. Mina's vanishing acts were always predictably followed by her reappearances. Six months later, in early May, and magically arriving at the stroke of midnight, Mina materialized, though it was not at all the same Mina who had disappeared. This Mina, who stumbled into the studio waking Besim with her ragged sobs, was beaten, bruised, barefoot, and visibly pregnant.

Throughout the unfolding early morning hours, while Mina allowed Besim to bathe her, washing away blood from her left cheek, above her right eye broken open by a fist, several scrapes from falls, and feet that had fled to safety without the protection of shoes, she could only offer Besim a compulsively repetitive, monotonously intoned excuse for her return: "He was going to kill me, so I had to . . . oh god, I had to . . . he was going to kill me . . ."

"Yes, of course, old girl, but you're safe now, and you did the right thing, didn't you?"

Although Besim was uncertain of what she'd done, of what guilt he was absolving her, these words seemed to do the trick. She released a shuddering sigh, rose from the tub, one hand on Besim's shoulder and the other pressed flat beneath the naked, dripping abundance of her torso, as if securing its weight to her otherwise slim body, which Besim wrapped in his old paisley robe since none of her former clothes now fit. Mina smiled drowsily, acknowledging what had become a recognizable gesture of reconciliation between them, and then fell into what appeared to be a profoundly dreamless sleep.

Once again, Besim never learned where she'd been, but only because she'd returned from a place that did not exist. There was no indication from Mina that she'd been missing all those months or that she would be a mother to another man's child. When she refused to leave the studio in order to be measured for a set of maternity clothes, Besim offered to hire a woman to come by one afternoon to do this for her, but Mina claimed she was perfectly capable of altering the dresses she already had. There was no sense in squandering good money on clothing no one would see, and in service to a physical condition that was, as far as she'd observed in other women, a temporary metamorphosis, after which she would return to her original slender self. Besim yielded to Mina's common sense, and refrained from commenting when instead of altering the waist lines of her old dresses she opted for padding about the studio in the nude. This seemed not so much an act of flaunting her belly but a sensible concession to the discomfort of discovering oneself pregnant during an early summer heat wave.

For the first time since meeting Mina's original slenderness nearly seven years ago, Besim began photographing her again. Mina offered no resistance, posing absently, lethargically, and the hazily wistful tone of the resulting images are perhaps due to the subject's inwardly pensive mood rather than any skill on the part of the photographer. That August, Besim received a gallery showing of his portrait series, and primarily due to the presence of these studied, strangely intimate, though disconnected meditations on his wife, which juxtaposed nicely with his more abruptly invasive snapshots of hostile strangers he'd captured while prowling the Bowery, Lower Eastside, and Greenwich Village alleyways. By some coincidence the gallery was located only a few blocks from the theater where the fourth and final play by Andrew Brennan was being performed, and both play and photographs opened to the public on the same evening. The intersection of both events, the first of which Mina saw advertised in the Sunday arts section of *The New York Times*, the second she refused to attend, finally forced her into constructing a dress that conformed to the girth of her eight-month expectant belly.

While Mina waddled westward, skirting the southern edges of Washington Square Park, turning down MacDougal towards Houston, where she would sit in a darkened theater and witness the worst of Andrew's delusional ravings, one might have seen, if one were looking for such a thing, a dignified old man and his elegant, silver-haired, beak-nosed wife wandering through the gallery where the photographs of Mina were displayed. The couple had no real reason for being there other than their innocent desire to kill some time; neither had much interest in photography, as neither could see the validity of any artistic purpose it might serve. Silently suffering these amateurishly pretentious portraits documenting nothing more than the invariably mundane conformity of the human face, they passed by each photograph with glazed eyes, dragging their feet, until they arrived at the triptych of Mina. The old man stopped and stared. His wife graciously sipped on a glass of cheap champagne that had been offered her, glancing at her wristwatch and noting the time. She refused to acknowledge the photographs. They had an unsettling quality, and not because they stood out in contrast to the rest of the photographer's uninspired efforts, but they made a point, whether intentionally or not, of calling to the viewer's attention the limitations of any photograph in its ability to reveal the truth of its subject's identity. Indeed, this is what Vasili Novikov saw and what his wife denied seeing:

In the first portrait of Mina, she is trapped in full profile, head uplifted as if in sexual ecstasy, eyes languorously closed; in the second she is presented face forward, eyes still gently closed, as if sleeping, musing on other worlds, all the inner dimensions of her private, unknowable self; in the third, she is captured fully nude, fully fleshed, but fully turned away, as she leans face forward against a blank wall, the sinuous curve of her spine confronting the viewer with all that it conceals. It is clear, in all of these pictures, that she is evading the camera eye, evading our eyes, refusing to become ensnared, and for this, we are all the more intrigued. Such a lovely woman, the viewer murmurs, hoping to unravel the enigma of such beauty, which itself evades the possibilities of language.

Vasili hadn't realized he'd murmured these words aloud until his wife breathed a small sigh of disapproval, linked her arm inside the familiar crook of his elbow and led him away. They shuffled out of the gallery, crossed the street, and found their seats in the theater where what they saw over the next two hours diminished any lasting memory of those photographs. If they'd been allowed to see what the photographs had intentionally hidden, they might have had a very different or at least more fully informed impression of their son's play. Mina had tried to rectify this omission by demanding Besim also display the self-portrait she'd taken of herself, in which she is posed before a mirror, face forward, eyes open, the undeniable swell of her full breasts and bared belly offered in open communication with the viewer. Besim had argued no one wanted to see a pregnant woman, especially a naked pregnant woman. In reply, Mina informed him of her decision to attend Andrew's play, since she could at least stomach more easily *his* distortions of reality so grossly inflicted upon her sense of self. It was a double entendre wasted on Besim but one Mina would later regret having made.

She should have anticipated the harm Andrew's play would try to inflict upon not only her but also his parents. She should have been prepared, since she was already familiar with the paranoid delusions Andrew had concocted as evidence of the betrayals he believed had been perpetrated against him by Mina and his father. She'd never thought, based on the last time she'd seen Andrew, that he was actually sane or sober enough to translate his lurid fantasies into a coherent plot. It remains debatable, though, whether *Antiopa* was a success, in spite of the Pulitzer Prize awarded to the author after he'd been committed to a psychiatric ward at Bellevue, his madness apparently confirming his genius.

The entirety of the play takes place on a brutally bare stage, void of props, painted scenery, or scrim, this absence of any visual design indicating to the audience that we are nowhere, in a place that doesn't exist. A young man and young woman, who may or may not be incestuous lovers, argue fiercely, passionately, about their versions of the past, in which they seemed to have tortured each other with prolonged separations marred by infidelities. They then torturously quibble over the lifelong obsessions they have nurtured for their adulterous, selfish, and obscure father, who may or may not be one and the same man. This old man makes an occasional spotlighted appearance on the stage, sitting in a rocking chair on a raised platform staring down at these miserable creatures, making no comment other than a gleeful cackle whenever they say something unwittingly stupid or cruel. The play ends with the young woman admitting she is pregnant. The young man embraces her tearfully, interpreting this news as a promise that she will never, ever again leave him. In response, she smiles sweetly, falsely, and joins the old man on his platform, sitting on his lap with her head nestled against his scrawny neck. The house lights fade on the young man's horrified look of disgust until a single lingering spotlight remains on the old man, his lips stretched in a triumphant leer, hands resting on the girl's belly, and then complete darkness descends. The audience is left wondering: *Who* is the father of the child?

The following morning, *The New York Times* would print a review of *Antiopa*, which was interpreted as a scathing satire offering in its darkly comic family romance the condemning critique of a repressive society in which love could only be bartered at the price of incest, madness, or death. For Mina, as well as the Novikovs, it was merely proof of Andrew's clinically deranged imagination, though the author had intended every word of this insane twaddle to be taken quite literally, for that was the spirit in which it had been written. Because he was their son, the Novikovs shambled off backstage in search of Andrew; Mina remained seated, oblivious to the people around her taking their leave, ignoring the waves of contracting pain stabbing at her from somewhere deep inside her belly. She was still sitting there when Vasili and Deirdre emerged from the wings, without their son, and walked up the aisle heading blindly towards the theater exit. Vasili, at least, failed to see her, his head hung low; Deirdre, though, steely-eyed as ever, and never missing a thing, expended one long heartless glance in the direction of the heavily pregnant woman sitting alone. Mina would never forget the brief, pointed, naked look of loathing and fear the older woman directed towards her before guiding Vasili out the door, to their hotel, and their decision to return to Europe so they would not have to face the disgrace of having their son committed to psychiatric care.

Mina would not learn of this decision until several months after that horrific night when she couldn't move from her seat, even when the house manager was threatening to lock up. She knew she could not possibly be waiting for Andrew because Andrew had vanished a long time ago. She knew her water had broken, and that she had to ask for help, but there was no one to ask. She knew the woman crouching beside her, urging her to her feet, and into a taxi, but she couldn't remember her name. She did not know why Sara Sorrell, whose name she cried out when it suddenly came back to her in one sharp pang of recognition, yes, why Sara Sorrell of all people would be the one to help her home, or why she would take it upon herself to knock on all the doors in the building demanding the assistance of any woman who knew anything about childbirth, which resulted in three mother gooses boiling water, shredding sheets, positioning Mina's legs so that one could peer between them while another held the poor girl's head against her chest, pushing her to push and push and push until the dead weight came dropping out into the large-boned hands of all people, Sara Sorrell. She didn't know where Besim was throughout all of this, only that he was absent, and when he did return, stinking of alcohol and another woman's sex, Mina screamed and screamed at him until he was forced to flee down the stairs, followed by the hissing disapproval of the impromptu midwives. He never did see the child. Mina never spoke of the child. All she knew was that if it had been a girl (she hadn't wanted to know its sex), she would have called her Sara, which Mina knew originally meant princess, or she who laughed, because as the story goes, or so her father taught her when Mina was a little girl trapped in his study every morning learning her bible lessons alongside medieval philosophy and ancient tragedy, when the first Sara was told at the age of ninety or some such quarrelsome age that she would become a mother, she laughed in God's face.

Mina could not stop laughing the day she read a letter from Sara informing her that Andrew had been sent to the loony bin, and although Sara believed marriage to be a great institution, she did not believe she was ready for that kind of institution, a feeble observation if there ever was one, from which Sara hoped Mina might receive some small consolation. After misinterpreting Mina's crazed cackle over Sara's poor pun, Besim insisted on leaving New York as soon as possible. By the end of that year they were securely settled in Italy, where the lush and sultry Tuscan sun allowed Mina the possibility of obliterating every last desire or hope for happiness she might have once conceived.

CHAPTER SEVEN
Duende

Now seems as good a time as any to introduce more fully Andrew's younger brothers, since now is when their lives begin to intersect with Mina's, if only peripherally. Nearly four years after Mina and Besim left New York, Jamie Brennan was on his way back there, forced to return to the country from which he thought he'd escaped. Throughout the tedious voyage, Jamie had been overwhelmed by a barrage of memories battering away at him, daily breaching the barriers he'd long ago established between his life in Paris and his childhood in America. As he sat in his deckchair, faced with an unending horizon of sea and sky, he began to recall small details from the first time he'd made this journey at the age of four. He'd never fully understood, then or now, the exact circumstances that had led to their father's decision to uproot all of them to America. All he knew was that Vasili had often reminded his sons, whenever one of them failed him in some way, that he and their mother had sacrificed more than they could possibly imagine during their family's exodus from an increasingly fascist Europe into the safe haven of democracy.

Their departure, however, had not in any way seemed planned but rather a frantic, last-minute affair. Jamie clearly remembered observing the strain of anxiety creasing his mother's brow, as she awkwardly maneuvered around their cramped two-room sublet, one hand protectively propped on the obtrusive bulge of her belly, the other shoving haphazard articles of clothing into already overstuffed suitcases. He was seated on his father's lap, listening to him read aloud the lecture notes Mama had helped translate into English, of which Jamie had little understanding. Although his mother was British, or from Northern Ireland to be precise, after an assassin's bullet had silenced her father for his political agitations, sending her into fifteen years of exile in Berlin and then Paris, she rarely spoke her native tongue, except with Andrew, who for ten years had been her only child. Now, though, with their imminent relocation to a college campus in upstate New York, where Papa had accepted a Professorship in Comparative Literature, and to facilitate the entire family's acclimation to American culture, it had been decided that English should be the Novikovs' primary form of communication. Papa was a polyglot god, the realms of five languages at his command, and the only way of effectively communing with Jamie's multilingual parents was by mastering the art of code-switching, a conversational flair his older brother often smugly demonstrated (though eventually relinquished as soon as he realized the easiest way of rebelling against their father was to become far more Americanized than Papa had ever desired, which simply required one to remain willfully ignorant of a second, let alone third, language).

Jamie instinctively tried to suppress any childhood memory of Andrew, yet once again he was shivering violently, standing at the railings of the upper deck, still a child of four, watching his older brother helplessly hunched over as he vomited all over his shoes. They could still hear, or at least imagine hearing, their mother screaming like a wild animal in their cabin two floors below, from which both boys had been evicted. Sometime later, still standing on the upper deck and staring out at the churning, foaming, moonlit trail left behind by the ship's passage through the cold, black Atlantic Ocean, Andrew had informed Jamie that now the new baby was born, their mother would no longer love him since that's what happened when new babies decided to arrive. As for their father, he'd throw Jamie overboard. Jamie had nothing to say in reply to this, because in that moment Andrew's threat was not beyond the realm of possibility.

That night was when Jamie decided to stop speaking altogether, which seemed the only sensible thing to do in a family that loved to hear the sound of its own voice. Papa's authoritative statements boomed off the walls, claiming the smallest spaces and tightest corners of all the rented houses they inhabited. Mama's voice was the redounding echo of Papa's every thought and command, though more genteelly refined, sliding underfoot across worn-thin carpets in her sibilant yet sonorous inflections. Andrew forever grumbled his ferociously defended opinions at the dinner table, situating himself as the illogical centrifugal whirlpool whipping around their father's imperious locutions. Colin cheerily chirped and gurgled above the madhouse din. Jamie refused to compete.

Fortunately, Jamie's lack of verbal interaction was for the most part indulged, his refusal to speak implicitly accepted within the family as his autonomous stance. Not for a minute did anyone consider there might be a faulty glitch in his internal mechanism transferring him out of his mirror phase into the realm of the symbolic. His father rejected all notions of symbolism. In this world there were only patterns and puzzles to piece together lest they unravel beyond our doubtful control, and because Vasili vociferously condemned psychoanalysis to be at best a form of unqualified quackery, Jamie was never made to endure any of those games with anatomically correct dolls or flash cards of grotesque blotches. These were insidiously pathologizing tricks, Vasili grumbled, often inflicted upon many wise children who had adopted muteness as a much more preferable mode of speech.

However, Jamie's first-grade teacher, a Miss Melody Kline, was not as agreeably accommodating, insisting his unruly silence disrupted her class. In a teacher-parent conference with the Novikovs, she bluntly suggested there might be something mentally or physically deficient in their child, something slightly un-American, since every normal, healthy, red-white-and-blue-blooded child learned early on the value of speaking one's opinions, whether elicited or not, and at the highest volume possible. Miss Kline assured the skeptical parents, who were obviously of Eastern European origin, that this was a tried and true lesson that prepared young Americans for the day when they would be forced to tackle the cutthroat mechanisms of their capitalist society. Mr. Novikov might have laughed this off as harmless twaddle; he'd prepared his family to accept such jingoistic sentiments as a common though harmless feature of American life, but as soon as Miss Kline recommended sending Jamie into weekly counseling sessions with a Lacanian therapist, he was pulled from the public school system and taught at home by Mrs. Novikov.

Jamie and his mother took equal pleasure in this arrangement, as their morning lessons stretched into afternoons of uninterrupted solitude. Colin eventually acclimated to the social life of babbling preschoolers, Andrew vanished into some New England prep school, and Vasili preoccupied himself with the petty politics of academia and the adulatory demands of his students. Jamie would patiently listen to his mother as she read out the lessons in her soft, lilting voice, which never demanded a response. Confident this more than sufficiently fulfilled her role as instructor, she left Jamie alone with his books and theorems and written exercises, which she would cursorily review the following morning. While Jamie educated himself, Deirdre went about her domestic chores, and if there were no secretarial tasks Vasili had left behind for her to complete, then she had an hour or so to do whatever she liked, though no one in the Novikov household could have guessed what that might be.

Nor did anyone suspect Jamie of forming a friendship with a frail, blonde little girl his own age, equally sparing with her words, and a far more intelligent and receptive playmate than either of his brothers. Nadia would drop by to visit Jamie when papa and mama were cloistered in the study, papa's deep-barreled voice dictating his lecture notes to the rhythm of mama furiously clacking away on the typewriter. The children would sit cross-legged facing each other on the floor of Jamie's bedroom with the door firmly shut, blocking out the noise of the adults down the hall. Nadia listened to Jamie elaborate on the books he'd read, the ideas they inspired, the complications he could only untangle with the presence of her smile urging him to reach the conclusion that seemed just out of grasp. Sometimes Nadia would debate an especially thorny point that Jamie stumbled over, but for the most part she comprehended everything as if she'd thought of it on her own.

Jamie thought of Nadia as the fraternal twin his mother had failed to produce, though as far as anyone knew Jamie had been the only zygote to replicate itself in Deirdre's womb during his term of residence in that obscurely fleshy domain; he was also the only one who could see or speak with Nadia. This led to a number of embarrassing instances when his mother overheard one of his rambling monologues. Although it had been established that it made no difference at all when and with whom Jamie chose to speak, Deirdre would knock on his door before opening it, choking down an inquiry while studying her son's innocent face, and attempt to reflect back to him his own placid gaze. Receiving no indication that anything was amiss, she had no choice but to turn and shut the door.

Nadia's visits became increasingly sporadic as soon as Jamie turned twelve and was sent off to the same prep school Andrew had been forced to attend. Fortunately, Andrew had long ago been expelled and was living his questionable life down in New York City, and now that Jamie was physically removed from his family, he rediscovered his voice, eloquently rising to the top of his class. During visits home, he would revert to silence, acceding to the expected monosyllabic adolescent grunt in lieu of fully articulated morphemes, and besides, Colin naturally took it upon himself to perform all conversational duties. Andrew was by this point a name rarely mentioned at the dinner table, his prodigal status saving Jamie the embarrassment of their parents discovering Jamie's one disastrous attempt during his final year at Harrington to run away. If Andrew had been on speaking terms with Deirdre or Vasili, the secret of Jamie's failed truancy would have slipped off Andrew's tongue and into their parents' uncompromising ears.

Jamie, seventeen-years-old, had just been accepted into the Sorbonne. It was an accomplishment that would oblige him to carry the entire weight of Vasili's paternal pride, sorely in need of bolstering since his eldest son appeared to be an utter disappointment, squandering all his early promise of creative success on booze and floozies, or so Vasili often grumbled. As for Colin, though an exceedingly sociable, bright, and witty boy, he revealed no academic aptitude whatsoever and was thus shamefully relegated to remaining in the American public school system. Jamie was expected to be everything his brothers were not. In fact, he was to be nothing less than the perfect imitation of his father's intellect. Jamie had vomited all over his acceptance letter, and then took the first bus to New York. Throughout the long, equally nausea-inducing ride, Nadia had sat beside him, her serene smile granting approval of his impulse without the slightest hint of anxiety as to its expected outcome.

When Jamie arrived at Andrew's apartment, which ostensibly belonged to some dance-hall floozy with whom Andrew claimed to be passionately in love, his brother had no interest in Jamie's stuttered explanations. Instead he insisted on getting Jamie stinking-puking drunk, and although exceeding his ambition of introducing Jamie to every disreputable dive located between the Bowery and Times Square, he failed to induct him into a life of debauchery. Whenever Andrew vanished in the direction of the toilet, Jamie took the opportunity to palm off his drink to the grizzled drunk who sat propped beside him; when they were booted out of the last bar in that evening's endless crawl, Jamie picked his slobbering brother up from the street, soberly walked him home, ensured that he passed out face-down on the bed so he would avoid choking to death on his vomit, and then took the first bus back to Harrington and his future of ascetic conformity.

Ever since that misadventure, Jamie consumed no more than a glass of watered wine with his evening meal, as conspicuously abstemious as his brothers were not (Colin surpassing Andrew in their mutual love of drink, as Jamie was about to discover). In the ten years since he'd left his family behind in the American wilderness, confident he'd constructed for himself an identity no longer generated by any allegiances to the past (having at least imbibed the Emersonian myth of self-reliance), Jamie had only written the occasional letter home, and had not once thought of Andrew, at least not until recently. Their father had sent him Andrew's published scripts, requesting a diagnosis of Andrew's mental illness through a psychological investigation of his plays, something Vasili could not do since this interpretive approach violated his sense of aesthetic integrity. He was, however, not above demanding that others take such desperate measures if it meant discovering a cure, any cure, which might free his child from the imprisonment of his own mind.

Whether the father's or the son's mind, Jamie could not be certain. Andrew's plays seemed to be trapped inside the worlds of Vasili's novels, and Vasili's novels, at least his most recent one, spun wildly out of his son's madness. More perplexingly, each plagiaristic play persisted in an obsessive evocation of the same elusive female character traipsing in and out of every scene. Andrew's numinous nymphet was nothing more than a transparent, ghostly echo of their father's mysterious muse, who was entirely imaginary and not at all based on any real person, which Vasili heatedly insisted when Jamie telephoned to share his conclusions. He knew his father would disregard anything he had to say. Vasili had always made it a practice of asking his sons for their opinions only to discount them as either adolescent diatribes or unfounded arguments (which in Vasili's opinion amounted to the same). Jamie, however, had long ago stopped falling for his father's puerile ploys. When Vasili demanded he travel all the way to New York to see his brother in order to make a more fully informed diagnosis, and then attempted to corner him into the journey by insisting it was the least Jamie could do after years of conveniently removing himself from any familial obligations, Jamie shrugged this off. He easily recognized the strategy as yet another of Vasili's shoddy efforts at displacing his guilt onto anyone other than himself.

Vasili continued haranguing him with an endless volley of telegrams transmitted from Lausanne, where he and Deirdre had retired soon after their decision to abandon their eldest son. In spite of his father's geographical proximity, Jamie was able to continue coolly ignoring him. Then Vasili showed up unannounced, huffing and gruffing and blowing down all of Jamie's defenses. The moment he stepped across the threshold, his larger than life presence exuded its usual command of deference, more so now that he'd put on some considerable weight (an inevitable side-effect of finally giving up what had become a four-pack-a-day habit); yet he also seemed pathetically reduced, arms akimbo, stranded in the barren minimalism of Jamie's sparsely furnished apartment, his mournful eyes, slack jowls, and hang-dog expression seeking absolution from one son because he could not request it of the other. That night, while Jamie lay on the sofa listening to his father's snores coming from the bedroom, he regressively longed for Nadia to reappear. She would shimmer seductively, solidifying briefly, no longer a little girl but always as old as Jamie himself.

Time left nothing unravaged, not even the people solely inhabiting one's imagination, and even knowing this, Jamie was not adequately prepared to confront either of his brothers, which was why, upon disembarking at the New York seaport, he took the precaution of booking a berth on the next available trans-Atlantic crossing, two days from now. Since it hardly seemed worth dragging around, he left his luggage in the care of the ship's porters, resigned himself to the obligatory delay of having his passport stamped by some greasily pomaded, pimply, and deliberately disagreeable clerk at the customs office, and then slowly began to make his way on foot towards his brother's apartment. The long walk through the twisted maze of Lower Manhattan, emerging into the economical, logical grids of the Upper West Side, would allow him enough time to prepare for seeing Colin again in the flesh.

By chance, or more likely paternal dictum, Colin would also be in New York: he'd been granted a reprieve from whatever film set he was working on in order to take advantage of this momentous occasion when all three brothers would be present in the same city, much less the same continent. Jamie had last seen Colin ten years ago, the day Jamie boarded the ship taking him to Paris, his family waving their farewells from the docks. Vasili and Deirdre had appeared to all the world two proud and forlorn immigrants, sending the pride of their fleet back to the old country as proof of their success, yet not quite certain why their fortunate son should want to return to the site of their former miseries. Andrew, as usual, had stood some distance from them, arms crossed, resentful of his required presence. Fourteen-year-old Colin had skipped through the crowds, whistling, hooting, and hollering, as rambunctiously naïve and in love with the idea of adventure as any American schoolboy.

Jamie had easily preserved this image of Colin, who five years ago began showing up in numerous Hollywood confections, all of which Jamie had reluctantly gone to see as soon as they premièred in Paris. Each celluloid representation of his brother's boyish ebullience held Colin in a permanent state of suspension, unchanging in character or appearance, and playing out the same character with the same farcical fate in every film. Colin seemed perpetually consigned to the role of outlaw-soldier-cowboy, the archetype of American rebellion, resourcefulness, and resilience enlarged to mythic proportions upon wide-screen Technicolor vistas of sweeping skies and surging seascapes of rolling hills, amber fields of grain, and vastly unchartered plains. More miraculously, or mundanely, depending on one's point of view, Colin had transcended to the greatest American myth of all: movie-star.

This, of course, exasperated their father, who would never be able to comprehend how his eldest and youngest sons had chosen to forego university educations; nor could he understand why they had preferred to pursue careers in the tawdry worlds of Broadway and Hollywood, both of which made a practice of sacrificing high art for the lowest common denominator of mass entertainment, and so Vasili took scarce comfort when either son had achieved apparent success. Indeed, when Colin had informed his parents of his ambition to become an actor, claiming, though not in so many words, that this did not require the refinement of one's intellect, but the manipulation of one's emotive experience, thus rendering the pursuit of a higher education entirely irrelevant, Vasili had become mired in a deep depression upon hearing such complete and utter poppycock.

Although it would have been a severe blow to his pride and principles, he should have pulled every string possible to secure his low-achieving son a place at Harrington, where they might have made more of an effort than the underpaid teachers at Riverside High to mold Colin's mind and inspire him to higher aspirations. On the other hand, the benefits of a private education hadn't made much of a favorable impression on Andrew, if one were to take him as an example, which he didn't. Instead, Vasili mournfully berated himself for having allowed Colin to run wild with his hooligan friends, all of whom dreamed of becoming the next Dillinger or Capone. Although Vasili's boyhood hero had been the Scarlet Pimpernel, he at least had a dash of wit and literary merit; whereas Colin's gangsters were two-bit, two-penny, two-dimensional magazine serials, most of them rife with sloppy spelling and grammar, as well as a plethora of slang. Vasili, however, took furtive pleasure in all those idiosyncratic idioms so unique to the American teen, inserting them with masterful command into his American masterpiece, *Dolores*, published the year Colin graduated high school with an unexpected distinction imprinted in scrolling Latin on his degree. The boy had laughed, insisted it must be some mistake, and then tossed it aside with his cap and gown and all further obligations to make his parents proud.

Vasili had known better, because unlike his brothers, Colin never felt obliged to do anything; life, for Colin, had always been effortless. This had been his charm since the moment he'd emerged from his mother's hemorrhaging womb, the favored child if there'd ever been one, if Vasili had ever been asked to choose, which he had, which he did. He'd spoiled the boy, indulged him with far more affection and far less discipline than he'd ever extended to his older brothers. Vasili didn't think there were any deficiencies in his other sons; Colin was simply so much easier to hold, to adore. Andrew and Jamie were inflexible, prickly, always demanding attention, approval, admiration, all the desperate needs of any child, for which Vasili wanted no responsibility since he too had never stopped needing these things. Or perhaps, knowing the struggle Deirdre had endured during that third pregnancy, and remembering, always, the unspeakable horror Vasili had been faced with when it was clear Deirdre might not survive, and when he'd finally held Colin in his arms, and knew, then, that there would not ever be another child, he had unswervingly stuck to his promise to love this child with all that his heart had left to spare. It was a promise he thought he could keep, that he could give Colin everything, because Colin asked for nothing.

When Colin told his father he was going to California and asked Vasili for his blessing and assistance, Colin was informed he'd be given nothing of the sort. If he wanted to run off in some pedestrian quest for stardom, then he could do it like all the other fools: start off at the bottom, on his own, and hold onto his delusions for as long as he could feed them. Colin laughed, because that's what Colin always did, and had said, "Okay, pops, s'pose ya gotta point, so's I'll sendja a postcard when I'm rich an' famous." Then he was gone the next day, and Vasili regretted his passing moment of stinginess, because he would have given in, would have given him anything if given enough time to put aside his disappointment and sense of betrayal. The problem with all of his sons was that none of them had the patience to wait out the storm of Vasili's moods until he was feeling more munificent, a frame of mind he always eventually arrived at, which was why Vasili and his sons always ended up with so many misunderstandings and impassable distances between them. It didn't matter, at least not with Colin, because everything came easily to him, even forgiveness.

Less than a year after Colin took over from Andrew the role of prodigal son, Vasili received his postcard. The location was some unidentified beach where white sands stretched into eternity and the waves crashed relentlessly into the supine form of a man and a woman melded together in a tangle of legs and arms that obscured their faces. The back of the card boasted in bold capital letters: **LAST STOP**—then in all lower case and identifiably written in Colin's childish, heavy scrawl: **see ya there, pops!!!** This was followed by an inscrutably silly smiley face. Vasili could not decode any of it, leaving the matter of translation, as usual, to his wife, who informed him, because she'd always made a point of speaking with her sons on a regular basis even when their father stubbornly refused to speak their names, that the postcard was a publicity still for the film in which Colin had been given a substantial part; *Last Stop* was the title of the film; the addendum was their son's invitation to the première, and as she'd already accepted the invitation, the extraneous exclamation marks were notations indicating Colin's enthusiasm for their impending arrival. As for the smiling symbol, that was both Colin's signature and his good-natured way of telling his father, "I toldja so."

"Told me what?" Vasili asked, genuinely perplexed.

"That you were wrong, dear, and he was right," Deirdre quipped, leaving the room and her husband to figure the rest out on his own.

Vasili had no notion, ever, of being wrong. He did, however, go out the next day and buy a used Buick, into which he packed three suitcases, a crate full of notebooks, a typewriter, and several nets and mounting boards, anticipating that a cross-country road trip would be the perfect opportunity for pursuing his lepidopterous passion, and then settled himself into the passenger seat, for he did not (nor would he ever know) how to drive. This, along with many other trivial details and tasks, he left to his wife, who had no complaints, because she, at least, knew who was in control. She knew Vasili needed a holiday and some distance from his present preoccupations, which more or less revolved around their eldest son.

Claudia's Revenge, Andrew's latest play, and the scene they'd witnessed after its première, had disturbed his father to the extent that he'd felt compelled to spend numerous weekends down in New York. He'd argued Andrew was in need of parental guidance if he were to save his marriage, much less his career. Rather, this was Vasili's lame defense when Deirdre accused him of spending too much time away at the expense of his latest novel. She knew Vasili had no interest in saving Andrew's marriage, but would be invested in saving his own, no matter how long a leash Deirdre gave him, and had always given him. The invitation from Colin had been one of those fortuitous coincidences Deirdre often employed to her advantage whenever she needed to maneuver Vasili back in the right direction.

They spent three weeks traveling westward, enjoying every mile of their American odyssey, until they arrived at the edge of the American frontier, the last stop, Beverly Hills. Colin rented them a beachside bungalow and took them to his première, which they did not enjoy. Seeing their child projected back to them on a fifty foot screen transformed him into a stranger wearing some sailor's suit, swigging whiskey, throwing punches, seducing an admiral's daughter, and dying in her arms from a gunshot wound to the heart, all the while winking, grinning, swearing, crooning, and moaning in Colin's own particular manner, which they cherished, but could not reconcile with the character on screen. Afterwards, he took them to a series of parties where both Colin and the Novikovs were toasted and adored by the glitterati. Unbeknownst to them, while on the road, Vasili had become as much an overnight celebrity as his son. *Dolores* had escaped censorship and was successfully scandalizing the American conscience, which never tired of morally outraging itself.

Only two days after their arrival, they ran into a former acquaintance from Berlin, where they'd lived nearly thirty years ago. This was not so fortuitous, for it morosely reminded Vasili of a time when he was young, happy, and in love, while Deirdre was forced to recall not only the reasons for her unhappiness during the early days of their marriage, but also the underlying reason for their present sojourn out west. With Vasili, it was always, always the same insipid infidelities, which Deirdre could put up with when she was young, but not now, not when she was old, when he was old. She knew there was nothing she could do but patiently wait it out. Vasili spent weeks presumably holed up with Stanislaus, writing the screenplay of his novel for a film he would end up detesting. When he was supposed to be acting as a script advisor during filming, Deirdre knew he was not on set. If he had been, then the film might not have turned out so disappointing, but at least this way Vasili could disown it without anyone arguing otherwise. Deirdre never argued, not with Vasili, not with anyone. People would do as they please.

As it turned out, people were thrilled with the film version of *Dolores*, if only because the majority of them had not read the book, and of course, according to the perverse trends of modern publishing, the film had an inordinate influence in raising Vasili's sales. This then transported the name of Novikov beyond the insular coterie of academics familiar with his work and into the realm of widespread recognition, even if the majority of Americans could not, or would not, correctly pronounce his name. No matter how many times, in interview after interview, he insisted on a phonetic transcription just to clear up any confusion, the public insisted on mangling it into a tortuously drawled Nawveekawv, and should anyone follow the author's preference, then it was disparagingly viewed as a sign of affected elitism (without the accent on the "e"). Meanwhile, throughout all this hoopla expended over the father, when it should have been the child's proverbial moment in the sun, not once did Colin betray any sign of begrudging his father's theft. Besides, most people failed to make the connection between the two. Colin had followed his brothers' examples and adopted his matronymic, simply because this was a much more useful stage name. Brennan was pronounceable and emphasized his Irish heri-tage, as opposed to the Slavic-Semitic mix also roiling around somewhere in his mongrel blood, an indelicacy his agent, Mable Montgomery, wasted no time in pointing out, since she at least was in it for the money.

Colin's obliviousness to his sudden stardom in fact caused his agent considerable distress. She found it impossible to believe anyone could care so negligently for his increasing fame and bank balance, but her client kept insisting he was only in the picture business for the adventure of it. At most, Mable thought this was an effective byline, and only a week after his first première, Colin was a hired gun, leaving his parents in California for Montana, where in the guise of Jesse James he rode around sharp shooting, cattle stealing, bank robbing, whooping and hollering and eventually getting himself assassinated. Then he was off to location in Dublin, where he would spend most of his time, when not shooting, stealing, screaming, and getting himself killed for being a Republican revolutionary, hanging about in pubs learning how to drink, curse, brawl, and weep like a poet. This became the public persona Colin ended up cultivating with a great degree of talent and instinct for what his fans and his agent wanted to see. This was not the version of Colin that Jamie was expecting to meet. Actually, Jamie did not know what to expect, only that Colin was expected and had kept his brother waiting on the front stoop of his W. 76th Street brownstone for nearly three hours by the time he finally decided to make an appearance.

"Was it today you said you'd be here?" Colin laughed, abruptly materializing and smelling of strong spirits, as if he'd been doused in them.

"My ship docked this afternoon," Jamie stiffly reminded him. "I walked up from the seaport and arrived here several hours ago, where I've been waiting—."

"You said you walked all the way up here?!" Colin cut him off, astonished by the feats of daring and bravery his older brother was capable of performing, though Jamie wondered if there was not also the slightest hint of sarcasm underlying his exaggerated incredulity.

"It really isn't much of a distance, only a few miles, perhaps seven at most," he offered in the same condescending tone he used when delivering a lecture to his students.

"But why in hell would you sit all this time *here*? There's a coffee shop just down the road, on Broadway. You'd of easily caught me coming up from the train—."

"I wasn't aware," Jamie interrupted, putting an end to the discussion, which his brother seemed capable of spinning out to an absurdly hyperbolic length. He had not even thought to apologize, but Jamie decided to brush this aside in favor of a brotherly handshake. Colin yanked Jamie into a huge and happy embrace, startling Jamie with the physical contact, and not because they were virtual strangers, but Jamie always reacted to hugging of any sort with pained embarrassment. His brother remained blithely ignorant of Jamie's discomfort, embracing him for much longer than Jamie thought necessary, before stumbling back, belching, and then digging into his pocket for the key.

Colin led them up to his apartment, stumbled once or twice on the stairs, steadied himself with a grumbled curse, failed then succeeded to insert the key in the lock, shoved the door open for Jamie then slammed it shut, turned on one dim overhead lamp, and proceeded to pour out two generous glasses of cheap scotch, all the while asking Jamie about the details of his voyage, to which Jamie mumbled vague replies. Jamie accepted the drink his brother thrust into his hand, deciding it wasn't worth the effort to decline, sank into a low, lumpy, tattered armchair, fastidiously sipped on his whiskey, and studied the room where his brother lived. It was one of those cramped studio apartments boasting a claw foot tub situated between two windows facing onto an air shaft, and shoved up against the opposite wall, in the corner, a mattress with yellowing sheets and a single rumpled coverlet. A motley collection of junk lay strewn across the floor: old newspapers, battered scripts, wine bottles full of ash and cigarette butts, pulp novels in the hardboiled detective genre, a towel stained with what looked like blood, a broken typewriter, numerous discarded socks and ties, and for some reason, incongruously, various items of ladies lingerie, as well as what appeared to have been, in better days, a blue silk dress. Jamie shut his eyes on the foul accumulation of all this detritus and then eyed his brother, now seated on a stumpy three-legged stool next to the tub, pulling off his boots, shirt and trousers until stripped down to his underwear.

"Perhaps I should check into a hotel," Jamie suggested.

"If you want," Colin shrugged. "I could get you a room on the sly over at the Moritz."

Jamie stared at his vagabond brother, appalled and impressed by his sincere lack of pretension when it came to money or class. He decided to stay in Colin's ridiculously sordid apartment, and so waved his hand in dismissal, as if the suggestion of a hotel had been his brother's. Colin dismissed Jamie's mute gesture of resignation by taking a hefty gulp of whiskey and lighting a cigarette, then without warning, plunged into the discussion of a dilemma Jamie himself had proposed but not ever anticipated having to defend, because he had not included Colin as one of his intended readers.

"So, Jamie, I dug into your book, or at least I tried, but got stuck at the first chapter. I mean, how is it possible to think about time without being present in time? It's impossible, you know, because I did try to imagine it, but it put me into a complete mind-fuck. I mean, the thought is fucking terrifying if you really try to play it out in your head, like some huge abyss opening up and swallowing you into oblivion, a black hole of nothingness, because to imagine time without imagining ourselves in time, well, that means you're one dead man walking, right? You can't very well fucking conceive of time without you being there, alive, part of the fabric, or whatever you called it, the construct of time, or you'd just go absolutely shitting bricks mad, right?"

"Precisely," Jamie murmured, too exhausted, too disinterested; he knew what he'd argued, and he knew what Colin struggled to articulate, yet none of it mattered because Colin had uttered the one word that would lead them into a discussion neither wanted to have.

"Shit," Colin scowled.

"It doesn't matter," Jamie sighed.

"Have you read papa's new book?" Colin tried changing subjects, though for some infernal reason persisting in holding a literary discussion.

"Yes, of course," Jamie grimaced, and then took his own hefty gulp, draining his glass, which Colin immediately refilled.

"He's fucking written Andrew all into it, hasn't he?" Colin flicked a match to yet another cigarette, ran a hand through his closely cropped black hair, and offered Jamie a cigarette, all in a sequential fluidity of grace displaying an economy of gesture one could only learn from performing or viewing the same scene repeatedly in countless films. Jamie took the cigarette, against his inclinations, just as he'd accepted the drink, and only because it provided an opportunity to moderate his response.

"Yes, I think that would be a fair reading," he exhaled, and coughed, taking another moment to consider when exactly Colin had taken up the habit of reading. Jamie had no way of knowing and he would not be rude enough to ask.

"That fucking Tebonik character!" Colin protested. "What was papa thinking?!"

"Exorcising his guilt," Jamie offered blandly, but both he and Colin knew this was not an acceptable explanation. "It is clever, though."

Too clever, Jamie thought. He'd also been bothered by Tebonik, a madman who denied and disproved his insanity with such a flair of arrogance, charm, and precision of detail, that even the reader was seduced into accepting his version of reality, at least until the end, when the reader realizes it's all been a cruel joke. For by the end, one is cornered into admitting that Tebonik is no more than a character created by an author, and that we are fools to have believed otherwise. Tebonik's identity, his past, his present, his heroes and his villains, his tragedies and triumphs, it is all a convoluted history like any fiction we might come up with to explain the narrative of our lives. This was the clever bit, which in the manner of many Novikovian tricks, often irritated rather than pleased his readers, who were perhaps not wrong in suspecting that the author was having a hearty laugh at their expense. Neither Jamie nor Colin, however, was the average reader, and they were not annoyed by their father's latest novel because they felt duped. They were too clever to fall for such sleight of hand; or, they were usually in on the con from the start, knowing their father as they did.

Rather, because the rule had always been that the personal details of their family relations were never fair game, could never be mined for novelistic purposes, or any such public airing, they felt personally affronted by their father's decision to violate this sacred law he himself had inscribed into stone. The character of Tebonik, no matter how witty a device, was too imitative of Andrew's obsessions and illness. These had been documented by his psychiatrists and shared, unethically, with Vasili, who'd demanded to have a copy of his son's medical files, read them in horror and disbelief, and then stole from them in order to present Tebonik's madness as so convincingly real one could not resist believing he was sane. Although critics praised the novel for its mad stroke of genius, its hall of mirrors distorting the reader's perception through a series of sly reversals, twists, and inversions of truths and falsehoods, Colin and Jamie saw only the madness of their brother and the shallow solipsism of their father, who'd plagiarized his child's pain in the service of artistic license, but only to perpetrate a clever narrative ruse.

"Papa is always clever," Colin sighed, and Jamie did not have a response, since it was a statement that could not be debated. Neither of them had the courage to contest whether their father's genius was reason enough to excuse his deplorable conduct; or whether the monstrous magnification of his many fears, desires, and obsessions, the delineation of which could be discovered in all of his novels, were in fact as common as the next man's.

Jamie glanced over at the small table to his right, seeking a distraction but finding none. A short stack of books sat atop the table, and Jamie noted the titles with some displeasure. On the bottom of the pile, Jamie's own obscure book, which perhaps only Colin had attempted to read. *Red Moon*, their father's novel, the one Jamie hoped was no longer up for analysis. *Antiopa*, Andrew's last play, and topping off this literary shrine, if compared to the flimsy five and dime novels flung forgotten on the floor, a slim hardcover volume that bore no title or author's name. The lettering, which had been gilded onto the spine, seemed to have suffered from an act of attrition, caused by time, the hands of a reader, or both. While Colin silently, sullenly, tucked into his third cigarette, musing on whatever private thoughts he chose to entertain, Jamie picked up the book, opened its cover to the title page, and learned it was a collection of poetry by John Donne. His recognition of the name only brought to mind the memory of reading, when still a student at Harrington, some lugubrious sonnet about death and pride and that was all, for Jamie had never taken a specialized course in literature other than Greek tragedy. He hadn't the faintest idea why Colin would have this book in his possession, or why he was reading poetry, of all things, but decided these were irrelevant questions, and so laid the book aside.

"Do you ever see him?" he abruptly asked.

"Sure, when I'm in town," Colin slurred.

"How does he seem?" Jamie persisted, in spite of Colin's incapacity to continue any further discussion; he was now hunched over on the stool, his head nodding in a losing battle to remain upright, while the cigarette in his hand burned down to its stub in a tenuous cylinder of ash.

"He seems like Andrew," Colin mumbled.

"What does that mean?" Jamie demanded irritably.

"Means whatever it means, brother," Colin stumbled over to the bed, took the blanket, and wrapped himself in it, indicating the decrepit mattress belonged to Jamie if he wanted it, then lay down on the floor and promptly passed out.

Jamie remained in the chair, and in the middle of the night, woke to the raucous rumbling of Colin's snores. Of course Colin snored. Colin could not help making noise, and Jamie suddenly remembered all his sleep-less nights when they'd been children and shared the same room before Andrew left home and his bedroom unoccupied for one of his siblings to claim as their own. Jamie would lie awake listening to Colin's fitful grunts and groans, and resented even the sound of his brother's breathing; now, Jamie was comforted by Colin's sleeping presence, the familiarity of it. He closed his eyes, and in the morning, observed Colin still sprawled across the floor and showing no signs of waking up any time soon. Jamie decided there was no point delaying, and so splashed a handful of tepid water from the rusted tap onto his face, studied his splintered image in the cracked mirror above the sink, and then left, confident, determined, and refusing to consider how Andrew might react to Jamie's unexpected visit.

An overweight orderly led Andrew into the room where Jamie had been kept waiting nearly an hour. Jamie rose, smiling, and Andrew stared through Jamie as if he were yet another faceless, nameless doctor. They sat at the table across from each other in the restrained manner of two people about to hold an interview for which neither had prepared. Jamie frowned when the orderly left the room. With no one else present to observe their conversation, he wasn't sure how to proceed. He fell back on his usual defenses, studying Andrew dispassionately, analytically. His brother's hair was noticeably thinning, his body thicker, heftier, due to a heavy regimen of lithium, his complexion sallow, and his hands spasmodically fidgeting, incessantly picking at his ragged cuticles, the patches of dry, flaky skin on his palms, scratching his forearms, his neck, his scalp, intermittently pulling at his hair so that it stood wildly in all directions, as if Andrew were determined to look as well as act the role of madman.

Jamie was not startled by any of this; he'd observed the inmates of several psychiatric wards, where he'd conducted research for his doctoral thesis. Many of them had exhibited some strain of psoriatic condition due to the combination of their mental stress and the routine scouring with lye and ammonia they were forced to undergo as a preemptive measure against lice and innumerable other vermin. At least this was the expla-nation the administrative staff had offered Jamie; it had been his own opinion that the treatment was more disciplinary than medicinal, aimed at subduing patients with a form of water torture that instilled in them an obsessive attention to their bodies. For how could they harm the staff if they remained consumed by their own physical afflictions?

In this respect, Andrew seemed no worse than any other patient Jamie had seen, and his brother's compulsive urge to tear out his own hair was a recognizable, characteristic gesture familiar to anyone who might have known Andrew in his life before Bellevue. Its pathology could be traced as far back as childhood, and was a kind of physical twitch he'd always exhibited whenever he felt frustrated or furious with something beyond his control or understanding. Thus, Jamie concluded, Andrew's exaggerated appearance was simply the result of his present situation and immediate environs.

"Andrew," Jamie finally spoke, but his throat constricted. Andrew was mumbling something incoherent, addressed to the scab of dead skin he was now prying loose from the base of his palm, and so Jamie was reduced to using their father's endearment for his son, to which Andrew had always deferred, for it had only ever been used when Vasili wanted his scatter-brained, hyperactive child's undivided attention.

"Andrej."

Andrew raised his head, the dull glaze in his eyes glimmering with a pavlovian slaver of hope. His eyes then narrowed, suspiciously, knowing all too well he would not receive a reward for obediently acknowledging Jamie's presence. His head shook in a palsied spasm of denial and lowered again to resume an agitated dialogue with his hand. Jamie sat staring at him, helpless, because he did not know what he'd intended to say. What was he expected to say? Here I am, now you can start acting like yourself again. Jamie realized he'd never been convinced that Andrew belonged in Bellevue. He was just throwing a tantrum, having a childish fit, playing one of his pranks, one of his own cruel tricks, either to get the better of their father or at least his attention. Andrew was always goading Vasili and Vasili was always gullible to Andrew's ploys, because for some reason both had always believed they were competing with each other; perpetually trapped in a duel to the death, a battle of wits and will that neither would ever concede. It hardly required a gaggle of Freudians to come up with this transparently oedipal scenario, which had been the inevitable diagnosis offered to Vasili in his son's medical reports. Vasili had of course refused their interpretation, Jamie's interpretation, all interpretations except his own, presenting his version of the facts in his latest novel.

The facts were these: Andrew had suffered a schizophrenic break, and for whatever reason, the indicators for this had always been there, somewhere in the map of either Andrew's genetic or psychological blueprints, and there was nothing his father, the doctors, Jamie, or anyone could have done to prevent it. This line of thinking, Jamie knew, was the easiest way out, relegating the past to a scraped slate, a tabula rasa that released both the sane and the insane from culpability or comprehension. At the very least, a strategy of forgetting allowed Jamie to focus on what could be done for Andrew now, in the present, and possibly the future; though there was no foreseeable cure, one might offer him something approximating a palliative oblivion. Jamie knew the options, he'd read the latest medical journals before agreeing to observe Andrew in person, and had explained to Vasili the likely repercussions of the experimental surgery the doctors wanted to perform as a prerequisite to releasing Andrew from institutionalized care. He knew this was why Vasili had insisted on Jamie going in his place, because Vasili did not want the responsibility for making the final decision to erase all former traces of his eldest child, which, paradoxically, was the only way Vasili and Deirdre might have their child returned to them. Jamie, however, had foolishly chosen to believe that as soon as Andrew saw his younger brother sitting before him, he would immediately give up the charade and assure Jamie he had nothing to worry about; Jamie would sign the papers releasing Andrew, they would walk out arm in arm, meet Colin at the nearest bar, and they would all share a long laugh over the sublime joke Andrew had pulled at their father's expense.

Andrew refused to comply, forcing Jamie to give up the fantasy and face his brother unflinchingly. He was still preoccupied with peeling off the slivered scales of his psoriasis-inflamed hands, the flesh where he'd obsessively picked forming raw, red cracks and fissures embedded in his palms. He continued mumbling some inaudible, incomprehensible litany. Jamie cleared his throat, preparing to interrupt Andrew's concentrated dementia, but Andrew raised his voice, repeating his mantra in a furious, unpunctuated stream of scornful phrases.

"Teach me to hear mermaids singing to keep off envy's stinging or where all past years are go and catch a falling star get with child a mandrake root and swear nowhere lives a woman true," he paused for breath, raising his eyes to Jamie, conspiratorially lowering his voice. "If you find one let me know and though she was true when you met her by the time you write your letter she'll be false to two or three . . ."

Jamie opened his mouth, about to cut off this rhyming idiocy, but Andrew leapt to his feet, slamming his palms down on the table between them, and bellowed like an injured animal, face lifted to the heavens somewhere beyond the low-ceilinged room, "OR MORE!"

"Andrew, a decision needs to be made, but I need you to help me make it."

"Vain lunatic," Andrew laughed hoarsely. "You could argue against me, and win, but by tomorrow, you may think the same."

"Andrew, I don't have time for this. Sit down."

"Pedantic wretch, go chide late schoolboys and sour prentices." Andrew sat down. "Love is all alike, and knows no season, or hours, days, months, years, which are the rags of time. Tell me, who's injured by my love?"

Jamie's resolve to converse snapped because, of course, he was speaking to his brother and not a patient or research subject. "What the fuck are you going on about? I didn't come all the way here to listen to this nonsense!"

"For god's sake hold your tongue. Or chide my palsy, my five gray hairs, or ruined fortune, but let me love. It's none to do with you, or any but her and me."

Why was he here, Jamie asked himself, why put himself through this? He would sign the papers authorizing the doctors to go ahead with the surgery, and then his father could deal with the aftermath. Jamie decided he'd already seen and heard enough. He shoved back his chair, stood up from the table, and prepared to leave without saying goodbye.

"Do you have urgent business elsewhere, Jamie?" Andrew demanded.

Jamie sat down, hearing his name, clutching onto this tenuous sign of recognition. "Andrew, I can't make this decision for you. I'm sure you know they want to perform this operation, with or without your consent, but I won't let them if you just tell me . . ."

"In spite of the darkness that brought us here, being well, I would gladly stay," Andrew replied. "But being sick in love, I would go."

"So you want to leave, then?" Jamie attempted to follow the coded trail Andrew seemed to be laying out for him. "If that's what you want then you have to prove you're better and won't just disappear, like the last time."

"Hah!" Andrew barked. "Those were her very words, Jamie, her very words!"

"Who are we talking about, Andrew?"

"Who, who, who are we? Who am I, who are you, why are you always leaving? That's the worst disease of love, she said, the foul, the false, which love admits, but not the man who has business elsewhere and pursues his mistress—."

"Okay, is it Sara? Is that what this is all about?"

"Sara?" Andrew shook his head, as if suddenly startled out of a trance.

"Your ex-wife."

"Ex?"

"Yes, she divorced you."

"Why?"

"Because you disappeared."

"Where did I go?"

"I have no idea."

"Did I come back?"

"Did you what?"

"Did I ever come back?"

Jamie studied him for a moment, wondering if Andrew wasn't a lunatic, but only an amnesiac. "Yes, Andrew, eventually you showed up again, with that play, *Antiopa*—."

"I remember going there."

"Where?"

"Antiopa."

"Where is that?"

"Here. There. Nowhere. I was there with her here."

"No, Andrew. She was never here."

"Because she left me, but I left everything and everyone for her, and then she left me."

"All right," Jamie sighed, realizing this was only going in circles, and belatedly suspecting Andrew was not referring to Sara, much less any woman who might exist. "Let's figure out why you're here, now, in this place, and how we can get you out."

"I came here seeking solace," Andrew recited. "But now I am every dead thing, a quintessence from nothingness, from dull privations, and lean emptiness."

"Andrew, are you quoting Shakespeare?!" Jamie accused him.

Andrew clenched his jaw, squeezing his eyes shut, his fingers twisting into his snarled, thinning hair, yanking a fistful of it from his scalp. He opened his eyes, stared down at the tufts of hair in his palm, and resumed mumbling his poetic litany.

"Get with child a mandrake root and swear nowhere lives a woman true and if you find her let me know and by the time you write your letter she'll be false to two or three or more or more or so much, much more."

"Andrej! I need you to focus. I'm only allowed an hour's visit, and so you have to listen to me. The doctors are insisting on this procedure before they release you, but I'll only let them if that's what you want."

"What am I supposed to want?"

"To get better? Or at least, to get out of here?"

"And go where?"

"Well, papa says you can live with him and mama."

"Papa? Why would he, after everything?"

"I know, but he regrets it, truly, you should see—."

"He ruined me," Andrew insisted, regressing once more into his lyrical psychosis. "And I am re-begot of absence, darkness, death; I am the grave of all that's nothing."

The lumbering orderly chose that precise moment to return. He hefted Andrew up from his chair and led him by the arm towards the door, as if all of the madmen under his watch were invalids incapable of walking on their own. Andrew turned at the door, smiling lucidly across the room at his little brother, who remained paralyzed in his chair. Jamie recognized the ironic grin curling the corners of Andrew's mouth; the same mischievous smile he'd always offered when about to say something unexpectedly witty.

"Jamie," he murmured. "Call for me tomorrow, and you will find me a grave man."

Then he was gone, swallowed up by the white-walled maze of the ward, while Jamie sat lost in the mazy corridors of his confusion. He had no choice other than to return to the sloppy squalor of Colin's apartment. In that disarray of unwashed dishes, grimy blinds, molding linoleum and linens, discarded paperbacks, peeling plaster and the remnants of some unnamed, unknown woman's wardrobe, there in that haphazard room that belonged to his undeniably and affably sound younger brother, Jamie sat in the dim glow of the apartment's single functional lamp, nursing a whiskey and water, ignoring the constant wail of sirens on the street outside. He reasoned there must be a police precinct somewhere nearby. He waited for Colin to return. He wanted to leave and never come back.

When Colin arrived, it was late and Jamie was as drunk as his brother. Colin looked around the crowded, cockroach infested corners of the studio, blearily, cheerfully, as if it were a place with which he should be vaguely familiar, but couldn't for the life of him remember why. He noted Jamie occupying the same armchair he'd planted himself in the night before, and observing the bottle near his feet, Colin picked up the whiskey and took a slug before squatting on his absurdly tiny three-legged stool.

"That bad?" Colin proposed, one eye closed, the other cocked beneath the thick smudge of his black brow.

"You should have warned me," Jamie grumbled.

"What, that he's raving bonkers mad?" Colin laughed. "Jesus and Mary fucking Christ on a stick, where do you think he's been these past four years?"

"You should have told me he only recites poetry," Jamie insisted.

"And how would that make a shitting brickload of difference?"

"You could have warned me," he repeated, lamely.

"Go back there and you'll get the gist of it," Colin offered, which was not at all helpful, since Jamie had no intention of going back there. "He just says the same damn things no matter what *you* say," Colin continued, guzzling another generous portion from the bottle then emptying the rest into Jamie's glass. "I wrote it all down, soon as I realized he was repeating the same fucking things, over and over again, but I still couldn't make any sense of it. It's like fitting together the pieces of a puzzle that won't ever fit."

"Yes, yes," Jamie waved his hand impatiently, having already come to this conclusion. "Can I see? What you wrote down?"

"Yeah, yeah," Colin sluggishly looked around the room, expecting his transcription of Andrew's words to be lying somewhere within his immediate reach. "Actually, I don't know. I mean, Jamie, it's all on scraps of paper, and in this place, well, as you can see, but, you know, I'm rarely here as it is."

"Then why are you even living in this dump?!" Jamie spluttered, for some reason furious with Colin for no other reason except that he was Colin. "Stay in a hotel, or at least hire a maid! And what, do you just go out, get drunk, bring back random women, trash the place, and then leave for the next film? Who lives like that, Colin?"

"It's not mine."

"What are you talking about?!"

"This dump, which fucking hell you're right it is, well, it's not my apartment."

"When papa gave me the address he said it was yours."

"Okay, so technically, yeah, I bought the place, but it's not really mine. I'm just kind of looking after it temporarily, you know."

"So to whom, then, does it belong?" Jamie asked through gritted teeth, carefully enunciating every single stilted syllable.

"Andrew."

"Andrew?"

"Yeah, this is where he was living when he left Sara, and more or less exactly the way it was when papa and mama found him shacked up in here. So you can see why they locked him up in a nice clean padded room," Colin lamely grinned at his lame joke.

"But why keep it?" Jamie demanded. "Or at least why would you leave it like this?"

Colin sat scowling at the empty bottle, and Jamie's head suddenly felt stuffed with thick, plodding thoughts that refused to connect. He wanted to lie down, sleep, and wake in another room, his own empty, sterile apartment. Colin's voice came through to him from far away, as if Jamie were already there, back in Paris, swaddled in his carefully controlled life that had nothing whatsoever to do with his brothers' lives.

"I thought when he got out of there he'd want his own place, so it didn't seem right, messing around with his things, cause you know, the doctors said, he'd need familiarity, if and when he ever got out."

"And you think this is what they were talking about? Is that what you thought?!"

"I thought he'd want some sort of home," Colin refused the bait, because Colin never argued, not with anyone in his family. "He'd want a place that was all his own."

"You may as well get rid of it," Jamie advised. "If and when Andrew is released, he'll be living with papa and mama."

"Poor fucking bastard," Colin muttered.

"Yeah," Jamie conceded. "Look, Colin, I'm sorry, but—."

Colin shrugged off the apology. He began rummaging around the junk on the floor, though Jamie couldn't tell whether he was attempting to find the missing scraps of papers or a bottle of booze. Jamie was certain the conversation was over, and because he wasn't sure what he might say to initiate a new one, or if this was necessary, he turned his gaze to the same pile of books he'd perused the evening before. He assumed the collection of family publications was the only thing in this apartment, as it turned out, actually belonging to Colin rather than Andrew. It was a reasonable assumption, as each of the Novikov-Brennan books had been published after Andrew's committal. Again, Jamie ignored them in favor of contemplating the slim volume of Donne, opening it to a bookplate pasted on its inside front cover, proclaiming Mina Byrne as its rightful owner, the name written in a feminine hand with swelling loops and swooping lines.

"Who's Mina Byrne?" Jamie asked Colin, who'd finished what proved to have been a scavenger hunt for cigarettes; he was now seated on the ledge of the open window, smoking, and contemplatively staring out into the narrow abyss of the airshaft.

"Hell if I know," Colin sighed irritably.

"Where did you get this book, then?" Jamie waved the object in the air.

"I didn't get it from anywhere. It was already here on that table, so I left it with the others when I bought them."

"But it says it belongs to this Mina Byrne," Jamie persisted.

"Christ in fucking hell, how the fuck should I know?!"

Jamie returned his attention to the book and flipped through its pages, the words blurring. He found a postcard inserted between two pages of heavily underlined passages, but no matter how fiercely Jamie squinted down at the words he could not make them out. He lifted the postcard to his face, deducing it was a mass-produced replica of a photograph of some nude, her luscious posterior beguiling the viewer with her fleshy curves. Jamie fastidiously inserted it back into the book, which he then laid aside.

"I don't even want to know," he muttered drunkenly, or perhaps it was all in his head, he couldn't be sure. "Why is that?"

"Why does there have to be a reason for every fucking little thing, Jamie?" Colin challenged him; so he had been speaking aloud.

"Why ask why?" Jamie laughed.

"Fuck if I don't need this," Colin muttered. He stubbed out his cigarette, flung it out the window, and stomped towards the door. "I'm going for a drink."

Then he was gone, and Jamie felt sorry. He did not want to be this cold, cynical man, even when drunk. For the second time that day, he wanted to cry. He wanted to crawl back into his mother's womb and begin all over again. He wanted to know things for the first time. He did not want to be himself. He collapsed, fully dressed, on top of the unmade bed. Nadia was there leaning over him, her presence assuring him that he did not have to think about anything, only the veil of her hair, black now instead of blonde, rippling across his face. She was smiling, her lips spreading slowly in a lusty grin, her mouth engulfing him. She was mounted on top of him, swaying her hips rhythmically, her hands holding him down, imprisoning his wrists. He tried to squirm free, thinking this was somehow wrong; she was his sister, his twin, but then he thought, why? Why struggle? Why was it all wrong? She was thrusting herself into him. That was backwards, somehow, not the way it should be. Her face was inching closer to his. She laughed, whispering something, but not into his ear, into his mouth, the words losing their shape as soon as they were spoken. Her mouth stole everything from him, and he was drenched in her skin, the pure animal scent of her . . .

He sat up, gasping, soaked with his own sweat, only his own. He searched the room, attempting to pinpoint exactly where he was. The morning light filtered through the cracked blinds. Colin lay wrapped in a blanket, snoring, just the same as the night before. Perhaps it was the same night and Jamie had never gone to see Andrew, and that was yet to come. Jamie rose from the bed in his crumpled clothes, splashed several handfuls of rusty tap water over his face, and left his tie on the back of the chair. He picked up the collected poetry of John Donne, glancing furtively at Colin's shadowy form sprawled across the littered junk of their older brother's possessions.

Jamie opened the book to the page where he'd reinserted the photograph of the nude. He studied its grainy black and white image, now sober enough to see what he'd missed the evening before. Written in the white space beneath the image, in Andrew's bold block print, there appeared a single word: **DUENDE**. He then noted an X scraped across the image, as if someone had scratched it with a sharpened pencil before regretting this action and attempting to reverse the disfigurement by erasing the lead imprint. He was about to return the postcard to its hiding place when his eyes snagged on several heavily underlined verses, the pieces of Andrew's puzzle magically falling into place: *Vain lunatic, against these 'scapes I could / Dispute, and conquer, if I would; / Which I abstain to do, / For by to-morrow, I may think so too.* Jamie flipped through the book, scanning all the other annotated lines, marked a page with the defaced photograph, and closed the book. It was small enough to fit inside the inner breast pocket of his jacket, which was where he concealed it, ignoring the sharp pang of guilt as he stepped over Colin and out the front door without waking him to say goodbye.

He hailed a cab that wildly veered around the winding turns of the road running across Central Park, honking and braking its way through the early morning traffic crawling down Second Avenue, and eventually dumping him off on 19th and First. When he discovered himself sitting across from Andrew, again, both of them stared at each other as if they'd never expected to repeat yesterday's reunion. Jamie took out the book and slid it across the table towards Andrew's fumbling hands. Andrew stared at it in horrified recognition, refusing to pick it up, his lips sealed in a painful, cognizant frown. Jamie opened the book, pointed down at the title of a poem, and then while reading aloud, traced with his finger the under-lined words that had provided him with the necessary insight.

"*For having purposed change, and falsehood, you can have no way but falsehood to be true,*" Jamie concluded his reading of the relevant passages and then glared at Andrew accusingly. "That's what you've done, isn't it, this whole act of yours? Taken fragments from these poems, reversed every-thing on purpose, and made all of it backwards, out of order. Just to play some stupid game with your doctors who are too stupid to recognize what you're doing. The only thing I can't figure out is why. What's the point?"

Andrew made no response, providing neither defense nor denial. His eyes were riveted to the postcard, which Jamie had forgotten. Andrew bleakly studied the nude; one of his fingertips, the nail chewed down to the raw, red flesh, traced the lines of the woman's curves.

"Twice or thrice I loved her before I knew her face or name," he murmured, his voice trembling with regret and reverence. "In a voice, in a shapeless flame, like an angel, some lovely glorious nothing, but her every hair is much too much, and love cannot inhere."

Andrew suddenly slammed shut the book on the photograph and shoved it back across the table to Jamie. Although he began manically tearing at his hair, grimacing in consternation at either the strands yanked from his scalp or the fact that he still had any left to pull free, the direct stare he offered Jamie appeared reasonably sane.

"Duende," he commented in a tone as dryly pedantic as the one Jamie used when elucidating some arcane observation to his students. "A perfect word for an imperfect muse. First, an evil spirit. Second, inspiration. Or, we might combine the two definitions into one. The evil spirit of inspiration. Reverse it and you have the inspiration of an evil spirit. Yes, indeed, a word that by its very definition presents a perfect reflection of itself. Contained by a multitude of contradictions. Oh my newfound America!"

Jamie picked up the book. "So do you want this?"

"God, no!" Andrew shuddered. "Besides, they wouldn't let me keep it."

"Well, what do you want? Papa wants to get you out of here, if at all possible—."

"He'll dig open my grave," Andrew digressed. "He'll spy a bracelet of bright hair about the bone, and by the time he finds us, she'll be a Magdalene, and I something else, because first, we loved faithfully, but second, we knew not what we loved, nor why. There is no measure, Jamie, no language, should I decide to tell what a miracle she was."

"Andrew!" Jamie snapped. "I need to know what you want!"

"I want to forget her, Jamie," Andrew replied. "Let them do whatever they want, as long as it helps me forget."

"Yes, okay, fine," Jamie rose from his chair, giving in a little too quickly, because he wanted all of this over and done with. "I'll tell papa this is what you wanted."

"Tell him, Jamie," Andrew offered a glimmering ghost of a smile. "Tell him it would be more merciful to forget. He'll understand, but you have to tell him exactly these words. I want to forget. If I can forget, then I can come home."

Jamie was not quite sure what the word *home* might signify for his brother, but it had to be a place better than this. He clutched the book in one hand while with the other he awkwardly attempted to shake Andrew's hand, not knowing what else to do. Andrew also seemed confused, snatching his hand away the moment he realized Jamie was grasping onto it. They stood there forlornly studying each other, both of them once more transformed into strangers. All of this is a bad dream, Jamie thought, where nothing connects, where nothing ever will make sense.

"Well, goodbye, Andrew," he mumbled. "I suppose I'll see you again soon enough."

Then he fled from the room, ignoring Andrew's look of confusion, because Andrew knew he would not be seeing his brother again anytime soon. Jamie found one of Andrew's doctors, signed the necessary papers, and scrambled into a taxi. He headed directly to the seaport, and once he'd boarded his ship, when he was swiftly skimming over the ocean, back home, to *his* home, Jamie foolishly swore he would never revisit New York, no matter how desperately his father begged and bargained, because Jamie would not ever allow his father to show up unannounced at his door.

He thought about flinging John Donne into the sea, consigning his words to a watery, unmarked grave, where they might escape exhumation and absolve Jamie from ever having to disinter and decipher the method to his brother's madness. It seemed the only symbolic gesture of which he was capable, but he was safe now, and felt slightly ridiculous for even indulging such an impoverished fancy. Jamie could not throw away any book, no matter how detested or unwanted. So he stowed Donne at the bottom of his trunk, and when he was back in his sunny, tidy, austere apartment, he took out an oversized shoebox of old family photographs that he kept under his bed and buried the book inside of it. The *Songs and Sonnets* inscribed with the name of Mina Byrne would remain for many years closed and forgotten, holding within its pages her image turned away, her face forever concealed.

CHAPTER EIGHT
Lunar Voyage

"As if!" a toady voice croaked impatiently. "*Come se, bella, si potrebbe nascondere te così facilmente!* No, no, the self is not dependent on the *miraggio* of the past. *È al di là di convinzioni*, you are sitting there muttering such nonsense! No, *mio caro*, and I address you as such for you are a purely intellectual creature. I suppose it is your exceptionally developed masculine side, so you are surely only prodding me, *non è vero?*"

By the time Garinetti wrapped up this little performance, Mina could not recall what she'd said to inspire it. They'd already finished two bottles of Barolo and had ordered a third. She would have preferred an espresso but neither of her companions would look too kindly on her request. Although they sat at a table situated beneath the broad awning of Caffè Giubbe, and she wore a broad-brimmed hat of her own fashioning, the glare of the midday sun on the piazza and the withering heat along with the wine inspired in her nothing more than the urge to sleep.

"*Mi dispiace*," she offered one of her languorous dozy smiles. "*Cosa stavo dicendo?*"

"*Chissà?*" Giovanni interjected. "What is of importance, *mia cara*, is you must forget all notions of beauty, all so *in modo femminile*, so unworthy of our attention, when art must be of vigorous exertion. *Sì, bella*, your dainty poems must become *più muscolare*; they must show destruction and rage, rampaging with the rioting pleasure of the masses;

these are the only beautiful ideas worth writing, worth dying for! Oh, and *sì*, do not forget, *il disprezzo per le donne*, who of all miserable animals—."

"*Basta!*" Garinetti erupted. "You are only paraphrasing like some mindless monkey from my manifesto, which *La signora* has already read for herself, have you not, *mia bella donna*?"

"*Esattamente,*" Mina nodded, sipping from her wine, and wishing she could muster the energy or desire to remind Garinetti that she'd also thought the entire thing a pile of rubbish, at least those parts of it he and his acolyte were now rattling off for her benefit; they were in fact speaking over her head, directing their volleys at each other with simmering suspicion of the other's staunch loyalty to the tenets of their faith.

Mina tuned them out, and from beneath the wide brim of her hat, she drowsily observed the bustling life of the piazza, where street performers, merchants, and harassed tourists performed their daily circus, and eventually focused her gaze on the dismally grey sandstone figure of *Abbondanza* perched atop her plinth, from which she peered down at the eternal ebb and flow of commerce taking place beneath her. She seemed representative of the only positioning allowed a woman, securely situated on the pedestal of man's imagination and far removed from any significant interaction with the business of life. As for the limited imaginations of Italian men, Mina had come to realize that for them, Italian women were created for one purpose only: bearing children, and if not that, then providing food and pleasure, but only one or the other, never both at the same time. Thus the female sex had been neatly apportioned into the discreet roles of wife, mother, and whore, and if one were asked to compile a list, as Garinetti often did, it would be impossible to name a single one of them who'd made a memorable impression on history, unless of course one acknowledged a sublime soprano or murderous Medici.

Indeed, according to Garinetti, if there were any great ruptures in history for which women might be held responsible, it was merely owing to the fact that their base desires lured men away from those transcendent activities to which they should be devoted. Man's sole purpose was to develop the progress of culture by applying himself to the higher visions of art, philosophy, and politics; woman was an insurmountable barrier to the accomplishment of man's destiny; insurmountable because she was necessary to the propagation of more men; the logical conclusion, then, was to solve this whole dilemma by discovering some trick of agamogenesis, not a wholly unimaginable feat considering the great advancements in technology of which man was capable, if not for that pesky problem of woman; and therein lay the catch.

Mina almost felt a twinge of pity for Garinetti, whose impoverished imagination entangled him in a farrago of fallacies and feverish fantasies, none of which troubled his overweening sense of superiority since he failed to see the inevitable gaps in his logic. Although any self-respecting woman would have refused to associate with such an offensive character, Mina appreciated him for the fact that when in his presence she indeed felt a rare spurt of pleasure in prodding Garinetti with his own absurdist reductions.

Deciding to rouse herself into action, she disengaged from her lazy contemplation of *Abbondanza*, and interrupted the men, who were now debating the demerits of establishing a meritocracy to which women might also aspire to infiltrate.

"But darlings, if women have no outstanding merits, then all of this is a futile thought experiment, yes?" Mina reminded them.

"*Appunto!*" Giovanni squeaked. "I make this same point, *cara*, but Emilio as ever wants to drag on with such *sciocco dibattiti!*"

"*È vero*, most of your sex is seeming no better than *animali*," Garinetti conceded. "But even animals must have rights. *Perché no, dove si trova il danno*? They are too stupid to do anything with those rights. *Certamente*, this only applies to women in general, not to individual women of *avanzate natura*, such as you, *bella*. You are excepted from this rule."

Mina drained her wine, allowed Giovanni to refill her glass and Garinetti to believe she'd deferred to his empty concession. Her mouth felt weighed down by the Barolo, wanting for words that might reduce Garinetti's posturing to an amusing spectacle of vapid virility. He patted Mina's hand consolingly, then went on with his relentless campaign to cut Giovanni down to an egoless size while Giovanni bombarded him with impotent missiles of meager wit, both of them battling over the same bland territory men had been anxious to win since time began: the sexual favors of a woman. Mina sat pretending to listen, and although she smiled with vacant approval when either man solicited recognition of his brilliance, this only gave Giovanni the impression that he was rapidly losing ground, as her gaze seemed fixated upon Garinetti's far more ruggedly handsome and aquiline profile.

Mina was in fact silently composing a poem, or at least the bare bones of one, prompted by what she now observed to be the enormously dispro-portionate size of Garinetti's nose. Symbolic of what? No, no, *mio caro*, there mustn't be any hint of namby-pamby symbolism. Language must be action, words must do something, nouns must be verbs and verbs must be nouns. Very well, then. Your projectile nose intrudes in the sober business of the battlefield truffling the trail of the female. Oh dear, you've committed the crime of a rhyme there. Never mind. Your genius resides so much less in your brain than in your body, dealing exclusively with the priapic enterprise of extracting itself through the activity of thrusting things in the opposite direction to which they are willing to go. How's that for troubled syntax?

And then she grew bored with the game, tuning back in to the men's chatter, which seemed to be playing out some kind of histrionic opera of seething envy directed towards their rival, the insolent poetaster and incor-rigible casanova, Gabrunzio, who was holding court at Paszkowski's on the opposite corner of the piazza. Mina squinted and detected the suave slouch of her spouse seated beside Gabrunzio, and then, probably in reaction to some naughty joke Gabrunzio had just told him, the barrel-chested rotundity of Besim's amused guffaw reverberated across the wide expanse of the piazza and Mina wished in that moment she were sitting at that table rather than this one. Her head ached and so she closed her eyes, just for a moment . . .

"*Andiamo a casa. Lei è stanca e vuole andare a letto.*"

Mina's eyes shot open, her chin jerked up, and she observed the sun in its late afternoon descent achieving its daily auriferous illusion splayed out across the octagonal miracle of Brunelleschi's Duomo. She yawned, smiling bashfully as she did so, and graced the men with a coy shiver of mortification over her feminine indolence. Gathering her shawl and her purse, she rose from the table, and demurring with a husky laugh, rejected their offer to escort her home, which, if she'd accepted, would have only prolonged their scuffle over who had the greater privilege of crawling into her bed that evening.

"But the sun soon will be setting!" Giovanni protested.

"Not a good time to stroll the streets alone," Garinetti grumbled. "I shall take you."

"*Non è necessario!*" Mina coquettishly insisted, as if their misplaced gallantry amused rather than annoyed her. "My husband is just across the piazza with Gabrunzio, and I'm sure he'll be delighted to escape that wicked man."

"Is that not *Signora* Hayle salivating in your husband's lap?" Garinetti queried slyly. "That woman wears the most atrocious hats!"

"*Sì*, perhaps you should make for her one of your own *confezioni di buon gusto*," Giovanni peevishly chimed in, making an absurdly idiotic metaphor of which he was not aware, indicating Mina made cakes rather than hats, or rather, the hats of Mrs. Hayle looked more like towering cakes threatening to topple her head from her neck.

"Mrs. Hayle is perfectly content with her choice of fashion," Mina offered a composed smile. "And I'm sure Gabrunzio will be only too happy to entertain her while my husband sees me home. *Buona sera, signori, è stato un piacere.*"

Neither man bothered with offering a departing response, or rising from his seat to go through the motions of the customary kissing embrace. Giovanni scowled into his empty wineglass; Garinetti snapped his fingers for the *cameriere* to bring another bottle of wine; Mina strolled away with considerable relief. Abominable manners, indeed. She crossed the piazza to Pazkowski's where her husband lounged with his latest mistress and his latest chum. Mina could not decide who was the more deplorable of the two: Gardenia with her fawning desire to fuck any man she considered her social better (and yes, her atrocious hats poorly fashioned in the excessively demonstrative styling of the English uppercrust were a severe mark against her); or Gabrunzio, but only because he was a flat-out lecherous pig (though capable of far more charm than either Garinetti or Giovanni).

She knew Besim also felt the same hostile disregard for her two companions, so it all evened out in the end and neither made the effort of criticizing the other; to do so would have been in very bad taste, as tasteless as the people with whom they chose to consort; both consoled themselves with the observation that when deciding amongst the available options, it was merely a matter of determining the least of all possible evils, and at least their quartet of Gs, with their eccentric foibles, inappropriate provocations, wildly oversized egos, and outlandish appearances, proved themselves the most entertaining bunch of baboons Florentine society had to offer.

"Ah, *bella,* here you are at last to join us!" Gabrunzio gushingly greeted her with a smarmy leer. "Sit, sit, *la mia splendida signora,* we shall procure another glass for your pleasure. Gardenia, allow some room for *La Signora.*"

"The Lady Beresford does not have the slightest intention of joining us," Gardenia thinly smiled. "You look terribly peaked, my dear, one of your horrid migraines coming on?"

"Nothing of the sort," Mina murmured evasively before turning to Besim, who'd already risen from his seat, only too happy to avoid one of Gardenia's childish displays.

"Oh bother, I entirely forgot about our appointment," Besim took Mina's arm into the crook of his own. "Gabrunzio, old chum, you'll see Mrs. Hayle finds her way home?"

"*Per il mio enorme piacere!*" Gabrunzio winked.

"Oh, darling, must you?!" Gardenia wilted.

"There's no getting out of it, is there, old thing?" Besim sighed helplessly in Mina's general direction.

"No, nothing to be done for it," Mina confirmed. "But perhaps, Gardenia, we might manage to join you for tea later this evening."

"I'll depend on it!" she pouted, placated, perceiving Mina would never do any such thing but Besim would be permitted to do so; the little ninny was already plotting away as to how she might rid herself of Gabrunzio in time for her expected tryst with Besim, who was a far more estimable catch than the Latin lothario.

"Shall we, Besim?" Mina indicated her impatience to leave.

"Right-o, off we go!" Besim muttered. "Duty calls!"

"*Ciao, ciao, bellissima, bell'amico,*" Gabrunzio rose from his seat, effusively kissing their cheeks and painfully prolonging their departure, while Gardenia sullenly simpered.

"Yes, yes, and all of that," Besim grumbled awkwardly before pulling Mina away in the direction of Via del Calzaiuoli, where they turned south and began their leisurely stroll home. "Well, old girl, how was your afternoon?"

"I'd rather not discuss it," Mina snapped, depleted of all patience now there was no further need to put up their combined front of the Honorable Beresford-Berishas.

Upon arriving in Italy four years ago, they'd learned that the flagrant use of Besim's inherited title allowed them instant access to a much wider circle of social contacts than they'd ever thought to cultivate when in New York. This had been Besim's idea, as he believed, and perhaps rightly so, that their insulated marriage had done more harm than good, at least with respect to Mina's mental health. Mina agreed, if only because she'd belatedly realized her marriage too closely mirrored that of her parents, which was enough to push her into going along with anything Besim proposed. Besides, the Florentines had such an outmoded groveling respect for titled foreigners that Mina and Besim discovered they were able to rent a fashionable, oversized hilltop two-story villa in the Oltrarno, just beside the Boboli Gardens and boasting several lovely rooms with a view. Never mind it was slightly beyond their means; Besim argued they'd lived for too long in that cramped studio, and perhaps having separate rooms of their own might restore some kind of connubial bliss between them. Mina ignored Besim's faulty logic, allowed him the ludicrous pleasure of carrying her over the threshold the day they moved in, and even promoted the brief, prosaic fantasy that they might actually be capable of falling in love.

It was a necessary fiction, because before settling in Florence, they'd spent a dreadfully dull summer holed away in Vallombrosa, where Besim had brought her to recover from her nervous breakdown, depression, or whatever ailment had afflicted her. She'd lain in bed for weeks, refusing to speak or acknowledge Besim as he nursed her throughout every hour of her torpid misery. Besim never complained, because he knew Mina would eventually grow bored, and sure enough, one afternoon he woke from a siesta to find her packing their belongings, and when she saw him studying her bustling preoccupation, she primly, self-deprecatingly informed him:

"I cannot imagine anything less disputably respectable than prolonged invalidism in Italy. We are not at all that sort of British, are we?"

No, they indisputably were not, though Mina thought to all appearances they certainly seemed to be, in spite of their farcical affairs. Strolling lacklusterly down the Via del Calzaiuoli, their stiff silence in stark contrast to the roiling, boisterous din of the catcalling merchants and thuggish thieves and filthy children and ruddy washerwomen and their strutting husbands, Mina mused upon the tepid blot the hoards of English tourists impressed upon the messiness of Italian life-traffic passionately throbbing in the street; how the hips of women swayed among crawling children; half-rotten oranges openly sold at reduction; the barbershop imitation mirrors offered as prayers to Mary preserve our mistresses from seeing us as we see ourselves. She rather liked that last clever turn of phrase, storing it away for further use sometime further in the future when she might have the energy to write it down.

When they emerged onto the Piazza della Signora, overcome as usual by its magnificent juxtapositions of stately *palazzi* and tawdry tourist-cramped *caffè*, its beggars and poets and bandolier-belted patriots and Baedeker-baffled Lucy Honeychurches and a baker's dozen of brawling bambini and prowling bantams and barking pugs and the perambulating beau monde and one basking pneumatic and so much, much more, Mina stumbled slightly while Besim dragged her through the throng; and just once before scissoring their legs through the swarming, narrow *cortile* of the Piazzale degli Uffizi, Mina glanced back with inspired pleasure and stored in her thrumming head the precise angle of the sun slicing the whole lot in half, warming the folded hands of a consumptive left outside in the midst of all that methodical madness because her chair is broken and she must be wondering how we feel for we walk very swiftly scattering the pigeons into the dusky arches of the Loggia dei Lanzi and the foreshortened illusion of the streetscape between the wings of the Uffizi articulates only an idealized perspective because we know soon enough we will reach the Arno and speak of all the things we have pushed aside and isn't it time we just have it all over and done with?

Besim bypassed the Ponte Vecchio so they might prolong their walk westward along the Arno, once again slowing their pace to match the sluggish flow of the river. "Don't you think, Mina, old girl, it's time you gave up your infatuation with Garinetti?"

"I'd hardly call it an infatuation."

"Then why continue cavorting with him?"

"Cavorting? What a ridiculous word!" Mina laughed. "Besides, you're the one who said I needed to be around other people, and as you know, he's been wonderful for booting me out of my depression and into my most intensely productive period of—."

"You haven't produced a single thing," Besim reminded her, refusing to chastise her selective memory, though he'd certainly put up with quite a bit of Mina's nonsense, and Mina knew, now, no more, but that wouldn't stop her from putting up a fight.

"Well, at least he produces in me the desire to produce. He has all kinds of brilliant theories, and actually, if you must know, Besim, there all sorts of things I've begun working on."

"Mina, love, take it from one who knows, he's nothing more than a poseur and from all I've heard he's a brute to women."

"Yes, you're absolutely right," Mina conceded, and then began babbling in a lame effort to maneuver Besim away from the point she knew he would eventually make. "Absolutely, he's despicable. He's even said it's perfectly acceptable for Italian men to beat their wives, that rape is the procreative prerogative of victors in war, you know, life recreated out of death, or some such hogwash, and if he had it his way, all men would be able to bear their own children. Though he hardly deserves as much credit as you give him; he's completely harmless, just an old goat with all kinds of silly notions. Honestly, I'm quite grateful to him, because if it weren't for having known someone as repulsive as Garinetti then I would have gone on blissfully, ignorantly unaware of the battle between the sexes, which is perhaps the most significant issue of our time, well, of all time really, don't you think?"

"I think you sound like a nincompoop," Besim grumbled. "By the way, you're still not taking turns in bed with the both of them, are you?"

"No," Mina winced. "Giovanni figured it out and accused Garinetti of debasing all their higher principles. You know Garinetti went on at great length in his manifesto about how the adulterous triangle was one of the four intellectual poisons that should be abolished, or some such preposterous moralizing, but of course Giovanni takes anything Garinetti says on face value, so for him to discover Garinetti's insufferable hypocrisy pushed Giovanni into a suicidal tizzy, the whole fabric of his reality rent open and all that—."

"As if you hadn't a single thing to do with any of it," Besim laughed.

"Well, of course I was in the right, Besim, having acted entirely in the wrong!" Mina quipped, feeling somewhat encouraged by that laughter. "Besides, I've already decided I'm done with the both of them. Truly, Garinetti has become such an utter bore and as for Giovanni, the poor nearsighted thing just keeps getting narrower and narrower in his viewpoint. Oh, Besim, just today we had a lovely argument. I maintained that pederasty, or any form of pedophilia for that matter, was the most morally and physically abhorrent thing in the world, and gave the most conclusive reasons—which he couldn't deny—but I'd got him going in so many circles he ended up by saying the love of children was the noblest form of love one could conceive. So you see? Quite amusing if you think about it."

"None of it is at all very funny anymore, Mina," Besim sharply halted, forcing them to a standstill in the middle of the Ponte Santa Trinità. "I'm not sure why you waste your time, but I refuse to wait around until you figure it out, because when you do, old girl, you won't like it and I won't see you through another of your damned spells."

"Since when have you cared what I do, Besim?" Mina smiled carelessly.

"But Mina, it really is all so beneath you," he insisted. "And I'd rather thought, well, the both of us, that we might—."

"I imagine Gardenia will be waiting for you," Mina reminded him.

Besim blankly stared at her, stunned by her cold dismissal, but he should have known how she'd react. Mina always felt threatened when cornered; she needed to be left alone, and in the morning when Besim straggled back home she would open the door and this time also confess she needed him more than any other person in the world, just as she knew he'd been about to do, and it was all so trite, so poorly executed, this threat of an ultimatum hurtling out at her from nowhere. Yes, Besim really should have known better.

He knew enough to leave her stranded on the middle of the bridge, walking back the way they'd come, but continuing forward, onward, westward to the Excelsior where Mrs. Gardenia Hayle impatiently waited because like Besim's own mother she coveted the title of Lady Beresford, only going at it from the reverse, from divorcée to dowager as soon as Besim divorced himself from that Mina Byrne (who was not at all a lady), and married Gardenia. Yes, that's exactly what Besim should do, Mina decided, feeling slightly drunk, the haziness of dusk impairing what she'd thought had been her sober vision.

She walked as far as Santo Spirito before ducking inside to rest in its cool sanctuary, or else the remainder of her stumbling walk home might have led her back over the bridge to Caffè Giubbe where Giovanni and Garinetti sat mumbling to each other their misogynist monologues. Mina only ever visited the churches of Firenze to view their collections of art, which seemed to be their sole purpose for existing. She sat on a bench in the south end of the nave, feeling she'd committed some sacrilege, an adulterous woman, shamelessly intoxicated, daring to enter, head uncovered, the sacred house of a neglected God, and seeking absolution for a crime for which she was not entirely sure she was responsible. As if in reply to her confusion, a rumbling groan of thunder reverberated in the heavens far above the vaulted interior of the basilica. Mina nearly irreverently laughed in the face of this empty reprimand; oh dear, if her father could see her now. He would not know her, yet that hardly seemed of any great significance.

All that mattered was that Mina and Besim knew who they were; it was important to them, this being of who they were; they were bodily, transitively, repeatedly, disjointedly themselves, and they had come to believe they were quite complete. On Sundays they silently sat together in the balmy light of the parlor, watching the passing shadows from the gritty road outside playing intermittently on the cracked plaster of the white walls. On all other evenings they looked out of their two windows: on the floor above, Besim from the library converted to a darkroom and on the floor below, Mina from the sienna-stained kitchen, where she made an effort to cook, concocting all sorts of saliva-inducing treats. Ding dong goes the bell because at any hour Besim will want his dinner. Patience is an attribute Mina has learned and so prepares casseroles to dish up at any hour, all suitably delectable. Meanwhile, what had Besim constructed of his desires while developing his negatives, and Mina while among the pots and pans? One never asked the other and thus they wisely ate their suppers in peace—of what their peace consisted neither could say—only that he was magnificently man and she insignificantly a woman who understood understanding is knowing perceptively that to each his or her own; to man his labor, to woman her worship of unworthy men, and if in-between there were sometimes tender meals and an infrequent caress, so be it, it seldom is as it should be. All the while he pondered the dark of his darkroom, and while she created paellas instead of poems, they resisted the urge to peep in on each other, fearing there might be nothing to see. She resigned herself to hanging out the window at the precise hour when all along the sloping street one could hear the clacking of all the green shutters from which bits of womanly bodies variously leaned; their household duties complete, allowed at last to mingle eyes with the commotion of the world beyond their kitchens and beds; Mina becoming no different from all the women all shuttered up in their houses, all like marionettes jumping on the same shuddering strings; all intimacy thrust out into the street rather than remaining cloistered in matrimonial sheets, all watching for a falling star and when a star fell Mina wished Besim would still love her tomorrow, and as Besim never gave any thought to the matter, he did. All the while she wanted to become a woman who wanted everything to be everything, everything every way at once, infinitely variegate. She shifted infinitesimally from the Mina Besim always knew; conceding to monogamy with her mercurial aspirations and chameleon consistency, all the while every evening expecting unexpected intangibilities; and Besim remained monumentally the same, the same unpardonably dependable Besim, but if he had become anything else then Mina's world would whimper to an end; Mina without Besim and with no axis to revolve upon would discover everything that was anything dwindled to a full stop. So in the mornings she dropped miniscule crystals through devotional fingers, spooning saccharine star drops into his red enameled coffee cup, and in the afternoons went to market with a basket trimmed with red flannel flowers; when she was lazy she wrote a poem on the milk bill, the first verse *Buongiorno*, the second *Buonasera*, something easily learnt by heart, and gently pushed together because one day elided murmurously, uneventfully into the next . . .

Mina discovered she was crying maudlin messy tears. This was the sort of poem a lady would be expected to write, all purplish and pulsating with probing sentiments of dissipated love. Well if not love, what then? Something disparaging, something coldly, cleverly, caustically lampooning the sexual neuroses of men, and not her own failures or longings; no, not that; dull drivel indeed. She listened to the abating storm outside, rose from her bench, and peered at the frescoes installed in the chapels to either side of the south end of the nave: both by Foschi, one depicting the *Resurrection*, the other the *Immaculate Conception*, or rather, the dispute over the immaculate conception, which Mina thought slightly amusing, as if any man knew what any woman knew about the inner experiences of conception, gestation, or birth. Perhaps all these Old Florentines were envious of God fucking the unsuspecting virgin Marah, whose old Hebrew name translated into bitterness, and not at all blessed. Mina listened to the silence of the sky outside and exited through the south doors, emerging directly onto the Piazza Santo Spirito. She walked between its rows of rain-bespattered trees and turned onto Via Mazetta, taking the most circular route home.

Something might be salvaged, something someday to be written from far away on the benign peninsular of memory, but her feet dragged and her head was now pounding. She carefully descended down the road along the palazzo, gingerly stepping along the narrow footpaths fronting the shops selling innumerable assortments of *gelati* and leather handbags, veered right and then finally directly home up the steep and narrow street of Costa di San Giorgio though not so up as to reach the *porta* culminating in the fading fresco of the dragon-slayer. Mina unlocked the door to No. 54 and stuttered up the stairs, habitually finding safe harbor at the kitchen table where she kept pens and paper and useless blotter and thought that of all the poems she should write it would be the one about the intimate smallness of her days: the scrubbed ammoniac of the ash-wood table, the greasy cleanliness of the chipped chopper board, the multi-hued vegetables, the indentations of flour fingerprinted like traces of ghosts who refuse to erase, the flickers of straw-fanned charcoal arranged among the kindling of her audacious happiness, all the pet simplicities of her universe where circles of kneaded dough were simply round or ovate having no vices because there was no one but the woman who lived here and no one to interrogate the direction in which they, or she, decided to go.

The narrative no longer held any pleasure for Mina as soon as she stopped to think of herself in the third-person, because if one were looking from the outside in, he or she or they might comment, well, none of this matters, not a pinchful of salt or suspended doubt, because as soon as I/ we learned that the house inspiring such a dreadfully heartbreaking poem was inhabited by a mad woman then it was all beyond my/our patience for the inestimable deferral of disbelief. Mina decided to ignore this niggling of self-doubt and proceeded to write the poem that had been intending to come out of her since not the end of this day but the end of another evening when everything had slipped into an irrecoverable nothing.

Parthenogenesis

I am the centrifugal rapture
Of a whirlpool
From which I long to extrude
An extraction of this embryonic
Sliver of what remains
Between our nucleotides of belief
I am no more than a theorem
Of your spatial continuum
To which
Abandoning ourselves
I might circumlocute
Eternity in a nutshell . . .

In my congealed corpulence
Listening to the inchoate moon and
Beyond the threshold the thundering
Footstamp of a sepia-stained provocateur
Rushing inexcusably late into the room
Apologizing for his infidel intimacy
With the washerwoman a floor below

I am precipitating a cliffside
Peripheral to our institutionalized past
Transgressing myself while
A slick bloodied beast slips
Between my insensate thighs
Spilling out into the universe

Upon a mere mewl   then   silence

As pain blossoms infinitely
Into generative explosions
Of aborted villanelles

Some years later, when this poem was published along with all the refined versions of the poems incubated from the germs of inspiration prompted by this day, Mina, before approving the proofs, referred back to the original draft and found a small handwritten memo she'd addressed to herself, something she'd forgotten in all that had proceeded from the moment she'd put aside her pen: *It is a sorry but small pleasure to introduce the other sex to the inner meaning of childbirth. The last illusion is gone. There is nothing more to lose or conceal. I am sad.*

Mina did not have time to reflect upon this confused sentiment. An importunate knock on the front door a floor below repeatedly intruded upon her evening's hard-earned peace. As soon as she'd finished writing the poem, she realized the pounding in her head had subsided, but then she thought it might be Besim, locked out, deciding he was happier sleeping at home rather than amongst the overstuffed décor of the Excelsior. No, Mina could not stop internally rhyming, not in this incautious, too hasty moment of relief. She skittered down the stairs, opened the door, and with a gasp of distress, found Andrew, unsmiling and uninvited, and returned from the dead.

CHAPTER NINE
Vanishing Acts

Before filling in the gaps that were not addressed in previous chapters, and compressing ten years into a single paragraph, here is the brief history of Mina and Andrew: Once upon a time Andrew and Mina fell in love but married other people. Andrew wrote some plays; Mina painted some paintings; neither Andrew's plays nor Mina's paintings were understood by the other. Andrew destroyed Mina with his plays, Mina destroyed her paintings. Andrew became an alcoholic; Mina became depressed. Andrew left his wife and for the following two years his whereabouts remained roughly unknown; Mina did not leave her husband, who also failed to keep track of her whereabouts, but eventually noticed she'd begun writing poems. Mina and her husband lived in California for several months before Mina returned to New York, left her husband, returned to her husband five months pregnant, and at the end of another three months went to see Andrew's last play. On the same night Mina gave birth to a dead baby, Andrew attempted to kill himself; he was then committed indefinitely to a psychiatric hospital; his wife divorced him; and nearly four years later his brother signed the consent papers for an operation making possible Andrew's freedom. Meanwhile, Mina and her husband had moved to Italy, where she failed to find any happiness until one evening she wrote a poem, a generally good poem, or at least a start to something new; then Andrew showed up unannounced at her door.

For those readers who might still be confused as to why Andrew was the last person Mina wanted to find on her doorstep, let us retrace our steps back to the evening of *Claudia's Revenge*, which was the pivotal event in their relationship. It was on this night that Mina realized she did not resent Andrew's plays because they grossly misrepresented and maligned her character; rather, this latest play had revealed to her that she was exactly as Andrew saw her. Not once had she asserted her presence, deferring to the existence he'd assigned her, because she was lazy, because it was easier to allow him his interpretive delusions, making of her what he wished to see: a beautiful woman, evasively, seductively mysterious, always receding from view, and thus all the more desirable. Mina receded because in her truthful estimation, she had a clinical intellect, a cold heart, and a cynical distrust of romance; she was not moved by any of Andrew's passionate displays of love, which she found embarrassingly silly, and was more or less certain she had no particular talent when it came to sex. None of this mattered; Andrew insisted on believing otherwise, and Mina had not once discovered sufficient initiative or courage to set the record straight. She thought she was the type of woman who should insist on doing so, yet whenever the opportunity presented itself, she stalled, stuttered, stumbled into silent self-reproach, because she did not know if she liked the real version of herself.

So she destroyed her paintings because she'd also recognized she had no real genius for this sort of thing, let alone any genuine desire to be a painter, recalling her only motivation for becoming one had been Maître Regnauld's idiotic insistence upon it. Afterwards, she was not so much depressed as she was discouraged: by herself, by all her inappropriate choices, her vague sense of direction, her sense of loss now that she no longer wanted to paint or remain in love with Andrew, her confusion over what to insert in place of those two desires, leading inevitably to the obscure longing to become some other woman, and if not the real Mina, then at least someone she could live with, some version of herself that she and no one else had created. Then she received a letter.

Dear Miss Byrne,

I write out of concern for my son. He's confessed to me the details of your relationship as well as his confused desire to

139

no longer go on living without you. My immediate impression of you, Miss Byrne, gleaned from our regrettably brief introduction at the première of Andrew's latest bizarre play, is that you are a sensible, level-headed sort of girl, without the usual romantic fripperies filling your head. You are far too intelligent to fall for the impassioned antics with which my son indulges his need for dramatic displays, which are more often than not disproportionate to the matter at hand. However, this is the first he's ever communicated a suicidal wish, causing his mother a great deal of worry, and since it causes me immense discomfort to see my usually composed wife unnecessarily troubled by anything, I have taken it upon myself to act as intermediary between you and my son with the hope of easing this episode in Andrew's life into some sane manner of closure. He has seen the sense of this, and has requested I write to you (which should explain how I ascertained your address). He believes, and perhaps rightly so, that you will refuse to see him again; or, perhaps out of some misplaced paranoia, he has insinuated that should a letter arrive at your residence addressed to you in his own hand, your husband would demand to see the letter or suppress your reply, or like some jealous ogre, bar you from ever leaving the house again. These all seem overwrought details provided merely to persuade some reader of some outlandish plot, don't they, Miss Byrne? But it is life, and not a novel, as much as we wish it were, for then we might disregard the convolutions of my son's imagination as merely implausible. Be that as it may, my own desire for your response to my letter necessitates its own complications. My wife is not aware of my writing to you, and since she sifts through all our correspondence before I have the opportunity to read it myself, should she come across your reply this may cause her further distress. My son is of course in no mental condition to receive direct word from you. My proposal, then, is that we meet in person so you may have the opportunity of expressing to me your wishes concerning Andrew, which I may then filter back to him in a manner

that does not further incite his mania. If you find this an
acceptable solution to our dilemma then may I suggest . . .

Mina had stopped reading at that point, the words beginning to blur, tears of laughter pooling in her eyes. It was the most preposterous letter she had ever received. She did not know whether to be offended by its cool familiarity, its cruelly dismissive tone towards the author's own child, or its callous insinuation that Mina might readily agree to meet him in secret. Then she saw the scrawled signature, which caused her a brief spasm of disbelief, forcing her to review the past three years of her affair with Andrew, because not once had he betrayed to Mina the name of his father; he'd only mentioned in passing that he was a professor of literature at some traditionally liberal campus upstate. Mina dithered over whether to accept the signature as certain proof that the author of this letter was one and the same as the author of *Dolores* (a book Mina greatly admired, at least upon second reading), or if the signature was not some fraudulent hoax on the part of Andrew (recalling how he'd taken such offense over her initial appraisal of the book), or simply a case of mixed identities (for there could conceivably be more than one Vasili Novikov in this world); but then Mina decided, displaying that level-headed common sense for which she'd just been extolled, that Occam's law should apply, and so allowed the revelation of Andrew's father's identity to perform a number of reversals in her perception with regard to the letter's author and his son.

She was now inclined to feel flattered by the letter's presumptuous insinuations, all of which implied its author deemed Mina to be on an intellectual par with someone of his own kind, a compliment rarely doled out by men of such assured genius. She decided to ignore his overly mannered tone, resisted any further urge to question his motives, denied there was anything illicit in his request for a clandestine meeting, and because she so desperately needed even the most feeble spark that might reignite her sputtering self-confidence, allowed herself the fantasy of basking in the metaphorical glow of associating with a man of greatness. Moreover, the discovery that Andrew was so closely associated with such a man inspired in Mina the impulse to revise every aspect of their relationship, as she began to contemplate the possibilities of a different past and a different future between them. Andrew was suddenly reborn into a perfectly new person, a stranger with whom Mina might magically, mysteriously fall in love, and without the illusion of crossed stars. No, she did not allow the usual romantic fripperies to fill her head; her romances were no less than acts of razing to the ground all edifices of the past in order to pursue a single-minded project of resurrection, restoration, and redemption.

Apparently, Mina followed Vasili's instructions provided in his letter, met him at the secluded bar located several blocks from her studio on East 11th Street, chosen by Vasili simply because it was one of those rare public establishments where one did not have to suffer the intrusion of soft music played in the background. After Vasili expended with his usual awkward hemming and hawing, they more than likely brushed aside the topics of Vasili's son and wife and engaged in the business of getting to know each other. There is no reason to allow our imaginations to run lewdly away with us. Their conversational trysts, which continued over the course of the following year whenever Vasili found an excuse to travel down from upstate, remained limited to a passionate admiration for the other's intellect, or so Mina chastely believed, playing out her girlish fantasy of finding the Abelard to her Héloise. Mina's fantasies were always overly literate, but for a child who'd had nothing but books as companions while growing up, we might forgive her this.

As for Vasili, who can say? He enjoyed, like any aging man, the company of a beautiful, witty woman; he felt as usual the need to compete with his eldest son; he indulged in the occasional respite from his old faithful, eagle-eyed wife; he was in-between books and feared he would never write another; he saw in Mina a reflection of his own youthful ambitions, for he too had once wanted to be a painter but settled for poetry and then prose; or, he was reminded of a girl he'd loved when he was a boy, before the irrecoverable losses of time, tuberculosis, expatriation and exhaustion stole from him the gauzy glowing patina of his longed-for youth. One might settle on any number of these things; in the end, they are beyond the scope of our knowledge or interest. All I know is that Mina took from Vasili his encouragement to begin writing poems, and once Mina embarked upon this endeavor, we're not sure why she continued her relationship with Vasili, at least to the point of following him, with Besim blissfully ignorantly in tow, all the way to California.

Whatever the reason, it all ruptured and came to an abrupt end. Mina was sent packing back to New York, though she did not return to her senses, since we do know for a certainty that she returned to Andrew before straggling back, pregnant and beaten bloody, to Besim, who in one of many interviews explained that by the time the child was born, strangled with the cord around its neck, Mina had become so far removed from her former sensible self that she hysterically believed this was her punishment; for what, precisely, Besim hadn't the slightest idea. All he could do was remove Mina from New York, from all possible reminders of Andrew or Vasili; and once in Italy, she decided to put the past behind her. But then she wrote her own letter:

Dear V,

We have returned to Europe, as I am aware you and Deirdre have done the same. Andrew's wife informed me of as much, which is to explain, as I know you like to have these small details in place, how I knew where to send this letter. I do hope this reaches you, if only because I so very much need you to know that all is forgotten as much as can be forgiven. We spent the winter in Venice, where one is able to lose oneself in the watery reflection of one's face, and then the summer in Vallombrosa, where it seems one is forcibly required to rehabilitate oneself out of the sheer boredom of finding restitution from the mountain air. We've now settled ourselves into a lovely predictable rhythm of domesticity, in a middling hilltop villa in the Oltrarno, in the medieval mishmash of Florence (as you might gather from this letter's return address). I do not expect you to return anything, however, as it is now a question of moving forward, or so Besim makes a point of reminding me whenever I go for more than a day without walking out amongst society. Besim believes society is an excellent curative for whatever sadness afflicts me, never realizing of course that it is, as it has always been, the company of others which thoroughly depresses me, since it is the perplexing simplicity of society as a whole that confounds one's desire to live peacefully and productively. I know what you would advise, and so I shall do my best to continue constructing my little poems, progressing into the discovery of something much

*larger than myself. Something as large as life, and twice as
natural, through the looking glass, where one might agree to
imagine the fabulously monstrous existence of a unicorn as
easily as that of a child. Perhaps the only possible bargain
one might make with the past, yes?*

With all best wishes,
M

After waiting several months for a reply, Mina made an entirely
different bargain than the one indicated in her letter, proceeding to repeat
compulsively the Vasili-Andrew affair with their two poor duplicates,
the old Garinetti and young Giovanni, whose oedipal rivalry, delusions
of grandeur, argumentative fallacies, and misogynist fantasies seemed to
extract from Mina some kind of penance for some unforgiveable crime.
This was the quandary from which Mina felt she'd finally freed herself on
that evening when she walked away from Giovanni and Garinetti, allowed
Besim to say the words that would bring their fruitless marriage to a close,
wrote a poem exorcising the loss of her stillborn child, only to find Andrew
waiting on her doorstep, clearly there to dredge up the corpse of the very
thing she'd just buried. Mina's ripple of alarmed revulsion deterred her
from questioning why Andrew had felt the need to reappear, or what he'd
gone through to get there. Mina never took into account that Andrew, or
anyone else for that matter, might have a version of the past quite different
from her own understanding of it. Since I don't want to give the impression of suppressing Andrew's side of things, here is an alternative history
from his possible perspective:

Once upon a time Andrew fell in and out of love with a number of
people. His first love was his mother, who never loved him in return, or at
least never as much as she loved his father. His second love was Calliope
Wilcox, a freckle-cheeked, ginger-tressed, naughty imp, who during his
first American summer took him under the baseball bleachers and allowed
him to fondle her pert rosebud breasts while she fiddled with his unruly
black hair, twirling it slowly in her fingers until, with a sigh of unexpected
pleasure, she yanked a strand clean from his scalp. His third love was Giles
Vanderhoven, the third form captain of the Harrington rugby team and
the third son of a third generation shipping magnate and his third wife, a

triple bronze medalist in ladies' dressage; Andrew failed to remember any of the particulars, other than the usual horseplay the more discontent boys at any private school engaged in when left with nothing better to do in between expulsions. His fourth love was the nameless woman who relieved him of his virginity when he ran away to New York at the age of seventeen, forever finished with school and prosaically prepared to see his name in lights on Broadway; he didn't remember her name because he was paying her for the favor and it had all been over and done in a New York minute within the stall of a public restroom at Grand Central Station. His fifth, sixth, and seventh loves had been Maribelle Hawkins, Sadie Jones, and Felicia Fitzpatrick, a series of short-lived girlfriends who had no defining attributes other than that they were all members of the chorus line for the Ziegfeld Follies. His eighth love was his wife, Sara Sorrell, a former high-kick girl herself, and, as we already know, Andrew was no longer in love with her by the time he married her because he'd already met his ninth, last, and longest-lived love, whom he believed was like nothing and no one he'd loved before.

I have already covered the details of how, why, and to what extent Andrew loved Mina, having dissected the evidence of this in his plays, Mina's less than appreciative reaction to those plays, and all their probable conversations surrounding Andrew's confused versions of Mina. So let us skip forward to that missing period of time just after *Claudia's Revenge* and leading up to Andrew's ensuing period of insanity. First, it is highly unlikely Andrew asked his father to write a letter to Mina; he may have babbled out a few distraught details when Vasili cornered him into doing so, giving up her name, and as soon as Andrew had been sedated with a bottle of bourbon, Vasili riffled through his son's diary, copied out the address for a Miss Mina Byrne, left Andrew to deal with Sara on his own, and did not see or speak with his son for another two years.

Second, Andrew did not leave his wife; Sara asked Andrew to leave. She wasn't at all enraged or surprised by his infidelity; rather, it was that disastrously inane play, which had caused her a great deal of professional embarrassment. Her new agent, Mable Montgomery, had invited several film producers to the première of *Claudia's Revenge*, and though Sara had already suspected the play was doomed, she chose to believe her performance might just pull it off, or at least secure her a contract with one of the larger Hollywood studios. The morning after the play Mable informed

Sara that there were not any forthcoming offers, and that she would break off their own contract, which was more than merely professional, if Sara did not dump the dead weight of her husband.

Sara agreed to Mable's terms, though not so much to save her career, but she'd decided she would no longer continue cleaning up the messes of yet another drunk. Her father had been one, her mother had been one, her first husband had been one, even her first, second, and third agents; so she'd finally made the decision to act ruthlessly in the pursuit of her own interests instead of supporting, to her professional detriment, the tedious self-absorption of so many slobbering dipsomaniacs. Sara, however, did not see why she shouldn't retain her generously benevolent nature, and so found Andrew a tidy studio apartment on the Upper Westside, agreed to withhold his new address or any inkling of his whereabouts from his parents should they come asking for it, and for the next two years continued until their divorce to pay the rent on the apartment.

Third, then, and in an attempt to recover those missing two years, it seems Andrew spent a good deal of his free time, which is all he possessed when not drinking himself into a stupor, waiting across the street from Mina's studio for her to appear, and when she did, following her unseen back and forth between East 11th Street and the bar on East 3rd. He never approached her, never made his presence known, because he'd also observed nearly every other weekend his father entering and exiting the same bar always shortly after and directly before Mina's arrivals and departures. After a year of this, after establishing a consistent pattern, after assuring himself they never met anywhere else, not in some hotel or heaven forbid in Mina's home, after several months had elapsed without his father appearing, and after concluding that he needed to discover what was actually going on between them now that it showed signs of slowing to an end, Andrew went into the bar and slipped into the booth where Mina sat scribbling in a journal. She went on writing for several seconds before she raised her head, startled to find Andrew sitting opposite her, glaring at her with a wretched, desperate smile. After her eyes flickered briefly with confusion, panic and then guilt, Andrew knew all he needed to know. He ignored Mina's swift recovery, her sweetly false smile, her soft husky hello, and accused her with the one thing he knew she'd deny, because it was the one thing not even he was willing to imagine.

You're in love with him. *With whom?* You know. *Oh, Andrew, it's not at all what you think.* I think it's disgusting. *You haven't any idea what you're talking about.* What do you talk about? *Poetry and things.* What things? *Really, Andrew, nothing of importance, just poetry.* How could you? *How could I?* Betray me. *I haven't done any such thing.* Why him, of all people, why him? *He was someone to talk to.* You haven't any idea what he's like. *I know enough.* Well, my mother will put a stop to it; she won't let someone else take her place. *Andrew, that's ridiculous, no one's trying to take anyone's place, and besides, she knows all about it.* Of course she does, she always knows, but not because he told her. *That's not what he told me.* He's a liar and his lies like his books are like games, and we all just play along, always, just to keep him happy. *Andrew, I'm not following. You're not making sense.* You know exactly what I'm talking about, because you're just like him. *I've never lied to you.* Yes, you have. *When?* You just didn't know you were lying. *If I don't know when I'm lying, then how can it be a lie?* You know what I mean, Mina. *No, I don't, Andrew.* Have you missed me? *Of course I have.* Then prove it.

Mina allowed Andrew to put her in a cab and take her uptown to his squalid apartment, where for the first time she permitted him the pleasure of fucking her on a mattress, because it was his and not Sara's. They drank a bottle of bourbon and continued conversing in circles until Andrew passed out after proposing she divorce her husband and live out with him the happily ever after of Mina and Andrew forever and ever. Mina took a cab home, wrote a poem, went to bed, and the next day convinced Besim to take her to California, because that's what she'd already agreed to do when Vasili told her that's where he and Deirdre were going, had gone, three months ago, before Mina had seriously considered what would happen, what it would mean, for Andrew to discover she had been seeing his father.

Mina did not want to acknowledge the terrifying dilemma in which she now discovered herself; she could not continue any sort of relationship with both the father and son at the same time, nor could she choose one over the other, or even make the choice of living without either; they both answered something for her that the other could not. What frightened her most, having seen Andrew now separated from Sara, was that she did indeed miss him, and the possibility of Andrew and Mina until death do us part opened up into a gaping, vertigo-inducing reality. So she ran away, needing someone else to make the choice for her.

She knew that father like son Vasili could only take pleasure from his relationship with Mina as long as it remained a secret, or at least retained the pretense of remaining a secret. He could not excuse the deliberate cruelty of betraying his wife if it became public knowledge that he'd been seeing another woman. Though of course his wife was fully aware of everything Vasili did, and as soon as Deirdre was given the opportunity, she confronted Mina, discreetly of course, and advised her to return to New York where she might be more welcome; thus Mina had maneuvered Deirdre into pushing her back to Andrew and out of Deirdre's own marriage. Regrettably, since no one knew or considered what might be going on in Andrew's head, by the time Mina showed up, his perspective had become skewed to such a deranged degree of paranoia that the whole experiment of Mina and Andrew happily ever after was doomed from the start.

Mina had disappeared for three months without explaining where she'd been or why she'd reappeared. Andrew had spent those three months drinking himself into a perfect storm of suspicion, inventing scenarios of Mina dead or debauched or both by his father's hands, his father's insatiable lust for anything belonging to his son destroying the woman Andrew loved. When Mina materialized alive and unharmed, though never quite credibly untouched, Andrew had come to believe the only way of erasing or preventing all the imagined disasters he'd constructed was if she promised never to leave his sight. Mina agreed to this on the condition of his sobriety, and Andrew agreed in a moment of inebriated elation as soon as he realized Mina was truly promising to stay. Mina tidied the apartment, stocked the cupboards with food, and prepared a warm bath and broth, thinking this the most sensible plan for preparing to wean an alcoholic off his bottle. Andrew shivered and sweated everything out to Mina's satisfaction, while Mina sat beside him reading aloud *Songs and Sonnets* by John Donne. After Mina decided the worst of it was over, they shared a month of delirious happiness, pretending to become the versions of themselves they had always desired.

After Mina informed Andrew with alarming alacrity that she suspected she was pregnant, Andrew gave up the charade. He opened the bottles Mina had neglected to dump out, and in the course of the following four months, in the increasingly unpleasant haze of his distorted sense of time muddled by bourbon and disbelief over possessing finally the Mina he'd always wanted, he began to suspect she'd only returned because she was pregnant with his father's child. The first time Andrew accused Mina of using him as her stooge in some elaborate scheme concocted by Vasili in order to conceal the truth of his illegitimate child from Andrew's mother, Mina again did the careless, wrong thing. She laughed, because it was all so insanely preposterous, which is precisely what she told Andrew, who also laughed while continuing to imagine the worst. The more Mina's belly protruded, the more Andrew drank; the more Andrew drank the more Mina withdrew; the more Mina withdrew the more Andrew accused her of planning to leave him; the more Mina denied this the more he believed it, and the more he believed it and she denied it, the more he indulged his delusional fantasies until one night he dragged Mina out of the bed, shoved her across the room, and battered her until she stumbled against the table, and by some incomprehensible strength, lifted Andrew's type-writer and smashed it against his skull.

Andrew woke the next morning to discover Mina had vanished into thin air. All of her belongings remained: her blue silk dress, her under-garments, her hairbrush, the lingering scent of her sex, and even her beloved John Donne. He staggered over to the mirror, saw a fissure of crusted blood spreading from his left brow to the hairline just above his left temple, dabbed at the blood to discern the depth of the cut, and when it was clear he wasn't in need of stitches, washed his face, taped over the cut, drank his last remaining bottle of Old Grand Dad, and then flung the empty glass into the mirror.

Because he needed to rid himself of the throbbing ache of what he knew would be his final play, Andrew didn't drink for two weeks, or at least limited his intake to a bottle of red wine a day, nothing more than that, nothing stronger. Because the typewriter was irreparably broken, and he couldn't have afforded ribbon or paper anyway, he scribbled out the first and only draft in a cramped spidery script inscribed in pencil on blank leaves torn from the pulp detective novels he'd taken a penchant for reading in the year he'd spied on Mina meeting his father. Because he could not think of any other available options, when the draft was finished he gathered his scraps of paper, stuffed them in an envelope and mailed the whole lot to his mother. He included a note instructing her to type up a clean copy, mail the copy off to Sara, who would know what to do with it, and to keep all of this, every bit of it, from his father; it was a surprise, a great big surprise of a substantial piece of work that would finally make his father proud.

Presumably, Deirdre fulfilled her son's request, and Sara performed her expected part, for the play found a producer, a director, some actors, and a theater. Vasili was certainly surprised, but never proud, only stricken with guilt and shame over his son's apparent psychotic break. As for Andrew, he never showed up to the première; he'd forgotten all about the play the moment he'd dropped it in the post, and had remained holed up in his apartment, memorizing passages from Mina's favorite poems while drinking himself to death, committed at last to following through on the suicidal wish he'd once confessed to his parents after the disaster of *Claudia's Revenge*. He could not, would not, live without Mina, and Mina no longer existed for him now that he'd written his last play. As soon as the curtain had closed on the première of *Antiopa*, Vasili and Deirdre stumbled backstage seeking their son and only finding his wife, from whom he'd been separated the past two years (although none of this was truly news to Deirdre). Sara gladly handed over the spare key to Andrew's apartment, and there they found him with one clumsily slit wrist and lying comatose on the rubbish strewn floor.

Three days later Andrew woke up, wrist stitched, stomach pumped, forcefully sobered, and in a white padded room at Bellevue, where he remained incarcerated for over three years, pretending madness because it seemed the only sane thing to do, because no one had explained to him how he'd ended up there. He suspected his father had something to do with it, all part of his scheme to murder Andrew and marry Mina, but that was impossible, wasn't it? Mina was already dead and buried and Andrew was safely hidden here, at least until his brother appeared and reminded him of everything with that photograph Mina had sent Andrew from the afterlife sometime between the night he'd murdered her and the morning he'd decided to kill himself. So when he told Jamie what he wanted, it was the sanest decision he'd made in years, because if it removed his cancerous memories of Mina, then by all means, let them shove an ice pick into his frontal lobe; let him go home to his father and mother so he could forget and be a child again.

Now, though, in the ever after of their asphyxiated happiness, Andrew stood before Mina begging silently, desperately, drooling like a dumb dog at the door, to be granted yet one more impossible chance, one more scrap of hope, and never mind it had already been gnawed down to the marrow with nothing left but gristle and grief. Mina saw the grief in his eyes, and though her heart slammed shut, she opened the door an inch wider, allowing him just enough space to squeeze past her defenses, cross the threshold, and enter her home.

He silently followed her up the stairs and into the dimly lighted parlor, sat heavily in a chair, and waited for her to reappear from the kitchen where she'd hastily disappeared, mumbling something about the need to prepare some tea. They still did not speak when she returned, but sat facing each other, sipping without pleasure their unsweetened Darjeeling. Mina studied Andrew, who in spite of his gaunt features had grown fatter, and was now balding, and had an ugly puckered scar running across his brow. He sat slumped, deflated of all his former manic energy, showing scarcely any spark of the Andrew she had always known and unreasonably loved, except for the fleeting glimmer of an ironic grin (because it was all so unlikely, his presence). Andrew stared at Mina, who would always be beautiful, though her luminous black eyes were now dull with unspeakable sadness, her once generous mouth pinched with weariness and disappointment and all the unbearable pain Andrew had caused her; he no longer knew why he was there, or what he'd wanted from her.

"Mina," he began but was not allowed to continue.

"How did you find me?" she demanded.

"I found a letter," Andrew mumbled. "One you sent papa."

"That was over three years ago," Mina stated, resentfully, as if the elapse of time was all Andrew's fault.

"Yes," Andrew replied, paused, and then continued slowly, stuttering in the face of Mina's glaring suspicion. "All I had . . . I didn't know . . . I was hoping . . ."

"What, Andrew? What could you possibly be hoping?"

"To find you."

"Oh," she sighed irritably. "Well, why?"

"Why?" Andrew dumbly repeated.

"Oh, never mind. Where have you been?"

"Before now?"

"Yes, of course before now!"

"I thought you knew—."

"I mean after Bellevue."

"With mama and papa," he mumbled, again, forcing Mina to lean forward in her chair. "Mama brought me home, not papa, because he won't fly, he won't drive, so mama does everything papa won't do."

Mina stared at him, refusing to feel the slightest sliver of remorse.

"Andrew, what did they do to you?"

"They? They did nothing. They sat and stared and pretended nothing was anything, but it's not their fault. Nothing is anybody's fault, so nobody needs to remember."

"No, Andrew, I meant the doctors at Bellevue," Mina whispered, assuming he was referring to his parents. "What on earth did the doctors do to you?"

"Oh, them," he made a choking noise, a stifled sort of laugh. "They punched a hole in my brain and mama took me home and we flew on a plane because papa doesn't like to fly but—."

"Yes, okay, Andrew, it's okay." Mina smiled gently, saving him from going on in this endless loop of information and because she was now prepared for him to answer her first question. "Why did you want to find me? Why did you come here?"

"I didn't decide, Mina," he told her, then shook his head, shut his eyes, and took a breath before delivering his disconnected, ponderous sentences, which took more effort that Mina could possibly imagine. "I found your letter. I can still read, which makes them happy, but I know they're not happy as long as I'm there, reminding them of everything that's nothing. I told them I wanted to go here, some place I've never seen. They don't have to do anything for me. I have my own money, from my plays, papa published them, and they gave me a prize for a play I wrote. I don't remember writing it, but that doesn't mean anything. Now I'm here and you're here—."

"And if I wasn't?" Mina interrupted, losing patience. "What if you came all the way here and didn't find me?"

"Don't worry, I have a hotel," he informed her.

"No, Andrew, I meant—," and then Mina realized that he had been attempting a joke.

"I know what you meant, Mina. They didn't make me an idiot. I don't have the words anymore; that's all, not any words. Mama builds my vocabulary, her word, and papa calls it some other word I don't remember—."

"Aphasia, rhymes with fantasia," Mina murmured, inwardly cringing at the inanity of offering him this mnemonic.

"Yes, that, but not all of it," Andrew tried to smile in recognition of his own absurd reply. "I can speak and understand, but I sound like this . . . like

152

this . . . idiot . . . and I know what you want to know, Mina. If you weren't here I would still be here."

"You planned to stay in Italy?"

"Yes," he sighed.

"How long have you been here?"

"Today."

"Oh, I see."

"I needed to know."

"What?"

"If I would find you."

"And now you've found me?"

"I will find a house."

"That's it?" Mina couldn't help laughing. "That's all you want? Nothing else?"

"What else?" he frowned, or smiled, she couldn't tell. "I want a house, and no one to feel sorry for me."

"Oh, Andrew," Mina suddenly felt willing to forgive him anything.

"And the child," he blurted. "I want to know the child."

"There isn't any child."

"Yes, I thought so."

"So what is there to know? It died."

"It?"

"I didn't want to know. I didn't want to give it a name."

"I understand."

"Do you, Andrew?"

"No, but if I say so, it will make you happy, and I don't want to hurt you, Mina, not again. Do you understand?"

"Yes, Andrew, I understand."

She also understood there was something left unfinished between them, something that needed to be put right, a way of bargaining with the past without playing by the old rules. So she rented a studio overlooking the Piazza Santo Spirito, its single open, airy room containing all that one needed: a bed, a table, some chairs, and a large, claw-foot tub, the lavatory down the hall, and not anything resembling a kitchen; she would eat her evening meals in a trattoria located on the corner below, and settle for bread, fruit, and cheese in the afternoons. Upon learning of Andrew's reappearance, Besim did not ridicule Mina's faulty memory; he simply agreed to move to the Excelsior, where he shared an adjoining suite with Gardenia Hayle. Besim supported Mina with his dwindling inheritance, while Gardenia supported Besim with her inexhaustible alimony, having been promised she would be repaid with the honorific of Lady Beresford. Unfortunately, for Gardenia, neither Besim nor Mina ever discussed divorce, which seemed a bothersome technicality since neither had any immediate desire to marry someone else.

As for Andrew, Mina helped him find a small, furnished villa situated atop a hill just outside of Siena and graced by a magnificent tulip poplar. She spent the month of August (when all of Firenze was transformed into a shuttered ghost town) securely settling Andrew into what would be his last home. It also would be the last August of their romance, just as Mina intended, offering Andrew whatever remaining surplus of tenderness she had left to give him before finally, truly, moving forward into a different love, located somewhere on the unseen horizon of her future, but nevertheless there, waiting for her. She did not explain this to Andrew, nor did she think it necessary to draw for him a map delineating the boundaries between what was now possible and impossible between them, all of which she had clearly staked out in her own mind in an effort to reclaim herself, foolishly believing Andrew implicitly understood since he was no longer the old Andrew.

The new Andrew made no attempts to possess Mina, patiently waiting for her to come back to him according to her own terms. Because where else did he have to go; what else could he do? She brought him books to read, and food for her to cook, and slept beside him on those nights she stayed, which were most of those nights during that last imperfect August, both of them naked, but only because of the oppressive heat; they'd discovered he was incapable of responding to Mina's, or perhaps any woman's, body ever again. Something from the surgery had left him impotent, and Andrew began to cling to the belief that this was how their lives would always be, until the day he died, because he did not think he could live otherwise, not alone with the emptied shell of himself, with his lobotomized loss of language, lust, and lunacy, all that had once answered for him who he was, with or without Mina; so it had to be with Mina, or nothing else, because she more than anyone might help him recover a small fragment of the man he'd once been, because it must have been much more than what he was now. Mina never suspected that the new Andrew was not so different from the old, still depending on her presence, or else she might have gone about things very differently.

On her last visit to the villa, she brought with her a phonograph recording of Puccini's *Gianni Schicchi*. Andrew had requested something to listen to on those nights when Mina wasn't there and he couldn't sleep. Mina didn't think Andrew needed anything tragic; thus her choice. They sat outside in the cooling evening air, beneath the tulip poplar, listening to the music drifting out to them from the house. When Lauretta sang her aria, Andrew, so very much like his old impulsive self, took Mina in his arms and waltzed her across the sloping lawn. Mina shut her eyes, pressing her mouth into Andrew's neck, huskily humming along to the words, and ignored Lauretta's plea to her father: *e se l'amassi indarno, andrei sul Ponte Vecchio, ma per buttarmi in Arno! Mi struggo e mi tormento! O Dio, vorrei morir!* When Andrew asked her why she was crying, Mina lied and told him it was because she was happy; she could not imagine being any happier anywhere else at any other time.

Andrew woke the next morning to find a photograph propped against the lamp on the bedside table; a small black and white image of a small pre-pubescent Mina leaning against a tangle of honeysuckle vines, wisps of black hair framing her diminutive face and her black eyes staring directly back at him, complacently challenging his gaze, as if she knew all those years ago when she was a child that he was here, in this now of her palpable absence. Andrew turned the photograph over, and there, in her looping feminine script, a column of words forming what almost appeared to be the wings of a moth or some other fluttering appendage:

> **Before knowing your existence**
> **Your existence was known.**
> **I was yours even then.**
> **Even then I was yours.**
> **Yours was I then even.**
> **Then even yours was I.**
> **Known was existence your**
> **Existence your knowing before.**

Yes, Andrew had known before even reading this clumsy palindrome that Mina was gone and would not be coming back. She would fade from his diminished life and eventually vanish from his memory, just as he'd wanted all those years in Bellevue, before the operation that disconnected his synapses, severing him from any remaining semblance to his former self. Now, having realized the doctors had botched the surgery, regardless if they'd assured his parents it was a complete success (hadn't their son's erratic moods been entirely eradicated?), and having realized his failure to capture Mina once and for all, Andrew decided it was better to remember the Mina who seduced rather than abandoned him. He walked into the village, ordered a case of Chianti, and after three days of drinking while belaboring over the composition of his letter to Mina, which required him to trawl his memory for the exact words and appropriate tone of injured sentiment, Andrew walked out of the house and stood beneath the tulip poplar, where he had known his last moments of happiness.

CHAPTER TEN
The Judas Tree

He discovered his son suspended from the tulip poplar, and he would never comprehend why anyone had been so foolish to plant this tree in the Tuscan countryside. It did not belong here. Just as his son, he thought, was an inappropriate extension of the tree. He sniffled indignantly, staring at his child, trapped in some strange phenomenon and rebelliously floating in midair, impervious to the authority of gravity. The world Vasili came from did not permit his son to dangle like that from the bowed limbs of tulip poplars. With an abrupt shudder, Vasili began to place in categorical order the natural environment of this very unnatural universe. Applying names to unknown specimens of human experience made them far more conceivable, and so he confronted the tulip poplar, because it was the most troubling part of this scene.

Yes, the *Liriodendron tulipifera*, of the family *Magnoliaceae*, a deciduous, lovely blooming tree, native to the eastern United States, with yellow-rimmed leaves and golden green flowers: three sepals, six petals, numerous stamens, many pistils, and a cone-shaped cluster of samaras. Such a beautiful word, *samara*, which translated into winged seed. There were other names, many things had many names, and the tulip poplar was no exception, sometimes called whitewood, or yellow poplar, with extended relations to the mountain mahoe, the banana shrub, and the portia tree. Portia was a wise young woman remembered for reminding one that the quality of mercy droppeth as gentle rain from heaven and it is twice blest and angels and ministers of grace defend us, we do pray for mercy; though we have not bothered with prayer in many years, let our prayer now take wings . . .

Perhaps his son had hoped for wings. He had always flitted about in frantic leaps of nervous energy, irritating Vasili to no end with his incessant tics and awkward, misplaced gestures. The boy now wore a mottled, distended expression that did not belong on any living creature. Vasili felt the usual urge to repudiate all connection to his child, but then could not decide who this unfortunate boy might be if it weren't his son, Andrew, taxonomically identified as *Andrej*, belonging to the genus *Vasilievich*, and of the family *Novikov*, though he also had connections to the *Brennan* family tree, and was recognized by the general public under this classification ever since he'd absurdly repudiated his patronymic. Vasili decided none of that mattered now, relinquishing all nurtured resentments, all of which swiftly dissolved in the indescribable pain of his loss. He now lived in a world where the species *Andrej Vasilievich Novikov* had become extinct, and there was no reversal or remedy for this evolutionary failure, no flights of angels that might sing his child to rest. There was no escaping this, not even when Vasili was offered, as some merciful serendipitous sign, the brief distraction of a rare Camberwell Beauty who had chosen this precise moment to flutter her seraphic wings in his tear-blotched face; it was said the *seraphs* had tongues of flame, and so they had been given this name; but there were no words or sense for any of this. He allowed the *Nymphalis antiopa*, with her blood black blue spotted limned in yellow wings, to waft away on the breeze, and turned his back on the boy because he was required to make the necessary calls that might bring help, regardless if there was no hope. All hope was hanged.

He thought perhaps he would also ask them to cut down that offensive tree, but sensed this would be yet another betrayal of his child. When he'd received Andrew's letter three weeks ago, his last communication with his parents, in which the boy had informed them of his decision to purchase the villa, and claiming his only reason for doing so was precisely because of the tulip poplar, Vasili had been irritated by Andrew's detailed description of the tree's massive trunk and trillions of twigs, stealing a phrase Vasili had once used to depict a tree in one of his old novels.

He had no idea why Andrew had chosen to live in Siena, since Vasili had not known until two days ago that Mina lived in Florence. After nearly a week of failing to get through to Andrew on the telephone, Deirdre had finally confessed to the whole business of that letter of three years ago, the letter from Mina to which Vasili had never responded because Deirdre had never given it to him. For some reason, though, she'd held onto it, and Vasili could not understand why she had shown it to Andrew, or why she'd kept so much to herself, so much that might have been avoided if he'd only known what she had known.

In her defense, Deirdre had argued that knowing him, her husband, as she did, she was sure it never would have made any difference; and while they'd spent an entire morning heatedly disputing the past, squabbling over all the trouble that had ensued because of that woman and Andrew's obsession with her and Vasili's meddling in their affair, which had turned into his own obsession; and even as they bickered about who was to blame if Andrew had found Mina again and all of his old madness returned; and as the morning blurred into an afternoon of questioning whether they were simply overreacting, assuring each other they'd done as much as they could for Andrew; and in the several hours it took to settle upon what should be done next, conceding to agree there really was no need to fret like this over him, based on the evidence of the year he'd lived with them since his operation, during which he'd never shown any signs of regressing; and upon deciding that evening, just to relieve themselves of any lingering worries, that Vasili would take the next train to Florence and then a cab to Siena and drop in on Andrew for a visit, just to see how he was settling in, and if there was anything he might need; yes, while they'd been doing all of this, deliberating and dithering, Andrew had been drinking himself into despair before swinging a rope over one of the lower sturdier branches of the tulip poplar, climbing up into the tree, fashioning a noose around his neck, leaping, and hanging himself there as an accusation of all the ways in which Vasili had betrayed his son, because he had never wanted to know who he was, and had traded him in to the Bellevue quacks in exchange for his own small reprieve of having to face his failures as a father.

Vasili found the back door unlocked and the phone where it had been left off the hook. He dialed the operator, requested *la polizia*, and when finally connected, struggled through his shoddy but serviceable Italian until the situation was adequately explained, leaving him afterwards with nothing to do but wait. So he sat and waited in a ratty armchair observing his son's shabbily furnished home: its rustic artifacts, its cluttered miscellany, its hot, stifling air still crowded with the peculiar odors belonging to Andrew. Vasili could not look out the window, or pick up the phone once more, as it waited ominously for him to make that one call he should never have been forced to make. So he simply sat there remembering a morning forty-one years ago when Deirdre had woken up in his arms, her face suffused with a blissful, sleepy glow, and had informed him they were going to have a child, their first child. That was as much as he allowed himself, because now, to imagine Andrew born meant having to proceed inevitably to the end of the narrative, when before it had always remained open, unfinished, a work in progress. Vasili, in that moment, did not think he would ever be able to write again.

When he heard the sound of a motor approaching, stalling, and then shutting itself off, he lumbered out of the chair and did as much as was expected of him, since the only useful thing he could do was explain to a group of strangers how he'd found his son hanging from the tulip poplar. They did not need an explanation for why Vasili was there, only how long it had been since he'd spoken to his son and if you please, *signore*, what was his state of mind? When Vasili said he'd never known the answer to this question, they left it at that; they did not care why his son had died, only how. With a surprising efficiency, they brought Andrew down from the tree, inspected his body, surveyed the environs for foul play, and upon discovering none, categorized the incident as self-inflicted. Then they allowed the coroner to take his body away. It was not until after he'd answered all their remaining questions and signed their papers, after they'd proffered their morose condolences, and after they had finally vanished, leaving him alone once more, when Vasili realized inexorably, insuffer-ably, that his darling, inane, bewildering son had also vanished and would never manage the trick of reappearing again.

He stood holding a thin sheaf of paper in his hand, and a black and white photograph of a young girl. These items had been discovered in the left breast pocket of Andrew's cambric polo shirt, one of those silly, passé, unflattering shirts he'd always insisted on wearing long after he'd outgrown his schoolboy days. The *inspectore* had declared the piece of paper was Andrew's *suicidio nota*, but that he did not know the meaning of the photograph, and because neither of these things seemed to hold any great significance, had left them with Vasili. When he finally glanced down at the note, reading it in one swift swoop of the eye, Vasili burst into a strangled laugh as he read the poorly transcribed poem, which, to anyone not familiar with it, would appear to be a long rambling sentence written by a character out of a Jacobean revenge tragedy:

When by thy scorn, I am dead, and even though you think yourself free, then my ghost shall come to your bed, and you, false whore, in worse arms shall see your sick taper begin to wink, and he, whose bed you lie in then, being tired, will, if you stir, or pinch to wake him, think you call out for more, and in false sleep will wither and shrink, and then, poor aspen wretch, neglected sow, bathed in a cold silver sweat you shall die, more a ghost than I; what I will say then, I will not tell you now, should that preserve you; and since my love is spent, I'd rather you repent, than by my threatening allow you to sleep still innocent.

It was much too much, more than he should have to bear. He should have torn it into a thousand pieces. Instead, he'd methodically refolded the slip of paper and placed it inside his own breast pocket, and now resigned himself to studying the image of a girl he'd never known but immediately recognized. It was all just as he and Deirdre had feared. Mina was here; Andrew had found her; Andrew had died because of her. No, that did not sound right. Mina was far too sensible a girl to have let something like that happen. She would never have encouraged Andrew's delusions; she had never done so in the past, so why would she now; but what did he know, really, about their past? He hadn't known about the child. Deirdre had known. She'd known Mina was pregnant, and had never said anything about it to him, had never even made the effort of finding out what had happened to the child. But it seemed clear by her letter that it had died, Deirdre had explained, finally allowing him to pore over the letter with his own eyes; yes, Vasili agreed, why would one need to imagine the existence of a child unless that child had never existed in the first place? Vasili could only imagine what that apparent loss might have done to Mina; no, he could more than imagine, because within the space of two days he'd learned that both his grandchild and child were dead. It was not the first time he'd seen this image of Mina as a small girl, but holding it again, he indulged the belief that it provided some small hint of what Mina's and Andrew's child might have looked like. Had Mina given his son this photograph so that he would have the comfort of imagining the same? Vasili's heart throbbed with tenderness and grief; then he turned the photograph over, saw what was written there, and felt capable of murdering the woman who had abandoned his poor, fragile boy with nothing more than this glib, shallow, and incomprehensibly cruel bit of cowardice.

Vasili knew Mina well enough to suspect she'd left his son without honestly, bravely explaining her reasons for doing so; he knew this because Mina had abandoned Vasili in much the same manner when she'd left California without warning, without any indication of where she'd gone or if she'd ever return, leaving behind a print of this same photograph, which Vasili had burnt to cinder in a hotel ashtray after discovering it waiting for him in an empty room where the flesh and blood Mina had failed to appear; so yes, he could imagine precisely the devastation of Mina's departure. As he turned over in his mind all that he now knew, sifting through the wreckage of all that had been lost, Vasili allowed the first shivering spasm of inspiration for his next novel to transform his grief into something more manageable, and for this he knew he could never be forgiven (and I know this because I've read that novel he would eventually write; I have read all of his novels and am confident of presenting Vasili's thoughts in a manner closely reflecting his state of mind).

Vasili stored the photograph safely out of sight, lifted the receiver of the phone, and while instructing the operator to connect him to a residence in Lausanne, did his best to ignore the sudden realization that someone would soon have to terminate its connection, box up his son's paltry possessions, and resell the house. The line rang for an interminable length of time, and when it was answered, the woman's voice came through breathless, ragged, and short. She must have been pottering about in the garden, enjoying a day miraculously left free to do whatever she pleased without anyone (that is, Vasili) intruding upon her privacy. He could see her peeling the canvas gloves from her arthritic yet still elegant fingers, brushing aside a silver strand of hair, and pursing her lips at the distraction of a phone that would not desist from ringing until she obliged herself to answer it.

"Hello?"

"Deirdre."

He could not say anything except her name. She'd loved that first foolish boy for so much longer and perhaps so much more than the other two foolish boys who'd followed him. Surely the quaver in his voice would be enough to tell her what he did not want to say aloud.

"Vasili, where are you?"

"*Andrej*," he replied, savoring the sound, because soon this would be a name neither he nor his wife would allow themselves to utter ever again.

"May I speak with him?" she asked, ignoring her suspicion that this was and always would be a futile request.

"No," he told her.

"Why?" she persisted, and then demanded, "How?"

"The tulip poplar, the one he'd gone on about in his last letter. He loved that tree."

And with that final verb presented to her in its conjugation of past simple, she could no longer continue denying the very complex fact it revealed about the present location of her son. The response she offered Vasili was not the expected wail of maternal grief, but something far worse: the injured whimper of a small helpless animal that has no sufficient language to describe the wound that has been inflicted on her.

"Deirdre," he whispered, after an unbearable stretch of time. "Please."

"No, Vasili, we will not discuss this. It is not possible."

"You will be here tomorrow."

"Yes, of course, I will take the first train. And you?"

"I must return to Florence."

"Oh, yes, I see."

"Deirdre, she should be told."

"You're absolutely certain he was seeing her again?"

"It seems likely, yes."

"But you're not entirely certain?"

"I'm certain, but would it truly matter? At the least, I should be the one to tell her."

"Yes, I see."

"No, you do not see."

Then he heard an abrupt click and the static emptiness of the line deliberately cut off. When he returned to Florence, somehow he was standing before his dead son's lover (he'd had the improbable luck to arrive at 54 San Giorgio just as Mina's former landlady was showing the villa to its new tenants and had been directed to No. 10 Santo Spirito), and when Mina offered him the same flicker of horrified recognition with which she'd greeted Andrew when he'd appeared unexpectedly at her door, Vasili lost all memory of why he was there. He was not sure he could explain it to himself much less Mina.

"Vasili!" she gasped. "Have you been to see Andrew? Is everything all right? Did you argue? Well, I refuse to get involved, not again, Vasili."

"No, Mina, there's no need," he cut off her nervous, prattling chatter, shoving a piece of paper and a photograph into her hands, and brutally, cruelly informing her, "Andrew hung himself on the tulip poplar."

She stared in bemused horror at the portrait of her childhood self. Scanning the contents of Andrew's suicide note, she recognized immediately its plagiarized sentiments. She lifted her eyes once more to acknowledge Vasili, murmuring idiotically, "The tulip poplar, such a lovely, impossible name for a tree."

"Perhaps you should write a poem about it. One of your monstrously clever, cold little poems. I'm sure my son's death is worth at least that much to you."

"Please, leave," she rasped out. "I do not ever want to see you again."

Because these were the words he'd needed to hear, the ones his wife had denied him, he walked away, refusing to remember, even when trying to recapture Mina in one of his books, the abyss of her black eyes, reflecting nothing of himself back to him; and, when he faltered at the door, turning briefly, he was certain to repress the sound of her infinitely anguished scream of rage, chasing him down the stairs into the dazzling glare of the sun as it mercilessly beat down upon the Piazza Santo Spirito.

"All happy families are alike; each unhappy family is unhappy in its own way."

—Some Russian Author at the Start of a Famous Novel

An old man sits in his garden surrounded by his sons; his wife stands at her kitchen window observing each of them seated in their various poses. Vasili shifts in his chair, seeking a distraction, imagining a hoard of butterflies hiding in the honeysuckle vines. Jamie sips his tea, left leg slung over right knee, spine upright in the posture of a pedant who has never done a day's hard labor in his life. Andrew is slumped in a hunch of shoulders caved inward over the pot-bellied flaccid folds of flesh he acquired during his three years at Bellevue, which everyone refuses to acknowledge. Colin fidgets, sprawled in his chair, grinning carelessly, impatiently at nothing and no one, because it is all so absurd, this impromptu gathering of people who long ago stopped wanting anything to do with each other. All of them simmer insufferably in the late autumn haze of an afternoon that appears as if it will never end, because none of them know why they are there, other than that Deirdre has demanded it of them.

Vasili believes it is due to one of her post-menopausal, old woman's whims. He thinks it is because of Andrew; now that they have brought him home she wants a glimpse of her boys gathered together for one final family photograph to be pasted in an album no one will ever see. He'd informed her it was a silly sentiment, because she could not, by force of her desire, negate the intrusion of the past onto their present; Vasili, in his typical, arrogantly obtuse fashion, is wrong. She notes the smug smile of mistaken comprehension, the glaze veiling his eyes whenever he removes himself from his present misery to go meandering through his private terrain of remembered, thus never lost, happiness. He is thinking, even now, of Mina; even now he believes Mina remains his preciously hoarded secret.

Deirdre has tired of Vasili's treasured tokens of nostalgia, to which he clings like an overgrown child who refuses his favorite playthings to be taken away. Even after excising Mina from his life, after convincing him to retire to Lausanne, where he need do nothing but write, where finally, without the imposition of looking after their sons, without the stress of poverty and the need to teach for a living, without the intrusions of students, fans, agents, publishers, without any further distractions, still he nourished his obsessions. She knows, as she always does, because she types out all his facsimiles, that for him time and distance are meaningless; he keeps every one of his ghosts alive, even when they are better off left forgotten. Even now he is planning his new novel, and Mina will be buried in every page. He can't help himself, especially now that Andrew is here, a reminder of the woman neither of them ever truly possessed.

So, yet again, in the interest of preserving her marriage, Deirdre has decided she has no other choice. She has already shown Andrew the letter, certain it will set him off on some foolish quest to recover Mina; and if that's what it takes to regain the veneer of happy solitude she and Vasili had managed to establish between them, then why insist on Colin and Jamie coming to visit? Because she knows, by some instinctive maternal twinge, which she long ago learned to suppress, that this is her last opportunity to play out the fantasy of a family that never existed, yes, her last remaining chance to see all of her children assembled together again.

She ignores the lump in her throat, the maudlin welling of tears, because Andrew suddenly lifts his head, sensing the weight of his mother's gaze boring through the glass of the window and latching onto his haggard profile. Complicit in the secret of the letter, he smiles the same sweet, foolish grin he would offer her as a child whenever he'd done something naughty and Deirdre promised she wouldn't tell his father; they'd keep it a secret just between them. Deirdre is paralyzed; she senses that she has committed some unforgiveable, unnamable crime, and not only against Andrew but each of her children. Suddenly she desires their departure; all of them, Colin, Jamie, Andrew, even Vasili; each of them have conspired in their overwhelming presence to remind her of all her failures, an intolerable reminder, on this day of all days.

Today is her birthday, which they have never once celebrated, because Deirdre has never permitted the slightest gesture of candle-lit cupcake or crayoned card. Sixty-two years ago, on her seventh birthday, her mother had unexpectedly died, an anniversary that until his own unanticipated death her father had never allowed her to forget, and so she has always nurtured the dull pang of her motherless guilt and subsequent lack of affection when confronted by any of her children. Contrary to all appearances, she is passionately in love with each of her sons; it is a love that is immeasurable, unbearable, threatening to dissolve all boundaries between her needs and each of their exclusively infinite demands. She attempts, as she has always done, to decide which of them she loves best in case she is ever asked to choose one over the other two. It is a futile thought experiment, because she cannot imagine a reality in which any of them did not exist; even to recall their absence from the world, the one she'd known before their births and childhoods, shatters her sense of time and space, threatening to cleft her body into a thousand inconsolable fragments. The imagined pain of losing any of her children is much too much.

Deirdre turns away from the window, vanishing into the dim corners of the house, where she will live out the rest of her life trapped in a permanent state of expiation for all the selfish and surreptitious choices she has made, always at the cost of abandoning her sons to their own fates.

Ten years after the last time he saw either of his brothers, Jamie Brennan sat alone in a first-class compartment on the journey from Paris to Lausanne. He contemplated the countryside revealed to him like a film played out in reverse motion across the transparent, though slightly smudged, screen of glass. Eventually, he could no longer ignore the reflection of his face imprinted onto the rolling scenery passing by, the optical illusion presenting a seeming paradox, as if he were simultaneously present in two spatial and temporal realms. He recalled, with some irritation, that his father had once observed in one of his novels, though Jamie could not isolate in his memory the exact novel, this very same experience of uncanny, involuntary doubling.

He retrieved a black and white photograph from his left breast pocket, studying the small girl's sullen, suspicious scowl, her eyes coldly, contemptuously challenging whoever stood behind the camera. One look into her eyes and Jamie had known she was the revenant of that lost child repeatedly evoked in nearly all of his father's books. Upon receiving the photograph from Mina, who'd shown up unexpectedly on his doorstep, Jamie had pulled down each of his father's novels and methodically searched the relevant passages, glancing occasionally, anxiously at Mina as she slept on his sofa for the better part of two days. When she finally decided to speak with him, he'd summoned the nerve to present his theory. She'd laughed, misunderstanding, and remarked, but your father actually never knew me as a child. No, of course, he couldn't have, Jamie had conceded, but the photograph still lay between them as evidence, as a reminder.

Jamie now willed himself into a doze, refusing to dream, declining to wake until the train pulled into the station. There would not be anyone waiting for him at the platform. No one was expecting him. He hired a taxi to drive him to his parent's villa, and because he had not brought any luggage, having purchased a return ticket for that evening, he had nothing to set down by the front door to announce his arrival. A meaningless gesture, since Deirdre now depended on a hearing device, which she rarely deigned to attach to her ear. Vasili would be sitting beneath the broad shade of the tulip poplar, which he had uprooted, transported and transplanted from the property in Siena to the garden in Lausanne—a morbid memento for Deirdre, yet Vasili seemed to take comfort from the tree, sitting out there most afternoons counting all the real and imagined butterflies floating above his head, until Deirdre forced him to retire for the evening.

Deirdre, as usual, was found sitting at the kitchen table sorting through the neverending pile of unsolicited manuscripts, bills, and correspondence from the outside world. Jamie gave her bony shoulder a gentle squeeze and sat down across from her; she absently murmured hello while perusing the letter in her hand, making him wait until she decided to slip her spectacles from her dignified nose and directly acknowledge his presence.

"You should have told us you were coming."

"It's only for the afternoon."

"Your father will be disappointed."

"How is he?"

"Why don't you go say hello? I'm sure you have very important matters to discuss."

"Actually, there's something I need to tell both of you."

"Oh?" she lifted one thinly drawn brow into an arch, an incomplete question mark, as if she simply had to wait and sooner or later the information would be revealed to her without expending the energy of acquiring it.

"I'm going to be married," Jamie blurted, knowing it was the only way.

"You are too old for marriage," she coolly reasoned. "Really, Jamie, you are nearly forty-years-old. Can you imagine what our lives might have been like if I'd married your father when he was that age? It would have been quite impossible!"

For once, Jamie refused his mother the opportunity to distill the unknown complexities of his life into a convenient analogy that mirrored Vasili's stubborn peculiarities. "I appreciate your concern, mama, but it's already decided. I only wanted to tell you in person."

"Oh, dear, how considerate of you. Does this mystery woman have a name?"

Jamie inwardly cringed. He had no choice. "Mina Byrne."

Deirdre did not erupt into a tempest of fury; she simply slipped on her familiar, glacial mask, though Jamie detected the faint trace of appalled outrage in her eyes.

"You're aware of what this will do to your father," she stated.

"It won't destroy him. Nothing, no matter how awful, is capable of destroying him."

"So you'd like to make a go of it yourself. Just like your brothers. My God, you know *nothing*, Jamie, nothing at all, because if you did—."

"I know everything, mama. I know what happened, the night Colin was born, and that was long before Mina ever came into the picture."

"Go talk to your father," she dismissed him, resetting her spectacles on the perch of her nose. "When you're finished, you may leave by the garden gate. I'll call you a taxi."

Jamie rose, hoping this would not be the last time he saw her. His father, also, did not immediately acknowledge him, remaining pointedly immersed in the book he held in his lap. Jamie sat and observed his gnarled, spidery blue-veined hands, their joints protruding in a deformed, arthritic contortion, like the hands of an ogre in a fairy tale, though Jamie could only see their frailty, or at least their imagined frailty. Vasili eventually glanced up at his son, scowled, replaced the bookmark in the slim volume, slammed shut its spine with considerable force, and then lifted the book in the air, shaking it gleefully beneath Jamie's nose.

"It just arrived by post, first printing, hot and steaming! This one will throw them all off the scent. Once again, I've slipped a wrench in their clumsily cogitating brains!" he laughed inanely, to which Jamie could only reply, "That good?"

"Oh no, my boy, it is far from good!" Vasili exhorted. "It is the most ingenious disappearing act man has ever devised for himself. The great Houdini would grovel in envy and shame! A fatal sucker-punch if there ever was one! Have you read it?"

"Yes, papa, of course I have."

Jamie had, in fact, not read it. When he'd received the galleys, he'd handed them over to Mina, allowing her to translate Vasili's convoluted sense of humor. Apparently, in this latest of the great Novikov's books, Novikov had cleverly concealed himself behind the mask of Novikov, and this achieved, just as Mina had remarked, a sinuously spiraling, self-referring, if not self-parodying, ever-receding hall of mirrors. Jamie, however, had not come here to discuss the enigma of his father's slippery intellect.

"Papa, there's something I must tell you . . ."

"What, you thought it was too daring, too arrogant of me—."

"No, papa," Jamie interrupted. "I'm getting married, to Mina Byrne."

When Vasili comprehended his son's words, he shriveled and slumped into a very old, very frail man. Somehow, Jamie discovered the courage to hand over the photograph of a young girl who'd eluded Vasili's knowledge, which might have consoled him in his old age. Vasili accepted the unexpected gift, smiling in inconsolable, though mistaken recognition. For what seemed like lifetimes, they listened to the insistent clicking of the cicadas, and the faintly imperceptible fluttering of a butterfly's translucent, filmy and iridescent wings.

"Why her?" the old man finally asked.

Upon hearing his son's stumbling explanation, the trajectory of Vasili Vasilievich Novikov's life reached the precise point where every pattern wove itself into a fabric of the most sublime, the most perceptibly cruel, yet the only possible recovery of all that had been lost.

"I never knew," he mumbled, concealing his face with those large, bulbous, twisted hands.

Jamie rose, turned, and walked away, because he could not bear to see the image of his father weeping. He left the garden gate unlatched, knowing Deirdre observed his departure from behind the safety of her kitchen window. After Jamie vanished, swallowed up by a future she refused to consider, she stepped out into the garden and firmly shut closed and barred the gate.

Twenty years before the last time she saw her last remaining son, Deirdre dreamed she was driving a limousine, her children in the back seat, her husband nowhere to be seen. The road ahead stretched flat, straight, directly perpendicular to the unchanging horizon, beyond which, she knew, the world vanished; she and her children would plummet over the earth's edge and all would be forgotten; all would instantaneously vanish in their long descent into the cavernous, gaping maw of an abyss without end, without sorrow or regret for what might never be explained, excused, or forgiven. As soon as she accepted the inevitability of this, Deirdre was no longer driving but seated in the rear compartment of the car, with her children, barred by the black opaque tint of a glass divider from seeing who was now at the wheel. It didn't matter; nothing mattered except her children.

Colin nestled in her lap, his sticky fingers entwined in her hair, gurgling gleefully as he pulled at her unruly black curls, the same glossy raven's hair all the boys had inherited from her. Andrew sat curled against the curve of her left breast, telling her all about the monsters inhabiting his night-mares, poking his brother's portly baby belly with his insistently envious fist, which only made Colin laugh and kick his feet. Jamie, on the opposite seat, held a porcelain teacup balanced on his knee, spouting verbatim, in the clipped consonants and rotund vowels of the radio BBC English of her childhood, the memory of some weather forecast portending storms at sea and sunny skies in Strabane. Deirdre ignored their competing voices, her eyes clinging to the sympathetic smile of the girl sitting beside Jamie, returning Deirdre's gaze with infinite wisdom and forgiveness. Barbara. She'd promised Vasili that if they ever had a daughter he could name her, but she would have called her Barbara; for her mother. My god, she looks just like my mother . . . then Deirdre woke, clammily feverish, and with Vasili holding her hand. They were still in the hospital, though Deirdre struggled to recall why, what for, when.

She tried to smile, to offer Vasili the reassurance that all would be well, all would be as it once was before, but every benign and malignant cell of her body resisted her command to do as she wished. She closed her eyes, because she'd wanted to ask if the operation had been a success, but could tell by Vasili's grim smile that nothing would ever again qualify as a complete success, that there would never be a full recovery, even if she outlived him and their children. The cancer had been cut out, along with the removal of her lump-laden, formerly milk-giving breasts. They had so looked forward, in secret glances and naughty chuckles, to the day when Colin graduated high school and left home, leaving them finally the freedom to romp as noisily and lasciviously as they liked, just as they had thirty years ago before Andrew's arrival. A fool's fantasy if there'd ever been one; she fifty-nine and he fifty-five, too old and eroded in their desires, but never their devotion—that, at least, might be spared. When she opened her eyes, she saw in his eyes both her fears and certainties confirmed. He would never leave her; he could not live without her, but he would never look at her or touch her in the way he once had. Fine, she could live with that.

Then Mina disrupted all her preciously preserved illusions, forced her to confront all that she'd lost, and Deirdre could not live with that. Love will compel any of us to do that which is beyond reason or sense. I can only imagine this is why Deirdre committed so many small, silent sins and sacrifices, desperate to defend her claim on the one person she believed rightfully belonged to her, because she had relinquished everything for him, even her children.

"Piece by piece the fragments are returned; the body, the work, the love, the life. What can be known about me? What I say? What I do? What I have written? And which is true? That is, which is truer? Memory. My licensed inventions. Not all of the fragments return."

—Jeanette Winterson, *Art & Lies*

CHAPTER ELEVEN
The Prodigal Returns

". . . and what do we win when we become exiled from the past, from all signposts that have formed us, from all that is tangible in our memories? What do we lose when compelled to return to these boundaries and circumlocutions of the self? We perhaps win an inestimable, terrifying, freedom that releases us from those loyalties that once constrained us. We certainly lose, upon return, the illusion of such sublime freedom, because paradise never existed, was not ours to claim. Instead, *we* are claimed, conquered and beholden to a history that by its inexorable will does not permit us that freedom we so fervently believed was our inalienable right. The contexts of this history, its temporal and spatial continuums, are not conceptually useful; at least not to our comprehension of a life and the ways in which it has attempted to imagine its own existence. Imagination is entangled and imbued with memory; and memory is not at all the same as history. How foolish of you to expect as much!"

Mina was jolted awake by the man's exclamatory inflection disrupting his own monotonous drone. She turned her head slightly to study the ghost of her father, whom she imagined, if he were sitting here beside her, might have gazed at the speaker with rapt attention, as if they were in intimate communion with each other. As for the man occupying the seat where her father should have been, he was snoring softly, a dribbling of drool salivating from the corner of his mouth. She'd found him hunched on the corner of Infirmary and Nicholson Streets, and in spite of the balmy breeze, swaddled and shivering in layers of rags. Mina had offered him the spare ticket her father had left behind and an invitation to accompany her to the lecture, where he'd receive an hour's reprieve from the chill with which he seemed interminably inflicted.

The bum eyed her warily, fingering the ticket in his arthritic hands before insisting with a rheumy wink, "They'll nae let the likes o' me in wi' ye, lass, but thankin' ye for the kindness."

"Nonsense," Mina had curtly replied. "The ticket is paid for and I may bring anyone I damn well please. They'll not say a word, not to the likes of me. So come along."

And so he'd followed her, chortling in anticipated pleasure of the promised warmth, and when they submitted their tickets, no one said a word, but Mina, conceding to the refined senses of her fellow audience members, took chairs in the rear, which considerably minimized the intrusion of the one person present who clearly had no right to be there. Before the lecturer had even been introduced, before he'd stepped up to the podium, cursorily skimmed his papers, cleared his throat and began speaking, Mina's grubby companion had hunkered down in his chair, arms crossed, chin lowered, and promptly fell asleep, forcing Mina to acknowledge that she never should have come.

It was a sentimental gesture, and one she was sure made no difference to the dead. Her father had purchased the tickets several months ago, failing to anticipate that neither he nor his daughter would have much use for them. When he'd shown them to Mina, he'd insisted it would give them both the opportunity to enjoy some time together, alone, and beyond Maggie's oppressive, ever-present purview. Mina had glanced down at the tickets, noted the name of the lecturer and the title of his paper, and was about to invent some implausible excuse for why she would not be able to go, but then saw the desperate, pleading expression on her father's face. She'd smiled, thanked him, and generously lied that it was a wonderful idea and she would look forward to attending.

The tickets had been all but forgotten until this morning, when Mina finally entered her father's study to sort through the items of his desk. She'd found them inserted into his diary, marking the date of July 16. Adam Byrne had purchased the tickets on April 11, collapsed on his way to bed on the evening of April 23, was informed the following morning by Dr. Caldwell that his heart would not last him another week, lay in his bed waiting to die throughout all of May and June, and on July 9, got out of bed, sat at his desk, was put back to bed, and upon giving his daughter his final words, stopped breathing.

Now, Mina was sitting beside a particularly smelly but harmless stranger, and because she'd never intended to be here, she occupied herself by studying the plaster and marble busts of long dead literary, scientific, and mercantile worthies, set on plinths lined up between the spaces of broad fluted columns extending down the narrow rectangular length of the room and up to the barrel-vaulted, arched and coffered ceiling of Library Hall, Old College, where Dr. James Brennan delivered his densely incomprehensible paper. Bored, and fearing what she might do if she stayed until the end, suspecting the only reason she'd decided to come was to introduce herself to Andrew's brother, as if that might diminish rather than heighten her grief, Mina got up and left, abandoning the old man she'd brought in with her, confident he or someone else would see that he found his way back to the street.

Emerging onto the south side of the quad's courtyard, Mina gulped in air and sunlight. The afternoon was too lovely to waste sitting indoors listening to some stupefyingly dull lecture, and knowing there would be another one waiting for her back at the flat, Mina chose to turn south down Nicholson in the opposite direction of her father's empty study and Maggie's obstinate glare, mutely chastising Mina's laziness, her lack of tears, her indecisions, her very existence. Mina eventually turned left onto Montague then took St Leonard's Lane all the way to its end, cutting through the trees and into Holyrood Park. She continued in a south-easterly direction, up the sloping incline of the Queen's Drive until she reached the steep west-face ascent of Arthur's Seat, which she had no desire to climb. Instead, she took the scrubby, generally horizontal path through Hunter's Bog. Here, between the Crags and Dasses, removed from the drab gray and smoke-stained slate of the city, enclosed on both sides by the verdant isolation of a wild highland landscape, Mina felt she could finally confront the loneliness welling up within her, ever since Andrew's death and her sudden departure from Italy, running away from Besim, from herself, from her inability to live independently, having squandered any faith she'd once had in her desire or capacity to do so.

What she'd done was unforgiveable: she'd abandoned Andrew; rejected whatever small happiness they might have shared between them, for as long as they lived; refused to become trapped in some distorted, domesticated fairy tale ever after. What was wrong with wanting the fairy tale? Isn't that what all women wanted? Mina had no idea what other women wanted; she only knew what she wanted, which was to be excepted from the norm. She'd been a fool; she'd gone about things horribly. Besim had said as much when she'd gone to him after Andrew's death, relying on his indulgent dismissal of all her flaws. No, she would not begin missing Besim, of all people, who should have offered her—what? What could he have offered other than the money needed to send her packing back to Britain?

Mina had refused any other option, insisting she could not stay in Italy another day, that she would never return (and she never did). She could not resume the pretense of marital relations with Besim, who had shot down that possibility when Mina proposed they leave Italy together and take up residence in the Belfast townhouse now that old Bess had died; it was just sitting there, empty and shrouded in white sheets. Besim insisted the house could rot for all he cared; he would never step foot in Ireland again (and he never did), and he would not agree to leave behind Gardenia Hayle (as Mina insisted), with whom he was quite happily settled; or, he was settled on learning how to be happy with a woman whom he knew would never be as infuriatingly, incomprehensibly desirable as his wife. Besim wanted Mina to go back to Paris, where he and Mrs. Hayle would soon be relocating, but Mina could not possibly face her aunt, not now, not after so many years of neglecting to visit, and Mina felt too ashamed to ask anything of Rosalie when she had nothing to show for herself; because Mina had failed to prove she was worthy of all those high expectations, and considerable financial assistance, Rosalie had invested in Mina.

For some perverse reason, neither Besim nor Mina was willing to consider divorce, and thus the only logical, respectable solution was to return Mina to her father. Like damaged goods, Mina had muttered, but gave in, because by that point, after weeks of arguing with Besim, weeks of refusing to weep over Andrew, she was too exhausted to put up much more of a fight. She was, honestly, relieved that Besim never offered to start again, to begin from the beginning, to pretend they might forget all their mistakes, as Andrew had thought possible. There were no complete breaks; the past was always there, waiting with all its reminders of all that had been lost, which Mina now knew. She'd run home only to discover home was no longer where she'd thought it should be.

Soon after her mother's death eleven years ago, Adam had moved to Edinburgh, because this was the birthplace of all the great philosophers of the modern world, and this was where he would write his magnum opus, the one he should have completed before he'd committed the error of marrying Lauren Lowell. Thus Mina found herself displaced to another city, of which she had no knowledge, no means to locate herself; the degree to which she felt suffocated by her sense of claustrophobia was far worse than she'd anticipated. She was thirty years old, once again living in her father's home, as dependent and helpless, as isolated and estranged from her fellow inhabitants and the rest of the world, as she'd been throughout her childhood.

She imagined the pain of her return home might have been eased if she'd returned to the familiarity of the Devonshire cottage, its untended garden, its spaces, sounds and smells, her old room and bed and books, all of this part of some small territory she might have reclaimed. Instead, she now needed to acclimate not only to negotiating her adult self in relation to the father she had not seen in thirteen years, but also the cluttered rooms, unreliable plumbing, creaking stairwell, and dim hallways of the cramped flat occupying the top two floors of a four-story split-level reconverted townhouse. Never mind the intrusive noise of the foot-traffic and lorries clattering below the parlour windows facing Canongate, or the rattling of trains pulling in and out of Waverley Station's southbound tracks, which Mina's north corner bedroom overlooked. Rather, it was Mina's own intrusive presence that seemed to be the cause of general disruption, which was not so different from when she'd been a girl, but at least she and her parents had worked out a comfortable routine. Now, Mina was blatantly unwanted, an usurper who had purposefully arrived to displace the other female occupant in the flat, or so Mina had convinced herself, since reverting to her marginalized role seemed the natural regression required of her, the position her parents had fated her to uphold ever since she'd arrived as a prickly reminder of their ill-suited union.

Although Adam had never remarried, he had set up house, and very much in the idiomatic sense, with Margaret Wren, a local woman he'd hired to cook and clean in exchange for room and board and a bit of pocket money thrown in. This arrangement was nothing more than a charade, constructed for the sake of decorum, though Mina was not sure whom her father had feared insulting. He'd rarely left the flat, locked away in his study, as always. He had no friends calling in to visit, and if he did, Margaret perfectly played the role of anyone who might be in her position: dourly dressed in widow's weeds beneath cook's apron and cap, grudgingly serving tea, humming happily only when she ironed, scrubbed pots, or set off to market, thin-lipped, imperiously silent as she knitted by the hearth, withholding all comments on the behavior of others, except when chastising her father to finish his soup or remember to wear his housecoat and slippers. Indeed, Maggie, as Adam affectionately called her, appeared exactly as she was, and no one would have suspected her of being anything else.

At least, in the ten months Mina had been living with her father, she had misidentified Maggie as merely the housekeeper, interpreting the uppity woman's suspicious frowns and sour glances as nothing more than resentment towards Mina for having stolen her bedroom, since there were only two in the flat. Mina never thought to question where Maggie was expected to sleep, assuming there must be some maid's quarters tucked behind the kitchen downstairs. When Mina finally wandered into the kitchen a week after her arrival, scrounging up a furtive snack before Maggie returned from her shopping, she discovered only a scantily-stocked pantry. When she asked her father where Maggie now slept, since she did not seem to have taken lodgings elsewhere, her heavy footsteps detected at all hours of the night, she was vaguely informed of a hide-away room just off the study, and that this was where Maggie had always slept.

Even if the location of Maggie's quarters seemed unorthodox, since her father's study connected to his bedroom, Mina accepted his explanation; the only thing that remained unexplained was Maggie's continuing hostility towards her. Did the silly woman think Mina would want her fired, or desired to take over her kitchen, or dictate meals and shopping items, determined to unsettle the general order of Maggie's general rule over all things domestic? Mina had not once expressed any such inclination, for the most part sticking to the relative seclusion of her bedroom or leaving for hours to walk aimlessly through the city and Holyrood Park. Or did Maggie expect Mina to take a greater part in the daily running of the house, because it might lessen her own burden, or it was simply expected of any woman residing in a home where she was dependent on the beneficence of the male provider? Perhaps Maggie thought Mina should have shown towards her father more of the dutiful daughter's adulation and fawning servitude?

Mina was incapable of unraveling any of these mysteries. She and her father behaved as they had always done: with a reserved respect for the other's intellect; without the expectation that one should behave contrary to one's character; with the implicit understanding that familial connections were arbitrary and did not automatically require undying devotion or obedience. On the other hand, Mina still desperately longed for her father's admiration and approval, no less so than she did as a child; and her father struggled to understand and accept his child according to her own autonomous idiosyncrasies. Neither of them knew how to express the depth of their love for the other, because these were not words they had ever declared openly, to each other, or anyone. Both regretted, now, Mina's long absence, ever since the day he'd put her on a train to Paris, because with her sudden, unexpected return both had become strangers living under the same roof. Perhaps it was the impenetrable oddity of this that Maggie found impossible to understand and so resented Mina for returning to cause her father such discomfort in his old age.

This was the most likely answer, now that Mina knew the logic behind Maggie's excessively solicitous care with which she'd watched over her employer. The night Adam died Mina had been woken by Maggie's insistent pounding on her door. Her father had gotten out of bed, without his robe and slippers, to resume working on his unfinished manuscript, and had collapsed at his desk, where Maggie had found him after waking to discover him missing. Why was Maggie sleeping in her father's bedroom? Mina did not bother to ask, since Maggie had also recently taken on the role of nursemaid, stationed in the chair at Adam's bedside should he need anything from her in the middle of the night. After hefting Adam's now diminished weight between them, which Mina stingily estimated Maggie might have managed on her own without wasting the time of dragging her out of bed, they got her father back into his own bed, and then Maggie left Mina there beside him as she rushed wordlessly out to bring the doctor, which Mina also suspected would be an unnecessary intrusion of someone else's sleep.

She sat watching her father die, the increasingly shallow rise and fall of his chest, his ragged, struggling breath, the ashy pallor, the glazed look of panicked fear, knowing this was the end, while Mina took his dry palm in her own and offered meaningless reassurances that all would be well, that she was there and the doctor was coming. Yes, Mina thought, these were all the appropriate clichéd components of any death-bed scene; she was performing her part as it was expected of her, when in truth, she wanted to return to her bedroom and allow her father to die alone and with dignity, without the intrusive, watchful stare of those who would be left behind, still alive. Mina did not hope to receive any final words of condemnation or blessing; if he'd had nothing to offer her in these last months, then what was there? Nevertheless, she could not move, fearing that if Maggie returned to find her father alone, there would never be a way for her to explain. It was easier to wait and watch, as much as she wished to be else-where, anywhere . . .

"Mina," her father groaned. "You must . . . forgive me."

"There's no need . . ."

"Should have done more," he insisted. "Sorry . . . didn't take care of you."

"You did your best."

"No, you . . . don't . . . understand," he gasped out his last words. "Always thought you could take care of yourself . . . but now . . . I see now . . . didn't have time to change . . ."

And then his body seized with a sharp intake of breath, which he expelled in a long sigh, and that was it, nothing more, ever. Mina closed his eyes for him, folded his arms over his chest, snugly arranged the sheets and coverlets around his torso, because that was what one did, and then left the room. She went into the study, tidied up the scattered manuscript pages in no particular order, and found the tiny cubbyhole of a room where Maggie kept a narrow clothespress, chipped washbasin, tatty armchair, a small trunk presumably filled with her unimaginable trinkets and hosiery, several baskets of knitting, but no bed. Mina took all of this in, as well as its obvious implications, without any sense of shock or disapproval; she felt no emotion whatsoever other than a slight disappointment in herself for not having reached this conclusion sooner. When Mina returned to her father's bedroom she found Maggie weeping softly, inconsolably over Adam's body. Maggie lifted her head briefly to inform Mina that Dr. Cald-well would arrive within the hour, and so Mina kindly left Maggie alone. She dressed, went down to put on the kettle, let in the doctor, offered him a cup of tea, and then led him upstairs to view her father's body.

"Will you want a priest, then?" Dr. Caldwell inquired, observing a now perfectly composed Maggie clicking a string of rosary beads.

"That won't be necessary," Mina replied, ignoring Maggie. "My father was an atheist."

"He's tae be buried in Greyfriars," Maggie informed them. "Priest or na priest, that's whit th' dear mon wished tae be dane fur him whin th' time cam."

"Will there be a wake?" Caldwell addressed Mina.

"I shouldn't think—." Mina furrowed her brow, because she had no idea what was expected, or what her father would have preferred.

"He didnae waant ony sic palaver." Maggie rose heavily to her feet, as if prepared to defend Adam's corpse. "Mr. Dalkeith th' Undertaker kens what's tae be dane. Mr. Byrne made a' th' arrangements, sae I'll juist gang th' noo fur his wee jimmies tae come collect th' body. Mr. Dalkeith wull tak' care o' everything."

And with that both Caldwell and Mina were dismissed from any further responsibilities, for which Mina felt greatly indebted. After Adam was buried in Greyfriars, with the vicar attending and no one else, Mina and Maggie silently returned to the flat. Mina claimed the upper floor; Maggie stuck to the kitchen and parlour, where she now slept, refusing to lie in Adam's bed, as if to do so would commit Maggie to some grievously presumptuous insult against the dead man and his daughter, whom it was now assumed held ownership of all his property. Mina lay in her own bed staring at the water stains in the ceiling, the patterns in the carpet, the droplets and streaks of rain on her window, lazily forming animal shapes and human faces, pondering nothing and no one, not even the shape of her hazily obscured future. She remained pleasantly listless until that morning, when she was forced to go down for some breakfast, which Maggie had failed to deliver with the customary knock on her door. Maggie sat at the kitchen table, purposefully waiting for Mina to appear.

"Time tae decide whit's tae be dane," she informed her.

"Done with what?" Mina asked, truly perplexed.

"Wi' yer da's remains," Maggie grumbled.

"But I believe we buried his remains six days ago," Mina tartly replied.

"Ye ken gey weel whit a'm oan aboot," Maggie admonished. "Sae, wance ye'r finished wi' yer scones 'n' tea, aff ye gang tae yer da's study, sin it's as guid a steid as ony tae begin."

Though Mina still struggled with translating Maggie's impenetrable brogue, she easily gathered the sense of it and did as she was told. This task of facing her father's death, of having to root through his private belongings, afraid of what she might or might not find, was not something Mina wanted or thought herself capable, but she obeyed Maggie, because what she truly wanted, as usual, was someone to make all the necessary decisions for her. Mina only got so far as sitting down at her father's desk, opening his diary and finding those tickets.

She realized, now emerging from the park and strolling past the gated entrance to Holyrood Palace, knowing that she would soon have to turn up Canongate, that her decision to attend Jamie's lecture had not been prompted by the desire to delay the distasteful task of riffling through her father's private papers, but rather from her inability to determine what she should do with her life next. Where should she go, how should she live, and with whom? Andrew was no longer alive, somewhere out there in this world, and with that unbearable knowledge, she'd thought she could meet with Jamie, that he might offer her the needed commiseration and closure. As soon as she'd sat down and detected the shock of dark unruly hair, the ghostly glimmering of an ironic grin, as if he knew something about life no one else could know, she realized Andrew would never agree to remain dead and buried.

Before arriving at 195 Canongate, Mina side-stepped into a narrow wynd, intending to take a circuitous, unnecessary route home, the extended delay ensuring her more time to sort through what she would say to Maggie. She desperately needed the advice of another woman who clearly knew how to cope with the mundane details of going about one's daily existence. It was now painfully apparent to Mina that she was not equipped to live a life less ordinary; she had never felt so lonely in all her life, and now regretted that she had never acquired a single female friend. She'd never learned how to go about doing such a thing, or even thought it necessary; women frightened her with their subtle hints that they shared some common wisdom exclusive to men's realm of experiences. Mina only knew men and their competing versions of Mina. In fact, Mina felt discomforted by her extended spell of celibacy, and despairing that she might ever attract another man again, decided somewhat irrationally that the most appropriate answer to this dilemma would be to cut off all her hair.

On North Bridge, she found one of those élite, high-end salons boasting a receptionist who could not comprehend why someone as fashionably degenerate as Mina would attempt an unscheduled appointment.

Mina persevered, and was rewarded, because she at least knew how to silence other women with her own coldly contemptuous stare. While waiting for the next available stylist, she was offered a glass of wine, which she accepted and drank, and as a result felt slightly tipsy once she was settled in front of a mirror and asked what she wanted done. Mina studied the chic young woman reflected back at her, with her sleek angular bob, as she studied Mina, the palm of her small hand resting on the crown of Mina's head, gently turning it from left to right. I'll have exactly the same as yours, Mina instructed. Aye, that'll suit ye nicely, she briskly agreed, and then, in a haze of insobriety, Mina watched her snip away with such a determined expression of achieving perfection that Mina could not help but admire and envy the girl's single-minded concentration, her focused dedication towards producing something so ephemerally aesthetically pleasing.

When she returned to the flat, the back of her neck uncomfortably naked, she fought the urge to go upstairs and hide in her room. Instead she sat down on one of the overstuffed plaid-print sofas directly across from Maggie. Multi-colored skeins of yarn, knitting needles, unfinished jumpers, hats, scarves, socks, doilies, and tea cozies lay strewn across the carpet, chairs and divan. The hearth fire crackled, Mina coughed, and Maggie continued looping one stitch after another, needles clicking at a furious pace until it became clear that Mina would not be ignored and simply go away. Maggie lowered the bundled mass of scarlet wool into her lap, and eyed Mina warily.

"A've hud hee haw tae keep me raisin' mair deils than ye can lig wi'oot yer da pestering me," she explained, incomprehensibly. "Ah begin th' yin, forget whit it's meant tae be, 'n' sae shift oan tae th' neist."

"Sounds like a poem," Mina smiled graciously.

"A dinnae ken aboot that," Maggie huffed. "It's juist a thing tae dae 'til th' neist thing comes alang."

"Maggie, why are you still here?" Mina asked, merely curious and not at all intending to be rude, which was exactly how Maggie chose to interpret her question.

"Waiting oan ye," she muttered. "Adam asked me tae keek efter ye, 'n' that's whit a'll dae 'til ye decide otherwise."

"Why would my father—," but Mina didn't see the sense in continuing that question or hearing its answer, as she had no idea what she was about to ask. "Honestly, Maggie, I don't know what to do, with any of this. I don't even know what to do with myself."

"A'd say ye ken weel enough tae chop aff a' that bonnie heid o' black hair," Maggie noted wryly, resuming her knitting, as if that was the end to the conversation.

"But it was the only thing I could think of," Mina laughed, a note of hysteria rising in her throat, and then the tears fell uncontrollably, shamefully. "Please, Maggie, what *should* I do? I don't know, I don't know, I don't know! Tell me, please, what am I *supposed* to do?!"

Maggie once again lowered her knitting, but did not rise to sit beside Mina and press the poor girl's sorrowful head to her hefty, consoling breast; she simply sat stonily studying the overgrown child. "O' coorse ye dinnae ken, wi' yer da gaen noo 'n' yer mither lang in th' cauld ground, bit ye'll figure it oot in a wee bit enough."

"But what if . . . if . . . I don't?" Mina choked back another ugly, gulping sob.

"Then lee wull figure it oot fur ye," Maggie platitudinized. "Yin wey or th' ither it aye pushes us whaur we need tae gang. If yi'll waant mah advice, lea it a' behind 'n' shift oan."

"Where?" Mina asked tremulously.

"Wherever ye think ye need tae be," Maggie offered in her most stentorian, oracular, self-evident tones. "Frae a' that belongs in th' bygane. It's whit we a' maun dae wance we na langer huv oor mither 'n' da tae run hame tae whin we tak' a coup 'n' cannae git up. We cannae gang expecting others tae keek efter us forever, noo."

"But you just said you promised my father—," Mina argued, because none of this was what she'd wanted to hear from Maggie.

"A've na mynd tae staying oan 'ere forever, lassie!" Maggie cackled. "A've mah ain daughter, 'n' her wee bairns, tae hulp keek efter. A'm gaun back up tae Fife as in a wee bit as ye git yersel' sorted, 'n' ah didnae expect that tae tak' mair than th' fortnicht!"

"Yes, well, indeed," Mina clipped out in response, tears dried, face composed, as she hastily, haughtily rose from the sofa. "I'll have everything wrapped up by the end of the week, at the end of which you're free to leave, and with full wages of course."

"Mingin' Sassenach besom," Maggie muttered, mindless of whether Mina heard or not, for it seemed she'd understood scarcely a thing Maggie had said to begin with. "It wilnae be in a wee bit enough 'til ah huv mah hauns free o' ye 'n' ah dinnae yer dosh!"

Mina retreated upstairs, fully exhausted after having had a good cry, not to mention the nearly futile task of following Maggie's side of the conversation. Although it hadn't been much of a conversation, not at all of much use to Mina who still hadn't the slightest idea how to proceed. Quite silly of her to expect someone of Maggie's ilk to provide assistance, and so she had no choice but to sit back down at her father's desk and begin going through its contents, hoping he'd left behind a list of instructions, or even a damn will, but there didn't seem to be one, and there was no attorney to offer guidance because her father, like any common fool, had distrusted lawyers, having styled himself, in his doddering dotage, as far more intellectually exceptional than actually proven. This was evident from the passage Mina pulled out of his unfinished philosophical treatise, randomly selecting an ink-stained page from the manuscript, which she read with increasing disappointment:

"And so we must accept the following as a universal law: man is only capable of potency and productivity when he is restricted by a horizon; if he discovers himself helpless in circumscribing such a vista for himself, whereby he may also reveal a solipsistic refusal to transcribe his vision within the embrace of another's doubtful reality, then he will either languish and inexorably decline, or accelerate headlong into his apposite demise. To further elucidate our axiom: Belief in the present hinges on a distinct borderline that isolates the luminous and perceptible fullness of being from the indecipherable and shadowy void of nothingness; on one's persistence in forgetting and remembering at the suitable time; on the possession of an indestructible impulse for experiencing one's immediate self through the irretrievable past and the illusive future. This, in a word, is the proposal the author now provokes the reader to reflect upon: *the future and the past are uniformly indispensable for the dynamic vitality and growth of an individual, and the world-view he must necessarily cling to and yet aspire to transcend.*"

Mina burst out laughing, casting the sheaf of paper, and her father's madness, aside. He'd left behind nothing more than a pile of pedantic piffle, as obscurely elusive as Maggie's garbled speech. Mina suspected the whole lot of it was a poorly plagiarized transcription from some other philosophical rigmarole; she had the distinct sensation of having encountered it elsewhere. Perhaps, then, these were only the scribblings with which he'd amused himself when he was bored, when he was without ideas for the real manuscript, which she was now determined to find. Mina began tearing through his desk, searching for a book that never existed. She pulled out drawers, ravaged book cases, hurling tome after empty tome onto the floor; she dragged furniture away from the walls, hoping to discover a secret safe or niche, but found nothing, nothing at all. She collapsed in the armchair, heaving, nearly weeping for the second time that evening, when her eyes landed on the black and white original of herself, eleven-years-old, a sullen slip of a miserable girl, gazing back at Mina as if she'd known, even then, that she would always feel betrayed by life and what she'd expected it to offer her. Not for the first time, Mina wished the photograph had never been taken, never been reproduced and given away, twice, and she couldn't comprehend why her father had kept his copy hidden away inside some book.

Mina snatched up the photograph, turned it over, found scrawled across the top, LAST WILL AND TESTAMENT, and then in one winding, unfathomable sentence: "I, Adam Byrne, being of sound mind and temperament, leave all that I possess, including an annuity of £200 held in trust with the Royal Bank of Scotland, to Mrs. Margaret Wren; I leave my daughter Mina to her infinite pluck, panache, and pulchritude, and to the good and generous beneficence of Mrs. Wren, if so needed." It was dated November of the previous year, a month after Mina had come to stay, and signed by her father, and no one else: no witnesses, no notarized stamp, nothing. Mina might have had another good long cry, or laugh; instead, she took up a sheaf of blank paper, and wrote the following poem, all the while, as if for inspiration, intermittently glancing down at the image of herself as a girl.

Chrysalis

Monstrously proportioned imago
bisecting in binary evolution
nebulous nostalgia from sludge:
mystery summing obscurity.

Truly the corruptible creature
is merely a diminutive nymphet . . .

NOSTALGIA

Dilatory wings
bellow from her scapulae
the susurration of souls;
pupates, as desire determines,
intuition with delusion.

Muse upon my
metaphases:

Childhood's spindling
abduction into Delirium.

Mina folded the poem and stored it away in her skirt pocket. She spent the remainder of that long mid-summer evening burning in the hearth all of her father's books, his diary, fake manuscript, unpaid bills, blotting paper, old sermons and letters, scraps of absent-minded notes, every consumable item he'd left behind for his daughter to incinerate. Lastly, because yes, she possessed if anything a great deal of pluck and panache, she burnt the photograph. He had after all confessed on his deathbed that he wished he could have changed, done more to take care of her, and so Mina was only carrying out his last wishes. In the morning, she would hire a lawyer, who would attest to her legal rights, as her father's only living heir, and obtain for her the annuity. In all fairness, Mina would sign over ownership of the Canongate flat and all the property therein to Maggie; she could do what she liked with it, saving Mina the trouble of dealing with anything extraneous to her own immediate desires and needs, which translated into leaving Scotland as soon as possible.

When Mina finally retired to her bedroom, the sky outside her window was an inky blue blotch, threaded with tendrils of iridescent cirrus clouds veiling a gibbous moon. She sat within the alcove of the window seat, knees pulled to chest, chin resting on knees, staring out, and thinking slowly over all her available options. She listened to the sporadic screech and lurch of late night trains pulling in and out of Waverley, and at one point, her gaze blurring sleepily, she observed two silhouetted bodies, one in the form of a man and the other a woman, emerging from the darkness to meet midway on the upper southern slope of Calton Hill. Illuminated by the moon and performing an optical illusion, they embraced, becoming briefly melded into one amorphous, incipient creature, and then, disengaging themselves, irreconcilably divided into two thin limbic figures walking slowly, inconsolably away from each other in the opposite directions from which they'd appeared. Mina sighed; she would begin again, and this time she would end up where she needed to be.

CHAPTER TWELVE
Une folie à deux

"As if, darling." Natalya's honeyed laughter oozed through the scarlet gash of her thickly lipsticked mouth. "Really, it's terribly silly of you, or any modern woman, to believe in such an outdated concept! What an oppressive notion, as if life is anything more than some comedy of coincidence and chance. No, *ma chère*, the only thing we women can rely upon is the predictability of always ending up where we least expect to find ourselves."

Mina felt bound to agree, since she now found herself, three years after she'd buried her father, surrounded by a circle of women for whom she remained a frustratingly inscrutable problem. During all their monthly afternoon teas, not once had she thought to offer a single narrative confession of even just one of her past affairs, persisting in her tight-lipped silence on this subject simply because the details of her romantic past seemed of negligible interest. As usual, Mina underestimated the importance of sharing the merest morsel of gossip, which she might have used as a passport into what remained for her the foreign country of female camaraderie. Indeed, Mina simply did not understand women and their ways, an accusation Natalya once again presented for the group's mild amusement.

"Natalya, you cannot blame Mina for refusing to convert," Daisy blithely announced, plopping down into Natalya's lap.

"But she should at least be allowed the chance for redemption," Natalya laughed, nuzzling Daisy's neck.

"And you'd be the one to redeem me?" Mina played along.

Natalya drily remarked, "Heavens, no, I'm already juggling three sinners as it is."

"And doing an awfully sloppy job of it," Daisy observed, disentangling from Natalya's lap and rising to replenish her drink.

"Oh, hush up, you made your bed so lie in it," Mable interjected. "Besides, Natalya's the one who completely supports the springs."

"If ya'll ladies excuse me," Daisy drawled. "I'll just go powder mah nose."

"Don't worry," Natalya assured everyone once Daisy sauntered off, as they all knew, to snort a pinch of cocaine. "I've always compressed more out of life than it actually possesses."

Mina sighed, exhausted by all the lame euphemisms and epigrammatic banter passed back and forth in the mere passage of one minute's dialogue. She wasn't sure if they had ever actually engaged in a conversation; instead, these meetings usually consisted of an emptily witty game of feeble thrust and repartee, a series of cattily timed comments aimed only at one-upping each other. All of which Mina found thoroughly disappointing, since their overdramatized entanglements and instinctive rivalries were not so very different from the behavioral tics she'd come to expect of men.

Natalya yawned. "Now, my dears, as for our Mina. It's no use trying to squeeze out *her* inscrutable essence. In fact, I spend many sleepless nights wondering if there's anything at all to discover behind that sphinx-like mask of feminine allure she has so artfully constructed."

"And if there were I can assure you it would consist of the most dull driveling nonsense," Mina quipped. "Such as, will it rain today, should I wear my hair up or down, do I have enough money to buy that silk scarf I spotted in the window at Le Bon Marché?"

"Was it that lovely green and gold Hermès?" Elyse giddily inquired. "I'll buy it for you!"

"The last thing Mina needs is a new scarf!" Trudie croaked. "If you want to go throwing your money around then set her up in a new studio."

"The one I have now is just fine, thank you," laughed Mina. "I'd much prefer the scarf, which I shall wrap around my head, solving the daily ordeal of what to do with my hair."

"Oh no, sugarplum, it's taken you long enough to grow it out," Mable scolded. "I have a whole pack of bobbed starlets who would die for that hair now that it's in fashion again."

"Nonsense!" Natalya snickered. "Other than the one prize bitch you keep on for best in show, you've got nothing more than a kennel of puppy-faced boys all clipped and groomed and on a tight leash whenever you let them out to play."

"True," Mable sighed. "But Myrna is threatening to retire and those puppies are my bread and butter, and yours as well, my darling, so don't play the hypocrite with me."

Natalya offered her own sigh. "Just once, believe me, I would like to see a woman attract the same kind of box office numbers as those impossible, undeserving little runts."

"Sweetie, I've been trying for years to get you to sign on my Margie La Mont for one of your big-budget song and dances!" Mable insisted. "She's a real pro, just had a smash hit on Broadway, and with a bit of—."

"Don't be ridiculous, Mabs," Daisy returned, sniffling noisily. "You can't expect to make a film star out of any woman past forty, no sex appeal, and that silly fake name—."

"Change her name and she's in our next picture," Natalya abruptly decided, for she was over forty, still in her prime, and quickly tiring of Daisy's insouciant charm. "It's an epic, shooting down in Mexico City, and with a meaty part for a bordello Madame who runs all the men out of town, just perfect for your vaudeville queen. In fact, with a role like this, I'll transform her into the greatest screen goddess the world has ever known, larger than life and twice as natural! What *is* her real name, by the way?"

"Sa-ra Sor-rell," Mable enunciated the syllables in an elongated, exasperated yawn, causing Mina to flinch, painfully, perversely. "Which really won't do at all, I know, but she's blessed with an abundance of breasts and hips and a voice just sticky with sex, every man's wet dream."

"Because of course we all dream of screwing our mothers," Daisy muttered. "Besides, changing a name won't change the woman—."

"A rose is a rose is a rose," said Trudie. "What about Sasha Weston? It has a softly sibilant sound, sophisticated, seductive and not too sinister, because if you're making your very own goddess then of course you don't want her to scare off all the men."

"That is precisely what I've been saying all along!" Natalya gushed. "Women like Mina, with that veil of contrived indifference, just hinting at a volcano of sexual voracity about to erupt, those are the ones men, and women, I might add—."

"Natalya, I'm hardly capable of being so disingenuous," Mina coolly interrupted, concealing the depths of her misery and discomfort. "The only mystery to me, or any woman, like this Sara Sorrell or Sasha Weston, or whatever you choose to call her, is how we actually manage to survive in a world that offers very little—."

"But that's exactly why we women need to believe in our own mystique," Natalya hastily recommended. "After all, every woman must create her own myth, which is really the only power allowed us in the politics and practicalities of everyday life—."

"Which, we all know, is in the domineering hands of men." Juno inserted her voice into the discussion only when it occurred to her the point had already been made.

"Oh, please, none of you are the victim of any man," Mina laughed, exasperated. "Really, except for Trudie and Elyse, I think each of you merely pretend to love women simply because you've yet to find a man capable of meeting your severe standards."

"Touché, darling, I'd no idea you had it in you!" Natalya approved begrudgingly.

Mable asked, "What was that about?"

"Well, I think it was all in very bad form." Daisy curled up for a nap, slightly defeated by her last drink rather than Mina's accusation.

"I believe," Juno yawned, "Mina was pointing out that we are nothing more than the dupes of our own self-delusions."

"But I truly love women," Mable insisted. "We all do."

"*Et c'est le but, n'est-ce pas?*" Rosalie stirred impatiently in her shadowy corner; as usual she'd nodded off as soon as tea had been served but was now very much awake.

"Yes, Tante, that is precisely the point," Mina confirmed. "You all love women yet to the absolute exclusion of men."

"Well, when you *appreciate* women as we do, what use are men?" Natalya asked, and then prodded, because she couldn't help herself. "Other than making for conveniently disposable husbands, as *you* very well know, my dear."

Mina ignored the jab. "Men are hardly useless. After all, if men did not exist then you would not be half so pleased with yourselves, since in your desire for women you've rejected the rule that says you should only desire a man."

"How clever," Elyse murmured.

"Fascinating," Trudie muttered.

"And so you are saying that a woman's desire for another woman is the most supreme form of desire." Natalya offered what seemed, at least to her, the most logical conclusion.

Mina replied, "I am saying no such thing. All I'm trying to say is that women need men to exist, and men need women, or how would we ever know which one we prefer?"

Then they barraged her with their usual ripostes that seemed to ignore anything she had just said. Really, my dear, what could you possibly know about this? How could you understand the slightest truth about what women see or desire in each other? You haven't a leg to stand on, having only slept with men, and so why insist on arguing against us?

"Well, I'm sure if you got me drunk enough I might renounce my wicked ways, but what I wouldn't give, even then, for one cock amongst you," Mina laughed, because her only defense was to make a bawdy, awkward joke of it, and they laughed as well, relieved to feel the tension dissipate. They were all staunchly terrified by any hint of outright hostility, which certainly indicated, in Mina's experience, an appreciable divergence between the sexes.

Overall, Mina thought the whole raison d'être of the group was slightly suspect, unconvinced that the accident of shared biology was a viable justification for solidarity. Besides, they were all so much more interesting on their own merits, but when herded together, all of their individual quirks disappeared, each of them conforming to some kind of feminized standard that not only society but they themselves expected of each other. All of which led Mina to question: Who were any of them alone, unseen, without the pressure to stick to the script? Who was Mina when no one was there to insist upon her performing her gender? How could she ever know this without the corrupting element of another's gaze?

In the past, Mina had not wasted so much time troubling herself over such unanswerable questions; indeed, the question of her feminine politics had never interested her as much as it did now that she was required to define who she was in relation to other women and not *merely* in contrast to men. It seemed a far more complex issue than she'd bargained for when she'd graciously, albeit skeptically, accepted Natalya's invitation to serve as the token *amante des hommes* within her newly established Académie des femmes, which, beyond its vague justification for existing (as a feminist answer to its exclusively male counterpart), had been formed to promote women's writings. They'd been introduced at one of Trudie's literary salons, where one often found far more men than women, but at the time Mina hadn't been counting. After hearing Mina breathlessly present one of her poems, which Trudie had insisted upon after receiving Mina's breathless admiration of Trudie's own satirical sketches, Natalya had taken Mina aside and informed her that she was the most breathtakingly modern and inventive poet of all time. Mina had humbly and audibly very much doubted this, but thought a willing audience and possible publisher for her work, a role Natalya indicated she herself would play, seemed as good a reason as any for befriending other women writers.

Even then she'd cringed at this term. After all, didn't it impose upon her artistic vision the same diminished worth that men often applied to women's creative efforts, confining and reducing the scope of their imaginations to the trivial concerns of their sex, whatever men imagined these to be? Mina had attempted to articulate as much in the poem she'd agreed to present that day, a promise Natalya now abruptly demanded she fulfill, and perhaps as revenge for Mina's vulgar witticism. They all knew Mina detested the sound of her voice speaking words that seemed more suited to remaining unpunctuated marks on the page, and so she rapidly, awkwardly delivered the brief poem without a single pause.

Vindication of Her Sex

Dispossessed as we are by our fathers
we wander unknown among you
ignorant of our lustrous exile

Designated your consecrated fools
nourished upon tempests in teapots
consumable constellations of conception

Our desires are driven by
apostate visions
bewildering your decrees

You may call us daughter wife or mother
the whims of your prurience
are not our concern

They all applauded, assuring her they thought this was supremely her best bit of work so far, but offered nothing else in the way of critique. They simply liked it because it was exactly what they wanted to hear, exactly what they thought she should be writing. Mina did not know if she'd written this poem for her own enjoyment or because she'd wanted to please her audience. Thus, because she always sensed intuitively when she'd come to her limits, to the end of any sordid affair, she decided to contradict their approval, handing it politely back to them.

"Honestly, this is not at all the sort of thing I want to write."

"But the rhythm, diction, and syntactical idiosyncrasies are all very much your own," Trudie professorially assured her.

Mina made a face. "All the same. Something seems false."

"It doesn't live up to your expectations?" asked Elyse.

"No, it is simply not what I wanted to write," Mina insisted.

Trudie said, "Ah, so the conception does not bear fruition."

"That would imply the poem is a failure," said Juno.

"There's no such thing as a failed poem!" said Natalya.

Mina laughed uncomfortably. "Are you serious? Do you actually believe that? Of course there's such a thing as a failed poem. All art has the capacity for failure, or what would be the point? Why have aesthetic or even technical standards?"

"Whose standards?" Natalya demanded. "Men's standards? We do not hold to those, not here!"

"My standards," stated Mina.

"Yes, of course, the only standards are those created by the individual artist." Trudie again misinterpreted Mina's meaning.

"So it's as I said, it doesn't meet your expectations." Elyse congratulated herself on being right. She was wrong; they all were.

"The poem is perfectly fine on its own," Mina sighed, giving up, because she was tired and wanted them all to go home and never bother her again with their overbearing opinions and ridiculous pretensions. "Besides, I feel I'm done with poetry. I've more or less exhausted what I can do with it and I don't want to write it anymore."

"Well, what *do* you want to write?" Mable was the only one who finally thought to ask, and yet Mina responded by exhaustively defining what she did not want to write.

Not another romance, not a love story, not something domestic or gothic, not fairy tales, not histories or biographies, all of these, invariably, predictably, concluding in a marriage, the family safely reunited and reconstituted, where the good always win and the bad horribly lose, because in the end it is all about constructing the fiction of reassuring ourselves that life neatly delivers on our doorstep what each of us believe we deserve; and no, Mina protested before anyone could interrupt, it was not at all a question of creating more credible heroines or compelling villains since such categorizations were delusionary myths in and of themselves. It was only a question of style, of language, and here Mina finally got around to answering what she wanted to write, a novel that did not conform to generic expectations yet refused to pretend to offer an entirely new form.

Utterly baffled, everybody glared at Mina. Then Elyse said, "Oh goodness. What kind of novel would that be?"

"A novel solely concerned with exploring the terrain of the imagination but without falling into the trap of trying to translate the imagination into realistic terms; a novel constructed purely of fantasy and desire—."

"Well, isn't that all writing really?" said Natalya dismissively.

"If you were paying attention, my dear, Mina never said she was trying to reinvent the wheel," said Trudie.

Rosalie again roused herself. "Well, why the hell not? My niece can do anything she damn well pleases! She's a true artist, that's what I've raised her to be, and so she doesn't have to play by your silly rules!"

"Yes, thank you, Tante." Mina gravely, graciously accepted Rosalie's petulant outburst, for Rosalie took all of her own pronouncements quite seriously. If anything, the interruption indicated Rosalie's weariness of the women's company, providing Mina an excuse to bring the whole rigmarole to a close without demanding outright their immediate departure.

"Actually, I am writing a novel, something not unlike my poems, rather excessively stylized but aimed at dislocating the English language, to make it read as if it were in translation."

"What's the bloody point of that?" Daisy mumbled, uncurling from the divan, her nap disrupted by Rosalie's strident speech; the women mutely observed her stumble about the room vainly searching for her coat.

"Whatever the point, be sure it has oodles of sex," Mable finally advised, rising from her chair to assist Daisy towards the coat closet since Natalya seemed unwilling to budge. "You can experiment your blessed little heart out but it'll never sell without sex."

Elyse exclaimed, "Oh but won't that defeat the purpose?!" She helped Trudie lumber to her feet before joining the search for coats.

"Yes, my dear, why don't you write something without a sexual undercurrent?" suggested Trudie. "If you want to write a novel that has nothing to do with women's *real* lives, then I'm sure that'll do the trick."

"Unfortunately, I know nothing but life, and that is generally reducible to sex," Mina laughed, ignoring the sting of Trudie's sarcasm, ignoring how this statement contradicted everything she'd just said about what she'd wanted to write, only wanting them gone, all gone, incapable of comprehending why it was such an ordeal for them to find their coats, file out the door, and leave her alone. Why did women always feel compelled to make such a prolonged production out of saying goodbye?

"The only problem is that novels inevitably end up being longer than life." Natalya found a suitably clever quip, loudly orating for everyone's benefit. "No, darling, forget about writing a novel, it seems everyone and their mother is pumping one out these days. Stick to your clever little poems. You use enough far-fetched words in them to convince readers of your originality. In fact, send me twenty-five of your best, including the one you read today, and with your *Elegy for Andreas* we'll have a smashing collection. We'll get the first print out by March and I'll bring you back to New York with me in April for a reading tour. How's that sound, love?"

"Lovely." Mina presented her with her coat, leading her to the foyer where Daisy and Mable stood fiddling with their buttons and scarves, Elyse and Trudie already gone.

"Lovely?" Natalya rolled her eyes, Daisy tugging petulantly on her coat sleeve, pulling her through the doorway and down the hall. "I offer you fame, fortune, my undivided attention and undying devotion and that's all you can say? No, I refuse to leave until you say yes! Say yes!"

"Yes! Yes!" Mina called after her, knowing it was the only way of avoiding Natalya for at least a fortnight, each affirmative ringing in her head as a determined denial.

"Write whatever you please, Mina darling," Juno murmured, the last to leave with a lingering, affectionate kiss on Mina's cheek. "And if that secret lover you've been hiding from us fails to show up tonight, come by and I'll keep you warm."

"Off with you, now, you naughty girl," Mina teased, ushering her out with a playful wink, and then finally, blessedly closed the door.

Jonathon Redpath poked his head out of the study down the hall. "Are they all gone?"

Mina acknowledged him with a weary nod and he shuffled into the salon, bending over Rosalie to console her with a kiss on the white crown of her head and a gentle pat on the bony shawl-swaddled shoulder. "Shall I make us a nice hot cuppa, then?"

"Heaven forbid!" Rosalie spluttered. "I deserve a crème de menthe after all that fiddle-faddle! I swear in all my wealth of years I've never wasted so much time in the company of such an outrageously insipid gaggle of honking geese!"

"It does make one wonder . . ." Redpath trailed off to the sideboard, generously measuring out three cordial glasses, knowing Mina would leave hers untouched.

"What makes you wonder, my dear Jonathon?" Rosalie prompted, echoing the tail end of his thoughts without allowing him enough time to formulate what they might have been.

"What? Wonder?" Redpath offered his own abbreviated echo, handing Mina her unwanted drink and Rosalie her much deserved reward before settling in his armchair.

Knowing this could go on forever, Mina said, "He wonders how you are capable of such sublime patience."

"Pshaw!" Rosalie feebly waved her half-depleted glass, which Mina filled with half of hers before placing the remainder on the table beside Jonathon's chair. "All I can say is that's the last time I let you invite those ninnies over to my salon."

"If I recall correctly, you were the one who insisted I make friends with people my own age," Mina reminded her.

Rosalie directed her response to Jonathon, who smiled wanly, benevolently, in Mina's general direction, since she seemed to have vanished. "I told her to go out and befriend other artists!"

"Oh, yes, other artists," Redpath echoed.

"Those over-sexed harridans aren't artists," Rosalie continued. "At least not the sort I cavorted with in my day!"

"What about Gertie?" Redpath suggested.

"Who's Gertie? I never knew any Gertie."

Mina reappeared with her coat. "Trudie."

"Ah, yes, Trudie," Rosalie muttered.

Redpath finished his liqueur and reached for Mina's glass only to find it already emptied. "Trudie, yes, ah . . ."

"She's as fat and ugly as an overinflated bullfrog," Rosalie pronounced. "And I don't understand half of what she says, or writes for that matter."

"As a matter of fact, ducky . . ." Redpath accepted the bottle of crème de menthe from Mina, who'd anticipated his next move and had saved him the trouble of rising from his chair. "Yes, as a matter of fact, I think we deserve just one more tipple."

"Tip? You want a tip?" Rosalie accepted Mina's farewell kiss. "Go out and find yourself a young lusty stud, my girl, nothing like *une affaire discrètement torride* to keep you young and inspired. How do you think I've lasted this long?"

"Well, I certainly shan't stay locked up here with old age," Mina laughed, bestowing upon Rosalie one more kiss and Redpath her most charming smile, and then left in search of nothing other than the speediest route home.

She walked up Saints-Pères towards the Quai, resenting February's sordid slush-stained sidewalks and streets, and after crossing the Pont des Arts, found a taxi willing to take her as far as Église de la Sainte-Trinité, leaving her a few extra francs to purchase a bottle of wine and only a ten minute trudge home. When she arrived at Besim's old studio, there was no need to knock on the door since she was the only one who lived there. When she'd shown up homeless in Paris (or at least, refusing to live with Rosalie), Besim had generously given her the studio (which he only used now when he needed a brief reprieve from Gardenia), and Mina had immediately taken the liberty of redecorating. The four walls boasted a fresh coat of pristine ivory and along their upper borders she had applied a whimsical trim of sapphire, coral and topaz figures from some fantastical aquatic universe of her imaginings. Each of the three windows facing the street below had been pried loose, scrubbed to a renewed transparency and then adorned with creamy panels of translucent silk accompanying the blue painted shutters.

Hanging from the ceiling, ensconced in the walls, and set on the tables were lamps of Mina's own design, something she'd recently taken up to keep her hands occupied now that she no longer painted and had lost interest in making hats; the studio had collected a ménage of these celestial globes and immortelles, as Mina called them, as well as fanciful tulips, stars and Japanese lanterns; some were made of colored glass, others papier-mâché; sometimes she sold her peculiar constructions for a bit of pocket money. Often she kept only one or two of the lamps dimly lighting the room, casting obscene shadows along the bare walls, soothing her while she lay in the bed, as she did now, revolving in her mind the strangely satisfying seclusion of the past few months, between September and this frigid winter, and yet feeling more and more like an escaped lunatic whenever she held a conversation with anyone other than herself, or Lucian. Of course, Lucian didn't count, and Mina suspected he was about to vanish again, this time for good, which almost seemed a relief.

How was it even possible to induce someone as nebulous as Lucian Doru to take on solidity, which he refused no matter how often Mina attempted to convince him of his own existence? He first appeared when she'd attended the autumn exhibition of "Nouveau Surrealism," none of which Mina actually saw, each canvas melting into the next, except one. A monstrous abstraction of primordial shapes retreating into a deep blue haze illuminated by a lunar orb of light washed over her, enveloping her in the amniotic fluid of its cerulean womb. Something the shape of a man walked towards her out of the indeterminate dimensions of this purgatorial landscape. She couldn't breathe. Someone passing by made some garbled comment on the failure of the painting to portray anything coherent. Mina muttered, irritably, but there's no need to portray anything at all, and a voice in her ear replied, yes, the image simply emerges from the artist as an extension of himself. Of course, Mina murmured, nearly toppling over and exploding in pure waves of epiphanic laughter, in the act of creation we discover all our possible selves. And the man hovering at the peripheral edge of her vision whispered, *desigur, draga mea,* the art of being is sufficient for all of us, and life is the most supreme creative act, *nu?* Mina had wanted to ask, but is it an act of birth or death? Are we in process of becoming or disintegrating? But then she thought, better leave it alone; and, why not allow him to seduce her with his ambiguous philosophy? And so she'd allowed him to follow her home and lie down in the bed beside her.

At the time he was only a threadbare wisp of an idea, and she tried to formulate a series of adjectives that might provide him with a more substantial shape: eccentric, isolated, malnourished, alienated, haunted, dilapidated, degenerative, derelict, yes, only a derelict figment of her imagination with whom she felt an unfathomable kinship. Their affair slowly perambulated around a series of walks, visits to cafés, galleries and gardens. Whenever he refused to join her aimless wanderings, she would attempt to summon his presence in the beatific, harrowed faces of the bums and drug-addicts she passed by in the streets. Mina had always had a weakness for such figures, finding in them the kind of connection, or self-reflection, one might designate to the ineffable bond existing between two soul mates (never mind they reminded her of Andrew). She too felt cast aside, stranded in the dinginess of her impoverished solitude, yet determined to make something from it, something approximating a work of art. Survival, she had always thought, was a form of elegance. Was not the universe itself based on this principle of design?

Nevertheless, she struggled to construct a narrative around the tentative figure of Lucian Doru, whom she decided, after naming him, was a Romanian exile, a starving artist whose own survival depended on Mina's carefully lavished attentions. One night she fed him smoked trout for dinner, absurdly thinking this might help to fatten him up, but his plate remained untouched while he went on insisting, somewhat histrionically, "One must die, *draga*, one must die." He looked prepared to dematerialize at any moment, and in a moment of panic, she invited him to live with her. Since he scarcely took up any physical space it seemed harmless enough to lease him full room and board in her head. For weeks, as Mina locked herself up with Lucian, pages and pages of a novel piling up on her desk, the arrangement looked as if it might actually work out. She discovered, however, that the more Lucian intruded upon her mind the more she felt utterly dislocated from herself. One morning she woke to find the following confession scrawled across the page of the previous evening's tussle with her psychic double: "Instead of holding me together, he blasts me apart; I am losing all recognizable dimensions." Mina realized that she had created her own vampire, draining everything she had without giving anything in return; after reading through her thick stack of pages she'd discovered that whatever she thought she'd been writing was completely incoherent.

So she stopped writing. Throughout all of December she holed up in the studio, making lampshades, reading Andrew's plays and Vasili's novels, thinking they might teach her something valuable she had failed to learn from them. How did one construct a story? That's what she wanted to ask them now, nothing more. How did one take a glimmering of inspiration and transform it into living, breathing material? How was it possible to sustain the life of a character beyond one's own incipient vision? Both of their ghosts laughed silently, smugly, because she already knew all of their tricks. They had simply imagined her, and done what they wanted with her, without any respect for the truth. Mina did not think she was capable of doing the same. Even if it were possible to construct some sort of muse, even out of Andrew's long-buried body, what would she be able to produce from this? What could she possibly take from her memory of a dead lover that might supply her with an expanded, renewed sense of self? The recollection of Vasili's rumbling voice, offering her his advice (or had it been an accusation?), suddenly dragged her out of her lethargy: "You just walk into a man's brain, seat yourself comfortably in an armchair, take a long look around, and then afterwards, my dear, you write down all you have found."

She returned to writing poetry, and not one of her monstrously clever cold little poems (yes, Vasili had accused her of this), but a fragmented narrative lyric, exhuming Andrew's corpse only to bury more deeply the whole romance of nostalgia, because there were no illusions of lost happiness; their affair and its aftermath had nearly killed her. *Elegy for Andreas*, composed in the rapid intensity of three sleepless nights, became for Mina an act not of creation but of resurrection, and not of Andrew but herself, and she discovered a way to steal back the theft of her identity; she'd found a way to mourn Andrew without losing herself in the process. When the poem was completed Mina knew, without the adulatory praise of Natalya and her cohorts, that she had written something that achieved a transcendence rather than a loss of self, and having done so, now she might move on into new terrain, where there existed the possibility of loving another without becoming diminished or destroyed by the force of her own petty obsessions.

So when Lucian Doru came knocking again, she thought yes, now I might be ready for you. But no matter how easily the story began to unfold, Lucian had been abandoned for too long. He had started out as one thing and now appeared to have become entirely other than she had intended. Or perhaps it was Mina who had changed; she no longer thought him very attractive; his penchant for prostitutes, opium, and philandering platitudes left her numb. The spark, prosaically, had died, and her desire to write a love story along with it. Hence her speech earlier this evening, which had been an impromptu attempt to describe not so much for her audience but herself what exactly she hoped to accomplish with her now stuttering novel. But she couldn't just leave it unfinished, not after so much energy had been poured into it, so she rose from the bed, sat down at the desk and shuffled through the manuscript, skimming blindly over the last month's efforts. When she came to the blank space following the last sentence she'd written, describing Lucian's bedraggled request to return home to Mrs. Mooney, Mina sat idly twirling the pen in her hand, contemplating a suitable response for poor Mrs. Mooney, who was probably feeling as if she'd already put up with quite enough by this point.

Finally, realizing even Mrs. Mooney had her limits and deserved some chance at happiness, Mina wrote: "Despite my primitive affinity with a presumed madman, I had clearly failed to establish any reality between him and myself."

The expected rap on Mina's door saved her from further puzzling out how to move on from there. She did not bother getting up to answer, since her visitor had his own key. Instead she tidied the manuscript pages, and then, while Besim let himself in, grunting hello, she rummaged around for a suitable casket, and as Besim opened the wine and poured out two glasses, she shoved *Lucian Doru* into a small cardboard box, tied it with a tattered piece of twine and buried it beneath the bed. Later, when Mina and her far-from-estranged husband lay pleasantly, drowsily tangled up in each other's limbs, Besim inquired, as if it were a perfectly natural after-thought to their session of sex, "How goes the book, old thing?"

"Vainly imagining I'd finished, wonderfully," Mina sighed, disentangling herself from Besim's hirsute and heavy thigh to light each of them a cigarette. "I think I've just killed off Lucian, however."

"Poor chap," Besim mumbled, accepting the cigarette and doing his part by resting the ashtray on the broad plane of his belly.

Mina gnawed on her lower lip, removing a stray flake of tobacco. "He kept refusing to give me what I needed."

"So is this the end of it then?" Besim exhaled slowly, staring up at the tendrils of smoke rising above their heads. "All neatly wrapped up and waiting for a long life on the shelves?"

"Not quite." Mina stared down the length of her legs, wriggling her toes, and then abruptly stubbed out the butt of her cigarette, causing Besim to flinch with the cold and unexpected weight of the small glass receptacle pressing down into his stomach. "But I must finish the damn thing . . . it's very sad . . . I feel as if there's something wrong yet at the same time something right . . . leaving it alone . . . but if I don't finish it I'm afraid it will finish me."

Besim removed the ashtray, raised his knee to scratch a tickling itch crawling up his oddly scrawny calf, and then turned to smile fondly, mutely at Mina, who returned his smile, because in that moment she knew what needed to be done. The absurdity of carrying on an affair with her husband had never before seemed quite so extraordinary and mundane. Regardless if she'd been the one to initiate their half-hearted reconciliation, she now realized that her survival depended on making a clean break from everything and anything that might keep her locked, paralyzed, incapacitated, in a never-ending stasis.

"Besim, I think it's time we divorce," Mina proposed.

He chuckled. "What brought this on?"

Mina lay back with her head resting on his shoulder, her right hand holding his left. "Well, I . . . perhaps . . . I just thought it's time. Natalya has offered to publish a collection of my poems and she's bringing me to New York in April . . . so, I supposed since I'll be there I may as well finally file the papers . . . rather, I'll need to find a lawyer before that can happen since we don't actually have any papers. Oh, I don't know how these things are done, Besim. I just know it's time we got it done."

"We could just tear up the marriage certificate."

Mina laughed. "I don't think that would take care of it. Legally, that is. And besides, I thought Gardenia already shredded the thing in one of her silly fits."

Besim also laughed, kissing Mina's much-beloved hand. "Right, yes, so she did, the old stick. I suppose it's just as well, then, this official divorce business. Gardenia's been pestering me about shoving off to the tropics, so we're retiring to Trinidad . . . some decent cricket over there . . . and it'll make her happy to be the Missus rather than the mistress . . . so send me whatever you come up with and I'll sign . . . all expenses paid, of course . . . courtesy of Gardenia."

Mina, momentarily, felt her heart sink.

She didn't know why she'd expected him to resist. That would not have been within his character. Nevertheless, she resented that he'd given in so easily. Stupidly, Mina said something to the effect of prompting Besim to reply, "But that's utter rubbish, old girl, since between us, well, you always did think me a complete bore."

"No, between us, old boy," Mina insisted, "I've always suspected you were my truest love. That is, if true love is supposed to remain unrequited."

As she'd hoped, Besim burst into his much-loved belly-aching guffaw. After he left to give Gardenia Hayle her long-awaited proposal, for the first time in the past sixteen years, Mina realized she was truly alone. She did not bother dressing while she stripped the bed of its sweat-stained, sex-scented sheets, though she did not have the heart or energy to bathe. Instead she took out a starched sheet from the linen cabinet and wrapped herself in its white shroud. Pulling it over her head so that only her eyes, mouth, and nose poked out, she felt herself turning crustacean, encumbered with an enormous shell stiff as plaster, a creature barely formed within the clear glass of a murky subterranean tank.

Through the narrow slits in the blue shutters the streetlamps cast blades of silvery light along the boards of the floor, and on the whitewashed walls, blank as canvases, these nocturnal illuminations crossed and spread a double shadow. Meanwhile, the legs of the furniture began shifting about the room. Mina tapered her eyes into a thin slice of blurred, watery vision and witnessed an aquarium world emerging out of biomorphic silhouettes evolving in constant metamorphosis, an hallucinatory landscape where mists of chaos curdled into the churning organic development of a carpeted confusion as cramped as the clotted convolutions of her brain. Out of this vaporous sludge from which all things might grow, Mina decided every one of her possible selves might emerge, expanding to the point of dislodging every barrier erected between the internal and external worlds, and in this fluid reality, time and space no longer existed, releasing her from all the pains of poverty and aging, the anguish of apathy, and the irretrievable loss of all she had once loved.

Mina then projected herself out of this aquatic realm into the moment of her return to the New World, disembarking from the vessel that brought her back to New York, and though briefly she could only see a woman in a desolate landscape stranded under a threatening thunderous sky, endlessly watching for the signs that would inform her of which way to go, she shifted onto the concrete path of the sidewalk and began floating in a vast ocean of swaying skyscrapers and ethereal automobiles and suddenly the wondrous sense of timeless peace and of perfect happiness. And when she told all of this to Colin many nights after the first night of their fateful meeting, attempting to describe the intricate process of how she had arrived, finding him laid out in an alleyway at her feet, and after he asked what was her first thought upon seeing his face, all she could offer was this inscrutable and prophetic summation of their doomed romance: "How far my mind had traveled only to come back to where I began."

CHAPTER THIRTEEN
Of Moths and Mirrors

The night Mina and Colin collided, Colin was a very unhappy man, and so he might be forgiven his dim view of the events that unfolded that starry April evening. His inability to recall the details was not merely due to the fact that by the time he arrived at the party where they met, he was already on the hazy precipice of intoxication. Rather, Colin couldn't understand why he was there in the first place, and there was no reason to suspect that as soon as he stepped out of the black stretch limousine and onto a scarlet carpet unfurling like a gaping, lolling tongue from between the faux Grecian colonnades of a marbled atrium, that he had stepped into the watery abyss of his death, waiting for him a mere seven months subsequent to the split second he gazed upon the enigmatic smile of Mina Byrne.

Although Colin usually put on a cheerfully bleary smile, on this fateful evening, he stubbornly chose to wallow in his foul mood. He clenched his jaw, gritted his teeth, and scowled irritably at the insistent press of epileptic-inducing flashbulbs ushering him into the tawdry opulence of the St. Moritz. After sailing clear of the leeching papanazis, a crowd of sniveling sycophants and starlets stood between him and the last vestige of sobriety, as he feebly groped his memory for some minimal clue that might explain his presence.

The Franz! The Franz! Mable's clucking reminder squawked in his head. The very same Franz responsible for turning *Dolores* into such a monstrous hit, no thanks to your impossible father! I'm stunned they would want anything to do with you, family connection and all, but want you they do, and in one of their upcoming epics, and you know what *that* would mean! So put on your prettiest face, my pea-blossom, and your absolutely *best* behavior, *Colin*, and make them *adore* you, as anyone with good financial sense should, darling.

Colin often considered firing Mable, but he knew, in spite of all her ruthless pimping, that she was fiercely protective of his interests, and because she made a point of knowing more about his life than Colin seemed to know, he assumed she was aware that he'd been recently dumped by his latest leading lady, and that he was feeling somewhat wounded by the halfhearted heart-broken realization that he'd been half in love with the little ninny. She'd already been spotted simpering on the arm of one of his rivals, and Colin suddenly suspected he was not merely here to seduce The Franz, but that Mable might have orchestrated the entire evening anticipating a series of photographs capturing her client arriving alone, drunkenly disgruntled, confronting his former paramour and her new beau (assuming they'd be here), and demanding a duel of clenched fists (a performance Colin rarely failed to offer when it was expected of him). Was this all part of Mable's neverending publicity campaign? Colin decided he didn't care, though he was prepared to slam his fist into anyone who detained him from docking in the safe harbor of the bar. He was swiftly putting away his second whiskey when a woman's singular voice rose above the rustling din of the room, at first faltering, and then building with husky confidence. At least she knew what she was trying to say.

> *Brood of Romance*
> *depositing the estimable*
> *Porcine Cupidity of her florid mouth*
> *swilling the amorous offal*
> *"Happily ever after"*
> *Trawls a weevil pernicious rostrum*
> *amid barren chaff*
> *strewn in matricidal-memory*

Having no reason to believe that he or anyone else had been persuaded to attend, of all things, a poetry reading, Colin deduced that someone for some reason had begun making some sort of garbled announcement from a raised dais situated in a too dimly lighted corner of the room. He made a squint-eyed attempt to identify the woman speaking, or at least attach to her a more precise set of features, which would then decide for him whether or not he should listen to her, but his swimming gaze had become fixated on Rosaline Westby, crossing the room and thus his line of sight, clinging flirtatiously to another man's arm, giggling in his ear, and dimpling prettily for his pleasure. They then planted themselves, backs turned to Colin, directly in front of the shadowy form of the woman addressing a lazily assembled audience, most of whom continued chattering and clinking ice-filled glasses and flutes of champagne—so much white noise distracting Colin from hearing the lengthy poem being read to them, which only reached Colin's ears in intermittent snippets, as if it were an S.O.S. distress signal broken up by extended spaces of radio static.

Forced to observe Tyrone Cipriano lewdly fondle Rosaline's plump silk-clad bottom, Colin slugged back his whiskey, deciding he may as well enact the charade of discarded and humiliated lover, because he was bored, because it required little effort to do so, or because it was better to do that than reveal to himself or anyone the genuinely wounded, helpless, confused source of his grief and rage, which could not be explained or bartered off for the public entertainment of others. He gestured sketchily to the bartender for another shot, eyes still fastened venomously on the offensive couple. Colin had indeed been replaced a little more rapidly than was decently forgivable, and so he skewered Cipriano with the slits of his seething black eyes (borrowed from his repertoire of proven photogenic film stills), sizing up the man, and concluding that he could easily beat the living stinking shit out of that smarmy slab of ham. Colin then rehearsed the narrative of their broiling feud, which would be dramatized for the press in all the interviews Mable most likely already had lined up for him.

He'd first met the asshole five years ago on the set of *Winterwar*, which had been shot on location in Prague. Filming went two weeks over schedule because Cipriano persistently failed to show up for his scenes. The film, intended as a star vehicle for Cipriano, had catapulted Colin to undeserving (as some insisted) fame, his brooding charisma upstaging Cipriano's waning charms, and even more so after extensive post-production editing had left entire reels of the aging king of action-adventure blockbusters on the cutting-room floor. Cipriano never forgave Colin this usurpation of his stratospheric opening-weekend crown (as if Colin had anything to do with it), and took every opportunity (whenever the press remembered his existence) of snidely insulting Colin's overblown talent as no more than a sign of the public's lowered standards of good taste (which of course did him no favors in endearing him to members of said public, who preferred their fading stars to go gently into that dark night or at least make some kind of unexpected comeback, usually by pulling off a spectacularly tragic and sudden death, none of which Cipriano had the good grace or dignity to do). Colin had always shrugged off Cipriano for the grubby maggot that he was, but now, *now*, he felt inspired enough to smash the slime ball's smirk into smithereens.

He was just about to embark on this worthy mission when he found blocking his path Marcello Sullivan, his old mate and drinking chum from as far back as the first film they'd suffered through together, some god-awful high-seas Navy escapade that had been tritely titled *Last Stop*. True to form, Marcello appeared amiably sloshed while optimistically attempting to suppress Colin's flailing wrath, reprising his role of trusty sidekick, always good for comic relief.

"Brennan, you old git, let's buy you a drink." Marcello maneuvered Colin back to the bar.

"The drinks are free," Colin sneered.

"So is she, my good man, and overcrowded as an open bar," Marcello muttered as he motioned for another round. "Forget Westby! Just look at all these adorable sweet-faced cunts. Not one of them, I promise you, would think twice about murdering their own whoring mothers if it meant the chance to suck your cock."

> *I flood your eye in a venial pulchritude*
> *Infinity squandered in a daisy-chain*
> *Spiraling nebulas in an oasis*
> *Where geysers rappel fulsomely*
> *Until a mere dribble of slavering deceit*

Colin abruptly scanned the room, vainly attempting to catch one substantive glimpse of the woman whose words followed Marcello's crass observation like a smoothly sophisticated punch line, but finding yet again only a blurred sea of faces, he returned to his whiskey, savoring its burn, and finally, belatedly, allowed himself to laugh.

Colin raised his refilled glass. "Right you fucking are, old Sully. A toast to Westby, the hardest working cunt in town!"

"To Westby," Marcello toasted agreeably. "May she suffer the sweet stench of her short-lived success."

"To sweet stinking Rosaline," Colin tacked on, idiotically. "May she grant Cipriano a syphilitic death!"

Marcello cheered before whetting his throat. "Here here!"

Colin did the same, sinking happily into the anticipated, longed-for click in his head, informing him he was now well and truly drunk, while listening to Marcello rehash some raunchy joke, drowning out the woman's voice rippling through the room, still failing to reach him, or perhaps anyone.

> *Neither desire nor the nameless revulsion*
> *Simply a collision of illuminated limbs*
> *Hammering embers out of stones*
> *I am wedged in the feeble vortex*
> *Of your poppycock and scuttlebutt*
> *Confessing my obviated love*

And then Mable Montgomery was standing there wedged between both men, glowering, arms crossed over stingy chest, foot tapping at a terrifying tempo, clearly hell-bent on haranguing Colin with the whiplash of her tongue. Colin bravely stood his ground, glaring balefully over the corona of her wild witchy hair, a look she returned measure for measure, because Colin had done something, or rather, was failing to do something.

He took the opportunity of striking at least one palpable hit. "You were supposed to come here as my date."

She promptly flicked aside his ineffectual swing. "Oh, hush up you baby-faced sot! Now, you know how much I truly detest playing the incessant ball-breaker, but it seems, sugarsnap, you are the most distractible little puppy."

"The bar is not a distraction." Colin took a defiant swig and signaled for yet another round.

"Aye, ish the main event," Marcello slurred.

"Colin, sugarplum, you can drink yourself silly anytime you want, but not here, not now!" Mable smiled, ignoring Marcello. "The Franz has been asking after you and so run along, you dumb melonball, and just be your usual charming self!"

"Queen Mab commands!" Marcello loudly, rudely expelled a lengthy burp in her face.

Colin followed with a grumbling sigh. "And we are but poor sodden slaves . . ."

Then, because Mable always won, Colin abruptly lost interest in the game, turning his back on Marcello, who turned his back to Mable and slurped down the two shots that had just arrived. Mable watched Colin navigate a convincingly graceful weave through the crowd, and once sufficiently assured he was headed in the right direction, gave a sharp kick to Marcello's shin and stomped off before the insufferable slob had the sense to realize the crippling jab had come from her stiletto heel. Meanwhile, during Colin's slow, uncertain voyage towards the detested and detestable Franz, the audible waves of that same woman's voice washed over him, tempting him to alter his course, but remaining somewhere just beyond the horizon of his focus, which once again had become mired in the grotesque mirage of Cipriano possessively pinching the pert curve of Westby's ass.

> *The proliferating truth of you and me*
> *Pilfering lunacy and lecheries*
> *A man and a woman always lie between*
> *Promiscuous plenitudes of identity*

"Hallo, Natalya, Laurenz, great fucking party!" Colin brusquely hailed The Franz.

They turned their heads in unison, assessing Colin with baffled surprise and then subjecting him to a long, awkward silence. The Franz blandly studied him inch by inch, calculating down to the last penny the necessary risk should they decide to cast him in their upcoming celluloid extravaganza and if the profit margin could be expected to outweigh the expense. The Russo-German couple was a most formidable conjugal business machine, regularly pumping out best-selling pulp and smash hit films, and all at the highest quality of cheap entertainment. Indeed, their disinterested appraisal of Colin was only a shallow front, the bargaining chip they used to mask their greedy desire to get their hands on him at the lowest market price.

"Hello, dear boy, but do hush!" Natalya finally condescended to kiss both his cheeks in her pretentious Slavic manner. "Mina is trying to give a reading of her work, which we've just published to great critical acclaim!"

"Who's Mina?"

"Oh, never mind, munchkin," Natalya simpered. "It really is delightful to see you in the flesh! Doesn't he look lovely, Laurenz?"

"Looking hale and hearty as ever and grown since the last we saw you!" Laurenz approved, putting on his best avuncular act.

Colin blearily ignored the monstrously false geniality of The Franz. He needed another drink. He snatched up a passing flute floating by on a tray, and after guzzling it down to the very last evaporating bubble, contorted his mouth in a concentrated effort to suppress the attendant belch. Natalya and Laurenz observed Colin with yet another appraising look, recalculating his worth.

"Thirsty," Colin chuckled, offering one of his most reassuring, melt-in-your-mouth grins while refraining, for the moment, from grabbing up another buoyant glass.

"Those are wise that run slow, my boy." Laurenz horribly mangled his chosen adage.

Colin's jaw automatically resumed its cramp, his fist clenched around the stem of his glass, longing to snap its fragile neck and jab its ragged tip into the man's jugular.

Natalya said, "But not *too* slowly."

Colin warily eyed both of them. What in fuck-all were they babbling on about?

"Right, well, I see your point," Colin agreed, having learned this was the most effective response to anything he found either overwhelmingly uninteresting or incomprehensible.

"Colinoshka," Natalya gurgled, finally getting to the point. "You've read the script?"

Colin chirped, "Unh, yes, yes, I have!" He'd done no such thing; Mable was always giving him scripts, which he never read until after he'd signed a contract.

"And, you are amenable," Laurenz enunciated loftily.

Colin grinned through gritted teeth. "Amenable to *what*?"

"Why, signing on as our lead, darling!" Natalya gushed. "What did you think?"

217

"We would really like to seal the deal on this, Brennan!" Laurenz huffed.

"Well, I'd need to go over the details with Mabs before signing anything," Colin stalled.

Natalya blabbered, "Oh, but Colinieshka! You must promise here and now! Our director, the Great Fassellini, is adamant about casting an unknown, undiscovered, untainted nonentity, something about the integrity of his vision, but *we* are determined to have *you*, and once we do, we're confident Old Fussy will warm up to the idea."

"Fassellini?" Colin scowled, befuddled by this dispiriting surge of all things Italian infiltrating his life, innocuous enough to the ignorant observer, but for Colin, an offensive and unwanted reminder of his brother's ghost haunting some shady and forgotten corner of a cemetery in Siena. "Does that mean we'd be filming in Italy?"

"Oh no, Brennan, we'll be shooting on location in sunny Mexico!" Laurenz exclaimed, transforming himself into a blustering travel agent.

"Hmmm, sounds tempting." Colin arched a practiced brow to indicate the dubious appeal of something he had no real desire or intention of doing, a trick he'd picked up from his severely discerning mother.

Pulling the old Russo sob-story strings, Natalya said, "Colinievokeshka, my lovely, you really cannot say no to a fellow countrywoman!"

Colin succumbed to yet another floating flute and drowned it in one gulp, as there seemed no point in reminding Natalya he had never set foot in Russia, did not speak a word of Russian, and that his thoroughly Russian father would have flat-out denounced her as a fraud. Colin's stomach churned. He needed another whiskey, something more potent than this carbonated piss-water. He was fed up, and afraid of where the conversation might be headed, flooring The Franz with his most devastating grin and imprudently shaking hands.

"Agreed! Sold! I swear by the moon, I'm yours!" Colin recklessly laughed, and then quickly fled the scene, though not before Natalya passed along her warmest, most inappropriate condolences to his father and mother.

Colin suddenly floundered on the shoals of a stone cold, gut-wrenching sobriety. He was no longer on speaking terms with either of his parents, both of whom refused to forgive him: denying his father's name, denying them in their old age the comfort of his presence, their desire for one child, at least, whom they might count on to persuade them of their infinite wisdom and benevolence, their infinitely aggrieved sacrifices and self-absorbed conceits; most of all, they refused to forgive his absence from Andrew's funeral, for choosing instead to remain on location shooting his last picture, *Double Twist*, a formulaic film noir, and thus choosing to ignore the more relevant mystery of his brother's death. In Colin's estimation, there was no puzzle to be solved. Andrew was simply gone and now no one had the excuse of pretending Colin had been anything other than a substitute child to make up for some unnamable loss Vasili and Deirdre refused to admit: the failures of their marriage, their failures with Andrew and Andrew's failure to remain the same affably amenably singularly adored boy he'd presumably once been before Jamie and Colin intruded upon the scene.

All that Colin recalled of Andrew is that he'd persisted in ignoring the fact that either of his brothers had ever been born. Only once had Andrew acknowledged Colin's existence with something other than his glazed stare of blank recognition. Colin was four and Andrew nearly eighteen, an idolized hero, on the brink of leaving home forever, and never to be seen again, unless one counted those enforced family visits from which Andrew could not escape. They were alone together, exiled to the shabby sitting room in one of the many shabby rented houses they'd inhabited throughout their childhoods. Ignoring the muffled argument taking place between their parents from behind the closed door of their father's study, Andrew sat fuming in an armchair, flipping through *The New Yorker*, because he knew the argument was about him. Colin lay sprawled on the rug at Andrew's feet, poring over an assemblage of preserved specimens pinned and mounted in several square boxes, clumsily sounding out their Latin names:

Acherontia atropos; *Abraxas grossulariata*; *Zygaena filipendulae*; *Albuna oberthuri*; *Nudaurelia cytherea*; *Amphicallia bellatrix*; *Nymphalis antiopa*.

It formed an unintelligible poem, one Colin practiced repeatedly, soothingly, whenever his parents shut themselves away either to bicker or batter out between them another of Vasili's novels or lectures, forgetting all about the small boy who also lived in the house, who was often left to come up with his own small sources of amusement since his older brothers were usually absent, shipped off to school, where Colin also sensed he'd be sent as soon as he was big enough. Colin studied the spots and stripes and varied prints of each fibrous appendage, the feathered antennae, scaled bodies and bristle-based hindwings, seeking a clue that would answer for him which one was misplaced. Vasili had set up this game to distract his son, laying out segments of his collection, instructing Colin to find the one that did not belong, and then disappearing for hours in the study. Vasili would eventually emerge to pour himself a cup of coffee, indulgently, distractedly ruffle Colin's hair when he announced he'd solved the puzzle, and then shuffle back to his interminable shuffling of index cards, puzzling together the pieces of his afternoon's writing. Colin simply assumed he'd come up with the right answer, but never had anyone to translate the names printed out in his father's careful calligraphy, or even why his father thought any of this was an amusing task to set up for a child who would have been much happier with coloring books and crayons and comics.

He decided to take the rare opportunity of asking Andrew for help in solving the riddle behind the purpose of this game, a chance he might never be given again since Andrew was running away and that's why their parents were arguing, though Colin wasn't sure where or why Andrew was going, or why his parents were so angry about him going, and he did not think anyone would ever see the need to explain it for him, and so he asked Andrew, "Why does papa like butterflies so much?"

"Those aren't butterflies, but moths," Andrew grumbled, still flicking through his magazine.

"Mofs?" Colin lisped, troubled because it seemed his father had been trying to trick him, and he couldn't understand why, and so he insisted, "They look like butterflies."

Finally condescending to glare at the specimens, Andrew confirmed, "Well, they're not."

"What's the difference?"

"Moth's are nocturnal, butterflies aren't," Andrew mumbled.

"But how do you know?" asked Colin.

"One flies at night, the other during the day," Andrew dully replied, still flicking through the pages of his magazine.

Colin spluttered, "No, here, now, these," because clearly these moths weren't doing any flying, and it was not nighttime and there had to be some other clue Andrew was withholding from him. "How do you know?!"

"How do I know?" Andrew flung aside the magazine, glaring down at Colin's furious frown. "I know, dimwit, because of their names, and because that one, there, is clearly a butterfly and the others are moths."

Colin said nothing; his mouth twisted up in an angry pout, his brow furrowed over eyes now narrowed into suspicious slits; Andrew was teasing him. It was more than Andrew had ever given him, but Colin did not like it. He stood up, fists clenched at his side, and evidently threatening a tantrum. So Andrew chose to laugh and slide from his chair to sit on the floor, taking hold of one of Colin's chubby fists and forcing him to sit next to him.

Andrew said, "Right, so look. Unlike the others, this one has clubbed antennae and much larger hindwings, which are nearly proportionate to its forewings. That's the one that doesn't belong, if you hadn't figured it out."

"Did papa make you play, too?" Colin asked, ignoring the obvious answer to the puzzle in favor of exploring the realization of this unexpected connection he now held with his brother. "When you were little like me?"

"Yeah, when I was little," Andrew muttered, irritated for some reason. "But at least papa took the time to play the game with me."

Colin was still too young to envy his brother this crucial difference between their childhoods; he was only too happy to have Andrew's arm slung around his shoulder, holding Colin against his ribcage, as they now studied the specimens together.

"Anyway, this one's easy to solve, because it's papa's favorite and he throws it in everywhere, in everything, even his stupid games," Andrew remarked somewhat enigmatically, pointing to the blue-spotted and yellow-limned bruised-black velvety wings of the *Nymphalis antiopa*. "It's a Camberwell Beauty, and very rare, very difficult to catch, because it flies very fast and very high."

"Did papa catch this one?"

"Doubtful, though I'm sure he likes to pretend."

Colin chose to move on, pointing to the other samples. "What are these?"

"Death's Head Hawkmoth, Magpie Moth, Six-spot Burnet, Golden Clearwing, Pine Emperor, Beautiful Tiger." Andrew listed off tonelessly, as if reciting a poem by rote, but one far more lovely in associative imagery, at least to Colin's ears, than its Latin counterpart.

Colin asked, "Where do they come from?"

"Where does what come from?" Andrew was startled because he did not know if he was being required to explain how insects went about reproducing themselves, the process of pupation, their father's obsessions, or the origins of anything existing in this incomprehensible universe.

"The names," Colin insisted. "And how do you know it's a mof just cause of the name?"

"I know it's a *moth* because papa told me so, and for all I know he could have made up the names himself," Andrew sighed, preparing to disentangle Colin from his side, resume his lofty perch on the chair, or stomp out of the house altogether.

Colin repeated his first unanswered question. "So why does papa like them so much?"

"I don't know, maybe because his own papa was a lepidopterist," Andrew guessed, foregoing the chair and looking for his coat. He'd decided he was no longer going to wait for their parents to emerge from the study with their decision as to whether or not they'd help finance his move to New York. He knew that they would, because his mother always won every argument in his favor, and so there was no point sticking around listening to his father hold out against him. He was going for a walk, and by the time he got back there'd be a check waiting on the kitchen table and a note from his father ordering him to pack up and leave by morning.

Colin stopped Andrew in mid-stride. "What's a leperpederast?" He turned and studied his brother's earnestly puzzled expression and then exploded in a guffaw of pleased laughter. Colin's error may have been due to his syllabically challenged tongue, but he'd just produced a linguistic invention not even their father might have dared.

"Ask papa," Andrew grinned, winked, and then walked out, still laughing, the last Colin saw or heard of his brother for ten years, until they all went down to New York and had dinner with Andrew and that funny woman who later became his wife, and the next day, when they put Jamie on a ship to France and Andrew went on pretending he wasn't there, that he, Andrew, was the one who didn't belong in the puzzling picture of a family that didn't even know each other's names anymore because Andrew had decided to call himself something else. And so had Colin, eventually, still worshipfully emulating Andrew, running away at eighteen and deciding to become an actor, and only because he wanted to be in one of Andrew's plays, and now, just look at where that had got him: in a room packed with people he despised, suffocating and choking back his grief because he would never be able to prove to his brother how much more they were alike than different.

But how did Colin know? What were the distinguishing traits that allowed him to identify the two of them as belonging to the same species? What was the basis for this classification? What did he have to go on other than a shared name and the shared origins of two people who had certainly not been the same two parents? The gap in years between Andrew and Colin had inevitably resulted in two very different versions of Vasili and Deirdre; so in all reality, did they even come from the same family? How would he ever receive an answer to this, since Colin and Andrew (and forget Jamie, who'd always asserted he had nothing to do with any of them) had never been given the chance to confer and compare between them their experiences? They would always remain strangers; there was no possibility of amending this, and Colin wanted to weep with all his rage and regret over what was now permanently frozen in time, because Andrew had cruelly decided to abandon Colin to all his confusions, just as he'd always done.

Colin realized he was staring back at his own reflection as he muttered incoherently into the opacity of the bar's mirror a request for more whiskey. The bartender eventually intervened between Colin and his double, handing over an entire bottle and advising Colin that would be the last he'd get out of him. Colin left a generous tip, took the bottle while ignoring the accompanying empty glass, and stumbled over to one of the tail ends of the semi-circle of chairs where he'd spotted Marcello slumped and staring in the general direction of the rest of the audience's attention. Colin planted himself beside Marcello, took a swig from the bottle, then passed it over to his friend, who accepted, drank, and returned it without bothering to acknowledge Colin, whose own gaze had once again become glued to the preposterous Cipriano, who still rudely stood in the center of the crowd, still rudely groping Rosaline's ass while leering at the woman who stood on a low platform, *still* persisting in reciting her endless poem.

> *Once we nearly gave birth to a nymphalis*
> *With the travesty of our nightly dreams*
> *Embossed on its buttery blue-bruised wings*

Colin lowered the bottle from his lips, mid-swig, gasping as if he'd received a sharp blow to the gut. He leaned forward, certain he was about to vomit. He raised his head, squinting fiercely, fully concentrated on piecing together a clear vision of the woman's face. He didn't think he had the strength to stand and move closer to the dais, not without crossing paths with Cipriano, so Colin settled for slumping back in his chair and listening to her voice; it was her voice he fell in love with first, before he ever saw her face.

> *Perhaps we metamorphosed*
> *In the exhausted blindness of an instant*
> *Exchanging rhizomes zygotes antigens*
> *Chromosomally communing with god*
> *Litigious liturgies spattered on our*
> *Vinous tongues*

Colin decided he was beyond drunk. He knew he would not remember any of this in the morning, but right now, in this moment, he understood perfectly; she was speaking to him and only him, regardless if she hadn't the slightest knowledge of his existence. Colin took a final swig from the bottle and passed it over to Marcello, finally mustering the courage to clamber to his feet and begin an unsteady weave across the room, to stand before her and prove his presence, his undying devotion and—and what? He had collapsed in his chair, dragged down by Marcello, who had misconstrued Colin's intentions.

"Lemme tackaro thish, ol boy, I'll bash hish brainz in foree ever shees it cumin," Marcello rose unsteadily, bottle cradled in his arms as he sashayed towards the unsuspecting Cipriano.

Colin realized what was about to happen, but he didn't care, though he wished for the whiskey again, just a small drop, his tongue now cleaving to the roof of his mouth, caked dry, unbearably dull and knotted . . .

> *We might have danced to an aria*
> *Along the banks of the Arno*
> *Or blown bubbles beneath a placid pond*
> *Or chased the stars into dawn*
> *And like Arabian lovers*
> *Told stories without endings*
> *Until there were no words*
> *To begin again never having to end*
> *And never asking why*

Because Colin had long ago stopped wanting answers to all the things that couldn't be answered; because he had always known there was no reason, no why, for anything, at least when it came to understanding why we insist on loving those who refuse to love us in return; because Colin knew the breadth and measure of love, *as boundless as the sea, my love as deep*—he was about to get up and declaim these very words, but things began to whirl out of control.

> *Muteness shatters against margins of mania*
> *Devolves to the voluptuous slaughter*
> *Muscle sinew meat carnal tissue*
> *To extract an indissoluble desuetude*
> *Deliquescing into sighs a cessation*
> *Plaguing egoism with empathy*
> *Toward the superficial thud of dissension*
> *And rumble of evasive murmur*

Marcello, the imbecile, had chosen this precise moment to challenge Cipriano in lieu of Colin, who meanwhile sat as if comatose, but was in fact swiftly falling into an impromptu, reckless, ill-starred love. Marcello attempted a clumsy jab, which failed to miss its mark, allowing Cipriano the advantage of swinging a hard left into Marcello's jaw, sending him sprawling to the floor and inadvertently smashing the whiskey bottle Marcello had somehow managed to hold onto, so that when he lurched back to his feet he raised aloft the jagged glass of its broken neck, which inspired a crazed screaming from the onlookers as they foolishly made a mad rush for the doors or contributed their jeers of support for one side or the other. Marcello eyed the broken bottle as if stunned to discover it in his hands, and at an utter loss now as to how he should proceed, he began crying out for Colin to make a show of arms.

Colin stubbornly remained in his chair, watching the woman whose voice had waned and paused. Her eyes flickered about the room, seeking someone who might explain for her the absurdity of why she was there. Marcello continued bawling Colin's name, and everyone collectively, visibly turned towards Colin, for they knew who he was even if she didn't, and so her own gaze fixed upon the strangely, simultaneously slumped yet stiffly stricken man seated and staring up at her. Colin finally came to his senses.

He grumbled out a thunderous command: "Let the lady finish her damn poem!" The entire room fully shifted its eyes onto her, but she did not know whether she should go on now that she had an audience forced into listening to her every word. Colin beamed at her his widest, most insensible grin. Could she even see him? Was he, for her, anything more than a shadowy something approximating the shape of a man?

> *I no longer object*
> *To where the objects of the room decide to appear*
> *Or what is obscured in the gloom they solidify*
> *Or what unnamed creature might arrive*
> *If the curtains were not curtailed*
> *Permitting corners to dissipate*
> *Forming an ovoid abyss*
> *Expanding to the shape of my silence*
> *Gracelessly I go as all things indelibly go*

Then she sighed, relieved to have finished, and Colin bounded out of his chair with the single-minded intention of introducing himself to her. The Franz, however, were mauling her with their greedy paws, intent on dragging her off the stage while the crowd offered a drunken applause, which The Franz seemed to interpret as a rumbling roar of disapproval. Misinterpreting Colin's sudden lurch towards the stage, Marcello resumed his brawling stance, unconvincingly waving the broken bit of glass in his hand. Cipriano took the opportunity of landing Marcello out cold on the floor with a solid right and then blindsided Colin with a sneaky left, and from there, it was all very much over.

Ears ringing, Colin slammed his fist into Cipriano's mug, a spurt of blood erupting from his shattered nose; someone grasped at his arm, and Colin wildly swung at his unknown assailant, rendering him unconscious alongside Marcello. When he glanced down to survey his handiwork, Colin happily discovered his victim was none other than Laurenz Franz. Well, that took care of that! No moonlight bathing in Mexico! Colin then mercilessly began pounding Cipriano to the bloody pulp he'd envisioned earlier that evening. Cipriano, however, insisted on battering at him until they ended up rolling around on the floor, thrashing clumsily, idiotically, trying to strangle each other, and for the most part failing. Colin at last succeeded in toppling Cipriano onto his back, fist smashing into his jaw, snapping it back so hard his head cracked against the parquet floor, and there it was, that was that, Tyrone Cipriano was out of the goddamned picture. Colin stood triumphant, blood-spattered, and ludicrously grinning.

Someone, meanwhile, was shrieking her silly head off at him, enjoying her brief moment in the spotlight, and someone else was informing him he was a useless son-of-a-bitch.

"Go on and fuck yerself, Westby." Colin spat out a glob of bloodied saliva at her feet, and then, with immense satisfaction, said, "You're fired, Mabs." But there was still the matter of Natalya blubbering over the inert half of Franz and Franz. Colin continued grinning, feeling with his tongue for any chipped teeth, mildly amused by Natalya's antics as she demanded Colin's immediate expulsion from the premises. He shrugged off the summoned security, who considerately nudged him out the rear exit into a rat-infested alleyway.

So there he was, as soon as he regained consciousness, lying flat on his back and looking up at the stars, a rare vision usually obscured by the smog-infested clouds perpetually hovering over New York. And there she was, sitting beside him, refusing to help him to his feet but simply studying him, hands primly folded in her lap, a glimmer of disapproval in her eyes before she decided he was worth blessing with the miracle of her smile. He wanted to weep with joy, his heart cracking open with the long-anticipated sight of her, infinitely more beautiful than he'd imagined, but his right eye had rapidly begun to swell shut. He wanted to say her name, which he thought he should know, but couldn't remember how or why, only that somewhere, somehow he'd heard it before. Martina, Malinda, Marlena, Malvina, Malina, Marina, Mina? He tried to mumble out all of these possibilities, but his lower lip was split and swollen, a tooth had definitely been chipped, and his chest felt as if it might burst, as he laughed in spite of the pain, gasping for air, asking, "Who are you?"

"A little less than kin, but more than kind," she murmured, deliberately misquoting (because she already knew how this would end), then gently, kindly helped him to his feet, leading him home, wherever that might be.

CHAPTER FOURTEEN
Laura's Romance

I wish, as another memoirist repeatedly wished, that my parents had a mind to what they were doing before they went about making me, but like a stray, runty, and starved puppy in love with the first person to offer a kind word or morsel of meat, my father followed my mother home. This turned out to be a West Village one-bedroom on loan from Natalya, who brought her paramours there whenever Laurenz was laid up in their Hampshire house suffering from his latest bout with gout. Colin immediately staked his claim by stripping off his soiled, blood-encrusted clothing, and leaving shoes, socks, shirt and trousers strewn in a random trail leading towards the bathroom.

"Don't worry," he assured Mina, who stood leaning against the closed front door, blandly observing his stumbling and presumptive performance. "I'll sleep on the floor and won't say a single word to you."

Mina wandered into the bedroom, where she discarded her own clothes and lay naked in the bed, not because she was in any way seriously considering taking Colin as a lover, but the late April evening was oppressively humid and the sluggish ceiling fan incapable of doing anything more than circulating the muggy air above her head. She pulled the sheet up to cover her legs, hips and breasts, and lightly swaddled in this way, she lay with her left cheek pressed into the pillow and her right ear listening drowsily to the splashing sounds of the overgrown child bathing himself.

She awoke at some point in the middle of the night and discovered Colin had crawled into the bed and now had her wrapped in his cold and clammy embrace. Mina lay pondering the exhalation of his breath on the back of her neck. In the morning she turned and saw that he was already awake, propped on his elbow and smiling down at her; she returned his stare with a brief flickering of recognition and displeasure. His smile expanded into a self-deprecating grin; the grin evolved into an expansive burst of laughter, and Mina helplessly began to laugh, as if they'd just shared some intimate naughty joke. Colin then shamelessly leapt from the bed, without the slightest concern for his or Mina's nudity, and trundled off into the other room. He returned with a towel wrapped around his waist, a glass of milk and a plate of rolls slathered with jam, which he'd pilfered from the kitchen and commenced greedily gulping and gobbling while sitting beside her. Mina had yet to say a single word, and Colin, appreciating her silence, garbled out between mouthfuls that as soon as he was finished with his breakfast, and after they found him some clothes left behind by one of Natalya's heftier cross-dressing lovers, he would take her out to the country.

The "country" turned out to be the Sheep Meadow in Central Park, and as they lay beside each other in the dewy grass, staring up at the drift of clouds and naming the shapes they formed, Mina thought, this is ludicrous. As they strolled through the marbled halls of the Metropolitan, staring at frayed tapestries, tiled mosaics, painted frescoes, engraved steles, monstrous columns and granite tombs, Colin claimed he would take her to all their places of origin: Bayonne, Ravenna, Crete, Athens, Rome, Alexandria . . . and Mina decided, we are not going anywhere. Tramping all the way back on foot to the Village, his hand in her hand, perspiration dampening the back of her dress, blisters bubbling in her shoes, Colin's boisterous voice leading her through the cavernous city, Mina lifted her eyes to watch the sky reflected in the glassy exteriors of towering buildings, and she realized, I have already been here before. When they found a suitably obscure and shabby tavern, with high-backed wooden booths, a thick fug of cigarette smoke, and sawdust, chalk and peanut shells littering the floor, and as soon as Colin plunked down a bottle of wine, with one glass for her, and a bottle of bourbon, with one glass for him, Mina knew that now she had to reveal the truth, because if not now then she never would.

"Colin, I must tell you," she began, faltering but determined to be done with it. "We're not exactly strangers. I mean, yes, of course, we've just met, but I've known—."

"Oh, no, please," he interrupted, laughing, foolishly believing Mina was about to spill the contents of her heart. "Don't tell me you're like all the other women who fall right into my lap. At least put up a damned struggle."

Mina smiled tartly, misinterpreting his boyish bravado for arrogance rather than anxiety. "That shouldn't present much of a problem. I am perfectly capable of playing the whole silly game, and so now that's cleared up between us, let's proceed to get very drunk, as I don't see how you'll get me into bed otherwise."

Colin exploded into surprised laughter, which sent Mina's head reeling, her spine shivery with pleasure, and her resolve quickly dissolving in the power she had to make a man adore her; thus the matter of her previous entanglements with the men in Colin's family was never cleared up, because Mina thought, none of it mattered since it would never go beyond one more night. By the time they left the bar, dusk had long dissipated into darkness, and Colin had reverted to his stumbling drunkenness of the night before. Leaning into Mina as she led him home, once more, he announced that he'd fallen in love with her.

"You know what you should do, Mina?"

"What should I do, Colin?" Mina maneuvered them into the lift and pressed the button for the third floor, the doors briefly sealing them in the moment preceding the rest of their lives.

"You should fall passionately, madly in love with me." He sloppily pressed his mouth against hers and failed to elicit the passion he'd hoped to inspire.

This was not because Mina, in her own inebriated state, wasn't already feeling half in love with Colin, but she had decided she was not yet half as willing to give in. Upon entering the apartment, Colin again peeled off all his clothes, disappearing into the bathroom. Annoyed, Mina picked up after him, sure that this was a sign of things to come. She neatly folded the borrowed clothes, though of course they now belonged to Colin since he had discarded the ones he'd ruined in the previous evening's brawl. Had it only been last night? Mina felt they'd already lived an eternity of lifetimes, yet they had scarcely shared anything. She thought, convinced, this is for the best. We'll pass out and then I'll send him on his way in the morning, without an invitation to return, without any hint whatsoever that what I want, what I truly want but cannot have . . . but Mina never finished that thought.

Colin had begun singing in the bath some operatic nonsense, a baritone aria sounding like a child's fabricated notion of the Italian language. As if drawn by some oafish siren stranded out at sea, Mina stood in the doorway watching him bathe. He lay fully stretched in the tub, head back, eyes closed, bursts of elongated singing escaping his lungs, and observing him in this strangely meditative pose, Mina began piecing together all the moments of every moment since they met: the brute force of his fist slamming into another man's jaw, the ease with which he strode across a room, the elasticity of his grin, the way he collapsed in a chair, on the ground, the graceful fluidity of his every movement, gesture, infinitesimal tic and flicker and fidget of his hands, eyes and mouth, even now, as he lay perfectly still, droplets of water creating a chain of rivulets across the curved contours of his clavicle, scapula, and ribs, and the crevasse of flesh dipping down between the sharp ridge of his hips and flat plane of his abdomen, all of this articulating its own perfect, self-contained intelligence. Without considering the consequences, Mina decided to join him in the bath.

And from here I can go no further; there are limits to what I'm willing to imagine. So let us fast forward through the months of May, June and July, which consist of many similar nights and afternoons, as Colin and Mina consume the time by drinking away the hours until they are left in a giddy stupor, empty bottles of wine multiplying magically all by themselves. Because they drink they are capable of remaining absolutely present for each other, their conversations sneaking around unspoken confessions. When they tire of talking, they sit curled in the same deep armchair sharing the same inverted book, pretending to understand the words, their bodies unsatisfied and exhausted by their insatiable greed for the other's skin, wanting to dissolve all barriers between them and melt in the reflective haze of the broiling heat rising from the asphalt, glass and steel of the city through which they blindly wander all summer long.

When Colin is not there—and he often disappears, much like his unmentioned and unmentionable brother—Mina sits in this same chair waiting for him, thinking of his flesh, as if it were abstracted and removed from his name. She pretends her desire is not fixated on Colin. He could be anyone. He is no more than the iconography constructed for him by the silver screen: the embodiment of the American man; tall, terse and temperamental; his slightest glance expressing disdain for all things feminine because his greatest desire is to remain untethered, roaming across the vast plains of his unanswerable, indefinable longing. Mina knows he'll eventually reappear, unexpectedly, because at least that much is predictable, and she has convinced herself that she's only carrying out this affair because in the end it will make a good poem. She also recognizes the depths of her self-deception, but realizes too late the lie of the mind; because she discovers, when attempting to pick up a different lover during one of Colin's unexplained absences, that her body refuses to respond to anyone other than him.

She lies awake until five in the morning then sleeps until noon then lies in bed another two hours keeping the image of his body revolving in her mind. She refuses to entertain the fact that at this moment he's sleeping beside another woman and pretends she's the only woman he's ever loved. He tells her this and she chooses to believe it, though Mina knows all too well that throughout the course of any self-deluding romance, one plays out a number of roles and fantasies, and that any illicit affair is always dull outside its own parameters, its own moments of immediacy. It is only when he shows up, when he is viscerally present, that she is convinced of his reality. When he's absent, his existence, their tenuous connection, seems laughable; it is only a story in which she is not a participant, as if she is not the one pushing and pulling him back and forth between her desire and guilt.

He more or less accuses her of this one night after having stayed away several days. She hears his insistent knock on the door, slowly counts to five and then lets him in; he paces the room swaying and weaving between articles of furniture, insulting her with a litany of clichéd endearments: "You aren't as strong as you think. You don't know how to love a man without losing control. I don't want anything from you. All I want is to see you smile." Mina smiles and kisses him until he agrees to be silent. While she fetches him a bottle of cold beer, he sits hunched in sodden insolence (a phrase she thinks has a nice ring to it). When she returns, she sits in his lap, and asks what she has never asked, because it might reveal more than she wants to know: "Where have you been? Where do you go? Where do you live?" He replies nowhere, nowhere, and nowhere, and then mumbles in her ear the only original albeit nonsensical thing she has ever heard him say: "You'd be better off living with me in a taxi-cab where we can keep a family of aristocratic cats."

The next morning, considerably sobered and eating their buttered toast in bed, Mina swipes away at the crumbs and decides she better put an end to it, and so says the exact opposite of what she thinks: "Colin, love, I think we're seeing rather too much of each other."

He bursts up out of the bed, lumbering about the room like a dancing bear and growls at her, "So you think you've learned all there is to know about me, is that it?"

"Well, you've hardly bothered yourself with knowing me," she calmly, coldly points out, returning the fierceness of his glare until he has no choice other than to collapse back into the bed, laughing wildly, pinning her down.

"Christ help me, I love you, Mina Byrne." He kisses her. "You're unlike any woman I've ever known, an impossible egg to crack."

Mina thought, yes, all of this is impossible, but then, she thought, why not? Colin takes her in his arms and falls asleep and for the first time in all her life she feels safe, protected, securely moored beside another person who wanted nothing from her in return. There was something inexpressibly vulnerable in him, something that tethered him to her, and she to him. So Mina, in that moment, like any woman madly, blindly, insensibly in love, chose to believe everything might be possible, because not once did Colin demand that they tell each other the stories of their lives, allowing Mina the excuse of never having to conceal or confess any part of herself. And Mina thought this was redemption.

Then Colin was forced to go to Mexico to fulfill his film contract. And Mina was forced to remain in New York since she had not yet gone about the necessary task of finding a lawyer to dissolve her forgotten marriage, of which Colin had no knowledge, thus requiring Mina to devise a series of excuses. She could not follow him to Mexico, well, simply because she was not some common woman who just picked up and left everything behind to go chasing after the first man to promise her a life of dissolute adventure. No, Mina resisted, wryly observing with obvious cynicism, she was the epitome of the New Woman, independent, eccentric, and of course, at the moment, celebrated for her daring collection of poems. Besides,

Natalya had set up a reading tour out west, which she really couldn't get out of; it seemed they both had The Franz to blame for keeping them apart. Colin couldn't argue with that, and so he vanished into the sunset and Mina almost convinced herself that was indeed the end of that.

She negligently went about the business of becoming divorced, hiring a lawyer recommended by Natalya, who in typical fashion advised Mina to pump Lord Beresford for all he was worth. Mina advised the lawyer to draw up annulment papers since it had only been an arrangement of financial convenience, and since there were no children to prove other-wise, the lawyer agreed this would be the most sensible and hasty route in seeking closure to the prolonged sham. Mina signed without checking to see if the lawyer had arranged for alimony, trusting both he and Besim would have her best interests in mind. She left the papers with the lawyer along with the address Besim had sent her several months ago. Believing they'd find their immediate way to a villa just outside of Port-of-Spain, and would be returned to the New York family court in an equally speedy fashion, Mina considered her marriage officially annulled.

In no way did she then seriously consider running off to Mexico. Rather, she decided she should take the time to weigh her options. She'd received all kinds of propositions from variously eligible and admiring men, many of whom were far more reasonable choices than Colin Brennan, who was no more than an aberrant fantasy, or so Mina reminded herself now that he was no longer there, knocking on her door and sucking out all the air from her lungs the moment he walked into the room. To continue enter-taining even the briefest twinge of longing when she woke in the morning without him was foolish and possibly harmful, hurtful, because she knew if he should ever discover after all this time who Mina really was, as he must, inevitably, because such things always occurred in every tawdry romance novel through which she'd disdainfully flipped while lying beside Andrew on the floor of Sara Sorrell's loft, well, then, Mina couldn't go further. She firmly, for the last time, decided the whole thing was over. Then, in late August, he began barraging her with terse and tritely phrased telegrams, which, when compiled, formed the first and only love poem he would ever write to her:

> *I am lost without you.*
> *I want to marry you.*

NOSTALGIA

My soul is dying.
No woman could ever compare.
Send a lock of your hair.
Better yet come with all of your hair.

After reading and rereading each of these silly sentences, and on the day she was to board a train for Chicago, Mina exchanged her ticket for one headed south, and for five days she watched the world outside her sleeping compartment shift and unfold, noting very little of the American landscape because it was the country she was so anxious to leave behind. Upon crossing the border into Mexico, she devoured every last inch of its volcanic, glittering magnificence: the northern deserts drenched in the glow of an amber, violet, and scarlet sunset were transformed the following morning into rugged mountains concealing within their veined bellies silver, copper, gold, opals, and amethysts, and finally, as twilight descended, just beyond the last craggy ridge, they dropped into a bejeweled valley, the central node of all her desires, where Colin waited somewhere in that gleaming, glittering city unsuspecting that she had travelled so far to begin her life again.

Stepping off the train at the tail end of September, Mina was blasted by the unexpected cold, and riding in the taxi, nearly cried at the sight of so many bedraggled, beggared and begging hordes of children roaming the streets, and when she entered the less-than-opulent foyer of the Hotel de los Sueños, the first person she saw was none other than Sara Sorrell. The woman was evidently departing; she stood in a sharply tailored business suit that clung to all her ample curves, tapping her high-heeled foot while watching a bellhop carry out piece by piece all the pieces of her luggage to the taxi parked outside, presumably the one in which Mina had just arrived. Mina thought she might sidle by in the shadows; it seemed unlikely Sara Sorrell would recognize a woman she'd met only the once, and over ten years ago. Sara however had a keen eye, a remarkably detailed memory (she certainly recalled meeting Mina more than once), and an astonishing lack of tact, for any other woman would have allowed Mina to pass by unseen.

"My goodness, is that Miss Mina Byrne?" Sara loudly, lazily drawled. "What in all that's holy are you doing here?"

"Good evening, Ms. Sorrell," Mina politely replied, and then came to a stammering standstill. "I . . . I . . . I . . . well, I had thought . . . I cannot say . . ."

"Oh heavens, girl," Sara clucked, her suspicion giving way to sympathy at the sight of Mina's pallid features; she firmly took hold of Mina by the elbow and all but dragged her to the hotel's deserted bar. "You look on the verge of collapse. Let's get a stiff one in you and then we can have a quick chatter like two old friends."

"But, haven't you—." Mina tried to clear her throat. "Haven't you a taxi waiting?"

Sara chuckled. "Phooey! Long as they got the meter running these loafers will wait 'til hell freezes over, and I ain't the one paying for the ride."

While Sara ordered two tequilas with salt, lime, and a back of whiskey spritzed with soda, Mina considered her options. She was visiting Natalya, but then Mina remembered Natalya was in Barbados enjoying a three-some with Daisy and Juno; she could not imply she was meeting Laurenz, for that was far too implausible; in fact, there was nothing she could say beyond the truth, and more than she dreaded Sara's disapproval, she feared Colin might saunter in at any moment and then it truly would be all over. Mina could not possibly explain how she knew Sara Sorrell without lying about Andrew. So she observed the other woman lick the salt from her palm, toss the tequila down her throat and clamp her teeth onto the wedge of lime to see how it was done. She managed a fair mimicry and then guzzled the whiskey as if it were water. When she put down her glass to meet Sara's gimlet eye, she realized there was nothing to hide. Sara had smoothly puzzled all the pieces together.

"Well, that's put the English roses back in your cheeks," she grinned lewdly. "Take my whiskey. I never have more than one in a sitting, since I need my two legs to stand."

Mina wasn't sure if this was intended as some kind of double-entendre, but she took the whiskey and slowly sipped, listening to Sara as she chattered on, as promised, about the cinematic disasters of the past few weeks: the crew were a pile of drunks; the sets a shoddy wreck of plywood and paint; the director a gibbering maniac; the extras an indolent bunch who showed up for the catering and aimlessly wandered off as soon as the siesta hour hit; the script a farce; her own part she'd had to rewrite; and her co-stars, except Colin of course, were all hopeless amateurs. Her part of filming had finished, and none too soon, as the director had carted the whole rotten lot of them off to shoot on location in the tropical hell-hole of Veracruz now that her bordello Madame had run the entire revolutionary pack of dolts out of town, just as Natalya had promised she would, which reminded Mina . . .

"Are you still Sara Sorrell?" she asked, suppressing a burp.

"Of course I am," Sara laughed, betraying no confusion as to why Mina asked such an absurd question, since Sara seemed capable of taking all things in her wide, ambling stride.

"I didn't mean," Mina started, then stopped, then tried again. "I didn't think it would go as far as this. But it has, clearly, and he doesn't know. Not about Andrew . . . and me . . . or his father. I couldn't tell him, and I thought he'd forget about me as soon as he came down here."

Sara smiled at her, a smile that merely said she didn't waste her time passing judgment on other folks for mistakes she herself could have easily made. Then she offered Mina a word of advice, or, a warning, Mina couldn't tell, and she wasn't in any mental or emotional capacity to decipher it. She only wanted a bed, a long cry, and Colin's arms around her.

Sara paused, and realizing Mina had not heard a word she'd just said, resorted to giving her a sisterly squeeze of the hand. "You look in need of a hot bath and a solid sleep. He won't be back for another week, so just ask the porter for his key, Room 115, and tell him you're his wife or they'll treat you like a dime-store whore and never answer your requests for room service. They're terribly Catholic that way down here."

Mina nodded, and then accepted from Sara an address in New York scrawled on a bar napkin, blankly studying the black smudges of ink without understanding what they might be trying to tell her.

"I doubt we'll be running into each other again, dearie," Sara assured her. "But birds of a feather, I always say, so don't be a stranger if you're ever in need."

Sara watched while Mina dutifully inserted the napkin in her battered, scruffy purse, where it would remain buried for five months until Mina retrieved it, desperately in need.

"There we go, off to bed with you, and best of luck!" Sara winked and then she was gone like a whirlwind tumbling herself out of there.

Mina lodged herself in Colin's room with a bottle of tequila and the shades pulled down. A week later, she woke in the hazy muted glow of falling dusk on the last day of September with Colin's arms around her and his breath nuzzling her neck.

"I thought you'd finished with me," he whispered.

"But we haven't finished talking," Mina murmured, at last coming to life, and apparently, according to my calculations, by the following morning or thereabouts, I was already in the process of mitosis, madly, obsessively multiplying and dividing.

The film wrapped in mid-October and Colin announced he was done with the whole picture business. He asked Mina to elope, and when she asked where to, he suggested Buenos Aires, where they could disappear; no one ever needed to know where they'd gone; not knowing anything about each other's pasts, they would imagine a new life, new identities for themselves. Although Mina had no certain proof of whether she was actually divorced, she stood in the chapel of Guadalupe and vowed to love Colin until the breath left her body. The next day, they took a train to Salina Cruz, a scrubby but rapidly expanding fishing village nestled among the barren hills and along the pebbly shoreline of the Bahía Ventosa, and from there they would sail down the Pacific coast of South America. They could have easily booked a berth on any of the available steamships coming in and out of the newly built seaport, but in a moment of vagabond inspiration Colin chose to buy a rotting dingy and immerse himself in transforming it into a sail-worthy yacht. So they temporarily set up house in a rented bungalow, its windows and shingles rattling away every night while the brisk gales sweeping in from the sea rocked them to sleep. Mina busied herself with the shopping, cooking, mending of sails and generally blissful lethargy that overcomes most women who believe they are in love but are in fact pregnant.

Near the end of November, and despite Colin's claims that they had severed all ties to the past, Mina returned home to find delivered on their doorstep a package forwarded from Mexico City and addressed to Colin in his father's recognizable hand. The package was in the ominous shape of a book. Mina left it on the table, unopened, where it remained for several days, as Colin was preoccupied with putting the finishing touches on the boat. One day, when rain kept him indoors, and while Mina was out the entire afternoon waiting in a doctor's office for a simple enough diagnosis, Colin opened the package, sat down in a tattered armchair and read his father's latest novel. He was still reading when Mina returned home, for it was—is—a very long book, the longest ever to wildly spin itself from the intricately threaded loom of Vasili's imagination. When Mina entered the room to give Colin her news, he glanced up from the book, furious, betrayed, interpreting easily the truth, and right before they launched into what would be their first and final argument, Mina recalled and decoded Sara's warning.

"Of course he hasn't forgotten you," she'd said, blotting with her fingertip the lipstick smeared around the rim of her emptied tequila glass. "Women with pasts always interest men—they hope history will repeat itself, but just remember, my dear, when it does, their interest inevitably turns to contempt."

CHAPTER FIFTEEN
Sara Sorrell

Unlike Mina, her own history was comprised of learning when to cut her losses and move on. According to Dame Weston, she began her vaudeville career under the stage name of Margie La Mont, perfecting the blowzy charms that later translated so devilishly onto the Hollywood screen, the very same hallowed destination that had been the ambitious dream of Winsome Baby Weiss from her earliest days performing the Saucy Samba, which had been the precociously provocative opening act for her father's boxing-circuit tour that eventually went bankrupt after Solomon "the Bludgeon" Weiss was incarcerated for fixing his fights. This unexpected predicament landed his daughter and wife into a "financially vulnerable spot of desperation," to quote Dame Weston's exact words.

"But Mother got us a gig concocting costumes for the ladies in the late night nude revue at the Amphion, and soon enough I learned the high-kick and the shim-shimmy and, more importantly, that you should always save a boyfriend for a rainy day and another one in case it doesn't rain. Eventually I snagged me a real Daddy Warbucks. Saul Sorrell was some big-time producer on the Great White Way, and if you know how to put two and two together, then you guessed it; I married him, but gawd that was a long con if there ever was one. Tottering Saul was already hitched to some babushka from Bavaria who wasn't about to go down without her fair share of kvetching, so I put in my time as the mistress while Saul put me in the Follies, and from there it was bit part by bit part until I was sashaying and belting and earning all the primary applause. After all my trails of tears, after all those dog days in the chorus line, after all that bitter-sweet jazz, all dues were paid and sweet old Saul turned out a real mensch. He finally ditched his old broad, put a ring on my finger and my tukhus in his Madison Avenue penthouse.

"The deal was, though, no more hoofing it for me. I had to be respectable, see, learn how to wear my clothes tight enough to show I was a woman but loose enough to prove I was a lady, and I thought fine and dandy. I was getting on in years, a tired twenty-four and looking forward to becoming a mama bird clucking over her little brood, but that old sot Saul couldn't hold up his end of the bargain. I'm sure I don't need to tell you the reason why he failed to make an entrance. Believe it or not, I'd never before encountered this kind of glitch in the male apparatus. So what do I do? Like a schlemiel I go out and buy a whole library of those bodice-rippers. Goodness I've never read such nonsense, and contrary to appearances, I've read all sorts of thinking man's books. How did you think I got so far in life? Well, I was in desperate straits, so I devoured every bit of that trash thinking I might get some useful tips, but nothing, I got nothing. All I learned was that good sex is like a game of Bridge: if you don't have a good partner you'd better have a good hand, and more importantly, it's not the men in my life that count but the life in my men so I exchanged Saul for this reconverted loft and a handsome alimony and he got himself a new chorus girl.

"I deserved every penny squeezed out of the old putz for stealing nine years off my life, and though I was on the verge of bored and bitter, which ain't a pretty picture, well, you know what they call me, I'm the rebound girl. I always bounce back. First thing I did was start schlepping my shim-shimmy all over the country, touring wherever they'd take me, and why, you ask, if old Saul had set me up for life? Well, you can't quit the theater, you know, until it quits you and more than that I wasn't about to retire my laurels and die a divorcée shacked up with a bunch of stinking cats and stinking of gin. Besides, I'd been hustling my hips for so long that's all I knew how to do, but it was stink awful exhausting because if my time with Saul taught me anything, over a certain age all the juicy parts shrivel up quick as a lizard on a hot rock. It's no surprise I was ready for some rejuvenating, something to give me the boost I needed to keep going.

"That's how I ended up with your brother, but I didn't know about Mina until after the fact. At the time, when he'd proposed, I had no reason to doubt he was in love with me and well, it's like Mother always said, a man in love is like a clipped coupon . . . it's time to cash in, especially when you're a woman on the wrong side of thirty-five and mooning over her empty womb. So I cashed it in and what did it get me? Well, never mind, you already know all about the trouble I went through with Andrew."

Sara took a respectful moment of silence for which Jamie was sorely grateful, thinking she might have gone on until her tongue fell off. "Yes, well, that's all in the past." He cleared his throat. "Right now I'm more concerned with—."

"Believe it or not," Sara assured him, "if it weren't for Andrew I would have never made such a success of things. So frustrating, the dear old thing, as meshuga as they come; always disappearing without a word and then showing up the next morning, moping about the place if he wasn't writing and when he was writing off he'd go in some kind of manic fit. I never knew what to expect, but that was half the fun of it at first; made me feel like a girl fresh out of her silk knickers, but of course I wasn't and could only take so much of his antics. Most of our marriage I spent loafing around the country headlining musical revues. The rest of the time I spent in the bath, my one and only haven from Andrew's moods, and after all my hours of meditating I came up with the decision to start writing my own parts. I always had a flair for shtick ever since my old vaudeville days, and so I knew this was the way to go especially after Andrew promised but failed to write me any good material.

"No need to rehash *Claudia's Revenge*; we know how that turned out, and by this time I'd taken up with Mable. Mother always told me that when choosing between two evils you should try the one you've never had before, so I thought why not a woman for a change. Goodness, what a nudnik that woman's turned out to be, but she's kept me on the straight and narrow, and who would suspect, after all I'd suffered, that I'd find a bit of luck and happiness. And it was all thanks to Andrew; without him I never would have written *Stardust Lily*, which was a smash on Broadway, and then I just followed it with one after the other . . ."

And then she began to rattle off all the names of her one-woman plays and Jamie didn't know if any of this was leading to the point of his visit or if she was as bonkers as Andrew had been; he didn't have the energy to interrupt her, though, and so sat in a suspended coma, allowing the low drawling drone of her voice to wash over him until he forgot why he was there; or how he'd ended up running this errand for his father when he'd sworn after the last time he left New York that he'd never do Vasili's dirty work for him again.

". . . so that's how I ended up in Mexico City, and the only joy I had of it was working with that lovely hunk of a thing. Matter of fact you two could be twins. Has anyone told you? Anyway, he was a real professional on set, but a little lost puppy off of it. I took him for a drink one night to see if I could put the wag back in his tail, as it were, though mind you I never have more than one, but I felt it was a family obligation, considering we're mishpocha, more or less, and can you believe the odds we'd end up working on a picture together? Gawd, just remembering that sweet boychick I met all those years ago at that awful family dinner Andrew took me to when he—Colin, that is, not Andrew—was just a budding thirteen, or was it fourteen? Either way it puts a lump in my throat, especially since there was nothing I could do for him. He just sat at the bar with a stiff upper lip, not even cracking a single one of his adorable grins, but I figured soon enough it was a woman who'd got him so low. It's always a woman with you Brennan boys, isn't it?"

Jamie blinked, utterly baffled, shifting uncomfortably in his chair. "Pardon?"

"Oh dear, all I've done is jabber on like an old Rebbe delivering a megillah and without enlightening you the slightest bit further than when you first walked in the door," Sara chortled, and not so much at the thought of impersonating the role of a religious man but rather the sudden realization that James Brennan had never been in love, much less intimate, with a woman in all his life. No point then, really, in trying to charm him, but then, she thought, he's such an insufferable schmuck, she may as well torture him a bit longer.

Sara rose with a twitch of her hips, slimming down the tweed of her skintight pencil skirt as she shambled over to the sideboard, and after nearly forcing upon Jamie a generous snifter of brandy, because she always knew when a man was urgently in need of a drink, she wandered aimlessly about the room, all the while rattling off more inconsequential details of her life, the sound of her voice rattling in his head, which could only manage translating abbreviated snippets of unwanted information.

"The film turned out a complete piece of schlock . . . but it didn't matter since I stole everything but the camera . . . signed on for a five-picture deal with Paramount . . . California here I come . . . just turned fifty . . . give or take a few . . . looks like I've struck the golden age . . . ditching the Big Apple for good . . . next week as a matter . . . looks like you caught me in the nick of . . . believe it or not . . . this only arrived a few days ago."

Jamie looked down in his lap to discover a thin sheaf of paper; he put away his drink, hands trembling, and read; the words, like Sara's rambling narrative, only reached him in a kind of fragmented Morse code transmitting a frantic S.O.S. from some dimension of time and space just beyond his immediate comprehension:

"Dear Ms. Sorrell—birds of a feather—desperate—Colin disappeared—Buenos Aires—stuck—out of money—no access to funds—tried reaching aunt in Paris—nothing—don't want to leave—what if he—but very ill—wit's end—need money for berth—Trinidad—then can find him—can't bring myself to contact his family—."

Jamie's eyes began to sting. He refolded the letter, finished his drink, and waited for Sara to say something, anything.

"Of course I immediately wired her the money."

"Very kind of you, considering . . ."

"But there's been no confirmation the funds were received, and so I'm terribly worried. I was considering going down there—."

"No need," Jamie cut her off. "I'll leave immediately. Maybe he'll have shown up by the time I get there. Thank you, you've done more than could be expected, Sara."

"Sasha, actually," she laughed hoarsely, brushing aside his arrogant contempt, reminding her of the callous treatment she'd received from his parents during all those years when she'd done her best to look after their son, when they'd wanted nothing to do with him, before, during and after they'd needlessly locked him up in the loony bin. Because she'd learned long ago there was no point in stooping to the level of the Novikovs and their entire élitist ilk, she ignored Jamie's crass manners and politely deflected attention back onto her own cheerfully tawdry existence. "Wouldn't you know? I showed up for the screening of the film and when the credits rolled I was shocked to see my part attributed to some dame called Sasha Weston. Apparently the producers, a real pair of mavens those two, decided this was a catchier nom de guerre, but it makes no difference to me as long as

I get paid, so Sasha Weston it is. Keep that in mind if you're ever out west, you're always welcome to come on up and see me some time."

But Jamie had already walked out the door. Don't feel sorry for Sara; she wasn't sad to see him gone. In fact, as soon he'd shut the door behind him she was struck by the belated euphoria of freedom that comes with knowing one has escaped all further obligations towards a role with which one has long grown bored. Yes, Sara has admirably, beautifully, generously played her part, and that's the last we shall see of her as she shimmies offstage and onto the rest of her life, transforming herself into an American icon of pluck, wit, and bravado. By the time she died, she'd reached the pinnacle of success any immortalized sex symbol might hope to achieve: the woman and the legend had long since become one, and the name had nothing to do with it.

CHAPTER SIXTEEN
Anima

The morning after the cataclysmic rift responsible for severing them, irreconcilably, irremediably, though not instantaneously, Colin woke to discover his wife still in his arms. A nightingale chattered away in the acacia tree outside the bungalow's bedroom window. Actually, he did not know what kind of bird was singing or what type of tree stood parched and emaciated in their windswept and barren backyard. In fact he doubted if nightingales were native to this country, but he liked playing with the idea of a bird flown too far south to roost in a tree that probably had no business being here either. Colin glanced down at Mina, recalling a snippet of poetry . . . *my soul into the boughs does glide: there like a bird it sits, and sings* . . . and for the first time resented her ability to remain so closed, contained, so utterly concealed, even while she slept. She curled into an even tighter ball, as if protecting, even now, all her secrets, as she murmured some insensible string of syllables. Perhaps the nightingale had slipped into her dream, or more likely the bird was dreaming her, and as soon as its song ended, Mina would dematerialize in the feathery morning light. This too, was impossible to know, and he did not think anything would ever be clear to him again.

It had all seemed so obvious the night before, when he'd thrown his father's book at her, and she hadn't moved but only flinched as it struck her in the stomach, certain proof that she knew she deserved it. If that hadn't been enough to confirm for Colin everything he'd just read, then the look in her eyes as she stared emptily back at him, as if she'd been expecting this all along, that said it all. Mina had stooped heavily, wearily, to pick up the book, noting its title before placing it on the table, and then she collapsed in the chair Colin had vacated. He'd left the room, because if he hadn't he might have strangled her. When he returned nearly two hours, three beers and five shots of tequila later, he'd found her still sitting there waiting for him. He opened a bottle of whiskey, poured out two glasses, handed one to her, which she did not drink, and settled himself at the small round dining table, slumped and glaring across the room at Mina.

"How long?" he demanded, calmly.

A creature of some sort scrabbled over the rooftop above their heads.

"How long, Mina?"

An owl hooted, greeting the night in hoarse anticipation of the unseen but certain prey waiting in the shadows.

"Tell me, how long!"

A moth repeatedly crashed against the window pane, desperately wanting to be let in.

"Mina!"

She laughed, faintly.

"I don't know what you're asking me, Colin."

"How long before you were going to tell me?"

"Tell you what?"

"About this." He snatched up the book, then kicked it across the floor towards her feet.

Mina ignored the now much battered novel. "What am I supposed to say if I haven't even read it?"

"You know what I mean."

"Do I?" she smiled, lost, losing. "I thought the past didn't matter."

"Of course it bloody well fucking matters!" Colin barked, his tongue exploding in a language Mina had never heard him speak before. "It matters a fucking shitload when my father has written a whole goddamned book about you!"

Mina couldn't deny that, because her name, albeit transposed, was displayed on its front cover; nevertheless she made the feeble attempt to convince Colin that it was all a misunderstanding, his own mistranslation. "*Anima* means soul, Colin, as in *anima gemella*—soul mate—or *un anima in pena*—a soul in torment."

"I fucking well know what it means," he growled. "As in Mina the woman I thought was my soul mate but turns out to be the *animating force* behind my father's imagination inspiring him to write about how she hounded my brother into his grave, where he remains for all fucking eternity a soul in fucking torment."

Mina continued lecturing him. "Or it might be an allusion to the feminine persona existing in the male psyche, his shadow self, the source of his creativity, which would make sense since both your father and brother liked to pretend I was their muse locked away as their dirty little secret, their own little plaything waiting off in the shadows of their collective subconscious. Oh, but we know, don't we, that Vasili doesn't buy into all of that psychological quackery. He couldn't possibly have been so clever, though I'm sure the whole book is just a fantasy dreamed up by a madman who refuses to get a grip on the elusive passage of time, and so he creates some alternative universe, some otherworld through some looking glass where everything is turned upside down, in reverse, because that's the version of reality he prefers; oh and let me guess, there's a bit of incest thrown in just to spice things up. Have I got it right? Is there anything I'm missing? If so, I'll be happy to read the damn thing, and then we can really get to the truth, or at least an accurate interpretation of why he chose that particular title."

During all of this Colin had begun pacing the room, seething, slowly releasing an animal Mina had always suspected lurked within him, ready to pounce, rend her flesh to pieces and devour her whole. Then suddenly, he'd stopped, turned, and faced her wearing the face of a stranger; it wasn't Andrew's livid yet helplessly forlorn face when he'd confronted her about Vasili, all those years ago, which she might have been able to cope with, knowing how to diffuse, soothe, and circumnavigate his wounded betrayal with wry quips and calm denial. Colin had turned savage, snarling, because she'd just told him everything he needed to know, and it was not what he'd expected or wanted to hear. When he snatched her out of the chair, his hands brutally digging into her flesh, Mina had no choice but to defend herself as they proceeded to claw and hiss and tear into each other until they were on the floor, in the bed, weeping, falling asleep, clinging desperately to the last shreds of their innocence, dissolving in tears . . . *I told my wrath, my wrath did end* . . . and Colin suspected there was nothing left, but now, watching her sleep, he thought any words approximating forgiveness, and all the words spoken between them, all the poetry she had offered him and he had tried to offer in return, all those scraps of sonnets and soliloquies recalled from his erratic boyhood education, all of it had become a tarnished, corrugated heap of junk because someone else's words were now lodged between them.

Perhaps something might be salvaged. Her eyes fluttered, briefly, but she only descended deeper into her dream. She had become painfully unknown and all too familiar. He'd always known that one day she would vanish, but not yet; she was still his life, his love, yes, his anima. This could not change, as much as everything else had altered. He thought, it could not all be her fault. Not the tangled story of Andrew, Mina, and Vasili, which she'd finally told him, her version, which he chose to believe. No, she wasn't at fault for this, since his father and brother could have been any two men she might have known before Colin, and whatever had happened, it was long ago in the past; it had nothing to do with the story of Colin and Mina. Yes, she should have told him sooner, from the very beginning, but then, Colin realized, there might not have been a beginning, and with that terrifying, vertigo-inducing thought, he knew it wouldn't have mattered. He would have still chosen Mina, followed her to the ends of the earth, or asked her to follow him, and knowing this, it was impossible to leave her.

The betrayal was not all hers. He should have listened more carefully to her that night they'd first met, but most of it was a delirious drunken blur, and any remembered details most likely the product of a vaguely fabricated reverie, which had become part of the fabric of his love for her. Now, though, it was clear. The poem she'd been reading aloud had not been a private love song, but a public display of mourning, for Andrew, and once again Colin was haunted by his childhood, once again the substitute for a child, or even a lover, that never existed. *Elegy for Andreas.* How had he missed this? He'd read Mina's published collection all those weeks waiting for her in Mexico; he could have easily figured out the puzzle because it was right there in front of him; he just hadn't been looking at it from the right angle, and now that his vision had shifted and refocused, it was glaringly obvious that he was the object that did not belong.

Colin rose from the bed. He kissed her lightly and in response she moaned, dreaming. After a quick, hot bath, he silently dressed, leaving behind his shoes and leaving the house without once looking in a mirror. His heart unexpectedly burst with a leap of unadulterated, untethered happiness as he loped down to the piers, relishing the hot sun on his face and the gritty sand beneath his feet, and at the sight of the small yacht he released a small yelp of excitement, the joy of a small child greeting his favorite toy. His bare feet padded softly along the jetty, startling the solitary, wizened old man who sat with his mottled legs hanging over the side, dangling his line, patiently waiting for anything to bite.

"Holá cabrón!" Colin greeted the old man, who glared up at Colin doubtfully, grudgingly, as if he'd just been deeply insulted. Colin shrugged it off, ignored the old man's baleful stare and went about his business, untying the boat, flinging the rope aside, scrambling onto the deck, and nimbly readying the sails, which Mina had so lovingly repaired. Colin noted the mild breeze and blissfully clear sky, tinted a rosy-fingered-dawn.

"*Se avecina una tormenta,*" the old man grumbled. "*Debenámos esta aqui!*" Colin glanced down, nodded in thanks, but paid him no mind.

"*Se avecina una tormenta!*" he repeated, gesticulating with his gnarled index finger out towards the vast stretch of sea and then back at Colin. "*Debenámos esta aqui! Una tormenta! Se avecina una tormenta!*"

Colin offered the man one of his sloppy grins, only comprehending the last word. He cast off from the pier, and in response to the old man's wildly frantic wave, beckoning him to return, Colin hollered out a recklessly, ridiculously ebullient, "Adios, amigos!"

The old man glanced over his shoulder, searching vainly for whoever else stood about witnessing the *gringo* fool sail off to his certain death; discovering the pier deserted, he mutely watched the boat slowly fade into the horizon.

Meanwhile, Mina woke from a dream, gasping for air, for Colin, who was always there, offering a hand, a thigh, a caress, a grumbling breath, reaching out to silence her fears and bring her back to the semblance of safety that his body was capable of promising her. Realizing his absence, but convinced it was only temporary, Mina fell back asleep without doubting his return. Seventeen minutes later she stumbled down the hallway and plunged her head over the rim of the toilet, emptying her stomach until she collapsed in hoarse, retching sobs, disgusted by the noise. After rinsing her mouth and face, and then collapsing again beside the toilet, sensing another wave of nausea, she stared numbly at the absurdly carpeted rather than tiled floor and knew she would never see Colin again. The incontrovertible proof of this was found in the still damp impermanent stain of his footprints, left there by Colin when he'd emerged from the bath.

NOSTALGIA

Waiting for the morning's oppressive queasiness to subside while watching Colin's footprints evaporate, Mina could not deny that these were the last lambent traces of his body in all its undoubted gravity, the last segmented evidence she would ever have of his existence. Simultaneously, because the magic of the human imagination exists in its ability to believe two opposing thoughts at the same time, Mina listened for the sound of his footsteps crunching along the sandy path leading to their front door, the click of the key turning in the lock, the slight sigh expelled from his lungs announcing his arrival home, and afterwards, everything would go back to the way it had been before he'd learned who she really was. In this way she managed to get up from the floor and crawl back into bed. Colin would be there when she woke.

Meanwhile, again, she dreamt the same dream, in which Colin led her by the hand, black pearls dripping from the ocean of his eyes; butterflies chased stars through her hair and a small child ran laughing before them towards the slanting shadows of a sun setting on a horizon that could never be reached. The horizon could not be reached because it vanished. The dream shifted and Mina was alone in a gray fog, or more precisely, an absence of anything material that might define for her the contours of her own body. The longer she remained in this borderless suspension, the more acute her pain. When she thought it was no longer possible to continue breathing, a face and body appeared in all its precise dimensions and exactitudes of scent, sound, and semblance, and then she woke, gasping in incoherent grief. In her dream, Andrew had smiled at her, and he had told her she should not worry, and she should not be afraid, because he was not lost, only momentarily detained.

CHAPTER SEVENTEEN
Delirium

My mother's long journey towards me ended on a morning late in the month of May in the barrio of San Telmo five months after she reluctantly departed Salina Cruz on a Japanese steamship that chugged her down the Chilean coast and left her in Valparaíso from where she crossed inland on a train transporting her across Argentina until it delivered her to Buenos Aires and a one-room *conventillo* on Humberto Primo where she grew increasingly despondent with each day that her belly expanded and my father failed to appear. In his place, Mina was forced to confront his double, as she feverishly, foolishly opened the door persisting in her belief that Colin would materialize without warning and they would resume their lives as if he had never inconvenienced her by leaving her alone for so long. Instead, this man standing in her doorway was a stranger, as shocked by the sight of a heavily pregnant, destitute and delirious Mina as she was to see him, standing there pretending to be Colin when she knew it could not be Colin, because Colin's eyes were a crystalline blue and his brother's were as black and flat as Mina's own sunken, dejected gaze.

Certain he was a fleeting figment of her imagination, Mina returned to the bed. She lay there, immobile, palms splayed across her swollen belly, drifting into the memory of the telegram she'd received informing her of Lauren Lowell's death. Mina wished now that she had not been so cruel towards her mother, leaving her to die alone without her daughter at her bedside assuring her that she had always loved her even if she'd never told her so before. The thought of Lauren's emaciated body sinking deeper into her deathbed as the tumor ate away at her perpetual loneliness and regret for the life she should have lived only heightened Mina's motherless grief, washing over her in waves of unbearable guilt. She tried to imagine a memory in which her mother held her as a small girl, singing her Hungarian lullabies and telling her she was loved and everything in her life would turn out just as she dreamed; from there, Mina reconstructed a childhood in which Lauren and her daughter shared immeasurable moments of perfect understanding of the other's wants and needs because they had always known that they belonged to each other; that Mina could not have been born to any woman except the one who had smiled at her that day in the church and told her that she must always remember the happiness they had shared, briefly, without expecting or asking for it to be received.

To be honest I don't know if this is Mina's fantasy or my own; perhaps while I kicked and turned and prepared to leave her womb we shared the same dream. It doesn't matter because my uncle was there and he only wanted to know the same thing my mother wanted to know but refused to consider: What happened to Colin? Where was he? Could he be found? Was it possible to retrace all the steps that had led to his disappearance? Jamie was about to ask these impossible questions, but he wasn't sure whether he had shown up at the right address. There had been no mention in her letter to Sara of any pregnancy, and he had no idea of how to recognize the woman who had written that letter; he only had an address, and suddenly wishing that this was not the right address, for the woman on the bed looked in need of more than Jamie felt capable of offering, he hesitated, remaining awkwardly in the doorway, and Mina continued concentrating on ignoring the ripple of dull pain spreading from some indefinable place deep within the muscles of her abdomen.

Since I do not wish to leave the reader in needless suspense, the questions Jamie had come here to ask were never answered; and in this moment it could hardly make a difference as to whether or not anyone ever discovered the precise location and fate of Colin's body because I am impatient to be born.

"Miss Byrne?" Jamie cleared his throat in reply to her extended groan.

Mina refused to confirm her name. As he offered a stumbling explanation for who he was and why he was there—she only heard this information in fragmented bursts of unwanted and unnecessary information: "I've just come from New York—actually Paris—parents received a telephone call—he never returned from Mexico—so my father sent me—spoke with Sara Sorrell—I've come down as soon as—have you heard from Colin?"

Mina did not hear this question. If she had, she might have laughed. All she could think was why doesn't he ask about me? Is he not expecting some kind of explanation for my existence, as if I were put here on this earth only to explain over and over again why I had the absurd misfortune to fall in love over and over again with the same man? Is he here because he's the only one left and now it's his turn? I won't I won't I won't go through any of this, not now, not again because the last time I lost everything. So she lifted her head to tell Jamie to leave her alone to die but something warm and wet gushed out from between her thighs and Mina collapsed back onto the bed. Jamie watched as a dark stain spread across the front of her dress, refusing to give in to the clammy hysteria he sensed this should cause him, as if he'd been here before watching this same scene unfold, in another lifetime, long ago.

"Miss Byrne—Mina—is there anything I can do?"

Mina answered with a primal anguished scream. Jamie nearly turned and fled down the hall but not to find help; only to run and never look back. The woman from the neighboring room, however, poked out her head, saw Jamie standing in Mina's still open doorway and shambled over to stand beside him, her body smelling pungently of garlic and chili and something else as musty as molding mushrooms. She took one brief satisfied look at Mina, turned and then ordered Jamie to "*Espere aquí,*" and before waddling back down the hall towards the stairwell, muttered over her shoulder, "*Voy a traer una de las hermanas.*"

By this, Jamie assumed, she had gone to fetch whoever it was that might be of more assistance, and now that he felt certain there was nothing else he could do, or was expected to do, he chose to sit beside Mina and hold her hand and tell her everything would be okay. Mina stared up at him, eyes glazed with glassy recognition; she smiled, with difficulty, as if she had always known him and then she concentrated on refusing to scream for the next twenty minutes, which is how long it took for two Betlemite nuns from the Iglesia de Nuestra Señora de Belén to appear. They bustled into the room with an assured and unwavering faith that this and nowhere else in the entire universe was exactly where they belonged, since it was their order's mission to serve the sick and poor, the wretched and devastated, all the detritus of this world that their God had abandoned to their care. They certainly seemed to know Mina, tittering and cooing, calling her by name, admonishing her in their stern and tender and infinitely forgiving voices for failing to take better care of herself, or the child, as they'd advised. One of the sisters tried to shove Jamie aside, but Mina fiercely shook her head and began calling out Colin's name, wrenching on Jamie's hand. So that's where Jamie remained while Mina focused all her anguish on breathing and pushing; it didn't take long; I wanted out and less than an hour later I slipped out as slick as a seal with a fine coating of black hair, two blue eyes, ten fingers and ten toes and a greedy mouth which the nuns attached to my mother's breast. I gurgled and burped and because my mother's face was only a blur I trusted that she was looking back at me. She wasn't. Jamie was, though, and seven years later when we were finally reunited he told me that the moment he first saw me it was love at first sight, which is the very thing all children long to hear, from someone, anyone, even if he was not the one from whom I needed to hear these words.

Regardless, he was the only witness to my birth and for that I loved him in return. He held me while Mina slept for three days, only giving me up when one of the nuns stopped in to spoon soup down my mother's unwilling throat, forcing her to feed me, and then muttering ominously as they gauged the progress of her continuing fever despite their cooling cloths and wealth of herbal remedies. They did not waste any prayers. Mina seemed determined to die, or at least Jamie had convinced himself she was going to die. So in those three days he constructed an entire life for us, without my mother.

He would take me back to Paris and raise me as his own; he would teach me to swim and to play tennis; we would take automobile trips across the Alps or through the Pyrenees; we would holiday by the seaside in summers and spend winters huddled by a fire while he told me stories about my father because he could tell me nothing of my mother; and if my father by some chance was resurrected, then Jamie would hand me back over to him, as if I were a treasure he had kept safe until my rightful owner showed up to reclaim me. Jamie knew Colin would never reappear; he was rational enough to realize he was gone forever; and so in Jamie's mind, irrationally, I was already his and his alone, a foundling from some fairy tale, whom he would ensure never wanted for a thing, would always remain in the enchanted realm he had created for us. For these three eternal days he sat with me swaddled in his lap, drinking in a delirious happiness slowly creeping over him until he forgot how the world could have ever existed before I was in it.

Again, I cannot be certain if this was Jamie's fantasy or something I had reconstructed for myself; in any case, my mother did not die and even if she didn't want me for herself she could not imagine giving me to a complete stranger, which is exactly what they were to each other. They both realized this as soon as she asked for her child back. While she nursed me Jamie averted his gaze and Mina stared at him with a cold gleam of suspicion.

"Why are you still here?" asked Mina.

"There was no one else," replied Jamie.

"You could have left."

"It wasn't clear you were going to live—."

"Her father's not dead."

"Yes, well . . ."

"He isn't." Mina clenched her jaw. "I know that he isn't. He wouldn't just leave me."

"So what are you going to do?"

"Look for him."

"What about the child?"

"That's none of your concern."

"But she's Colin's child, isn't she?"

Shifting me to her other breast, Mina laughed, exasperated. "Of course she is. But she's not yours; she doesn't belong to any of you. I won't let you have her, because that's not what he would want. He didn't want anything to do with any of you, and neither do I."

"Mina," Jamie calmly spoke her name, since there was something frantic crawling into her voice. "How are you going to find Colin? With what money?"

"I haven't any idea. It seems I've already depleted the annuity my father left me. My aunt in Paris would help but I've heard nothing from her—."

"So let me take you back to Paris." He didn't mention the money Sara had wired and was probably still waiting to be collected from the bank.

"But how will he know where to find me? This is where we planned to start our lives, and I'm close to the docks. I go there every day waiting for his boat, like a fisherman's wife . . ."

Her voice trailed off in a whimper as she allowed me to fall from her breast, her head beginning to knock repeatedly against the headboard of the bed. Jamie rose and picked me up to nestle against his shoulder while he patted out of me a dribbling burp.

"Mina, you're unwell," he murmured softly, soothingly. "We don't have to go back to Paris. I'll stay here with you and help look after the child."

"For how long?" she eyed him warily, suspecting a trick.

"As long as you need. And once you've recovered your strength, if we haven't heard from Colin by then, if he hasn't shown up, then I'll help you look for him."

"Why? Why would you do this?"

"What else can I do?" Jamie smiled helplessly, but not at Mina.

Mina shut her eyes, drifted into sleep and Jamie stayed with us in that seedy tenement room for a week, watching over Mina as she watched him. I don't know what they said to each other, if anything, because that was never part of the story when I asked Jamie to describe for me, repeatedly, the day I was born, my favorite fairy tale in which I played the starring role; it didn't end happily though, at least not as Jamie had hoped.

He returned one day from looking for better lodgings in the Barrio Norte to find Mina had gone, taking with her whatever meager possessions she owned, including me. Jamie waited until nightfall for us to return, and when he finally thought to open the side table drawer where he'd stored an envelope full of banknotes for the down payment on an apartment, all the contents of his heart messily spilled out before it cracked and closed.

Apparently, my mother could not accept my uncle's offer because the thought of tying herself to the last available Brennan brother was beyond the limits of plausibility, and Mina was no longer willing to cast herself in a love story, not even a romance with her own child.

Three weeks after I was born, she arrived in Port-of-Spain on a small freighter, hired a cart and driver to take her to a hacienda five miles east of the city and knocked on the door until someone agreed to let her in, because her arrival was unexpected and unwanted, at least by the lady of the house, who was not in fact a lady but still merely the mistress since her husband was not yet divorced. When Besim informed Mina of this by way of explaining Gardenia's rude reception of her, Mina never asked why the papers had not been signed or returned to the lawyer in New York but only collapsed, heartbroken, realizing that she and Colin had never been legally married. Besim promptly had her put to bed in a room with thick drapes, where she remained nearly a month in a neurasthenic haze, which Besim indulged since after nearly fifteen years of marriage he had become inured to Mina's silly fits; eventually she would snap out of it, rising from the thick fog that enveloped her, and be on her way. Meanwhile, though, there was a child needing to be fed, and so I was given to Bertha, a local wet nurse.

The night before Mina left, after signing the new divorce papers Besim had hired a new lawyer to draw up, ones that actually provided her with a generous alimony, which the first agreement had failed to leave out, and because he was now the legal father of a child he could not disown, Besim asked her the only question that had yet to be answered.

"Mina, old thing, what name do you want to give the girl?"

Mina stared at Besim blankly, as if he'd reminded her of something she had never thought to consider, which in fact she hadn't, not once.

"Laura," she finally replied. "For my mother."

Then she was gone, sailing off around the world looking for a ghost; there were never any letters, postcards or telegrams; the only thing Mina wrote in all those missing years was a poem narrating her endless journey away from me.

The Undead

Can one who still has presence
remain displaced?

Crescendo
of love's charade
entails no plausible respite
beyond this too provisional role
of my nautical-haunt
bedeviling your unknown grave

Recalling the plurality I was beside you
inimical to imperfection
cracks tattered by minuscule sentiment
of memory's bedlam

NOSTALGIA

No supreme architect
raconteurs originary nebulae
imploding into necessary apocalypse . . .
retracing your vaporous location
to the unimaginable once before we were—

Allow me at least
this misconception
of mourning's indolence

Choosing
to float in Lethean lethargy
an unwilling Eurydice
refusing to return

CHAPTER EIGHTEEN
Luminosities

When Jamie opened the door to discover Mina standing there waiting to be let in, he nearly slammed it shut in her face. She should never have come, but he could not turn her away. Her face appeared gaunt and pale; the flesh beneath her eyes tinged a bruised violet; her hair pulled severely back in a coiled bun, unkindly stretching the skin across her high, protruding cheekbones. She studied his own face, her lips pressed firmly together, tense and drawn, as if she were biting down on the insides of her cheeks, hungry for something only he could give to her. He had nothing to offer; she should have prepared herself for this before showing up unannounced, uninvited.

"Hello, Jamie." Her voice cracked on a hollow note.

"I don't want you here."

Her lip trembled, on the verge of tears. "But I'm here."

So he allowed her to enter, shutting the door softly behind him, and with arms folded across his chest, Jamie leaned back against the door, watching Mina observe with those blank black eyes the Spartan severity of his home. She stared down at the floor, and then lifted her head and met Jamie's unrelenting gaze; she was now weeping in earnest, and Jamie wanted to hate her. Instead, he took her threadbare woolen coat and folded it neatly over the back of the chair that belonged to the desk. He led her to the sofa and then left the room, returning with a mug of steaming chamomile tea. After placing it into her chapped and shivering hands, he sat across from her, waiting for her to speak, to request from him whatever she'd come here to receive. When Mina discovered the empty mug in her hands, drained to a few flecks of bitter leaves, she looked up and saw Jamie still waiting tolerantly, comfortably reclining in the stiff leather of his armchair, and blandly, blankly watching her.

"I apologize. I would never have come here unless it were important . . . something only you could . . . you see, I was only hoping," she stumbled and then cleared her throat. "I was hoping you might have a photograph . . . of him . . . when he was a child. It's not for me."

"Who, then?"

"He's still alive," she ignored his question. "At least he is for me. I don't need to be reminded, when I see him everywhere."

"Then who?" he persisted. "Who do you need this for?"

"It wouldn't matter, not to you, not anyone," she met his gaze, levelly, fiercely defending the choice she had made seven years ago.

"Are you so sure of that?" And the wry smile tugging at the corners of Jamie's mouth transformed his face into the exact replica of his dead and missing brothers.

Mina stared at him, startled, defenseless, her expression revealing for a fleeting moment the ghost of the girl she must have once been, credulous, precocious, unmarked by any trace of guilt or pain. The briefest glimmer of a smile also played at the corners of her mouth. Then the shade was drawn over her eyes, and they became unreadable.

"I'll go now," she announced, rising hastily, searching for her coat. "I shouldn't have come, but thank you for the tea. It was most kind of you."

He gestured for her to sit back down. "Mina, please, there's no need to rush off. I think I have something."

He disappeared into the bedroom, trusting she would still be there when he emerged. Kneeling on the floor beside the bed, Jamie searched for the old shoebox where he kept family photos stored and hidden from sight. The floor was caked with a fine film of dust where he'd failed to sweep, but he ignored that, pulled out the shoebox and incautiously opened it, a veritable Pandora's Box. He sat on the edge of the bed and blindly sifted through the photographs, only seeking what she'd requested, his fingers reaching deeper through the pile until they brushed against an object that did not belong. He retrieved it, confused, sending a random pile of photos scattering across the floor and at his feet.

He dumbly stared at the book, and then felt the urge to explode in an irrepressible guffaw of comprehension, an echo of his long-dead brother's laughter. Jamie flipped through its pages, discovering the postcard of the nude exactly where he'd interred it nearly fourteen years ago. He glanced down at the page before him, skimming its first few lines, expecting to receive some arcane but prophetic message. *Now that thou hast loved me one whole day, to-morrow when thou leavest, what wilt thou say? Wilt thou then antedate some new-made vow? Or, say that now we are not just those persons, which we were?* He laid aside Donne, neglecting to reinsert the image of the sinuous curves of Mina's naked spine, buttocks, and thighs, the twist of her hair draped forward over her shoulder as if to conceal her breasts, and the burgeoning swell of her belly, which the viewer could not in any case see. Jamie furtively slipped the postcard beneath a pillow, as if the flesh and blood Mina Byrne would suddenly decide to follow him into the room, strip off her clothes, and like some demented succubus drain his soul until he became a hollow husk of desire, just as she'd done with his brothers.

Horrified by this unbidden image, and as if in accusation of some irreparable violation, he discovered his younger brother's angry, flashing, wary eyes staring up at him from the floor. Jamie studied the rare image of Colin, around the age of six or seven, displaying one of his savage scowls, appearing offended that his mother had been so rude as to snap a picture at such an inappropriate moment, and documenting for all time his intensely childish misery. This was not at all the brother Jamie remembered, and so he searched for a different photograph, one that would provide evidence of Colin's more recognizable loopy endearing grin, as if Jamie needed proof that such a boy once existed. The only one he could find was blurred, unfocused, not at all a precise likeness, but clearly Colin, running and laughing in the yard of some house where they might have once lived. He put it aside and continued searching, now obsessed with rediscovering the only Colin he was willing to acknowledge, and finally ended up with a shot of all three of them, aged four, eight and eighteen, posed against the immense abyss of the Grand Canyon, the last of their family vacations when they were complete, before any of them had gone missing. Andrew stood glowering, Jamie serenely bored, and Colin beaming. Yes, this captured nicely the hazy mirage of their individual personalities, not as themselves, but with the faces they'd always presented to the world.

Jamie gathered up all three of the selected images along with the book and returned to the front room, where Mina had remained in exactly the same rigid pose, but now wearing her coat, prepared to flee. When Jamie handed her the book, she looked down at its cover, confused. I believe this belongs to you, he explained, and after opening it to find her name, she simply closed it once more and laid it on the coffee table. She mutely accepted the photographs from Jamie and frowned, displeased, upon the three brothers, and then perplexed at the blurred Colin, and finally, with the third picture, she forgot, momentarily, to breathe, her fingertip lightly tracing the boy's frown, his unruly hair, the stubborn set of his jaw. She exhaled, smiling beautifully, and when her eyes lifted to acknowledge Jamie's presence, the phantom of her former self flickered once more across her face.

"Thank you," she murmured, the smile fading as she returned to him the photo of the three brothers. "You should keep this. I only wanted a picture of her father, for Laura."

"What does she look like?" Jamie asked, cautiously, hearing my name for the first time.

Mina cackled. "I haven't any idea. I haven't seen her since . . . since I left her in Trinidad . . . with my ex-husband who, well, who seemed at the time the best person . . . or it was the best place for her . . . as you know, I wasn't altogether . . ."

"Yes, I remember."

"I'm bringing her back to Paris." Mina sat down in a crumpled heap on the sofa, toying with the buttons of her coat. "Rather, Besim is sending her. He says it's time I stopped running away from my responsibility, and he's right, I'm tired, though I'm not sure I'll know how to be a proper mother, not after all this time."

Jamie sat beside her. "Will you be living here, then, in Paris?"

Mina nodded. "My aunt left me her apartment in St-Germain. It's been empty ever since she died, which was . . . actually . . . right before Laura was born. I would have left it to Redpath, her companion, but he was too batty to go on living there by himself . . . oh, it made no difference, he didn't last much longer without Rosalie . . . and I know none of this is to the point. Yes, we'll be living in Paris and so perhaps . . ."

Jamie caught his breath, refusing to ask anything of her. Mina shifted out of her coat, rummaged through her pocketbook and retrieved a photograph to give to him in exchange for the ones he'd offered her. The small girl stared back at him with a sullen scowl of distrust, partially veiled by a tumble of black curls framing her pale, heart-shaped face, slightly tilted to one side in a pose of defiance, her eyes coldly, contemptuously challenging whoever stood behind the camera. Jamie recognized her immediately.

"I'm told she looks like me, and perhaps she does . . . it's hard to say . . . but I used to have a photograph of myself when I was about that age, or maybe a little older . . . in fact, I gave a copy of it to Andrew once, and to your father too . . . I don't know why," and then Mina burst into tears, sobbing in Jamie's arms until she fell asleep.

She remained there on his sofa for nearly two days, for the most part sleeping, rising only to accept a mug of tea or bowl of broth, weakly smiling her gratitude, because not once did Jamie ask Mina to explain herself. He already knew all he needed to know, and beyond that he didn't care. There was something else, some other puzzle, far more important, that needed to be solved. Jamie sat in the armchair, occasionally glancing at Mina while she slept, as he continued to study the photograph of the girl he had once thought could belong to him, before he ever knew what might emerge from her puckered and perfectly peaceful infant's face. Yes, she vaguely looked like Mina, but comparing the photograph side by side to the one of Colin as a boy, anyone might have mistaken them for twins. A thought, a theory, then began to form, and everything fell into place; he pulled down his father's books, skimming through their pages to find the relevant passages, and when Mina groggily woke to find him gazing expressionlessly at the books piled on the coffee table, she defensively pulled the blanket around her shoulders, because she knew what came next, but what came next was not at all what she expected.

"She looks like Dolores, like Aveline, Myra, Lucia," Jamie muttered. "All those ghosts of poor doomed little girls repeatedly reincarnated . . . and you . . . of course you reminded him . . . if you looked at all like her . . . like the long lost daughter he never had . . ."

"But your father never knew me as a child," Mina murmured, misunderstanding, yet relieved because he'd been the first to comprehend, unlike his brothers, unlike his mother, that there had never been anything more to her relationship with Vasili, nothing more than an old man and a younger woman pretending innocently to be a father and daughter, at least until Vasili wanted more. "Besides, he wrote *Dolores* before he ever met me."

Which only confirmed for Jamie his carefully pieced together puzzle, "Colin had a twin," he stated, which only became true the moment he said the words aloud, and then all that he'd so vigilantly willed into oblivion, returned to him.

Incapable of suppressing their curiosity and their fear, refusing to obey their father, Jamie and Andrew had snuck below deck to the berth, from where their mother's screams had recently grown silent. They took turns peeking through the keyhole of the door. Mama lay unconscious on the narrow, blood-soaked bed, and lying on the blood-soaked sheets at the foot of the bed two inert barely breathing lumps of flesh, one large, swollen, and monstrously splotched and the other tiny, shriveled, and impossibly pale. Papa stood paralyzed, terrified, staring down at the debacle of a pregnancy and labor gone horrifically wrong. The ship's doctor paced the room, flipping through the pages of a book, mumbling over either his own or the manual's inadequacies, and then he stopped, perused the page before him, paused, glanced at the bed, then Papa, then back at the book, nodding his head uncertainly. Papa lost patience, snatched the book out of his hands and flung it across the room. The doctor haltingly informed Papa of his best guess based on the findings from his book compared to the evidence before them: monochorionic, identical male and female almost never seen, exceedingly rare, twin-to-twin transfusion, high rate of morbidity, almost certain mortality for one or both, the larger one has greater chance of survival but Vasili must choose. So Vasili chose, and without hesitating, he instructed the doctor in his list of priorities, and after Colin was fully swatted into life, the mucus cleared from his nose and lungs, he was handed over to Papa while the doctor turned his attention to staunching the blood spilling out of Mama; all the while the little girl lay forgotten and dying, and finally, when the doctor picked her up, there was no point in attempting to revive her, and Jamie and Andrew clearly heard him ask, what do you want me to do with her? Papa told him to take it away. The doctor wrapped the dead thing in a clean white sheet and after he left the cabin the boys emerged from hiding and discreetly followed him like phantoms down the passageway, up the stairs, onto the dark, windswept deck, tiptoeing towards the abandoned stern where they watched from a shadowy crouch the doctor throw the white bundle overboard and into the sea. When he was gone, Jamie and Andrew stood huddled and shivering at the rails. Andrew had vomited and Jamie was too frightened to return to either their mother or father, and so there they remained silently staring down together at the churning, foaming, moonlit trail leading away from their sister's unmarked grave.

"We should give her a name," Jamie had whispered.

"What's the point?" Andrew laughed bitterly.

"Mama said Papa could name the baby if it was a girl. Papa forgot to give her a name. Mama would want for her to have a name."

Andrew looked as if he might cry. "Okay . . . Nadia, that's what he would call her."

"Okay, Nadia," Jamie agreed and when he was finished sharing with Mina this memory, she whispered, exhausted, because now she understood, "But what choice did he have? And every book has been an attempt to bring her back to life, to give her back to your mother—."

"And look where it got him," said Jamie. "Everything died that night . . ."

And Mina thought, yes, perhaps, but there is always some way of beginning again; and she thought, I am tired of ghosts; and then, she contemplated offering Jamie the chance at happiness she'd once refused his brother. She doubted it would ever work, because she did not think she could ever be happy, but then she thought . . .

CHAPTER NINETEEN
Perpetual Departure

And so, for what it's worth, we became a small happy family for a very small wrinkle in time. Well, it is worth at least three paragraphs representing the brief duration of the three years of our make-believe. When I was seven Besim put me on a boat with Bertha. He told me I was going to live with my mother. I didn't know what a mother was supposed to look like; I'd thought Bertha was my mother even though we looked nothing like each other. When we arrived at Le Havre, a tall, willowy, unsmiling, middle-aged woman and a taller, stooping, bespectacled, grimly grinning man were there to meet us. They told me their names were Jamie and Mina. One was my uncle and the other my mother. Apparently my uncle was also married to my mother, but when we arrived "home," as they called it, I quickly realized they were not married like Besim and Gardenia since they did not sleep in the same bed, or even the same room. But more than Besim and Gardenia, they seemed to love each other, deeply, perfectly, in their own eccentric, affectionate, unspoken way. To sum up, they were the doubles of Rosalie and Redpath, or at least I have imagined Rosalie and Redpath based on what I saw of Mina and Jamie, as they pottered about echoing each other's sentences, indulging my every whim, and doing their best to transform me into the image of a daughter they had both created between them.

Instead of sending me to school, in the mornings Jamie gave me lessons in philosophy and history, and every evening Mina made me read poetry, and none of us thought this approach towards my education very odd since it was all Jamie knew, Mina had been educated in much the same manner when she was a girl, and I had never been expected to acquire any sort of education other than the stories of Creole folklore Bertha told me every night before bedtime. My mother and uncle now encouraged me to learn as many languages as possible because if one learned to love words in all their various forms then one would never be lonely or bored; so I dabbled in Italian, French, English, Spanish, even Yiddish; and when Mina hired a maid from Anstruther, I sat in the kitchen listening to her clatter on in her honeyed brogue as she told me all about the adventures of her girlhood when she went out to sea on her father's boat, catching selkies and conches and sea sprites in the wide sweep of their net. Mina insisted that because I was her daughter then I should develop my inherent creativity. I spent afternoons drawing and painting, but without lessons since Mina claimed these would kill the imagination, and she would advise me, whatever you become, my darling, do not ever become bourgeois.

When I became homesick, and after Bertha returned to Trinidad because the European winters were insufferable, Jamie brought home for me a Red Howler, who clambered and shat and chattered all over the apartment until Mina demanded he go back to whatever jungle he'd come from, which meant back behind the bars of his home in the Jardin des Plantes. Afterwards, though, and stricken with guilt, she allowed me to keep as many animals as I liked, as long as they were of the domesticated sort. Rosalie's flat became a menagerie of birdcages, stray tabbies, a spaniel and her yapping litter, expendable hamsters, and assorted reptiles. I had been uprooted and planted in my very own paradise where neither time nor the outside world was allowed to disrupt our fabricated family. Mina was not really my mother but a fairy godmother, magical, distant and serenely capable of providing me with the answer to every question I never asked, and Jamie was the magician who could make Mina laugh whenever she remembered things that had no name, and he told me every story I ever requested so that I would know precisely, expansively, who I was long before I became a small seed in search of my mother's womb.

One night Jamie died in his sleep, unexpectedly, quietly, from an aneurism, and Mina could no longer go on pretending. After the funeral, we visited an old man and an old woman who claimed they once knew my unknown father when he was a boy, and then Mina brought me back to

Besim before disappearing into the rest of her own life. The rest of her life hardly matters, and I wouldn't know how to begin filling in the gaps; there was no one left who could tell me anything about her, and although Besim sometimes agreed to give me clues, he had very little to offer other than what I've already told you. Besides, he died when I was twelve, and I don't want to revisit that memory. For the next six years Gardenia tolerated my presence, either because she had no choice or, as I'd prefer to believe, she felt sorry for me but only until my eighteenth birthday when, like Cinderella, my fairy godmother appeared in the form of a letter from a lawyer informing me I was the recipient of a trust fund from the Novikov-Brennan royalties, and, it seemed, the sole executor of their combined estates, a role assigned to me by Deirdre, who, having outlived her husband and the last of her sons by six years, realized she had no choice in the matter if she wanted to ensure it all remained within the family, so to speak.

I eventually tracked Mina down to a cluttered Bowery studio, filled with junk, which she called found art, and scribbling poems professing her devotion to all the drunkards, mongrels, and outcasts of the world, or at least, Lower Manhattan, which now demarcated the boundaries of her existence. She knew me upon first sight, and for that I was grateful, since she appeared slightly mad, not to mention ill with severe respiratory problems. She blamed her congested lungs on the evil vapors left behind by all the ghosts who visited her each night. I took her to a doctor, who assured me it was nothing fresh air couldn't cure, and Mina mutely nodded her agreement. So I moved her to Aspen, bought her a house, which is where she lived until she wandered out into the middle of a snowstorm, but we've already covered that, haven't we? It seems lifetimes ago. I flew up from Buenos Aires, buried my mother, and boxed up her belongings, all of which were donated to the Salvation Army to disperse to her beloved bums.

I kept for myself several small boxes stuffed with letters, photographs and unpublished manuscripts, one heavily underlined copy of *Songs and Sonnets* and one long autobiographical poem, *Luminosities*, which Mina had spent the last fifteen years of her life composing, and which took me some time to translate. While sifting through Mina's possessions, I also found my grandfather's last novel, *Lorelei*. Deirdre had sent it to Mina after his death several months following Jamie's sudden departure. Perhaps Deirdre believed the story had no worth, at least if it were to be published;

or perhaps Vasili had requested in his will, or on his deathbed in a Swiss hospital dying of pneumonia, knowing that it would remain unfinished, that it be sent to Mina. In any case, it now belongs to me, just as he had intended, and one day, but not now, I shall decide what to do with its fragmented narrative of marriages, muses, moths, mirrors, and madness.

Now, I have nothing else to write, not even the story of my own life, since I've spent a good portion of it writing this family history, nine years in fact, and it has nearly killed me, locked up in an attic, hacking away from a three-pack-a-day habit, nibbling here and there a bite of toast, curling up in bed with a bottle of Bordeaux, ignoring the outside world where I am told real things happen, things that people actually care about. It is presumed that because these things are real then they are all that matter; but I've spent my entire life making up my mother, and all the rest of my family, and this is the only possible story I could have told, the only ending I can offer you. Or, perhaps, there is one more thing, something floating between the hazy borders of imagination and memory . . .

CHAPTER TWENTY
The Tulip Poplar

An old man sits in his garden surrounded by the ghosts of his sons, all of them small boys scampering about his chair, clumsily chasing a cloud of *Nymphalis antiopa* fluttering above their father's head. He shifts his cumbersome weight, signifying the burden of his years, to observe the shadowy silhouettes of two women standing behind the kitchen window watching the girl they have sent out into the garden; neither woman appears very pleased with the other's existence, and if Vasili could hear their confession it would be more than he could bear.

Deirdre tells Mina, "I almost had a daughter once," and Mina replies, "So did I," and that is all either of them feel the need to concede. They observe the childless old man beneath the broad bows of a tulip poplar, its generous shade concealing the anxious, happy gleam in his eyes as he takes the lost child of his heart on his knee to tell her a story, and when he is done he asks her what she would like for him to call this story: Laura, Flora, Dora, Nora, Cora, or perhaps all of these? She offers him her solemn smile and tells him that he should decide. He detects her fidgety desire, now that the story is finished, to get down from his lap and wander through the garden, and so he gives her the ending that will allow her to proceed into the rest of her life.

"Now, my dear child, before we say goodbye and I let you return to your mother, who is impatiently waiting to depart, I will have you notice that not the least adornment of this chronicle is the delicacy of its whimsical detail: a grove of blossoming lilac trees; a mermaid dreaming of swimming in endless seas; a pretty plaything laughing among the fading forget-me-nots; spectral butterflies chasing stars along the margins of the universe; a moon limned view of the past stolen from the slanting shadows of sunlight setting on a horizon that can never be reached; and, if you can imagine, much, much more."

"I assure you that I am indeed a live being. But it is necessary to stay very unknown . . ."

—Mina Loy

ACKNOWLEDGMENTS

This is a work of fantasy and not intended to provide a factual representation of any person, place, or incident, historical or otherwise. However, Carolyn Burke's archival work and biography, Becoming Modern: The Life of Mina Loy (University of California Press 1996) supplied this novel with much more than I could have come up with on my own. A good portion of the dialogue in Chapters 8 and 12 come from letters and other notable quips by Loy and her contemporaries (also cited in Burke's biography). All of the poems by Mina Byrne (except "Beyond Berating," for which I must entirely take the blame) are mirrored distortions of Loy's poems (see The Lost Lunar Baedeker, edited by Roger Conover, Noonday Press, 1996), and the Loy epigraph (or, postscript) can also be found in Conover's introduction to LLB (pg. xii). Chapter 8 compiles several of Loy's "Italian" poems, liberally translated into prose, and the latter half of Chapter 12 borrows heavily from Loy's novel, Insel (edited by Elizabeth Arnold, Black Sparrow Press, 1991). The Winterson epigraphs from Art & Lies (Vintage 1995) can be found, respectively, on pp. 30 and 136.

Early versions of Chapters 2 and 10 were performed at the 2005 Edinburgh Festival Fringe as part of an author showcase, "Alternate Endings," produced by the St. Andrews postgraduate creative writing group, Naked on Stage. Jamie's visit home in the interlude section between Chapters 10 and 11 was published in New Writing Dundee 5 (2010) as the short story, "The Prologue (To Everything That Came Before)."

Since "books are made of other books," then profound gratitude is owed to the novels and imagined persona of Vladimir Nabokov, whom the author hopes, unlike the ghost of Hamlet's father, will resist from urging the executor of his estate to pursue a needless law suit. Vasili's little speech to Besim on p. 85 is a somewhat mangled Nabokovian adage (though as much as I've tried, I can't recall or recover the exact source). Chapter 20 owes something to the ending of A.S. Byatt's Possession and the last paragraph of course pays homage to the final paragraph in Ada, or Ardour. Stacy Schiff's biography, Véra (Mrs. Vladimir Nabokov) (Random House, 1999) most likely influenced and informed the Deirdre-Vasili marriage. Svetlana Boym's The Future of Nostalgia certainly shaped my reflective revisions of a narrative project that began (unknowingly) with the desire to play with her concept of the "off-modern," which "recovers unforeseen pasts and ventures into the side-alleys of modern history" (www.svetlanaboym.com).

Though by no means an exhaustive list, other sources of inspiration and influence include: Angela Carter and Diane Arbus (for several stolen phrases and photographs); Regina Spektor's "Chemo Limo" (for Deirdre's dream); Eric Hissom, Bram Stoker, Anne Rice, and Sam Shepard (for Andrew Brennan's dramatic oeuvre); P.G. Wodehouse and J.P. McGuire (for Billy Beresford/Besim Berisha); Orlando and Tristram Shandy (for lessons in how to write an auto/biography); Mr. Shakespeare, Mr. Donne, and Mr. Carroll (for obvious reasons); and of course the indomitable Mae West (for making an appearance as Sara Sorrell).

Many thanks to my parents, Deborah Cripps and Randall Jennings, as well as Laura Limonic, Rachel Marsh, and Sarah Taylor, for reading in various stages over the years and providing their encouragement and support. I am indebted to Professor Elizabeth Beaujour, whose comparative literature seminar at Hunter College, "Nabokov: Bridging Two Cultures," provided me with the early groundwork and inspiration for playing with language, time, and space (or else I might never have thought to throw together fictional versions of writers who in "reality" never crossed paths). Some of my later revisions were greatly enriched by the exchange of ideas with fellow scholars who participated in the seminar, "Mina Loy across the Arts," at the ESSE 2010 conference in Turin, Italy, with particular thanks to Esther Sanchez-Pardo, Linda Kinnahan, and Sandeep Parmar. Most deservedly, thanks to Christine

Junker for copyediting and reading multiple "finished" versions (and insisting this end up a much shorter book than it was to begin with). Thanks to D. Harlan Wilson and Anti-Oedipus Press for a beautiful cover and book design, and capturing perfectly all that I had envisioned.

Many apologies to anyone else, living or dead, real or fictional, whose name I've neglected to mention—if you are owed recognition, thank you.

NOSTALGIA